BREAKING BRENNA

A NOVEL BY

ANNABELLE WINTERS

Copyright Notice

Copyright © 2021 by Annabelle Winters
All Rights Reserved by Author
www.annabellewinters.com
ab@annabellewinters.com

If you'd like to copy, reproduce, sell, or distribute any part of this text, please obtain the explicit, written permission of the author first. Note that you should feel free to tell your spouse, lovers, friends, and co-workers how happy this book made you. Have a wonderful evening!

Cover Design by S. Lee

ISBN: 9798774280551

0 1 2 3 4 5 6 7 8 9

BOOKS BY ANNABELLE WINTERS

THE CURVES FOR SHEIKHS SERIES
Curves for the Sheikh
Flames for the Sheikh
Hostage for the Sheikh
Single for the Sheikh
Stockings for the Sheikh
Untouched for the Sheikh
Surrogate for the Sheikh
Stars for the Sheikh
Shelter for the Sheikh
Shared for the Sheikh
Assassin for the Sheikh
Privilege for the Sheikh
Ransomed for the Sheikh
Uncorked for the Sheikh
Haunted for the Sheikh
Grateful for the Sheikh
Mistletoe for the Sheikh
Fake for the Sheikh

THE CURVES FOR SHIFTERS SERIES
Curves for the Dragon
Born for the Bear
Witch for the Wolf
Tamed for the Lion
Taken for the Tiger

THE CURVY FOR HIM SERIES
The Teacher and the Trainer
The Librarian and the Cop
The Lawyer and the Cowboy
The Princess and the Pirate

The CEO and the Soldier
The Astronaut and the Alien
The Botanist and the Biker
The Psychic and the Senator

THE **CURVY FOR THE HOLIDAYS** SERIES
Taken on Thanksgiving
Captive for Christmas
Night Before New Year's
Vampire's Curvy Valentine
Flagged on the Fourth
Home for Halloween

THE **CURVY FOR KEEPS** SERIES
Summoned by the CEO
Given to the Groom
Traded to the Trucker
Punished by the Principal
Wifed by the Warlord

THE **DRAGON'S CURVY MATE** SERIES
Dragon's Curvy Assistant
Dragon's Curvy Banker
Dragon's Curvy Counselor
Dragon's Curvy Doctor
Dragon's Curvy Engineer
Dragon's Curvy Firefighter
Dragon's Curvy Gambler

THE **CURVY IN COLLEGE** SERIES
The Jock and the Genius
The Rockstar and the Recluse
The Dropout and the Debutante
The Player and the Princess
The Fratboy and the Feminist

ANNABELLEWINTERS.COM

BREAKING BRENNA

A NOVEL BY

ANNABELLE WINTERS

I
<u>SOMEWHERE BETWEEN MOSCOW AND KIEV</u>

The black metal door at the front end of the bunker screeched on its rusted iron hinges. Footsteps sounded on the concrete floor. Slow, ponderous footfalls. Heavy leather boots lined with sheepskin, studded with steel.

Brenna Yankova knew those boots. She knew those footsteps. She knew every sound of this place. She'd been here a week but could already tell one rat from another just from the way they scurried across the rough floor, prowled the straw-lined edges of her windowless cell.

Could smell them apart too. When you lose one of your five senses the others compensate for the loss of their sister. Technically Brenna still had eyes, therefore still had vision. But without light those clear brown eyes were good for nothing but tears.

"Quit your tears or else I will take your eyeballs with me when I leave," whispered the owner of those boots. He always whispered, never raised his voice. Perhaps he had learned it was more terrifying that way.

The threat was for the prisoner in Cell Two, three doors up from Brenna. The man in Two was new. He had been crying for seventeen hours by Brenna's count. She was good at counting the hours. No idea if her count was accurate, of course. It was just a game she played with herself. Something to remind herself she was still human. Still had a mind capable of rational thought. After all, if she could still count, it meant she wasn't crazy. Blind, maybe. But not crazy.

Not yet.

Brenna pulled herself up into a sitting position. She'd been lying on her side, curled up against the cold, uneven concrete, listening to the rats moving along the dark walls of her cell. They didn't bother her much. Didn't try to eat her face when she slept. They only did that if you had food stuck all over your lips. No chance of that happening in here. She'd eat her own lips if there were any leftovers crusted on there from the day's solitary meal of hardtack bread and lukewarm meat broth thin like dishwater. Probably a good time to start that low-carb diet.

The footsteps moved down the line of cells. The left foot dragged a little, like it always did. She called the man Boots. It was a cute name, like from a Russian fairy tale. Her father had read her some of those stories when she was little. A lot of boys named Ivan and girls called Ivana. Plenty of witches, all of them called Babayaga. As a girl she'd been afraid of those gnarled old witches. Now she wished she were one. She'd cast a spell on Boots. Spring the locks. Fly off on a mortar, just like a curvy Babayaga.

Breaking Brenna

But the magic of childhood was long gone, just like her father was long gone. Brenna was alone now. Alone again.

She backed up silently, a reverse butt-first crawl towards the rear of her cell. Her bare heels touched the rough wall and she sat back on her ass. She still had plenty of cushion left on her rump. Hell, maybe she could survive for years on her body fat. Bears did it, didn't they?

Brenna got her legs out from under her, pulled her well-scraped knees up against her chest, then hugged them tight. Her eyes were wide, but the darkness was so absolute she couldn't even see shapes. The blackness was thick enough to choke her. She wondered if today was her day, just like yesterday had been Prisoner Four's day.

Boots had come for him early, before the day's meal. They didn't want to waste a bowl of broth on Four. Of course, she had no idea where they'd taken Four. Perhaps he was being released. After all, she didn't hear gunshots from a firing squad. No solid *thunk* of the gallows floor opening up. Perhaps he'd been set free. Perhaps there was still hope. Maybe someone had come for Four.

Was someone coming for her?

Boots was past Prisoner Three now, left foot still dragging. Cell Four was still empty. Brenna was Five.

There was no Six.

Today was her day.

Fear crawled up her legs, starting from her toes. A new kind of fear. Not the persistent, gnawing fear of the infinite darkness that she'd experienced every moment she'd been here. Not the sharp, spiraling fear she'd felt a week ago when the Russian Secret Police stormed her Gorky

Park studio apartment, took her in the darkness, put her in that boxy Lada van, took her to a basement in the Moscow suburbs, interrogated her for three days, then shipped her out here like livestock to the slaughterhouse.

Nope, it wasn't that kind of fear. It was closer to the creeping, whispering, slithering fear that invaded her when she first looked upon the jowly, haggard face of Boots and wondered if he'd violate her body before or after torturing her to death. Maybe both, she'd decided.

That last fear still lived in her, but so far had not come true. The Russian Secret Police had been rough, fearsome, and brutal. But not in that way. And Boots had not touched her. Not like that, at least. She'd been beaten but nothing more. Boots had hit her the first day with a casual backhand that sent her flying across the room. She had a bump on her cheekbone from his iron-hard knuckles. It was a permanent bump. Boots had cracked her cheekbone with that single blow. As the bone fused unevenly, the scar tissue would form a permanent bump.

The other guards mostly stayed away from her. She'd seen them look at her, whisper, stare. But they never approached, like they'd been warned not to.

They were all bedraggled men with wild eyes, perhaps from amphetamines. The Russian military had a long history of handing out amphetamines like candy. Of course, back in World War Two all the armies were using those drugs to keep their young men awake and alert for days on end. Brenna wasn't sure why these guards needed to be alert. She'd seen the prison when they let her out of the van. There was a curved concrete wall rimmed with razor wire. Impossible to climb because of how it curved backward on you. Best she could tell they'd been driving East towards Ukraine. Perhaps they were already in Ukraine. Ukraine was its own country now, but the Russian presence was still strong. In some ways the Soviet Union never really died. It just went underground.

She thought of the fence now. It had given her some strange comfort. It told her that this was a prison all right, but it wasn't a *gulag*. Father had told her about the old *gulags* with a strange relish, like they excited him. They were so far out in the frozen wastelands that there was no need for a fence. A thousand miles of frozen desert was a pretty good fence. You wanna escape on foot? Go for it. Death would be certain. Does the cold get you or do the wolves take you first? That was the only question a Siberian escapee asked, Brenna's father had told her once. There weren't many dumb enough to run.

So the fence was a good sign. So was the distant glow of city lights on the horizon. Not many guards, and certainly not the A-team. This was an off-the-grid prison, but it wasn't max security, and it wasn't a place where the Russians sent you to die. That was what she told herself the first night. That was what she told herself every night.

The footsteps stopped outside her door.

"Yankova," came Boots's rasping whisper, barely audible through the iron door that seemed thicker than her thighs. Probably designed to be a nuclear fallout shelter. This was definitely a people scarred by the Cold War, the threat of a mushroom cloud near and present.

Brenna didn't reply. She hugged the oversized canvas jumpsuit around her legs, rocked back and forth, and waited.

There was a small barred window about six feet high in the door. It slid open with a sudden shriek. Light poured in through the slot, and Brenna yelped and slammed her palms over her eyes.

The pain of vision made her want to cry out again, but she hyperventilated and swallowed the sound. She kept her legs tight together as a slight breeze curled its way around her bare ankles. They'd taken her clothes when she arrived. She'd been given this musty jumpsuit. It was way too big and far too long. But it was warm.

"Yankova," Boots said again. "*Yankova!*"

The potato-shaped shadow of his face blocked the light as he peered through the slot. Brenna moved her fingers apart and peeked. She wondered if he was checking to see if she was still alive.

For a moment she considered playing dead. Maybe he'd open the door, come in to kick her body to make sure. Maybe she had enough strength left to plunge her thumbs into his eyeballs, all the way to his brain.

Brenna's father had recommended the move the night of her first real date, when she was fifteen. Bobby Marshall was taking her to see a movie. It was back when people went to theaters to watch movies. Back when Brenna still lived in New Jersey. Back when cinema houses had oversized cups of sugar-sweet sodas packed with ice, buckets of hot buttery popcorn big enough to wade in. Back when there was light.

"Go for the eyes or the balls," her long-haired, dark-eyed father Alexei Yankov had advised matter-of-factly, barely looking away from the three mammoth computer screens that were always alive and moving like a snake-infested jungle floor. Charts on one screen, numbers on the other, lines of computer code scrolling down the third, all against colorful wallpaper backdrops that looked like scenes from the apocalypse.

"Yes, the eyes or the balls, Brenna." He'd turned and grinned. "And remember, when you attack, you must commit all the way. Overwhelming force is what wins the day. Hit early. Hit hard. No mercy. No regrets. Better to go too hard than too soft. Do not stop until the enemy is broken, destroyed, demolished. Just like in *Doom* or *Halo* or *World of Warcraft*."

"Um, Bobby's a vegan pacifist. He just became secretary of the Chess Club," Brenna had said with a raised left eyebrow and a half-smile on her lips. But she'd tucked away that nugget, just like she had with everything her strange, intense father had said to her.

She'd grown up in awe of the looming, shadowy Alexei, partly because she'd never really known him. He'd never married her mother, but never quite abandoned her either. He was stingy with his time, but generous with his money. The direct deposits from Moscow International Bank arrived on the last day of every month. Month after month. Year after year. Same amount every month, just below the IRS reporting threshold. They'd started the month after Brenna was born, her mother had said. But they stopped three months before Brenna turned eighteen.

Those three months there was nothing from Alexei. Then, in early February, something arrived for Brenna.

Two things, actually, spaced only by a few days. Two sets of words, from two different sources. One set digital, the other analog.

The digital words popped up on the encrypted ProtonMail account that her father had insisted she use for all correspondence. It was a message from Princeton University.

An acceptance email. Early decision.

She'd wanted to go to Princeton ever since she'd learned Albert Einstein spent his golden years there. It was a thrill to get in, but also a relief in a weird way. At some level Brenna knew she'd get in, which made the thought that she might not get in terrifying. So when she got in it was thrilling but somehow also just meh.

The feeling told her that deep down she had confidence that bordered on arrogance. She knew she was smart. She knew she was strong. Straight A's from Middle School onwards. Varsity Softball Captain. She'd even outplayed Bobby Marshall and become Chess Club President—no need to put his eyes out or kick him in the balls to win. So yeah, getting into the old Ivy League University down the New Jersey Transit line from where she'd grown up hadn't been a great mystery.

The other set of words was the mystery.

It didn't come by email. It came in regular snail mail. A solitary black envelope of thick cardstock. Double-sealed with black electrical tape. A single sheet of quadruple-folded acid-free paper.

It was from her father, who'd been back in Russia for almost two years by then, completely incommunicado.

He'd always been a man of few words. There were thirteen words on the sheet of paper, which was like a record for a letter from Alexei.

The first word was Congratulations. Brenna wasn't sure if her father had simply guessed she'd gotten into Princeton or was hacking into her supposedly unhackable email account or perhaps even into Princeton's mainframe. She'd smiled, then read on.

Twelve more words.

Twelve totally random, absolutely unconnected, supremely mundane words.

There were no instructions. No directions. No explanations.

No follow up emails. No messages on her cell.

Brenna had stared at the words, excitement brewing in her breast. The good thing about having a father who didn't say much was that it was easy for Brenna to remember pretty much everything Alexei had ever said to her.

She thought of something he'd said on his last visit, not long after Bobby Marshall had been struck off the potential husband list because he'd taken her to see a cheesy Rom-Com that made Brenna want to put her own darned eyes out. She'd always been more of an action-adventure type girl.

"It is getting difficult to send money from Russia now," Alexei had said to her two years earlier, on the morning which turned out to be his last in America.

They were alone in the small den where her father stayed on the green fabric pull-out couch when he visited. Brenna's mother rarely entered the den when her father was visiting. It had always been that way and Brenna never questioned it much. Her mother Nancy was a strange, quiet person too. How Brenna was born with the gift of the jabberwocky was anyone's guess.

Alexei had glanced at one of his on-screen charts and then turned to face his daughter. "Russian government is freezing bank accounts, seizing assets of anyone they suspect of anything. American sanctions are also a problem. US Dollars are harder to come by, even harder to send." Then he'd winked and smiled, his bright Rasputin-like eyes flashing. "But there is this new thing called cryptocurrency. It has potential."

That was all he'd said. Those charts on his screens had moved, and he turned back to them. Hours later he was gone. Alexei left late that night, after an uncharacteristically warm hug. He even sought out Brenna's mother, entered her room and spoke to her quietly. Then he hugged Brenna again and walked out the door.

Brenna never saw him again.

And she never would see him again.

That was why she'd come to Moscow.

To say goodbye.

Not to the man himself. Just his plain, government-issued gravestone.

Brenna exhaled in the empty cell as those memories swirled through her mind. Princeton was ten years in the past now. But cryptocurrency was ten years in the future. Alexei had been ahead of his time back then, and thanks to him, so was Brenna.

She'd taken her father's comment as advice, and looked

into cryptocurrency. It didn't take long for her to figure out that cryptocurrencies were like electronic cash stored publicly but anonymously on the Internet in accounts called electronic wallets.

Anyone can see anyone else's wallet, see how much money is in there down to a thousand decimal points. Anyone can send money to anyone's wallet without permission. Just like sending an email. Simple.

As for getting money *out* of a wallet?

Actually spending that money?

That was simple too.

All you needed was an obscenely long string of letters and numbers called a Private Key.

Every wallet has its own private key.

If you know that key, you can drain the wallet, and nobody can stop you.

Nobody can get the money back.

You can convert it into US Dollars or Euros or whatever. Send it anywhere. Spend it on anything. It's yours. All you need is that Private Key. Once you have that, the wallet is yours. No one can reverse the transaction. No one can freeze the wallet like the government can with a bank account. No one can get that money back for you if someone gets your Private Key. It's a bearer asset, just like cash. The person holding it owns it. So if you own the Private Key, you own everything in that account.

And those twelve words?

They were a Private Key.

Or more precisely, the *key* to a Private Key.

It had taken a few hours before Brenna figured out that the computer nerds had created a cryptographic formula that used insanely complicated mathematics to hide a Private Key inside a sequence of twelve common English words. Easier to remember words than a long list of random numbers, they'd figured. So if you knew the twelve secret words, you could enter them into this program and it would decipher the Private Key for you.

A key within a key.

A number hidden behind words.

It didn't take long for Brenna to figure things out. The crypto program was open-source and online. She found it. Entered the twelve words. Sat back and stared at the cryptocurrency wallet Private Key that had been unlocked by the twelve words in her father's letter.

It contained over a quarter-million dollars worth of cryptocurrencies.

Just enough to cover four years at Princeton.

Just enough to launch Brenna into the world.

Except now her world had crashed, Brenna thought as the despair rolled in again like a dark tide. Her father was dead. He'd been dead for years, though she'd only just found out after running her DNA through a new database maintained by the Human Identification Project that catalogued DNA of dead bodies that had never been identified. They'd come up with a 50% match on DNA recorded by the Ukrainian police a decade earlier. The body was buried in what was now Russian territory. No name had been put on the grave.

Brenna was going to put a name on that unmarked gravestone.

There was nothing else of Alexei left. Just a few memories, some dust, some bones. The money was long gone, traded in for a Princeton degree which was depreciating in value every year. Fancy credentials weren't what they used to be.

She looked up at the streaks of white light surrounding the dark shadow of Boots' head.

"Yankova," he said once more.

"I'm alive," Brenna replied in Russian. She spoke it with an American accent, but she spoke it well. Her father had taught her the basics. Then four years in Princeton's Department of Russian Studies had made her fluent, albeit in an academic way.

Boots grunted. "Of course you are alive. Nobody dies here without my permission. Especially not if you are under my special protection, yes?"

Brenna didn't respond. She listened for the sound of chains outside the door. Prisoners were usually shackled before being taken out of their cells. There was no clink of metal.

Boots spoke again in his rasping whisper. "Who are you?" he asked.

Brenna frowned. An odd question. The Russian Secret Police had already asked her that. She'd answered all their questions truthfully. *It is a mistake,* she'd told them in her best Russian. *I'm not a journalist. I'm not a spy. I'm nobody. Just a half-Russian, half-American girl here to visit her father's grave. Alexei Yankov was his name. He died ten years ago, but I just found out. He was Russian. I'm an American. Can I get my phone call to the U.S. Embassy, please?*

They'd laughed at her. Asked her who she was again, what she was doing in Moscow. They threatened her, slapped her around a bit, threatened her again. Then they'd sent her here.

Why? To scare her? To break her? Did they really think Brenna was CIA or something?

Could be the Princeton degree, she'd thought at first. It was common knowledge in spy-circles that the CIA loved recruiting super-smart Princeton grads. She spoke fluent Russian. She was tall, broad, strongly built for a woman.

Shit, maybe they *did* think she was CIA.

Was that good or bad? Looked pretty bad so far—though she *was* still alive. Still, nobody else had questioned her for a week. No deals. No threats. No bribes. They were just holding her here. But for whom? Boots did say something about special protection. At least she thought he did. She couldn't be sure. Too long in the dark. Too long without a good meal. She prayed that they'd finally figured out she was nobody, and the ordeal was over.

"I am nobody," she said to Boots sullenly. If the Russian Secret Police didn't give a damn anymore, Boots certainly wouldn't. Except he'd asked. Why had he asked?

"Damyan Nagarev does not come out of the shadows for just nobody," Boots whispered. "You are somebody to Damyan Nagarev. Who are you, Yankova? Tell me the truth and perhaps I can protect you. But there is not much time. Damyan sends his man Mikhail for you. You are in Ukraine, not Russia, Yankova. Damyan is a legend in Ukraine. A god to some, a demon to others, but feared by all. He has called in favors to protect you from being ravaged by the men in this prison, and I have seen to it that you stayed alive. But when Mikhail comes I cannot stop him from taking you. Cannot stop him from doing what Mikhail the Tongueless likes to do. Nobody can. But tell me the truth and perhaps I try to hide you, yes?"

A chill ran up Brenna's spine. She knew the name Damyan Nagarev. Her father had mentioned him once, long ago. Alexei had spoken of him in strangely reverential tones, called him a man of vision and purpose. It was only when Brenna looked him up later that she learned Damyan's visions were of violence and his purpose seemed to be to kill as many Russian government officials as possible. She'd seen his name in the Russian news over the years. Followed his story now and then, mostly because her father had mentioned the name and Brenna had clung to every word Alexei had said to her.

Damyan "The Demon" Nagarev. Leader of an anti-Russian underground rebel group. A long, bloodsoaked resume including stints as a Russian Special Forces commander and then a senior Bratva enforcer in the Russian mafia's Ukraine operations.

Both previous careers had been cut short under mysterious circumstances. He'd disappeared for a few years, then emerged as the leader of something called UNA—the Ukrainian Nationalist Army, a group committed to freeing the Ukraine from Russian influence. Apparently Damyan had rediscovered his Ukrainian roots and decided it was time the Ukraine reclaimed its own roots.

Damyan's UNA broke on the scene by claiming responsibility for two high-profile assassinations of Russian officials in Kiev when Brenna was a sophomore. It was big news in Princeton's Russian Studies Department, and Brenna had paid close attention. After all, she'd already heard of Damyan Nagarev before that.

Question was, why had Damyan Nagarev heard of Brenna Yankova?

2
AXELROD RANCH
MARIETTA, GEORGIA
UNITED STATES

"Heard you have a big speech planned for Ax and Amy, Bruiser," said John Benson.

He gestured with his champagne glass towards the bride and groom, who were still surrounded by about forty-three guests, most of them current or former military. All branches were represented here, though of course the Navy was front and center. This was a SEAL wedding, after all.

Bruiser shifted in his cramped black dress shoes, rubbed the back of his tree-trunk sized neck, and forced a grin. He patted the left breast pocket of his rented tuxedo. Ordinarily he'd have expected the warm comfort of feeling his Sig Sauer 9mm handgun in that spot. Instead all he got was the anxiety-inducing crinkle of the folded sheet of yellow legal paper with his Best Man's speech written out in his oversized scrawl.

"I'm not a speech guy, but yeah. I'll do my duty like

a good Best Man. Embarrass the hell out of Ax. Get the bride to blush bright red." Bruiser's forced smile slowly relaxed into his characteristic big-assed grin. He could do this. He'd memorized the speech and rehearsed it eleven times, twice on video. No, he wasn't a speech guy, but he could handle public speaking—hell, he'd been a visiting instructor at BUD/S in Coronado Bay twice already, held the attention of forty sweat-soaked, blood-stained SEAL trainees with his words of infinite wisdom. But though he'd never admit it out loud, he had to admit the embarrassing truth to himself:

He was nervous as hell about this speech. Uneasy about the whole thing, really.

"You've never been married, have you?" said Benson, his wise gray eyes sparkling like Bruiser had seen before. It meant Benson already knew the answer. Hell, Benson probably knew more about Bruiser than any other living person did—Bruiser himself included. After all, just because Benson had quit the CIA didn't mean the CIA had quit him. Just like Bruiser leaving the Navy to join Benson's Team Darkwater Special Operations group didn't mean he was no longer a SEAL.

Once a SEAL, always a SEAL.

Hooyah.

Bruiser shook his head, shrugged, and grunted. Was that why he was feeling uneasy? Was Ax getting hitched making him reflect on his own needs, forcing him to look at his own life and see what was missing?

Stop that shit, Soldier, he told himself. You are *not* gonna get emotional at a damn *wedding*. Yeah, seeing Ax so happy is making you question your own assumptions about marriage, but it'll pass. You can't do what you do and still be a good husband, a good father.

Maybe Ax will be able to pull it off, but that's only because Amy's a special woman, Bruiser thought. It takes a special woman to make it through what those two went through with Prince Rafiq. What are the chances there are two kickass women like Amy Hadad in the world? Pretty darned low.

"You know what the secret to a good marriage is, Bruiser?" Benson said.

Bruiser glanced up, left eyebrow raised. "Don't know. Don't care."

Benson chuckled. "Touchy topic? Wanna talk about it, Soldier? Ex-spies are very good listeners, you know."

"Nope," said Bruiser, glowering at a waiter who slowed to offer him a glass of champagne but then hurried off at the sight of the massive ex-SEAL getting grumpy like a bear emerging from hibernation.

Bruiser patted his speech-script again, ran through the opening lines in his head, exhaled slowly to bring down his heartrate. He could stay calm in a firefight, but his best buddy's wedding was getting him jumpy. And John Benson seemed to be enjoying keying him up. "Most certainly do *not* wanna talk about it."

"I don't care what you want or don't want, Soldier," said Benson crisply. His gray eyes sparkled again, but with a different sort of intensity. "You'll answer my question and you'll answer it now."

Bruiser frowned, his fire rising briefly. But Bruiser

knew how to control his natural instincts to strike back at any jab, physical or verbal, and he took another long, slow breath.

On the exhale he understood.

He understood that Benson hadn't come over to shoot the shit with Bruiser. Benson wasn't a casual-conversation kinda guy. The ex-CIA man was working. Always working. Always one step ahead of everyone else.

His mind always on the next mission.

"What's this about?" Bruiser said softly.

Benson took a breath and let it out slow and steady. "It's about Boris Kowalski," he said coolly, looking straight ahead, expressionless like a stone wall. But those gray eyes were shining silver, and Bruiser damn well knew why.

"You know how I got the name Bruiser, right?" he growled, fists clenching as he fought back a smile that was fueled by some old anger mixed with a new respect for this crafty old bastard John Benson.

"Because bruising is what happens when someone calls you by your given name?" Benson said with a wink. He turned and looked at Bruiser dead on. "Boris Kowalski. Only son of Marcin Kowalski and Anna Mirkhova. Father is Chicago Polish. Mother is first generation Russian, from the ghettoes of Moscow. You speak fluent street-Russian, excellent Polish, and, best I can tell, pretty decent English, even through that thick Chicago accent."

Bruiser stayed quiet. He relaxed his shoulders, uncurled his sausage-thick fingers, letting them drum against his uncomfortable tuxedo trousers. In kindergarten and first grade he'd been teased relentlessly about being named Boris by his Russian mother. Then in second grade he hit a growth spurt. By third grade his new name was Bruiser. Enough said.

"You keep up with Russian politics?" Benson asked.

"Russian imperialism, you mean?"

Benson grinned. "We're all in the empire-building business, kid."

Bruiser grunted. He stayed silent. CIA guys were all about the politics, the compromises, the double-deals and the triple-crosses. Bruiser saw the world differently.

He saw it through the eyes of a soldier.

A military man who bled red-white-and-blue, never compromised on his loyalty to America, believed deep in his powerful heart that America was Good and Right, end of story.

Maybe it was simplistic, but it kept Bruiser clear-headed in combat, laser-focused in battle. It helps to have no doubt in your mind when you're facing an enemy who wants you dead. All humans have a natural aversion to killing another human, and it's a mind-game to push back that instinct and do your duty when it calls. That's what makes you an elite warrior.

That's what makes you a SEAL.

"We've had a guy on our radar for years," Benson continued. "Russian-Ukrainian. He went underground, but just popped up again. Damyan Nagarev is his name." Benson paused. "Heard of him?"

Benson raised his champagne flute and sipped. Bruiser noticed that the glass was still almost full. Bruiser himself rarely drank. Looked like Benson didn't drink much either, but the CIA man liked to pretend. Bruiser himself didn't give a damn what people thought or said about him. Unless they called him Boris, of course.

Bruiser thought a moment. Damyan Nagarev. The name was familiar. He nodded.

"SEALs did an informal joint session with a few guys from Russian Special Forces five years ago, back when things weren't so tense. I overheard some of the Russian guys mention Damyan when they were talking in Russian amongst themselves. I guess he's a legend of sorts in Russian Special Forces. They called him the Demon, I think." Bruiser chuckled. "Damyan the Demon. Real creative."

Benson didn't chuckle. "He's earned that nickname. Got kicked out of Special Forces for being too damn brutal, which is saying something. Half of the Russian SF trainers are ex-KGB guys who spent their youth torturing their own damn citizens."

Bruiser frowned. Excessive brutality in Russian Special Forces? That *was* saying something. "Where'd he go after that?"

"Straight to the Bratva. Started off as a regular enforcer in Moscow, but got promoted three times in a year. He was so ruthless and efficient they sent him to Kiev, in the Ukraine. Damyan was the Russian mafia's top enforcer in the Ukraine. Pretty much drove the local Ukrainian mob out of Kiev. Not an easy thing to do."

Bruiser grunted. He wasn't chuckling anymore, but he wasn't particularly impressed either. Thugs fighting thugs. Mafia fighting mafia. Hell, Bruiser was from Chicago. What the hell did Kiev have that Chi-town didn't?

Anyway, it seemed irrelevant to him. Bruiser didn't like talking in circles. He was a ram-straight-ahead kinda guy. "So why does the CIA care about some Russian enforcer in Ukraine? He's basically a grunt who's good at killing people."

Benson cracked a half-grin. "That's *exactly* why we cared." His grin tightened. "We tried to recruit him as an asset a few years ago," he said quietly.

Bruiser glanced at Benson, frowned, and rubbed his clean shaved chin which was roughly the size of the Matterhorn. "An asset. You mean an assassin." He shook his head. "You know, every time I think the CIA can't surprise me with how low they can go, you guys go lower."

Benson laughed. He faked another sip and glanced towards where Ax and Amy were posing with yet another group of military folks—this time six Marines in full dress blues.

Bruiser followed Benson's gaze, smiling when he saw how damn happy Ax looked. Ax himself was in a tux, since he was no longer officially military. He'd left the Navy to join Benson's covert Team Darkwater, taking the former SEAL Team Thirteen with him—Bruiser, Cody, and Dogg. But there was no mistaking that Ax was still a SEAL to the core, just like the rest of the old team.

"Hey, I surprise myself too when I realize what I'm capable of doing," cracked Benson. He turned his attention back to Bruiser, drawing Bruiser's gaze away from the happy couple. "But right now I need to understand what *you're* capable of doing, Soldier."

Bruiser tightened along his thickly muscled spine. "I'm

capable of doing whatever it takes," he said. No flinch. No blink. Not even a breath.

"Nobody doubts that," Benson said. "But this is a different sort of mission. Mind games more than war games. Finesse more than fighting. Maybe not quite the best fit for your skillset."

Bruiser bristled, hot blood rising up his back, the small hairs standing up along his neck. He'd always been the big guy in the group, starting from third grade onwards. Even amongst Ax, Cody, and Dogg he was the biggest—which was saying something, since Dogg was the "smallest" at six foot one and two hundred pounds.

But Bruiser wasn't just a grunt who was good at killing people. Sure, he'd been a killer defensive-end all the way through college, but he played for the University of Chicago, which was known more for its Nobel Laureates than its football program.

"My *skillset*?" he growled. "What exactly is my damn *skillset*, Benson?"

Benson narrowed his eyes. They flashed with mischief. Maybe something else. "Relax. I know you graduated Summa Cum Laude in Mathematics from the University of Chicago. You can probably solve a quadratic equation easier than most people can spell the damn word. But this isn't about pure intelligence, and it's not about brute force." He paused, took a slow breath, let it out even slower. "It's about a woman, Bruiser."

Bruiser took a quick, short breath and rumbled it out. He shot a glance at Ax and Amy, the married couple glowing with what Bruiser supposed was magical romantic love or something cheesy like that. He folded his huge arms over his barrel-shaped chest and looked down at Benson.

A woman.

It made sense now.

Why else would Benson ask him about marriage and bullshit like that.

"All right, I'll bite," said Bruiser. "What's the secret to a happy marriage?"

"You gotta lie like the best damn liar in the world," said Benson without missing a beat, like he had the answer ready, like he knew Bruiser would break and ask the question. "That's what true love is about. Lie like a motherfucker. Lie like a sonofabitch. Lie like a dog in the summer heat. When she asks what's wrong, you say *Nothing's wrong, baby*. When she asks what you're thinking about, you say *I'm thinking about you, baby*. When she asks what movie you want to watch, you say *That cheesy fucking rom-com, baby*."

Bruiser almost choked on the blast of laughter that burst out of him like a cannon. He knew Benson had been secretly married to Sally Norton, Amy's boss at the State Department. Sally had been killed by one of Prince Rafiq's assassins. All the members of Darkwater knew what Sally had meant to Benson.

She'd meant everything.

Benson's whole world was lies.

Sally had been his truth.

Still, there was a strange seriousness to Benson's quip. Bruiser composed himself and waited. Benson smiled, those gray eyes shining with a dark mist. Bruiser wondered if he was thinking about Sally. He wondered if Benson and Sally shared the same kind of love that Ax and Amy seemed to share. Was there more than one kind of love?

How the hell would he know. He'd never told a woman he loved her. Never wanted to say it. Never felt the need. Huh. Maybe Benson was right. Maybe this mission *was* out of his skillset.

"A woman?" Bruiser said. "I hope you aren't gonna ask me to assassinate a woman, Benson. I'll do anything for my country, but there are lines I'd rather not cross."

"Relax. I don't think you'll need to kill her," said Benson. He thought a moment. "Well, I hope not. You'll have to use your judgment when the time comes. Though if the time comes, it's possible your judgment will be compromised. That's why I'm hesitant to send you. Your combat record is perfect. Unfortunately your record with women is significantly less perfect. But you speak Russian like a street thug. You even kinda look like a Russian street thug. Hell, you *are* Russian."

"I'm *half* Russian," Bruiser reminded him. But mentally and emotionally he was more than fifty percent Russian, he knew. His mother's Russian influence had been dominant in his childhood. After all, she'd been born and raised in the Moscow hood, whereas Bruiser's dad was two generations removed from Poland—way more Chicago than Krakow. "Just half."

"So is she," said Benson. He glanced over at the raised platform where the bride and groom were still being harangued by selfie-seekers. Then he looked over towards the white-painted wooden double-doors leading out to the sprawling patio where the barbecue ribeye steaks were already hissing and spitting on the massive grills set up for the wedding dinner. "Let's take a walk, Soldier."

They stepped outside. It was four in the afternoon. The Georgia sun was still high, still hot. The Axelrod ranch was decorated with red-white-and-blue streamers flying from barn roofs, matching ribbons draped over painted wood fences. The pastures were green and lush. The gardens surrounding the ranch houses were well watered, perfectly manicured by Ax's mom June. And the barbecue was on. Hell yes, the barbecue was on.

Bruiser inhaled deep. "Spicy mesquite. Smoky hickory. Molasses dark and sweet like a French stripper's asshole."

Now it was Benson's turn to almost choke on a guffaw. "You know, when you say things like that it gives me confidence that maybe, just maybe, you're the right man for the job."

Bruiser grinned. He'd always pushed the limits with the wise-cracks. Violence to sex, nothing was off limits for him. It was battlefield humor. A reminder that you live on the extreme edges of society, where nothing is taboo, where you might have to kill a man with your bare hands tonight and be at the Thanksgiving table with the family tomorrow.

Ax, Cody, and Dogg understood it.

So did Benson.

The rest of the world, not so much.

To hell with the rest of the world.

Bruiser had forsaken the rest of the damn world when he committed himself to his country, to his mission, to this life.

They strolled silently to the edge of the wooden deck, away from earshot of the caterers who were diligently flipping the ribeyes and turning the turkey legs. Not a whole lot of veggies on the grill. This wasn't that kind of crowd.

"CIA Director Martin Kaiser called me," Benson said, leaning on the white wooden railing and gazing out at the proud, beautiful horses grazing in the distance. "Martin and I worked together trying to recruit Damyan back in the day. We failed. Neither of us handles failure well. I guess it always felt like unfinished business, so he called me when Damyan popped up on the radar after years of being underground."

Bruiser nodded. He knew that although Benson had quit the CIA completely, Director Kaiser still shared information with him. Although Benson never said it outright, Kaiser and he had an unspoken understanding that Team Darkwater could do things the CIA couldn't.

Maybe even things the CIA *wouldn't*.

"The NSA's voice-recognition scanner-programs picked up Damyan's voice on a cell phone call," Benson continued. "He called a number we traced to an unofficial detention center in Ukraine, just over the Russian border. It's a Russian prison, but in Ukraine for plausible deniability. It's like a holding area for off-the-books prisoners. Apparently Damyan is interested in someone the Russians put there. A woman. We got her name from the phone call. Ran her through the system." He paused. "She's American. Brenna Yankova."

Bruiser frowned. "Russian name. She's CIA? Black ops or something?"

Benson shook his head. "The Russians may have thought she was, which is why they picked her up. Things are tense with the Russians right now. CIA's been putting a lot of undercover agents in the field lately, so the Russian Secret Police have been particularly aggressive. She's a Princeton grad, bilingual, maybe fits the profile of a CIA analyst. But she's a civilian. Homeland Security shows her leaving the U.S. from Newark Airport a couple of weeks ago. Round trip flight to Moscow. Six week trip."

"How long have the Russians had her?"

Benson shrugged. He stayed silent.

Bruiser raised an eyebrow. "We didn't know the Russians took her?"

Benson grunted. Half-grinned at Bruiser. "You overestimate how much we know. She wasn't officially arrested. What, you surprised the Russians didn't give her a free phone call to the U.S. Embassy?"

Bruiser wasn't surprised. He knew why his mother had fled Russia. "So she's a hostage?"

Benson shook his head again. "Russians never contacted our CIA station in Moscow. There are back-channels they could have used to say they had one of ours. Could have used her to get something out of us, maybe just to humiliate us. But they didn't do it. They probably checked her out, sweated her, didn't get anything out of her. Which means maybe they don't believe she's CIA."

"You sure she isn't?"

"She isn't. Kaiser would know. He'd have told me."

"So they made a mistake," said Bruiser. "And it seems they know they made a mistake. So why hold her?"

Benson shrugged. "Maybe they're worried she'll go right to the U.S. Embassy and make a scene. Make the Russians look foolish. Get some embarrassing publicity. Some tense diplomatic meetings—which are tense enough these days." He touched his chin, moved his neck like it was cramping. "Or maybe there's something else going on."

Bruiser blinked, rubbed his own big chin. "Like what?"

Benson took a breath, glanced at the caterers. They were basting the turkey legs with mesquite and molasses, slopping fresh golden butter on the steaks. "Could be a cover. Could be Brenna Yankova is selling something to the Russians. Could be they make it look like a mistaken arrest. Make the trade behind prison walls, then spring her. If anyone was watching, it would look like a mistake. No harm, no foul."

Bruiser snorted, not sure if Benson was serious. One look at the CIA man and Bruiser was reminded that Benson was always serious. Even when he made wisecracks about rom-coms. "A traitor? You know that for a fact?"

Benson shook his head. "Kaiser's got someone doing deep background on her."

"What do we know so far?"

Benson thought a moment, like he was considering how much to reveal. Ax had told the guys that Benson might look like an old gray wolf but was wily like a damn fox. He never showed you all his cards. Always held something back. Always bluffing. Always keeping his options open. Didn't matter whose side you were on—Benson manipulated everyone when he played his games.

"She's Alexei Yankov's daughter," Benson said softly.

Bruiser stared blankly. "Who's Alexei Yankov?"

Benson smiled. "That's what we're trying to figure out. He's a nobody, so far as we know. He's also been dead for ten years, it seems. Brenna Yankova ran her DNA through the Human Identification Project. Got a 50% hit on an unidentified murder victim killed in Ukraine, buried in Russia. Got to be her father."

"So there you go. She just found out her dad died and is buried in an unmarked grave. She wants to visit the site. Simple explanation." said Bruiser when Benson paused.

"It would have been, if not for Damyan rearing his ugly head."

Bruiser chuckled grimly. "Still a big leap to think she might be a traitor. You think Alexei Yankov worked for Damyan? And Brenna is in cahoots with her Russian dad who died ten years ago? Still a stretch. There's gotta be something else going on, Benson."

Benson stayed quiet. He looked at his watch, a scarred black metal Fossil Chrono. "These are questions I'm going to be asking you in two days," he said casually.

Benson turned his head to the left, gazed past the barns, to one of the side roads. Bruiser followed his gaze. There was a cloud of dust in the distance. As Bruiser watched, a black Chevy Suburban shot out of the dust cloud, heading straight towards the ranch house. Bruiser estimated he had about four minutes. He didn't waste his time asking about logistics.

"There's still a chance Brenna Yankova is an innocent American civilian just visiting her father's grave," Bruiser said, thinking out loud rather than asking a question.

"Innocent civilians are of no interest to a man like Damyan Nagarev."

Bruiser rubbed a spot above his left eye. There was an old scar where a sniper's bullet had grazed his forehead. He'd heard the bullet coming even though it made no sound in the dry desert air outside Tikrit.

Nah, he hadn't heard it.

He'd *felt* it.

That sixth sense all elite warriors seemed to have. Axe had it. Bruiser had it. All four of them had it. That's why they were still alive. That's why they always walked into battle with an unshakeable faith that when the gunshots stopped and the gunsmoke settled they'd be the ones still standing.

"Forget Damyan Nagarev for a minute," Bruiser said, his blood rising again when he thought through it. "You're saying the Russians are holding an American woman in a secret prison and we're doing nothing about it?"

Benson's gaze softened for a moment. The softness didn't last. "We're doing something about it now, aren't we?"

He turned back towards the horses. Something

spooked them suddenly, and they bolted off towards the sweltering horizons of the vast pasture.

Bruiser watched the horses run. He thought of what Benson had said about Nagarev. About Brenna. Was she really a traitor? Or was she innocent.

Still, Benson had a point: Why would Nagarev be interested in an innocent American civilian? Why would a wanted, hunted man be interested enough to come out of the shadows, to risk having his voice intercepted on a cell phone call? Wouldn't Nagarev have a hundred cronies who could have made that call?

"Nagarev knew her name, and she's clearly important enough that he made the call himself. He didn't trust anyone else to make the call. Didn't want anyone else getting to her before he did," said Benson, his gray eyes studying Bruiser, perhaps running an assessment on whether Bruiser really was up to this mission. "Which means she has something important that Damyan wants. Or knows something important. Or *is* something important." He swallowed hard, stayed quiet, looked out at the horses, then towards the approaching Chevy Suburban.

Bruiser narrowed his eyes and gazed out over the impossibly green pastures of the Georgia ranch. His sharp mathematical mind put the pieces together in an instant, and he whipped his head back towards Benson.

"You want me to get to Brenna Yankova before Damyan gets there," he said. "Figure out why she's so important to him." He bit on his bottom lip, furrowed his brow, squinted into the sun. "But it's already too late, isn't it? When did Damyan make the call?"

"Four hours ago."

Bruiser snorted. "Even if I get on a plane in the next thirty seconds it'll be too late. No way I get there before Nagarev."

Benson smiled like he knew something Bruiser didn't. Of course he did. Spooks always held something back. It was habit. Instinct. A way of life.

Bruiser thought a moment. Then he shook his head, rubbed that bullet-groove on his forehead.

"Where did Damyan's call originate from?"

"Buenos Aires," said Benson with a grin.

Bruiser grinned back. He did the mental math. Argentina was a lot farther from Russia than Georgia. He nodded, glanced towards the black Suburban, then back at Benson. Two minutes till the car got there. Bruiser wasn't going to waste it talking. He figured Benson would tell him what he needed to know.

"Don't know much more right now," said Benson. "The car will take you to Robins Air Force Base. I called in a favor."

"Good," retorted Bruiser. "Because I don't want to owe those fly-boys any favors."

Benson laughed. He reached into his jacket pocket and pulled out a slim black phone with no logo on it. Bruiser took the phone, looked at it, then slid it into his interior jacket pocket. As he pulled his beefy hand out, he heard the crinkle of paper.

"Shit, my speech," he said, feeling his heart quicken again. It had been beating calm and steady while Benson was telling him about secret Russian prisons and terrorists nicknamed "The Demon." But thinking about his buddy's wedding made him sick with anxiety. Maybe he did have some unresolved issues when it came to women and relationships. Oh well, too late for therapy. Unless the driver was an Army Psychiatrist.

"Hand it over, Soldier," said Benson with a sly grin.

Bruiser raised an eyebrow. Then he pulled out the speech and handed it to Benson.

Relief washed over Bruiser. Then a pang of guilt that he was happy to be relieved of speech duties.

He looked past Benson's shoulder, caught a glimpse of the married couple through the open double doors. Ax was looking in his direction.

Bruiser met his old SEAL Team Leader's gaze. They locked eyes for a long moment. Ax nodded once. Bruiser nodded back. No words needed. They were brothers.

"You called in another favor for the car?" Bruiser asked as the shiny black Suburban skidded to a halt alongside the side fence, totally destroying June Axelrod's pansies. "CIA issue? Homeland Security?"

"Nah," said Benson, scanning Bruiser's hand-scrawled speech as he strode back towards the wedding reception. "Just an Uber. Turn on your phone, Soldier."

Bruiser grinned and shook his head. He glanced towards the Suburban. The driver was in street clothes, but a Jarhead by his haircut and ramrod-straight posture. Marine all the way through.

Bruiser grinned again as the smell of hickory and mesquite came to him on the hot Georgia breeze.

"Turkey leg or ribeye?" he called to the driver.

The driver turned, blinked, and swallowed hungrily. He was young, fresh, and green like he'd just come off the farm. Bruiser didn't wait for a response. He slapped two massive ribeyes on two plates, grabbed a stack of napkins, and hopped the fence without spilling a drop of molasses-heavy sauce or golden-cream butter.

They ate with their hands. The Marine handled his steak like he'd done this before. Bruiser got some sauce on his tux. It was a rental. He was going to lose his deposit anyway, since the tux was going to end up in an Air Force trash can. By the last bite, Bruiser was wiping his hands on his lapels with the perverse excitement of a child playing in the mud.

When the steaks were gone, the Marine glanced at Bruiser in the rearview mirror.

"There's something for you under the passenger side seat, Sir," he said.

Bruiser looked down and saw a black duffel under the front passenger seat. He pulled it up onto the back seat and unzipped it. He grinned when he saw the familiar shine of a Sig Sauer 9mm handgun, complete with three extra magazines. There was also a six-inch pigsticker blade. And, most importantly, there were clothes.

Real clothes, not the damn rented monkey suit. Black cargo pants and a black tee shirt. They weren't military issue, and when Bruiser looked at the labels, he realized they were Russian. He frowned. Benson hadn't told him shit about the operation. Bruiser figured Benson would brief him on the flight. Now he remembered the phone.

"Shit," he muttered, pulling it out of his jacket. It

was still off. He felt along the side for the power button. There wasn't one. There was just a fingerprint reader on the front. He pressed his big right thumb on it. The phone lit up with blue light. There were already messages on it when it started up all the way.

The first message was the complete file on Damyan Nagarev. Bruiser flicked through the summary. He'd read the details later on the flight. For now he tapped on Nagarev's most recent photo and zoomed in.

The face was lean, almost colorless. Oval and long, with a dull yellow widow's peak of hair shaved close to the skull. Razor-sharp cheekbones and thin grayish lips that were a straight line over a sharply cut square jaw.

The eyes were sunken and blue, but very much alive. There wasn't a hint of defeat in those eyes. They were the eyes of an alpha wolf, a man who'd been in many fights and won every single one of them. Bruiser immediately understood why Benson and Kaiser had wanted to recruit Nagarev: Better to have a man like this fighting for you than against you.

"Damyan the Demon," he muttered under his breath as he took a long look into those cold blue eyes and then double-tapped the screen.

The photo shrunk back to a little square of color. Bruiser flicked quickly through the next few pages of Nagarev's file. He stopped on another photo. Another man.

This man was bigger, with spiked blonde hair and tattoos creeping out above the collar of a black tee shirt. His name was Mikhail Gervin, and he was Nagarev's right hand man. The only man Nagarev trusted. Mikhail's last known whereabouts were in South America.

Made sense, Bruiser thought. Nagarev would keep the one man he trusted close. Even a demon needs someone to watch his back. Satan himself had a legion of them, right?

Bruiser frowned as he looked at Mikhail's file. There were three photos, all taken at different times. But the man wore the same clothes in all three photographs. Black cargo pants and black tee shirt.

Bruiser's frown deepened. He shot a glance at the clothes in the duffel bag. He thought of his own tattoos, a couple of which snaked all the way up his chest to his collarbones.

If someone were describing Bruiser and Mikhail, they might describe them with the same broad brush strokes. Big Russian street-thugs with tattoos. Always in black. Square jaw. Spiked light-colored hair. Green eyes.

Sure, nobody would be fooled if they knew Mikhail well or had a clear photograph. But chances were that if Mikhail were to show up at an underground Russian prison to pick up a secret prisoner, nobody was gonna be asking him for ID.

Was that Nagarev's plan? To send Mikhail to pick up Brenna Yankova?

But then why didn't Nagarev tell Mikhail to make the phone call? Surely a man like Nagarev understood that modern surveillance tech was basically science-fiction alien-level shit now. Damyan had to know he was risking his voice being picked up on a scanner. Why take the risk?

The answer came to Bruiser in a highlighted note in Mikhail's file.

Mikhail Gervin couldn't make the phone call.

Couldn't make *any* phone call.

He had no tongue.

Bruiser's back tensed up. Now he understood why Nagarev, a man who trusted no one, would trust Mikhail. And it wasn't just that Mikhail couldn't speak. It was *why* Mikhail couldn't speak.

He hadn't been tortured.

He hadn't been threatened.

He'd cut his tongue out himself.

A show of commitment.

A gesture of loyalty.

Proof that he could be trusted.

"Scared yet?" came Benson's voice from the phone.

Bruiser was startled but not surprised. "What else aren't you telling me, Benson?" he growled.

Benson was quiet. Bruiser could hear him grinning through the phone. It was all a game to Benson, wasn't it?

Bruiser understood it. All of them understood it. That sickening pit in your gut before a mission was adrenaline trickling into your system. The most powerful drug known to man. It was why they all did what they did. It was why a warrior wanted to be on the battlefield. Why a warrior *needed* to be on the battlefield.

"Getting her out of there should be easy, so long as

you get there before Mikhail and take his place," said Benson after a pause. "And you've probably already figured out not to say anything to the warden, since you don't have a tongue. Just grunt and nod. Should be easy for you, big guy."

Bruiser bit his tongue so he wouldn't say something he might regret. Benson knew how to push a man's buttons, but Bruiser was damn good at controlling his temper. Ax was the hothead in the group. Bruiser, despite his almost comical bulk, could cool himself down just with the power of his mind.

Made sense that Bruiser was the best sniper in the team. He could stay motionless and silent for eight hours on a chilly, windswept mountainside in the Hindu Kush. He'd done just that countless times, waiting patiently for his target, taking his time with the shot, making the first one count. Yeah, pretending he didn't have a tongue was gonna be manageable, he figured.

"So no lines for my role," he said with an exaggerated sigh. "Why do you even need someone who speaks Russian? You just needed a guy who matches Mikhail's description, right? The CIA has access to a bunch of big guys who can grunt and glower. It's a ten-minute mission. Pick up the girl, take her to the extraction site, hand her over to the CIA interrogators. They can figure out if she's a traitor or not. Why is this a Darkwater mission?"

Benson paused again. Bruiser could hear him breathe.

"When was the last time you heard of a traitor being prosecuted in the United States?" Benson said softly.

Bruiser thought about it. "It's been a while," he said finally.

"And why is that, you think?"

Bruiser thought some more. "Because we don't have any traitors?" he said hopefully.

Benson chuckled. It was a dark, dry laugh. "I'm a patriot like you, Bruiser. To the death and beyond. But I'm also a realist. We've always had traitors in our midst. Not a lot, but enough that it could be a public relations problem if we brought every traitor to trial."

He took another breath. A chill crept up Bruiser's spine as he locked into Benson's thought process, followed it to the logical conclusion.

A conclusion that sickened him.

"So we just don't bring our traitors to trial," he whispered. "We take them out in the field. Bury the bodies in unmarked graves. Make it seem like we have no traitors."

"Welcome to the shadowy world of spies and spooks, kid," said Benson. "No black. No white. Just gray. Lots of gray."

Bruiser chuckled. A dry, dark laugh that matched the mood. "I prefer the simple life of a soldier. Give me a target and an M-11 sniper rifle and I'm good."

"You don't have to do this, Bruiser," said Benson. "You're right. Kaiser can find someone who'll pass for Mikhail. They can extract Brenna Yankova. Interrogate her. Find out what she did or didn't do." He paused. "Get rid of her when they're done."

Bruiser swallowed. He looked down at his phone. The third message from Benson was still unopened. He tapped on it. It was another file.

Brenna Yankova's file.

He glanced at the summary as Benson's question hung

out there like a noose waiting for Bruiser to put his head in it.

It didn't take long.

Just about two seconds.

Two seconds that felt like forever.

Because he spent those two seconds looking at Brenna Yankova's photograph.

Looking into her big brown eyes.

Seeing something that he knew nobody else saw.

Something that nobody else could ever see.

"I'll take the mission," he said softly, pushing away the odd feeling he got from looking into her eyes.

A feeling that made no sense.

A feeling like she was his.

3
BUENOS AIRES
ARGENTINA

"She's yours after we get what we need from her," said Damyan Nagarev through a puff of heavy black cigar smoke. "Twelve words and then you can cut out her tongue and make her scream from the depths of her throat. You like that, do you not, Mikhail?"

Mikhail Gervin turned his head halfway and grunted through a sideways smile. Then he turned back to the woman swaying her wide hips to the Latin beat thundering through the black speakers nailed high on the red walls of the *Carnita Club's* private room.

The woman was large, just like Mikhail liked. He slapped her ass hard and watched her ample buttcheeks shiver. The woman yelped and turned around quickly, but Mikhail growled at her, grabbed her hips, and turned her facing away. With his big right paw he spanked her bottom again, this time so hard she screamed.

She tried to run for the door, but Mikhail grabbed her wrist and yanked her back towards him. He held her throat with his left hand, shoved his right hand between her asscheeks from behind, slammed her against the dark red walls.

Damyan watched for a few minutes, then lost interest. He sighed and looked at his watch, a heavy white-gold Patek-Phillippe studded with holes where there used to be diamonds. He should have sold the watch along with the diamonds, but it meant something to him.

"Eight minutes, Mikhail," he said in Russian as he stubbed out his Cuban cigar and stood from the tattered blue leather sofa. He reached into his left trouser pocket and pulled out a grimy roll of twenty dollar bills. If this plan did not work, soon he would be carrying one dollar bills, he thought in disgust.

In the old days he carried hundreds, all crisp and new.

Those days would be back again once he had Brenna Yankova.

There were some pesos mixed in with the dollars. He didn't usually bother with Argentinean currency. The corrupt government printed so much of it that it was only good for cleaning one's arse.

Though U.S. dollars were heading in the same direction, Damyan thought as he peeled off six twenties and slid them under the heavy cut-glass ashtray. That should cover the cost of the woman. Life was cheap in this part of the world.

And soon life would be cheap in *any* part of the world for Damyan.

As soon as he extracted those twelve words from Brenna Yankova.

Twelve words that opened up a digital wallet.
A private treasure chest.
Treasure that rightfully belonged to Damyan Nagarev.
Treasure that had been stolen from Damyan Nagarev..
Stolen by a man who was burning in Hell.
Whose daughter would repay the debt to the Demon.

4

"I never heard of your father Alexei Yankov," said Boots, his twisted face going slack and then scrunching up to its normal raisin-like texture. "But Damyan has many who followed him in the old days. Perhaps still."

He took a step closer to Brenna, then turned and pulled the heavy door closed behind him before advancing on her again.

Brenna hugged her knees tighter as she huddled back against the far wall of her cell. Boots looked very large above her right now, but she wasn't scared of him. She hated him for hitting her, but she wasn't scared he'd hit her again. She didn't have the energy to be scared right now. The lack of food had taken its toll. The foul-tasting water hadn't helped much.

But she was alive.

And by the looks of it, Boots might actually be interested in keeping her alive.

Maybe even keeping her safe.

Brenna nodded. She'd told Boots what she'd already told the Russians: That she was just here to visit her father's grave, pay her respects.

Brenna thought back to when Alexei had mentioned Damyan. It didn't sound like Alexei knew the man. But lots could have happened since then.

The back of her head pounded in that dull, sickening way like when you drink too much vodka and sleep three hours and then wake up sweating and thirsty. Could her father have worked for the UNA? For Damyan Nagarev? Was it possible?

Of course it was *possible*. Anything was *possible*. She'd asked Alexei what he did, and he'd just smiled and said *Oh, this and that*. She'd asked her mother Nancy, who'd just shrugged and said she didn't know, didn't care, didn't want to know, didn't want to care.

And then Alexei disappeared. Ten years ago. Brenna emailed, but nothing came back. She had no phone number. No address. Alexei had always come and gone like the wind and the rain. Unpredictable. Uncontrollable.

Nancy hadn't been concerned. If anything she'd seemed relieved. She was no help. She didn't care.

Brenna tried calling Police Stations in Moscow. Hospitals in Moscow. Searched online records for car accident victims and plane crash manifestos in the region. Set up Google Alerts for Alexei Yankov that never got activated. She searched. She prayed. She waited.

Nothing.

Not a word.

Not a peep.

Not for years.

Then she saw an article about the Human Identification Project run by an NGO that had pulled DNA from the unnamed dead from all over the world. She tried her luck, not expecting much.

She got more than she expected.

A 50% match on her DNA.

A parent.

Her father.

She arrived in Moscow a month later. Found her AirBnb in Gorky Park clean and fresh with excellent wifi. Three days later the Russian Police knocked on her door. Someone in the building had called it in. Said she was a sturdy-looking American woman speaking Russian. They came at four in the afternoon. In the old days they'd have come at four in the morning without knocking. She went with them without a fuss. It was a mistake, she told herself. A funny travel anecdote to be saved for later.

And now, a week later, she was here, looking at Boots, wondering if her father worked for a terrorist.

Ohmygod, was my tuition paid with stolen drug money or blood money or terrorist money or monopoly money, she wondered in a dreamy semi-panicked state that felt oddly like things were happening in slow motion. A part of her whispered that her electrolytes were so low that she couldn't even panic properly. She smiled a watery smile and looked at Boots.

Boots seemed excited to talk. "Twelve years ago I had one of Damyan's men here. He said nothing for three weeks. Then he started to talk to the walls. I listened to everything. Many things, he said. He told the walls about UNA, about Damyan and how he was truly a demon-god. The prisoner boasted about his own loyalty to Damyan. Claimed that even after the Russian Secret Police pulled out his fingernails and electrocuted his testicles he said nothing about Damyan."

Boots sighed like he was reliving a fond memory. "Then, when I had heard enough, I contacted the UNA and told them I had their man, that he was talking to the walls, that perhaps someone would hear him talk. Damyan thanked me. He sent his man Mikhail to take care of things. Alas, I was not at the prison that day when Mikhail came, so I never met the man. But he is also a legend like Damyan. Mikhail the Tongueless, they call him. Do you know why they call him that?"

Brenna raised her left eyebrow. Her broken cheekbone hurt. "Um, because he doesn't have a tongue?"

Boots frowned like he was annoyed Brenna had stolen his punchline. He rubbed his chin and grunted. "Mikhail the Tongueless cut out his own tongue as a show of loyalty to Damyan," he said with gruff admiration. "Proof that he would never speak against Damyan, never betray his master."

"Couldn't he just text or email?" said Brenna through that dream-like trance that was hanging on her like a heavy blanket.

"Eh?" said Boots.

"To snitch on Damyan," said Brenna, almost smiling like a precocious child pointing out that the teacher is a dumb-ass. "He doesn't really need his tongue these days. He could just use his fingers and thumbs. Unless he cut those off too. Now *that* would be something."

Boots glared at her incredulously, like he couldn't understand why she didn't understand.

"It is symbolic," he said.

He looked at his nails, which were dry and cracked, like Boots wasn't getting enough collagen in his diet. Then he looked at Brenna, grinning so wide she could see that he still had a couple of rotten molars left in the gaping black hole that was his mouth.

"Mikhail is the one Damyan sends for you," he said softly. He looked at his nails again, closing his mouth but keeping the smile. "The rumor is he likes big, strong women, Yankova. They last longer. The bigger and stronger the better. He will like you very much."

Brenna stared. Boots was going to die, she decided. Horribly, if she had anything to do with it.

She smiled with sickeningly sweet pleasantness, like a Russian fairytale witch about to cast a horrific spell. For a moment she was taken back to those days when Alexei told her tales of boys named Ivan and the mischievous Babayagas of mythical Russia.

"He sounds great, but I'm not really dating right now, thanks," said Brenna, trying her best to push away the image of a tongueless beast making her "last longer," whatever that meant.

She looked up at Boots as she summoned the dregs of her mental strength to plan out a strategy. Right now Boots was here, and he'd hinted at protecting her. She didn't trust Boots any more than she trusted that mangy rat who lived in the hole on the east wall of her cell not to eat her lips while she slept. But she had to start somewhere. It was either Boots the Toothless or Mikhail the Tongueless.

What the hell, she thought. If I'm living in a dark Russian fairy tale, I might as well commit all the way. Here goes.

"I have what Damyan wants," she said softly in Russian. "Protect me and I will give it to you."

Boots crept closer, leaned down over Brenna, peered at her like he was looking for something she'd hidden down her oversized canvas jumpsuit. "Where is it?" he rasped.

Brenna tapped the side of her head. "Up here."

Boots blinked. He rubbed the back of his neck, looked down at her, then past her at the wall. He shook his head, slowly at first, then vigorously. Finally he sighed and stepped back, his shoulders sagging like he was disappointed she didn't produce a ruby or a magic bean.

Brenna's heart sank. He was chickening out. She could see it. Smell it. Feel it.

"Damyan sends Mikhail for you," he said, shaking his head again. "Which means nobody can protect you."

Boots shuffled backwards in his iron-studded boots, still shaking his head. Brenna desperately tried to think of something to offer him, but she knew she'd screwed up. She'd made things too complicated for the simple Boots. Given him too much time to think, too much time to scare himself with the urban legends of Damyan the Demon and Mikhail the Tongueless.

But as Boots heaved open the iron door, lumbered through and closed it behind him, Brenna realized that Boots never meant to protect her. He couldn't protect her. He'd made the offer just to get her to talk. He just wanted to listen. In his lonely world, listening was pleasure.

Just like he'd listened to that man talk to the walls. Boots was a bully and a brute, but he was no schemer or criminal mastermind. He was just a toothless gossip who wanted to know what went on inside his little prison. He couldn't protect her.

And if Mikhail the Tongueless really was as fearsome as Boots said, no one else could protect her either.

5

"*Protect her with your life, because she's now your number one priority.* That's one helluva line, Bruiser."

Bruiser grinned at the phone as Ax's voice thundered out of the speaker. "Did Benson do my speech justice?" Bruiser said.

"He had the crowd in tears," said Ax.

"Interesting," said Bruiser. "Because it was meant to be comedy."

Ax laughed, and then Amy came on the line. "Hey, Bruiser. That was such a wonderful speech."

"Wish I could've delivered it myself," Bruiser said. "But duty calls."

"Ax told me," said Amy. "Listen, when you get back to the U.S., come visit us in Georgia. I've got a college friend at the State Department in Atlanta who's single. You two would be perfect for each other. Actually, let me text you her number. You guys can start getting to know each other."

Bruiser grinned and winced at the same time. He didn't want to be rude, but there was no way he was gonna try dating one of Amy's friends. None of his relationships had ended well—at least not from the women's perspectives—and he didn't want any tension with his best buddy's wife. Also, texting a woman just to get to know her was very much *not* his thing.

"Didn't your husband tell you my thumbs are too big for texting?" said Bruiser, grinning wider as he stretched out his long, heavy legs in the military transport plane that had taken off from Atlanta with just Bruiser as its cargo.

Amy giggled. "My husband told me a lot more than that," she said.

She giggled again, and Bruiser could hear Ax in the background.

"Hey man, I told her that setting you up with anyone she actually cares about is a *bad* fucking idea," Ax yelled from the background.

Bruiser chuckled. He could imagine Ax and Cody fist-bumping, Dogg doubled over with laughter. He listened while Amy and Ax playfully argued over whether Bruiser and her friend would be a good match, and then Ax came back on the line.

The background noise of the wedding reception faded away, and Bruiser figured Ax had walked out onto the patio.

"Listen," said Ax, his voice low and steady. "I should warn you about Benson. You don't know him like I do. The guy is a trickster."

"Yeah, I'm starting to realize that," said Bruiser. "He's always playing games. Never telling you exactly what's going on, what he's got cooking on the back burner."

Ax chuckled. "True that. But at the same time, I trust

him as much as I trust any one of you guys. It's just that he plays the game his own way, by his own damn rules."

Bruiser took a breath. He nodded. "Yeah, you told me how he played you and Amy."

"Played us to perfection," said Ax. "And I wouldn't have it any other way. There's a reason he put you on this mission, Bruiser. You and no one else. Benson has this weird, almost supernatural instinct. He likes to put people in situations and then sit back and see how they handle themselves. He'll hold back information, play mind games, even lie about shit if it suits him. But you still have to trust him. Don't know how else to explain it. It's just how he sees the world, I guess. Hard to describe it without sounding hokey."

"You're a married man now," said Bruiser. "Everything you say sounds hokey. So try me. How does Benson see the world?"

Ax sighed. He was quiet a minute. "You ever think about fate, Bruiser? Destiny? Meant to be?"

"OK, I'm hanging up," Bruiser said through a groan.

Ax laughed. "That's probably for the best before we both embarrass ourselves. Hell, Benson's probably listening in right now, grinning like the wily bastard he is." He laughed again, then took a breath and exhaled. "You take care of yourself, Bruiser. Just know that when the time comes, your team will be there for you. Amy is my number one priority, but she understands that we're all part of the same team, the same family, on the same damn mission. You got that, Soldier? So long as Cody, Dogg, and I are alive, you are *never* on your own, you hear?"

"I hear," said Bruiser, feeling an odd lump in his throat. He wondered if he'd have made it through his speech without embarrassing himself by bawling like an overgrown baby.

He snapped out of it by reminding himself that he'd taken men's lives without an ounce of remorse, hurled himself into battle with bloodlust and blind rage. He was on a mission.

But a mission different from anything he'd done as a SEAL.

A mission that felt like fate.

Bruiser ignored the thought. Ax had got him sentimental for a moment, but he'd get over it. Fate was a fairy tale. Destiny was a distraction. Only the mission was real, and if he didn't get his head into the game, he might as well stop playing.

Bruiser hung up and slid the phone into his left cargo flap. He sighed, grunted, then pulled the phone out again. He tapped the screen, swiped a few times, stopped at Brenna Yankova's photograph.

He'd looked at that photograph far too long already. He'd studied her clear brown eyes, those full red lips, smooth round cheeks. It was a New Jersey Driver's License picture, but probably the best one ever taken by the Newark DMV.

There was also another photo, taken from a distance, probably pulled from Brenna's Social Media pages. It was from a few months ago. Pretty recent.

Also just straight-up pretty.

Bruiser tightened in his jumpseat as he let his gaze fall

over that picture. Brenna was tall and broad, with wide hips, bold curves, and a killer hourglass shape. She was wearing a hip-hugging dark blue long sweater over black tights. She was leaning on an unpainted wooden fence, blue sky above her, the sun pouring through the open strands of her long brown hair. She was big in the most beautiful way, and Bruiser had to fight away the thought of what she'd feel like in his arms, her soft breasts against his hard muscle, her thick thighs wrapped tight around his rippling haunches.

He grinned and shook his head. "Damn you, Ax," he muttered. "You and your perfect wife and your cheesy-ass happily-ever-after got to me a little. Now I'm imagining snuggling with some woman who might be a traitor, someone I might even have to kill. At this rate I'm gonna fail the mission before this plane leaves American airspace."

The thought of the mission brought his focus back to the here and now, the present moment, the only point in time that was real. The past was done. The future was a dream. Only the present moment mattered. That's where the battle is fought. That's where you win or lose, live or die.

With a sigh Bruiser let the images of Brenna Yankova die in his mind. He flicked past the photographs and read through the text. He'd already read everything Benson and the CIA had on her, and he already knew more about her than he would after a year's worth of bullshit texts with some random woman.

But still he went through her file again. Ax had warned

him that Benson always had a plan behind the plan, a method to the mystery. Benson didn't do or say anything without a damn good reason. All that talk about marriage and women and relationships wasn't because Benson actually gave a damn about Bruiser's tender loving heart or future happiness. It was because Benson wanted Bruiser to think about that shit.

And why?

Because this mission was about a woman.

This woman.

Now the adrenaline kicked in, and Bruiser's well-trained mind ripped through the information like a machine. This woman wasn't just some ordinary chick from Jersey. She was something special. Smart enough to get into Princeton. Confident enough that she *only* applied to Princeton. Hell, that was confidence that bordered on arrogance, wasn't it? Careful with this one, Bruiser.

He read on. Brenna was disciplined enough to handle a double-major while also setting college all-time records on the softball team. He knew she'd grown up with her mother Nancy, a quiet woman with not even a parking ticket to her name. Brenna didn't have any parking tickets either.

But she had speeding tickets.

Nine of them.

Bruiser sat up straight, stretched his neck, grinned up at the painted metal roof of the C-17 transport plane. Brenna Yankova had been a speed demon, it appeared.

Interesting. Was it teenage rebellion? Acting out against her mostly-absent father? Drugs? Alcohol? General risk-taking behavior?

Bruiser scanned through the details again. No drug busts, and she'd even passed a drug test for a part-time job in the chemistry department at Princeton. No reports of underage drinking, and she'd been sober for all nine of her speeding tickets.

Bruiser narrowed his eyes, pictured that brown eyed woman from the photograph flooring the accelerator on the red Honda Civic that was the weapon of choice in her assaults on New Jersey's speed limit laws.

He thought back to his own younger days in Chicago. Bruiser hadn't been a speed demon, but he'd pushed the edges of the law with his fists, just barely getting away with a clean enough record that he was accepted by the SEALs after college. Bruiser had inherited some of the street-fighter spirit from his mother, who'd grown up hard in the ghettoes of Moscow. Had Brenna picked up the need for speed from her Russian father?

"Alexei Yankov," Bruiser said out loud, closing Brenna's file and going back to Benson's string of messages. He found Alexei's file and tapped it open.

The photograph was of a lanky, dark-eyed Russian with long black hair and a beard that rivaled that of Rasputin himself. The file was shorter than the others, sketchy information that seemed suspiciously shallow. Surely the CIA had more than three damn paragraphs on a long-haired Russian guy who'd made dozens of trips to the U.S. and appeared to work with computers, had hacker-level smarts?

"What aren't you telling me, Benson?" Bruiser whispered as he scanned through Alexei's file.

Most of the information was financial: A long string

of direct deposits from Moscow International Bank to the Newark Credit Union where Nancy and Brenna had their accounts. The money was all legit, it appeared. Alexei clearly had legal income in Russia, or else he wouldn't have been able to use the banking system to make international wire transfers to the United States. It would have all been seized by the all-powerful Treasury Department, which ruled the world's financial systems to the last ever-loving penny, ruble, or peso.

"You may have been an absentee father, but at least you weren't a deadbeat dad," said Bruiser when he traced back the deposits and saw that they'd started the year Brenna had been born. He'd never missed a payment—not for the first eighteen years, at least. Then they'd all stopped. Made sense, now that they knew he died around that time.

Bruiser frowned, rubbing his jaw and cracking his neck. He quickly flicked back to Brenna's file, looked through her Princeton records.

She hadn't asked for financial aid, Bruiser realized. Hadn't applied for any scholarships. So how the hell did she pay for Princeton? Four years at an Ivy League university probably cost two hundred grand, maybe more. Where did she get the money? It sure as hell wasn't from that part time job feeding lab-monkeys in the Princeton Chemistry Department. No records of student loans coming in. Her bank accounts never showed any large deposits.

Then Bruiser saw something in Brenna's file that he'd missed. It was in her list of accounts. Just a line item indicating she had an account with some company called

COINHOG. Bruiser pulled up a browser and searched for COINHOG. His frown deepened.

"A cryptocurrency exchange," he muttered. "She made a quarter million bucks trading cryptocurrency?"

But there'd been no money moving back and forth between her bank accounts and the crypto exchange. Which meant she was just using the exchange to sell cryptocurrency she already had. She was converting it to dollars and then using those dollars to pay her college tuition. Which meant someone had sent her a big-ass stash of cryptocurrency.

Sent it in secret?

"Nah. There are no secrets from the most powerful U.S. agency," Bruiser muttered. "An agency more powerful than the entire military, the NSA, and Homeland Security put together."

He tapped his way to another website, grinning as the page loaded, showing the crest and lettering that inspired fear in every American, from billionaire to farmer.

"Ladies and gentlemen," Bruiser announced, "I give you the IRS."

Bruiser logged in using the credentials Benson had sent to all Team Darkwater members. Backdoor access to all government databases, a don't-ask, don't-tell courtesy from CIA Director Martin Kaiser. It took Bruiser all of three seconds to pull up Brenna's tax records.

And that's when he knew the game was on.

Because Brenna Yankova had indeed been audited by the IRS just after she paid Princeton with freshly converted cryptocurrency.

The trusty old IRS had indeed sniffed out some

cash-money that might be laundered or undeclared or whatever. And they'd gone after it like the bloodhounds they were.

Except they didn't get a cent of it.

The audit had been terminated.

Dismissed.

Sealed.

"Who can do that?" Bruiser wondered aloud. "Who can overrule the IRS, the most fearsome, darkest, deadliest agency in the history of civilization?"

He knew the answer, of course.

Damn right, he knew the answer.

6
CIA HEADQUARTERS LANGLEY, VIRGINIA

"You going to answer that, Martin?"

CIA Director Martin Kaiser glanced at the black hard-plastic phone that was beeping and blinking like a fire-truck on its way to the towering inferno. He reached out with his left hand, lifted the handset off the cradle, and let it drop back. The ringing stopped. The lights faded to black. He took a breath, then slid open the top drawer of his walnut desk.

"Cigarette, John?" he said softly, pulling out a crisp pack of Dunhill filter cigarettes. He held it out for Benson. There were eighteen cigarettes left in the pack of twenty.

Benson shook his head and smiled. "I only ever smoked Winstons, Martin."

"I remember," said Kaiser. He placed a Dunhill between his dry, cracked lips and lit it with a badly scratched golden Zippo. He took a puff, then leaned back on his black leather swivel, blowing the smoke directly at the ceiling smoke detector. "Took out the battery years ago," he said.

"What if there's a fire?" Benson deadpanned.

"I'll go down with the ship like a good Captain," Kaiser deadpanned in return. "We're all going to burn in hell anyway, right?"

Benson grinned. Martin Kaiser was a salty old CIA dog with no illusions about what they'd done. He could see the past with dark humor, accept it without regrets, without conscience, with an unshakeable sense of duty and self-sacrifice.

Kaiser was also an ex-Navy man, just like Benson himself. Just like all the men of Team Darkwater. Each of the military's branches was special, but everyone secretly knew the Navy was tops.

Not that any of the other branches would admit it, of course. Certainly not the proud Marines. Nor the cocky Fly-boys. And forget about asking the Army who's the best—unless you're itching for a fight.

Those Rangers do know how to fight dirty, though, Benson thought with a half-grin. But of course, nobody fights dirtier than the CIA.

"You sure about this kid Boris Kowalski?" said Kaiser.

"I'd suggest you call him Bruiser when you meet him."

Kaiser exhaled and looked at his cigarette like he was puzzled by it. He stubbed it out in an empty whiskey glass with the 1970s CIA logo on its side. "You should have told the kid everything," said Kaiser.

"He'll figure it out."

"A man who calls himself Bruiser might not have the capacity to figure it out."

Benson smiled thinly. "He doesn't call himself Bruiser. Other kids started calling him that—and not because he bruised easily."

"I've read his file," said Kaiser. "He's smart, sure. But there's too much he doesn't know. You've given him nothing about Alexei Yankov."

"We *have* nothing on Alexei Yankov. Nothing we can rely on, at least."

Kaiser tapped the fissure beneath his lower lip. "You should tell Bruiser about the crypto account. He needs to know what he's looking for."

Benson shook his head. "I don't *want* him to know what he's looking for. I just need him to start looking."

"She's not going to just blurt out the twelve words that unlocks that digital crypto wallet for us, Benson. She knows that Alexei converted the entire UNA treasury into cryptocurrency and hid it in her old college crypto account. She has to know. And so she's gonna pretend like she *doesn't* know."

Benson shrugged. "Brenna had already emptied out the account for her tuition. She might never have checked it again. Look, if she's innocent, she won't know the money is there. If she's playing us, it's best Bruiser doesn't alert her to the fact that we know the money's there, that we're watching the account from the public view-only address."

"You don't think she's playing us?" asked Kaiser.

Benson shrugged. "That money's been sitting untouched, growing exponentially for ten years as crypto prices skyrocketed. If she knew about it and didn't touch one damn cent, it's pretty good self-control."

"You didn't answer the question, Benson." Kaiser looked at the ashtray, then back at Benson. "I think she's playing us. She knows the money is in there. Alexei must have sent her a message that we missed. She's waiting it out, being ultra cautious with the money. Probably didn't dare touch it while in the States. Maybe she was waiting for Damyan to emerge before accessing that money. She could be a masterful player, Benson. Princeton grad. We recruit from Princeton, you know. Russian Intelligence might too. Hard to know what's cooking in her mind."

"All the more reason I want Bruiser in the dark. She needs to trust him, and the only way to make sure she trusts him is to make sure he doesn't know what he's looking for."

Kaiser was silent. He turned that whiskey glass around and ran his thumb over the etched CIA logo. "John Benson waving his magic wand, sprinkling pixie dust, whispering spells and incantations." He looked up, his blue eyes softening for a moment. "How are you doing, John?"

Benson stiffened. He knew Kaiser was asking about Sally. He'd lost her, and that was it. Anything else was his own damn business.

"Don't patronize me, Martin," he growled. "My head is in the game. My judgment is clear. This is how I operate. You know this, Martin. You know I pick the players, set the scene, and then let the game unfold according to the plan."

"Ah yes, the *plan*," snorted Kaiser. He leaned back and waved his arms in the air. "The universe's grand plan, right, John? Fate. Destiny. Magic."

Benson's lower lip tightened. "It's not magic. It's physics. Quantum mechanics. Fundamental principles of how life and death works, how time operates. Fate and destiny are just hokey words for probability distributions and event horizons."

He stopped abruptly before he said too much, revealed his unshakeable belief that love was the universe's most primitive force, most powerful energy, that both sex and violence emerged from the vast ocean of love, that every game was won and lost in that single arena. Martin Kaiser had no patience for that whimsical bullcrap. Not many people in this line of work did.

But elite warriors understand it, Benson considered as those memories of Sally Norton merged with thoughts of how Ax and Amy had met, how everything had revolved around the energy generated by those two. Their love was the center of that story, the arena where the battle with Prince Rafiq took place.

Would it be the same with Bruiser and Brenna?

Or was Benson kidding himself.

Was he going to be wrong this time?

Or be right in that beautiful way that made him love the game?

It was certainly possible that he was wrong about Bruiser. He'd been wrong about recruiting Damyan Nagarev. Perhaps he would be wrong about Brenna Yankova too. Perhaps she would betray her country, betray them all. If her father was a rogue, might she not be one as well? After all, blood runs thick, doesn't it?

But the river of love runs thicker, stronger, faster, Benson reminded himself as Martin Kaiser's desk phone rang again. This time Kaiser answered, holding the phone close and swiveling his chair around and away from Benson.

Benson looked at his old black Fossil watch that was battered gray. It still kept perfect time, just like the universe did. He smiled and stood up, moved the wooden high-backed chair against the side wall, and then walked out the door, out of the past, back into the future.

7
SOMEWHERE BETWEEN ARGENTINA AND RUSSIA

The future of the Ukrainian Nationalist Army depends on you, Mikhail.

Mikhail Gervin picked his left rear molar with the long, hooked stainless steel toothpick he carried with him everywhere. His jaw was so large that there were big spaces between his teeth, and chunks of the stringy Argentinean beef often lodged deep in the crevices. Nobody would describe Mikhail as a particularly clean man, but he did pay close attention to his mouth.

Mikhail found the offending piece of beef, hooked it with the metal pick, and pulled it out carefully. He sniffed it out of habit. Vaguely odorous, which meant it was from yesterday's meal, not the steak he'd wolfed down before taking the charter flight a few hours earlier from the private airfield that shared a runway with Buenos Aires International Airport.

The Learjet plane was owned by a local rancher who had benefitted greatly from Mikhail and Damyan's skills with handling extortionists. Still, it had taken almost a week to organize the flight. Without money, even friendship starts to become strained.

And the money was getting tighter every year, it seemed to Mikhail. He'd noticed that Damyan had left just six twenty dollar bills under the ashtray to pay for disposing of the woman at the *Carnita Club*. Last month it had been eight twenties a woman. Ten years ago when they first arrived, Damyan would pay a thousand to the club even if the woman was still alive when Mikhail finished with her.

Sometimes Mikhail liked to leave them alive. He liked imagining how they would adjust to life without a tongue. It was not as bad as one might fear, he thought. You can still make sounds, still communicate well enough. The most surprising thing was that you do not lose your sense of taste! It was shocking to Mikhail at first, but later he read that a man's sensations of taste are mostly related to smell, not the taste buds on the tongue. Who knew the human body was so complicated?

"It is not a complicated mission, Mikhail," Damyan had said as they drove to the airport in the silver Range Rover Discovery that had lasted ten years now, the bulletproof glass still thick enough to protect them. There were at least three governments who wanted Damyan dead, by Mikhail's count, and so they'd spent money on this battle tank when they had the cash.

Mikhail had nodded, staring straight ahead. He wasn't stupid, but did not take it personally when Damyan spoke to him like he was slow.

Mikhail was Ukrainian through-and-through, a child

of Kiev's streets, orphaned or abandoned, he wasn't sure which. He was old enough to remember Soviet Russia, and young enough to hate the New Russia. As a student he'd taken a keen interest in government, had dreamed about running for office, doing something good for his country. He was neither intelligent enough nor charismatic enough to hope to go very far at the national level, but perhaps he could have been a minor player in local Kiev city politics.

But the Ukrainian government was firmly under Russia's iron-studded boot at every level, and no criticism of Russia's influence was tolerated. After two failed city council campaigns, the second of which ended with Mikhail being beaten by Russian-paid thugs with sand-filled lead pipes, Mikhail decided on a different career path.

The Ukrainian mafia.

He started as a low-level knee-breaker for the loan-sharking operations. Mikhail was big boned, and during those years he added pounds of heavy, hard muscle and an impressive number of tattoos.

In his third year he killed two Russian Bratva men who had tried to muscle in on some of the Ukrainians' territory. The kills were bare-handed and brutal, and Mikhail got promoted to Enforcer. Suddenly he was a big man in the little corner of Kiev that was his territory, and for a while Mikhail was almost happy.

Politics would not have worked out for him anyway. By then his appetites for sex and violence had mixed to the point where he shocked and horrified even his own men sometimes. That might have been a problem for a public official. He was pleased how fate had led him to his true calling. When one door closes, another breaks open, yes?

But brutal indulgences with the curviest women of the Ukrainian brothels aside, what pleased Mikhail the most was the kind of violence that had nothing to do with sex. The Russian Bratva was making moves in Kiev, and Mikhail was thrilled to get a chance to kill Russians. In a way that was what he'd always wanted to do, and now he was doing it for a job! Funny how the universe finds a way to get you to your destiny, yes?

And that was what it felt like when he came face to face with the Russian Bratva's top Enforcer in Kiev.

It felt like destiny.

Damyan "The Demon" Nagarev. A wiry, lean, ex-Russian Special Forces killer who joined the Bratva and got shipped out to Kiev to muscle in on the Ukrainian territory. With Bratva money and Russian weapons at his disposal, it didn't take Nagarev long to drag the Ukrainian mafia to the negotiating table.

Mikhail Gervin stood guard at that table, watching his Ukrainian boss's back. But in truth he had spent more time watching Damyan Nagarev.

Listening to Damyan Nagarev.

The man was called the Demon, and judging by what Mikhail had seen of his victims, the name was well deserved. But in person Damyan was seductively calm, eloquent and measured, his cold blue eyes sunken in his head but alive with an eerie light. Damyan spoke of his own Ukrainian roots, freely declared in front of his own Bratva men that he hated Russians and working for the Bratva was just a job, not a calling, not a mission, not a passion.

It had been a strange meeting, and in fact Mikhail had been ready for a double-cross—given the bloody street-battles where Damyan had ordered beheadings and disemboweling, tactics he had learned from his days fighting the Afghanis with the Russian Red Army.

Rumors were that the Afghani tribesmen had learned the value of shocking brutality, learned how it instilled terror in soldiers who expected that the worst that could happen was a bullet or a bomb. Damyan had learned that there were few things more terrifying that hearing your brother scream in the darkness as his belly is slowly slit open and his intestines are fed to him while he is still alive.

"You will all be left alive now that we have made peace and your territory has been surrendered to the Bratva," Damyan had said matter-of-factly. "You may all go on your way." Then he'd looked directly at Mikhail, his blue eyes startlingly bright. "Or you may stay, if you choose."

The moment had been electric. It was a job offer, Mikhail slowly realized as he recovered from the shock. Damyan Nagarev was famously untrusting, and was rumored to have no close associates, no trusted inner circle, no right-hand man, no personal bodyguard. After all, he was an Enforcer, a man to be feared. He did not cower in underground bunkers, shield himself with bulletproof armor, hide behind the bodies of other men.

He was Damyan the Demon.

You cannot kill a demon.

At first Mikhail had been too tongue-tied to speak. Everyone in the room was looking at him, it seemed. Ukrainians and Russians, mob bosses and enforcers. Nobody spoke.

Then Damyan stood from the cold steel chair. He placed his fists on the long wooden table, looked past the seated, defeated Ukrainian mob boss, right at the bewildered Enforcer Mikhail Gervin.

"Of all the Ukrainians we fought, my men feared you the most," Damyan said in that even, almost robotic voice. "They still fear you, even though the war is over and we have won. That is an admirable quality, to inspire fear in fearsome men."

Mikhail nodded in acknowledgement, still tongue-tied. He glanced at the back of his boss's bald head, still bowed in defeat. Then he looked up at Damyan, who stood tall and broad, his wiry frame tight like he was studded with steel.

Something clicked with Mikhail in that moment, a feeling he could not explain. He understood the feeling, though. It was a feeling of kinship, connection. But not an equal connection. It was the connection of a master with his servant, a relationship as old as war and peace, victory and defeat.

Mikhail took his place at Damyan's side after that, and the two grew close. Perhaps too close. Because while for a normal man closeness brings trust and bonding, for a demon closeness gives birth to the serpent of suspicion, the moving shadows of doubt.

Now Mikhail forced his mind to switch off, to push away the memory of that night when Damyan accused him of treachery, challenged his loyalty, struck a blow that hurt Mikhail more than anything physical ever could. The big man closed his eyes and let out a guttural throaty cry, the stump of his tongue twitching like a toad in its death throes.

Thankfully the roar of the Learjet's twin engines drowned out his animalistic cry, and the two pilots did not turn their heads to see if a pig was being knifed in the belly behind their cockpit.

Slowly Mikhail settled back down. That was a long time ago. He was a different man back then.

And so was Damyan Nagarev.

8

Damyan the Demon sends his man Mikhail the Tongueless for you.
No one can protect you now.
He will like you very much.
Brenna's fever broke. Heavy beads of cool sweat poured down her face, rivulets from her temples down past her ears, all the way to her neck. The viewing window in the door had been left open, letting in a yellow shaft of light split by the shadows of iron bars.

She stared at the pattern on the concrete floor. She saw old bloodstains on the concrete, black with age. She closed her eyes so tight her head hurt. She'd hated the darkness. Now she hated the light.

Somehow Brenna stood up and walked to the sliver of light. She peered out and saw an unpainted gray concrete wall. Face squished sideways against the bars she could see down the hallway to the iron-studded door at the far end.

As she watched, it opened.

It was Boots, and she recoiled at the sight of him in better light. It did him no favors. She almost felt sorry for the grotesquely twisted jailer, but the throbbing

Breaking Brenna

pain in her broken cheekbone chased away any sympathy. Damn him to hell, she thought.

Boots stepped through the doorway and stopped.

Behind him a shadow appeared.

A man.

A new man.

Broad as a bridge, tall like a tower. He wore all black, a tight round-necked shirt and heavy black canvas cargo pants. His eyes flashed green as he stepped into the light.

His hair was thick, drawn up into spikes of dark gold. High cheekbones that caught the light in a strangely beautiful way. Neck thicker than a stallion's. Arms like cannons, biceps like cannonballs, tattoos down past his tight sleeves, peering out above his black collar.

Brenna let her gaze drop down along his gigantic frame that was a perfectly designed masculine V. Massive thighs that made Brenna's buttocks tighten. She glanced back up at his face. She knew who it was, of course.

Mikhail the Tongueless.

She glanced at his mouth. Bold, symmetrical lips that glistened in the golden light. But the lips were clamped together, square jaw shut tight, like it couldn't move, didn't need to move, because he couldn't speak.

Boots spoke to him in Russian. "She is in Cell Five."

The man grunted from his throat. He strode past Boots and looked down the row of cells. His eyes immediately found hers, and she froze when their gazes met.

Mikhail the Tongueless kept walking, his strides long and heavy, but measured. He walked with military precision, she thought. Like a soldier. Was Mikhail ex-military?

Damyan had been Russian Special Forces, but she didn't know anything about Mikhail the Tongueless. Except that he had no tongue. And that he liked curvy women because they lasted longer.

She looked down at herself and frowned. Brenna had always been a curvy girl, and she'd never been self-conscious about it, certainly not in a negative way. She'd inherited her mom's wide hips and full breasts along with her father's height. Being bigger than all the girls and most of the boys might have made grade school uncomfortable for someone else, but Brenna had also been blessed with a perfect mix of Nancy's subtle confidence and Alexei's who-gives-a-damn-what-anyone-thinks attitude. She'd been teased a few times for being bigger than most, but she always gave as good as she got, never let it change her unabashedly high opinion of herself—both body and mind.

She was who she was.

You could go fuck yourself if you had a problem with that, because she certainly didn't.

Still, there was something about this whole "Mikhail likes the curvy women because they last longer" thing that made her so mad, angry as hell, enraged more than scared.

There was so much old-world misogyny, so much ignorance and hatred, so much over-the-top cartoon-villain level bullcrap baked into that statement that Brenna wanted to kick someone in the damn balls. Again and again. Hard and with authority.

Mikhail the Tongueless had balls, didn't he? Well, let's see how long the Tongueless One can last with my hard shin-bone firmly lodged in there, she thought as she curled her bare toes, tensed her strong glutes, clenched her fists. They'd be calling him the Great Ball-less One after she was done.

Mikhail strode past Cell Three in his measured military march. Brenna swallowed when she saw his pectorals move under the tight black T-shirt. She knew the man was a murderer, a misogynist, probably a maniac. But she couldn't push away the annoying thought that he might almost be handsome if he weren't so detestable, almost be attractive if he weren't a madman who was into murder and mutilation, a beast who deserved to die slowly and horribly for what he'd undoubtedly done to other women, was going to undoubtedly do to her.

Her body started to tremble as Mikhail thundered past Cell Four. She could smell him now, a strong earthy aroma that was not altogether unpleasant. She'd expected him to smell like rotting meat—perhaps hoped he'd smell like that. But she found herself taking a deep breath of his masculine musk, picking up notes that reminded her of fresh cedarwood and smoky hickory and maybe even a hint of mesquite.

She swallowed hard, realized she was salivating, swallowed again hungrily. She blinked rapidly as her head spun from the stress and the starvation and the sight of this beast bearing down on her.

Then suddenly the door at the end of the hallway behind Mikhail clanged open.

A guard shouted in Russian.

"There is a man outside the gates!" shouted the guard, his voice high-pitched and urgent. "He dresses in black, very big, many tattoos. He does not say anything. Makes sounds from his throat. I have not opened the gate. What should I do, Sir?"

Boots turned, frowning, scratching his head, rubbing his chin. He glanced at Mikhail. "He is one of your men, yes? Driver, perhaps?"

Mikhail nodded quickly, grunting once and gesturing flippantly with his hand.

"Is there a problem, perhaps?" Boots said to Mikhail. "Perhaps he has an urgent message. Perhaps he needs the bathroom. I can ask my guard to bring him inside. No problem at all. Damyan Nagarev is a great man, and his name opens all doors in Ukraine."

"Nyet!" barked Mikhail, somehow forming the word with his throat and lips. He glared at Boots, then shot a killer look at the guard.

The guard stayed where he was, hesitant and shaky, not sure what to do, what to say, whether to stay or go, freeze in place or start dancing like a bear in chains.

Brenna frowned as she considered the description of the man at the gates: big guy, black clothes, tattoos, grunts and doesn't speak? Sounded like Mikhail's evil twin. Or good twin.

Weird. Maybe Damyan forced all his men to rip out their tongues to prove their loyalty? An army of tongueless beasts. Seemed a bit extreme. Maybe she *was* in a dark Russian fairy tale. Oh, if only she were Babayaga with her wand and spells and flying mortar.

"Get out," snapped Boots to the guard. "Go. I am busy with Mikhail Gervin, can you not see? Tell the driver to wait. What are you staring at, you weak-minded fool? Go before I pluck your eyeballs out and eat them!"

The guard stared at Boots, then looked towards Mikhail, who had stopped a few steps away from Brenna's little caged window. She could feel Mikhail stiffen, even though he showed no outward sign of it. His green eyes sought hers out, and for a brief moment their gazes locked once again.

Brenna blinked as her heart jumped like it had skipped a beat or perhaps two. Electrolytes, she thought blankly. Your heart needs potassium and sodium and magnesium to beat in rhythm. Just relax, she told herself as Mikhail's eyes narrowed and then widened like he was trying to tell her something.

Then, as Brenna stared at the monster's annoyingly handsome face, his dark red lips parted.

He winked.

And then he stuck his tongue out at her.

Brenna yelped, then clamped her palm over her mouth. Her eyes went so wide it burned, and she backed away from the window gasping. What the hell was going on?

"Forgive the interruption, Mister Gervin," came Boots's voice from outside in the hallway. "My guard is a stupid man. Slow in the brain and weak in the mind. A fool whose mother dropped him on his head ten times a day as a child."

Brenna tiptoed back to the window and looked at Mister Gervin, who clearly had a tongue—and some balls too, metaphorically speaking. She still wasn't certain what was happening, but the man's military-style walk gave her a pretty good clue.

He was the cavalry.

Somehow, some way, by the grace of God or the Devil or the Angels or the Fairies, someone had come for her!

Brenna almost collapsed where she stood as relief washed over her like a waterfall. She grabbed onto the bars of the little window, leaned against the cold iron-studded door, pressed her nose between the gap and grinned like a weak-minded fool about to pass out.

The monster grinned too, his back still to Boots. It was a sudden grin, spontaneous, like he couldn't help himself. Immediately he regained composure, frowning briefly like he was annoyed with himself. Then he was back in monster-mode, scowling and whipping his big body around to face Boots.

He let out a guttural growl that made Brenna's toes curl. Boots seemed to understand—even an animal would understand a growl like that.

Boots turned back to the bewildered guard, who was still frozen. "You are still here? Get out before I eat your eyeballs!" he shouted in Russian.

The guard finally retreated and slammed the door shut. The fake Mikhail let out a disgruntled sound of satisfaction.

Then there was another sound.

This time from Boots.

"Oh, shit," Brenna whispered, blinking her dry eyelids rapidly over her burning eyes as she watched in the weird kind of disbelief that comes when you're having a fever dream and the colors are so bright and vivid you can smell them and taste them and hear them singing.

Boots wasn't singing though.

Not with fake-Mikhail's big palm over his mouth, the other arm locked around his neck.

Crushing his neck.

Brenna stared with a weird excitement as Boots was lifted up off the floor by the hulking, green-eyed, tattooed beast who might not be tongueless, but was most certainly a killer.

Indeed, the fake Mikhail barely flinched as he snapped Boots's neck in the crook of his elbow.

Brenna watched with a sickening satisfaction as Boots went wide-eyed and died with her smiling face as his last image.

She was too far gone in that fever-dream to question what she was feeling right now. She'd never seen anyone die. Now she had. And she didn't feel bad about it all. Not one damn bit.

Enjoy hell, Boots, she thought. Hope they eat your eyeballs. You liked that cutesy little threat, didn't ya? They say hell is made out of your worst fears, buddy. Eat up, now. Slurp slurp. Gobble gobble.

Brenna was almost drooling as she watched the man toss Boots aside like a sack of rotten cabbages. She touched her broken cheekbone unconsciously as the man walked to her cell door. He was too tall for the peering-window. He stooped and looked in.

"You all right?" he said in English.

"Keys," she said, surprised that she was thinking rationally, annoyed that he wasn't.

"Right," he said, blinking and turning away, but not before Brenna saw his face redden with sulky anger that he hadn't grabbed the keys first instead of asking a totally pointless question.

At first she was mortified at seeming ungrateful for being rescued. But she got over it real quick. What the hell kind of question was that, anyway? Of course she wasn't *all right*. She was in an underground Ukrainian prison with rats for buddies, a broken cheekbone, and probably twelve different infections from a million unknown microbes. It was nice of them to send someone, brave of him to take the job. But the job was by no means done.

Get the job done and I'll drop to my knees in gratitude, she thought. I'll write to the President to give you the Medal of Freedom, go on every talk show to sing your praises, get them to make a movie about you starring Mark Wahlberg and Tom Hanks and every other Hollywood star who plays Great American Heroes. But get us out of here first. Please. Pretty please. With molasses on top, cherry filling inside, chocolate roses all around. Get us the hell out of here first.

Now Brenna felt a sudden panic, a desperate fear that this wasn't real, that it was too good to be true, that she'd wake up from this fever dream and find herself chained to the wall, being licked by the tongue-stump of the real Tongueless One while Boots watched with milky-white eyeballs, timing her with an old-fashioned stopwatch, whispering about how long she was lasting.

At last the man rolled over Boots's body and pulled out his keys. They weren't as impressive as she'd expected. She'd imagined a massive keyring with a million heavy iron keys like in some medieval dungeon. But it was a single master key on a nice key-chain that had a little leather-covered squeezy light at the end. It was something you might get free from a bank teller or a real-estate agent.

"Keys. Right," the man said under his breath as he stuck the key in the hole and turned it. "Sorry, I was distracted for a moment. Dumb question. Are you all right. Of course you're all right. You're standing upright. You're breathing deep from your chest and stomach. Your eyes are clear and focused. Your skin is smooth and flawless. Your . . . um . . ."

He turned red again and quickly looked down at the lock. She saw his big Adam's apple bob as he swallowed. She frowned and looked down at her chest.

What did he mean by "breathing deep from her chest?" Were her boobs heaving up and down as she hyperventilated? Did he notice?

She touched her face. Was her skin actually looking flawless? Wasn't it cracked and filthy and bloody? And no way her eyes were clear and focused, were they? They burned from dryness, and they must be hugely dilated from a week of darkness.

She looked in puzzlement as the guy finally sprung the lock. He was still looking down, like he was embarrassed or flustered. She blinked and touched her hair. It felt like the straw that lined the edges of her cell. Oh wait, there actually was a piece of straw in her hair. She pulled it out and tossed it casually aside just as he pulled the heavy door open.

"I take it back," he said when the full light of the hallway bulb hit her from the front. His face crinkled with genuine concern, then twisted into an angry grimace. He raised his left arm, and with surprising gentleness touched her bruised, swollen cheekbone with the back of his middle finger. "You aren't all right. Your cheekbone is broken. You've been starved of nutrition. Been drinking bad water. Haven't bathed in days, maybe weeks."

Brenna frowned and looked down to her left, trying to sniff herself without making it obvious. She didn't smell anything, but she knew that after a point you can't smell your own stench. She touched her hair again, then raised her head and looked directly into his eyes.

"I liked it better when you said my skin was flawless," she said through a vaguely amused frown. She looked past his broad torso, to where Boots was lying dead with his eyeballs the color of sour milk. "Thank you for doing that."

The man glanced at her cheekbone, that look of barely-restrained anger coming back in a red rush. "He did that to you?"

Brenna nodded. She touched her hair again, looked down at her bare feet, tried to straighten the neckline of her oversized canvas jumpsuit that was about as flattering as a well-used potato-sack.

"Wish I'd know before I killed him," the man said. "Would have made it last longer."

"Lots of people are into making it last longer, it seems," she said with a darkly sarcastic eye-roll. "Is it trending on Social Media or something?"

The man frowned like he didn't get it. Brenna didn't explain. She glanced towards the door leading out of the cell block. Then she looked back at the man.

He had a black handgun in his right hand, and he was scanning the ceiling and walls.

She followed his gaze. No cameras. This wasn't that

kind of place. They were less worried about escapees than about having any digital evidence of what went on in here.

Brenna shivered along her spine, took a step farther away from the open door to her cell. She didn't want to look at it again. She'd save that for when some therapist forced her to revisit the past so she could release her trauma. Then she'd punch the therapist in the mouth and run out of the asylum screaming in tongues. That would show them she wasn't traumatized.

The man quickly walked down the hall, glancing at the other cells along the way. The other prisoners were quiet like mice in daylight. Nobody begged to be let out. They were probably smart enough to know their odds were better inside their cozy little cells. Too many monsters prowling the hallways that lined the path to freedom.

"The real Mikhail is here too, isn't he?" Brenna whispered when the man walked lightly back towards her after listening at the door. "Outside the gates?"

He shrugged like it was no big deal, like he'd expected it might happen, planned for it. "I'm Bruiser," he said.

She turned her head slightly, raised her right eyebrow. "Bruiser? That's so 1950s. Do you have a brother named Bif?"

Bruiser raised both eyebrows and stared. Then his big face relaxed into a broad, easy smile. His eyes softened, and Brenna thought she saw a glint of admiration in there.

"Battlefield humor," he said. "Impressive. You've been locked up in solitary a week. You're half starved. You've been beaten and threatened and hell knows what else. You've probably been expecting to die. You just saw a man die." He grinned and shook his head. "And you can still make wisecracks."

Brenna shrugged like it was no big thing. She realized she was blushing like it was a compliment. Was it a compliment? Was it a good thing to make wisecracks while teetering on the brink of starvation and after watching a man get his neck broken? Sure. Let's go with that.

"I was serious about that 1950s thing," she deadpanned. "What's your real name?"

Bruiser ignored the question. Brenna noted his reluctance. "Tell me or I'm gonna start guessing, and you won't like my guesses."

Bruiser glanced at the door. "How about we get out of here first. Real names can wait."

"That bad, huh?" she quipped, feeling slap-happy now as the adrenaline got her high like a kite. The relief that she might actually get out of this alive was adding to the almost delirious excitement she was feeling right now.

Sure, they were still in a prison. Sure, there were guards outside, not to mention the real Mikhail Gervin. But although she'd been genuinely scared at how Boots described the Tongueless One, for some reason she wasn't scared now. Not with this man in front of her, by her side, watching her back.

She looked at Bruiser's broad back, ran her gaze down his tree-trunk thick arms, along his pillar-sized thighs, all the way down to his massive feet. The black military style boots seemed longer than her forearms. She felt oddly safe near him.

She took a long, slow breath and held it in. Yup, cedarwood and hickory in his natural scent. But there was definitely some mesquite mixed in there, like he'd eaten barbecue recently. Oh, God, what she wouldn't give for a barbecue chicken wing right now, smoky-sweet and hot off the grill.

"My real name is classified, Ms. Yankova," Bruiser said stiffly as he looked back towards the door again.

"Oh, so I'm Ms. Yankova now? I was Brenna earlier."

"I never called you Brenna. This is the first time I'm using your name."

Brenna frowned. She was usually really good at remembering what people said. Bruiser gestured to her to follow him. They crept towards the hallway door, Bruiser shielding her easily with his thickly muscled bulk.

"Boomer?" she asked from behind him.

"What?"

"I'm guessing," she whispered.

"Stop guessing," he growled.

"Bertrand?" she whispered.

He didn't say anything.

She thought a moment. "Got it." She giggled. "Bubbles!" she whispered triumphantly.

Bruiser whipped around, his face red and indignant, cheeks bulging with barely stifled laughter.

"Bubbles?!" he roared in the loudest whisper ever. "You think my name is *Bubbles*? What am I, a damn circus monkey?"

Brenna started to laugh uncontrollably, and she knew she was losing her shit. Bruiser was laughing too, his face crinkling up around his flashing green eyes.

For a moment Brenna felt she was somewhere else, anywhere else, everywhere else.

Then she was dragged back to the dark gray reality by the creak of the door on its iron hinges.

It was the guard whom Boots had called a weak-minded fool. Brenna couldn't tell if he was or wasn't, but she knew enough to see that he was messed up on methamphetamines, just like all the guards she'd seen in this place. Bruiser seemed to know it too.

"Listen to me," he said to the guard calmly in perfect Russian. She looked at him in surprise, but held her composure well enough. "I will be taking possession of this prisoner, as per my orders from Damyan Nagarev. Your warden has released her to me. He is checking on the other prisoners. Is my man still outside the gates?"

"I . . . I think so," said the guard. "He was very angry when I told him he would have to wait. I have not gone back outside."

Bruiser grunted, nodded once. "You go on and open the gates now. Escort my man inside so he can use the bathroom. He has a weak bladder, so do not mention it. He is sensitive about his little-boy parts."

The guard stared at him, looked at her, then blinked in the overhead light. Brenna could see him struggle to make sense of who was whom, what was what, which way was up. She'd never done any drugs, but had read enough about America's meth epidemic to know that chronic use fried your brain circuits like bacon. It was unlikely this guard had put all the pieces together well enough to realize there was tomfoolery, skullduggery, and plenty of shenanigans afoot. Brenna attempted to look docile with a hint of misery, a dash of despair.

"Yes, yes, he must want to go very badly," said the guard earnestly. "He is very angry. He speaks in a way I cannot understand. Makes this sound from his throat." The guard mimicked what Brenna supposed was Mikhail the Tongueless making angry noises. It sounded like a buffalo being strangled. "I could not understand what he wanted. Now I understand. A weak bladder is a very intimate problem."

Bruiser nodded sympathetically. He looked past the guard, towards where another sentry stood at the far end of the brightly lit anteroom. There were no windows. Gray concrete walls studded with white LED bulbs in metal cages. Like someone had taken an old World War II bunker and upgraded the electrical systems.

The other sentry was shifting nervously from one foot to the other, jittery and wired. He had headphones on, the spongy kind from the 1980s. He had a handgun in a well-worn buttoned-down leather holster and a battered rifle slung across his back.

Brenna wasn't a gun expert, but she knew what an AK-47 looked like. She'd played *Call of Duty* on her Playstation for about a year before giving up video games because she read an article about the dangers of excessive dopamine release on the brain's neurocircuitry. It was in a peer-reviewed academic paper. She had checked the references twice, run the data analysis in her own spreadsheet, then donated her Playstation to Goodwill and never looked back.

Bruiser looked back at her when the guard left to open the gates for the real Mikhail and his fake weak bladder. He glanced down at her bare feet. Looked up into her eyes again.

Brenna wiggled her toes and shrugged. The jittery guard was looking at her. He was startled when she looked directly into his eyes, and she held her gaze until he averted his bloodshot, meth-wired eyes in confused paranoia. His fingers curled into claw-like fists like a chicken going into rigor-mortis. She almost felt sorry for him. Almost but not.

"Shit. No shoes is a problem. You won't get very far very fast in bare feet," Bruiser said. He shot a glance at Jitterbug with the AK-47. "Thought I'd take Mikhail as he walked in, catch him by surprise. But I don't know if it's a good idea with AK-47s in the room. That guy is in the clouds, but I don't trust him not to shoot up the place." He moved his thick neck. Brenna heard it crack in a weirdly satisfying, oddly reassuring way.

"I can run in bare feet. I think. Do we have far to go?" she asked, looking for a window but of course there weren't any. "Where's the pick-up site?"

Bruiser didn't answer. He blinked and scanned the rest of the anteroom. There were three more doors along the side. Large metal doors like the one leading to her cell block. More cell blocks, obviously. Wait, what about that last door?

"Sleeping quarters. Galley. Bathroom," said Bruiser, reading her mind and shaking his head. "Only one way out."

"I don't hear a chopper," Brenna said, smiling nervously. "What about backup? Where's the rest of your team? Are they outside the gate in armor-plated Humvees?"

Bruiser's lower lip twitched, like he was going to say something but then didn't. "I don't want to fight him in here," he said under his breath. "Two amp'd up guards with AK-47s will pretty much kill us all if shit gets crazy in an enclosed space like this."

Brenna frowned. "Wait, do you not have a team? No backup? No choppers, Humvees, tanks, air-support? What kind of a rescue mission is this? Who the hell are you? Ohmygod, are you not American military? Ohmygod, are you just another thug? Do you work for Damyan's rival or something?"

Bruiser looked at her in a strange way. Outside the main door they could hear metal gates screeching open. Or maybe screeching closed—which meant the real Mikhail was on his way inside.

"Relax," he said softly. He let his hand brush against hers, his rough fingertips grazing her knuckles, making her shiver with an intoxicating, electric chill. "Trust me, OK?"

She looked up at him, that buzz working its way through her entire body. "OK," she said, confused but agreeing. Like she had a choice. She was barefoot, unarmed, and half-starved. "What should I do?"

Bruiser took her hand gently in his, squeezed, and then let go.

"Go with him," he whispered just as the front door started to creak open.

Brenna was distracted by the door and glanced towards it.

When she turned back to Bruiser he was gone.

9

Bruiser closed the door to the guards' quarters just as the front door swung all the way open. He stayed still, pressed his ear against the door, clenched his right fist, bit his lower lip so hard he tasted the copper in his blood.

Leaving Brenna out there alone was the hardest thing he'd done in a life of doing very hard things. A part of him had wanted to just shoot both the guards, then walk to the gate and put a third bullet between Mikhail's eyes. But there were too many unknowns, too much risk. AK-47s were notoriously inaccurate rifles, and in full-automatic mode they could spray hundreds of bullets around the room in a few seconds. Add some amphetamines to the mix, plus an unknown number of guards in the other cell blocks, and there was a damn good chance Brenna took a bullet or three.

And even if he shot all the guards in the place without getting Brenna killed—a big if—he still had to get her out. There was only one gate, and it would be barricaded by Mikhail, who would see Bruiser coming a few hundred yards away. Benson's intel suggested Mikhail would be alone, but his firepower was an unknown.

Bruiser was deadly with a handgun, but no handgun is a hundred percent accurate past thirty feet or so. An AK-47 was even less useful at that distance. If Mikhail was a good shot and had a rifle, he might hit a big target like Bruiser from outside Bruiser's range.

And if Bruiser went down, who would protect Brenna?

Bruiser couldn't risk that.

He wouldn't risk that.

And so he'd made the decision to leave her there.

To let Mikhail take her.

That would accomplish at least half the mission.

It would get Brenna past the gates.

Bruiser just had to make sure he got past the gates right after them.

Before the gates closed.

Mikhail would have driven here. The prison was in the middle of nowhere, forty miles from Kiev. There were no trains or buses this far out. Bruiser briefly wondered how Mikhail had gotten here so quick. Argentina was a good three hours farther from Kiev than Atlanta. Bruiser's Air-Force ride had landed at the Ukrainian Air Force's airfield on the other side of Kiev. There had been a five-year-old white Toyota Land Cruiser waiting for Bruiser to commandeer. He'd driven as fast as he dared, knowing that he didn't have the backup of the U.S. Government, that if the local cops stopped him, he would be delayed and Mikhail would beat him to the prison.

The GPS and maps had been pretty good but not perfect. Two dead ends, one closed road, and two hours later Bruiser had screeched into the wire-fenced parking lot behind the prison. He'd beaten Mikhail there, but clearly not by much.

Still, the math didn't work. Mikhail should still have been a solid ninety minutes away, considering he'd have landed at Kiev International Airport, which was also on the far side of the city. Benson's intel must have been off. Because Bruiser's math was never off.

He took a quick glance around the large, long, dormitory style room. There were twelve cots, metal frames with canvas slings. Ten of them were empty. One had a guard sprawled face-down in a sweat-stained undershirt. He was dead asleep. Two cots away another guard was sitting and staring. Not at Bruiser but at the needle stuck in his arm.

Bruiser watched as the shirtless, skinny man pushed the plunger in all the way. The guard let out a shuddering groan of pleasure, then collapsed in his cot, the needle still in his arm.

Heroin, Bruiser figured. Amphetamines keep you up. Heroin puts you down.

He shook his head and listened at the door, ready to storm through at the first sign of violence. He hadn't had time to coach Brenna on what to say, how to play it. He wasn't sure what the guard had told Mikhail. Did Mikhail know someone else was in here? Would the hopped-up guards mention it to Mikhail? Would it even matter to Mikhail, since Brenna was right there, barefoot and helpless?

He heard voices through the door. Russian. The first guard was speaking haltingly.

Then a grunt. Mikhail the Tongueless.

Bruiser listened for Brenna's voice as his heart thundered in his chest, his hand closed around the doorknob, his legs braced in case he needed to rush the room and start killing anyone and everyone who threatened Brenna.

Somewhere in the back of his mind came Benson's warning that she might be a traitor, that this wasn't a simple rescue mission, that he wasn't there to bring her home like in some damn American-hero movie.

His mission wasn't to break her out.

His mission was just to break her.

But right now Bruiser couldn't consider any of that. The feeling he'd tried to ignore when he'd seen Brenna's photograph had only come back stronger when he looked into her eyes through those iron bars, saw her bruised and battered, starved and shaking, but somehow strong and beautiful even through the filth and fear and stench.

Hell, he actually liked how she smelled, it occurred to him. It wasn't an odor but an aroma. Warm, earthy, and natural. Like wildflowers freshly plucked, clean dirt still on the roots.

Not that he knew what a damn wildflower smelled like growing up in Chicago. But he knew what her scent did to him, did to the man in him. He could smell the woman in Brenna, and it made his gut tighten.

In fact he'd been so turned around by the pure physicality of being close to her that he'd actually lost track of the mission. Never happened like that before.

Fear never got to him.

Danger never bothered him.

Breaking Brenna

Pain was no distraction.

Threats were meaningless.

But Brenna had gotten to him before she said a damn word. She'd gotten into his head, his body, his damn soul.

Not for long, but long enough that he'd stood there like an idiot and asked if she was all right instead of getting the damn keys and busting her out of there. Hell, if he hadn't delayed for those few minutes, maybe they'd have been out of there and in his Land Cruiser before Mikhail showed.

Bruiser tried to do the math in his mind but couldn't. He'd lost track of time during those electric moments when he was alone with Brenna, when they were going back and forth, slap-happy like children, excited like teenagers, teasing and flirting like this was a game, not a mission involving death, treason, and conspiracy.

In fact all that seemed like the side mission, not the real one.

It felt like *she* was the real mission.

Bruiser's phone vibrated in his left cargo flap. Benson, he figured. He didn't bother with the phone. Now wasn't the damn time.

He tensed up when he heard footsteps outside the door. Was Mikhail really going to visit the bathroom? Did that idiot guard blurt out something and make Mikhail suspicious?

The footsteps stopped outside the door. Whoever it was paused, then turned on his feet.

A moment later the outside door creaked open on its rusty hinges.

Bruiser felt the dry, crisp outside air creep under the crack beneath his door. He listened hard. Heard Brenna's bare feet being dragged towards the outside door. He thought a moment, then turned and ran towards the back of the dormitory.

Benson had sent him the blueprint of the prison, and he knew there were no windows and no back door. The place wasn't designed to be a fire-safe building. Either you run out the front door or you burn. Place wasn't too far from hell anyway, Bruiser figured.

He pushed through the door leading to the galley. It was filthy, with an industrial steel stove that was covered in hardened black soot. Bruiser leapt up onto the stove, sending an empty saucepan clattering to the stained tiles. He didn't care about keeping quiet. He only cared about getting out.

"Please be wide enough," he grunted as he reached up and punched out the grease-covered metal screen above the stove. According to the blueprint there was an outlet leading to the curved roof of the bunker. It looked just about wide enough to squeeze himself through.

It had to be.

He didn't want to chase Mikhail and Brenna out the front door. Brenna would immediately turn into a hostage, and Bruiser would immediately prove himself to be a damn fool with no sense of strategy, no command of tactics, no possession of self-control or good judgment under pressure.

But Bruiser started to question that judgment when he wriggled his big body up the dark metal-lined shaft.

The top of the outlet leading to the roof was covered with a metal plate. Hard steel, bolted in place. He should have picked up a clue from the soot-stains on the galley walls. This may have been a chimney years ago. It wasn't one anymore. They'd sealed this place up good and tight.

Bruiser's boot-tips and forearms were jammed hard against the metal sides of the shaft, holding him in place with outwards pressure. A metal plate wouldn't normally be a problem, except he couldn't use both hands to smash it without falling straight back down like a clumsy oversized ninja.

He took a breath and sighed it out. Then he let his arms go slack so he'd drop down a bit. One more long breath, then a slow exhale. He tucked his tongue firmly behind his teeth, tightened his jaw, flexed the thick, sinewy muscles in his neck.

Then he propelled himself upward like a rocket blasting off, leading with his torpedo of a head.

The bolts ripped out of their metal grooves, and the plate went flying off the top like a discus being hurled by a superhuman Olympian. Bruiser kept the upward momentum going, scrambling his boot-tips up the last few inches of the shaft.

A moment later he was on the curved roof. He dropped down to his butt and slid off the side onto the dead grass, landing softly for a big man, diving forward and doing a roll, coming up with his Sig 9mm drawn and ready.

He was about a swimming-pool's length from the parking lot. The twelve-foot high razor-wire fence had a human-sized opening in it leading to the lot. The warden had opened the gate for Bruiser when he arrived, and it was still open.

Bruiser scanned the floodlit parking lot. Something wasn't right. There was his white Land Cruiser. There was the beige Lada that he figured belonged to the warden. And a beat-up Russian Jeep knockoff painted military green but with no discernible logo. The Jeep had been there when Bruiser arrived. So had the Lada.

So where was Mikhail's vehicle?

He couldn't have driven off already. Bruiser's headfirst exit had taken eleven seconds, maybe twelve. Even if Mikhail had parked right near the front gate Bruiser would still see the car, still be able to follow.

A chill crept up Bruiser's back as he rose to almost full height and jogged along the shadowy side of the bunker, toward the front gate. Had he screwed up? Was Mikhail still inside the bunker? Had he taken Brenna to one of the empty cells, shooed away the guards, shut the door, turned out the lights?

Bruiser almost lost his mind at the image of that tongueless beast putting his meaty paws on her. It was a visceral, instinctive reaction, from someplace deep down in Bruiser, a place that didn't question the insane thought that she was his woman and she was his mission and nothing else mattered. Not a damn thing.

"Get your head straight, Soldier," he growled under his breath, forcing back the vicious need to barrel his way back into that bunker, guns blazing, fists flying, ready to maim and kill, demolish and destroy, take back what was his, what he knew was his.

"You're losing your damn mind, Soldier. This isn't the time to finally snap. You're trained not to lose your shit even if you run out of oxygen a mile underwater and you're fighting sharks with your fists. You are *not* gonna lose your shit because you're flying into a possessive, protective rage."

Bruiser closed his eyes and shook his head like a wolf in a rainstorm. Maybe Benson was right to have doubts about Bruiser being able to think straight in this situation, to keep his cock and balls and machismo out of it and just pursue the mission with a cool head, a dispassionate heart, an even keel.

But Bruiser had read the report on Mikhail. He knew the man's hobbies, knew what he liked to do, knew what he'd done many times. A man like that doesn't stop doing that shit. It only escalates. Only gets worse. Darker. More deranged. Deadlier.

Bruiser was about to go back in there, take his chances that the guards had finally found their warden dead and were beginning to freak out. But then he saw movement in the darkness past the front gate.

He squinted and saw them. Mikhail and Brenna.

Moving fast, cutting across the lifeless yellow grass between the driveway and the frontage road that led to the closest highway. Mikhail was carrying her draped over his shoulder like she was a sack of vegetables. She was slumped over his shoulder, bare feet dangling, hands swinging.

Immediately Bruiser knew she was unconscious. Either she'd finally passed out or he'd drugged. her. He refused to let himself consider that he'd hit her. Bruiser knew that in this strangely deadly, manically possessive state he might not be able to control himself.

Then it hit him, and he grinned.

He didn't fucking *need* to control himself.

Not anymore.

Because for some dumb-ass reason Mikhail was on foot. Maybe he'd parked a bit away, hidden his car in the woods along the highway. Maybe he did in fact have a driver waiting for him. Whatever the reason, Bruiser could run him down in the darkness like an animal being hunted. Bruiser was big as a bear, but stealthy like a lone wolf stalking his prey. He raised his head and felt the wind on his cheek. Grinned wide like that wolf. He was even upwind of them.

Now he moved, agile like a panther, quick like a viper. He made it out through the sliding metal gates just as the automatic winches started to whir, the gates started to scream closed on their tortured rails.

Mikhail looked back as the gates screeched. Bruiser was ready for it, and he flattened himself on the ground, staying off the road. He kept his head down, closed his eyes. He knew for a fact that humans, just like animals, know when a pair of eyes are focused on them. Instinct was a real thing. Evolutionary drives were more powerful than even the most rigorous training.

In fact, the best military training was nothing more than awakening a man to his primal drives, showing him how to use them in battle. After all, every man and woman alive today, even the most cowardly of the lot, are descended from an ancestor who at some point was in a fight for his or her life.

A fight that they won.

Which means every human carries the ability to kill inside them. Bloodlust pumps through every man's veins, every woman's heart. Even a pacifist vegan who would weep for a squished mosquito has that instinct buried in his trembling heart.

It's in us.

Most of us are taught to suppress it.

An elite warrior is taught to accept it.

To use it.

To fucking love it.

Adrenaline surged through Bruiser's veins as he picked up the chase again. Mikhail was carrying Brenna effortlessly, but he didn't know he was being followed. He kept a steady pace. Bruiser did the math. He figured he'd close in on them at a rate of thirteen feet every twenty seconds.

He wouldn't move too fast until he was close enough to draw his six-inch pigsticker and pounce on his prey. Bruiser couldn't risk taking a shot when Brenna was draped over the asshole's shoulder. The good thing about Mikhail having to carry her was that he'd have to drop Brenna to draw his gun. The idea of Brenna hitting the hard ground sickened Bruiser, and he played out a scenario where he cushioned her fall and then immediately hurled himself at Mikhail. He'd have to see if he could work it. He hated the thought of another bruise on her battered body, but she'd survive. She'd survive and she'd heal. He was sure of it.

So sure that it felt like fate.

Like destiny.

Like he was meant to be here. Just him. Only him. Him and her.

Again he pushed those thoughts away. And again they assaulted his mind and heart like an unstoppable force. Bruiser knew those thoughts were coming from that deep place in his subconscious, the place where instinct lives, the place where that ancient animal-brain lives, the part that cares about only two things:

Survival

And reproduction.

Bruiser almost lauaghed at the thought, but he knew damn well that every drive and need, thought and emotion, action and reaction boiled down to those two things. There are just two drives. Two drives that kept the human race going.

Kill my enemy.

Take my mate.

Those two drives wrote the story of every man's life, whether he was a soldier, a shepherd, or a damn circus clown. Everything else was just a footnote.

Bruiser's foot hit a half-buried rock and he stumbled, landing hard on his right boot-heel. Immediately he dropped to the ground and lay flat, completely motionless, not even a breath, so still he'd fool a possum.

He sensed Mikhail stop, turn, hesitate.

Then he heard the big man's footsteps continue.

Bruiser hadn't been made. But he'd lost time. It was going to add about twenty-six seconds to his timeline.

He counted to nine and leapt to his feet.

And then he stopped and stared.

Listened and groaned.

"Motherfucker!" he shouted when he saw two bright lights snap on down the highway.

They were too far apart to be a car's headlamps.

He heard the roar of twin engines.

The whine of high powered jets.

No wonder Mikhail had gotten here so quick.

No wonder the math felt off.

"Damn your intel, Benson!" he roared when he saw the silhouette of Mikhail tossing Brenna's heartbreakingly limp body into the plane through the open side door.

A moment later Mikhail clambered in after her. The door slammed shut. The plane started to taxi down the highway.

And Bruiser broke into a dead run.

10

Mikhail was dead tired by the time he strapped himself into his double-sized seat and mopped the sweat from his leather-wrinkled brow. He was out of shape, breathless, slow and lumbering. He felt strong as ever, and there was very little fat around his heavily muscled midsection, so it puzzled him a moment. Ah yes, he realized. It was the cigar habit that he had picked up from Damyan. He would stop when he returned to Buenos Aires.

The woman moved in the seat across the aisle, and Mikhail turned to look at her in the full light. He hardened immediately, uncomfortably, uncontrollably. The Latin women suited him just fine, but this woman clearly had Slavic blood. Mikhail could barely wait for Damyan to finish with her and hand her over for Mikhail's use.

She groaned against the rough seat cushion, licking her lower lip that was cracked and dry. The sight of her red, luscious tongue made Mikhail's heart pound like a bass drum. He was sweating again. He had to adjust the seatbelt to handle the heavy breaths he was forced to take at the sight of this woman so close but untouchable.

Yes, she was untouchable for now. Certainly Damyan

would not care what state she was in so long as she could still talk, still tell him her secrets, those twelve words that unlocked a digital treasure chest. But Mikhail knew himself very well. He knew that once he started, he would not stop. It was better not to start. Bringing a tongueless, broken body to Damyan would not be a good idea.

Besides, it was only a nine hour flight. He could wait. Perhaps he would take longer with this one. She was dehydrated and half-starved, but she would quickly fill out to her glorious natural shape.

Brenna Yankova was her name. She was the daughter of Alexei Yankov, a man Mikhail had never liked, never understood, certainly never trusted. But Damyan had brushed off Mikhail's garbled protests and used Alexei Yankov anyway.

"He has computer skills none of us can even understand, let alone master," Damyan had said. "The UNA is bankrupt, Mikhail. Now that so much money is just numbers on a computer screen, Russia and America have seized our accounts, stolen millions of dollars of our funds, claimed them as spoils of war. It is almost impossible to hold dollars or Euros without the damn Russians and Americans sniffing it out and siphoning it away. Those two countries may be enemies, but when it comes to taking the money of groups they call terrorists, groups of freedom fighters like us . . . yes, on such matters Russia and America seem to agree just fine. Bastards. Criminals. *They* are the damn terrorists, Mikhail."

He'd taken a puff of his cigar, shaken his head and laughed. "Did I ever tell you how the American CIA tried to recruit me, Mikhail? Two of their top men, they sent. Benson and Kaiser. The man Kaiser is now Director of the CIA, can you believe? Hah. I should have accepted. Gutted them from the inside out, like a parasite hatching in a pig's belly, eating its host from the inside." He'd chortled, run his hand over his close-shaved head, the stiff yellow hair like shorn wire. "They offered money too. Lots of money. No matter. Once we recover the currencies Alexei had secured for us before his unfortunate death, we will be back in business. A new sort of business." He'd paused again, taken a long, slow, smoky breath. "They label us terrorists when we are freedom fighters. Well, perhaps now we will live up to that name. Yes, Mikhail. The UNA will do to Russia and America what you do to your lovely ladies. Rip their tongues out. Run rampage on their bodies. Make them beg for death."

Mikhail had grinned, then opened his maw and wiggled his stump. He knew how grotesque he looked when he did that. The stump was uneven and hideous, gray fibrous scar tissue covering its thick edge. He'd cut it out himself, and it had been harder than he'd imagined. Not so much because of the pain or the natural revulsion to mutilate oneself. No, Mikhail could handle that just fine. What he couldn't handle was the slick, slippery, blood-and-saliva soaked tongue that thrashed and squirmed as he sawed at it.

He forced himself to look away from the woman. But she moved again, moaned again, fluttered her eyelids, licked her lips.

She'd passed out cold outside the prison. Dehydration. Starvation. Probably a lot more than that. In fact he was surprised she'd been able to stand at all.

She was filthy, her cheekbone was badly bruised, her lips dry and cracked. But nothing else appeared damaged. Mikhail had glanced at the crotch of her prison jumpsuit as he lifted her. No bloodstains. Damyan still had some influence. It protected her in a savage place. Even the men in such prisons would have been raped by the guards. A woman would be dead by now.

The plane started to vibrate as it approached take-off speed on the bumpy makeshift runway. Mikhail glanced out the window. The cabin lights were bright, and all he saw was his own reflection and that of the woman across the aisle.

Her eyes were open now. Her lips were moving. She was saying something, but her voice was weak, her lips and tongue too dry for the sound to carry.

Water, she was saying. She was thirsty.

Ordinarily Mikhail would not care. But Damyan wanted her alive. He sighed and leaned his heavy body into the aisle, looked toward the small galley with a fridge and some cabinets stocked with nuts, beef jerky, perhaps some fruit.

Beyond the galley was the cockpit door. It was a reinforced steel sliding door, and it was closed. There were two pilots inside, he knew. During the flight one of them had served Mikhail hot coffee and chilled vodka.

But the pilots were both occupied now. Besides, they were not accustomed to communicating with a tongueless man. It would be easier to go to the galley himself. Some water would be enough for the woman until they were airborne.

The plane was close to taking off, but Mikhail snapped off his belt and stepped into the aisle. He had the powerful haunches of an ox, and was very stable on his big feet. He lumbered down the aisle, grabbed a bottle of water, stomped back towards her. He unscrewed the cap and made her drink.

Her eyelids fluttered open and then closed again. But when the water touched her lips she began to drink hungrily.

Mikhail watched her throat move as she swallowed. His hand shook. His pants felt tight as he bulged with that insane need. His free hand reached out. He let his fingers stroke her smooth neck.

The sensation almost made him explode in his pants, explode in his mind too. He pulled his hand back before his fingers tightened around her tender neck. A bead of sweat rolled down his nose, dropped onto her forehead as she gulped down the last of the water.

Mikhail closed his eyes tight. Soon he was mostly back in control. He exhaled and took a step back, straightened up and looked down at her.

Brenna moved in her seat beneath him, her body relaxing as the water did its job. She arched her neck back, and her oversized collar opened up a little, giving Mikhail a fleeting view of breasts large and heavy, perfectly sculpted and round, big enough to fill his massive palms.

He almost had a brain aneurysm. It took all his willpower to not take her right then and there. Take her savagely. Finish it with brutal quickness. He imagined reaching around her thrashing body and tearing out her tongue as he finished in her.

Somehow he made it back to his seat, his eyes bulging as big as his cock. He would not last nine hours, he realized.

And therefore neither would Brenna Yankova.

Damyan would not get to speak to her in the living flesh.

Even if by some miracle he kept her alive, she would not have a tongue to speak those twelve secret words.

Which left Mikhail one option.

He pulled out his phone, tapped the oversized black screen, swiped to where he could type Russian words for the robotic female voice to say out loud.

He typed his instructions. Then he rose again, leaned over Brenna. She'd fallen back into a stupor, so he slapped her on the cheek twice.

They were hard, sharp smacks, and she snapped open her eyes and recoiled. She swung her right fist, but he was too close for the punch to land. Her forearm hit his cheek. It felt like nothing. He grabbed her elbow and twisted.

She screamed, but he kept twisting until she realized he could pull her arm out from the shoulder like a chicken being de-winged. He told her with his eyes that he would do just that. Then he eased the pressure slightly, and she slumped down exhausted and defeated. He was used to seeing that in women. He liked to see it in a woman.

"What do you want with me?" she asked in English.

Mikhail understood English well enough, but hated the language. It sounded vile to his ears. He did not much like Russian either, his opinion of the language tainted by his hatred for the people. But he'd grown up speaking Russian, and he even thought and dreamed in the damn language. It was too late to rewire his brain now. It would have to do.

He smacked her again, then held her by the throat and tapped his phone. The mechanical female voice relayed his instructions in Russian:

"Give me the secret words and I will let you die fast," came the mechanized voice.

Brenna stared at him, her eyes bulging from the pressure around her throat. Mikhail eased up so she could breathe. He tapped the phone again.

"Give me the secret words and I will let you die fast," the robot messenger said again.

"You have the wrong woman or the wrong information," she replied hoarsely. Her Russian was good but with a filthy American accent.

Mikhail tapped the phone again. The plane went over a bump. It was still hurtling down the runway. Now the front wheel started to leave the ground, inclining the plane.

"I don't know any damn secrets. You've got the wrong woman," she said again, her voice trembling a bit.

Mikhail huffed out a breath. He let got of her throat so he could type. He tapped the phone again and held it out.

"Damyan Nagarev knows you have the secret words. He is never wrong. You have the words. Give them to me and I will let you die."

"I don't *want* to die," she snapped back in Russian. Her eyes were bright now. The water had brought her back to life. "Which means *letting* me die is not a very tempting offer. You'll have to do better."

"I do not *need* to do better," Mikhail roared, but of course the words only formed clear in his mind. The sound that emerged from his mutilated mouth was incomprehensible to man or beast.

Mikhail's temples throbbed as the blood pumped hot and hard in his head. He tightened his grip on her throat, his eyes bulging along with hers. He squeezed but then stopped when he remembered his orders.

The words.

Twelve words.

He only had to extract twelve words from her.

She would just need to say them once and he would remember. Mikhail was no genius, but he had a memory like a bear-trap, especially for the spoken word. Perhaps it was because he did not learn to read or write until he was twelve years old. He did not know the inner workings of the human brain. All he knew was that she needed to speak twelve words and he would remember them.

Then hours of bliss.

Many hours.

Of course he was lying about letting her die quick. He would keep her alive until he could hold back no more. Damyan would not care so long as he got his twelve words. Got his money. That was all Damyan seemed to care about these days.

"Careful," said Brenna with an almost smug half-smile as the plane tilted to the left suddenly, throwing Mikhail off balance for a moment.

In that moment Brenna slid down into her seat, raised her leg, and kicked out viciously at Mikhail.

Her bare heel got him in the abdomen before he regained his balance, and the big man stumbled back into the aisle. He grabbed onto the seat backs on either side of the aisle to stop from falling, but the plane took off just then, still listing to the left like there was a weight on the wing, and Mikhail swayed and swung like an ape in a windstorm.

Brenna burst out of the seat and tore down the aisle away from Mikhail. The lavatories were down there, and Brenna tumbled into one of them and slammed the metal door shut.

By the time Mikhail lurched his way down the lopsided aisle, the door was locked. He sighed and shook his head, ran his hand through his stiff hair, rubbed his chin and sighed again.

Then he heard something behind him.

He turned.

Stared.

It was a man dressed in black. Big. Broad. Fists

clenched. Eyes narrowed. Black Swiss Sig Sauer pistol in his right hand. Tee shirt and cargo military pants. Short dark blonde hair, spiked like wire. Tattoos creeping up over the collar, down along his big forearms.

He looked like a younger version of Mikhail. Fewer creases on his face. More light in his eyes. Their features were not very much alike, but without a clear photograph of their faces, the two of them would be described in the same general way.

Immediately he knew what had happened, why he had been made to wait outside the gates for the warden, why the guard looked so confused, why he'd made some odd remark about the warden being occupied with a very important visitor.

At first Mikhail wondered if it was a double cross by the warden. No, that made no sense. It was the Russians or the Americans. CIA or Russian Intelligence had intercepted Damyan's phone call to the prison. Damyan had been worried it might happen, that now the computers could even recognize voices on a phone. But the risk had to be taken. Of course Mikhail could not make the phone call and Damyan trusted no one else with this very important secret.

Mikhail dropped to his left as the man fired. He felt the bullet scream past his right ear.

He slapped his right hand down along his thigh and felt for his weapon. It was a Glock 19 handgun. Austrian made. Very simple. Very reliable.

He whipped the gun out, firing repeatedly even before he raised it all the way. His bullets pounded into the seat backs, sending white stuffing flying into the air like snowflakes.

Mikhail was jammed down behind two seats, slumped down against the window, listening for the other man's cries of pain.

None came.

No more shots either. The man must have realized Brenna Yankova was not in the seats therefore must be in the lavatory. He was afraid of hitting her with a stray bullet. Which meant he was probably an American. Weak. Afraid of taking a risk. Perhaps doubtful of his own abilities. Good.

Mikhail held his breath, considered his next shot. There were twelve rows of seats. The man was six rows ahead, probably slumped down just like Mikhail. A 9mm handgun could easily blast through one seatback, maybe two, possibly three. But it wasn't going to shoot through six of them.

Still, Mikhail had thirteen bullets left plus two spare magazines. Plenty of ammo to waste. He could certainly try his luck, especially since his enemy was hesitant to shoot in this direction, with the lavatory as a backstop to his misses. Mikhail would be shooting in the direction of the cockpit, but the pilots were behind two inches of reinforced steel. So long as that door stayed closed, the pilots and flight controls were safe.

The plane was all the way in the air now, and the wind noise was horrific. It felt like a damn hurricane in the cabin. Mikhail glanced down past his feet and saw why.

The door was open. The man had pried open the emergency door above the left wing. He hadn't broken a window. A careful man. Also someone who knew planes, knew that if you slide a long enough blade into the emergency door you can spring the latch from the outside.

It also meant this man had a knife. At least six inches long, with a sturdy blade that could probably cut through bone like butter. Army Rangers liked their knives. So did the SEALs. Was this man a Navy SEAL?

An odd chill went down Mikhail's spine. He grinned and shook his head. Even he was not immune to the hype around the famous Navy SEALs, the self-proclaimed greatest elite warriors of all time. Mikhail had killed forty-six men in his day, but most of them were mafia thugs, Russian police, and the occasional civilian. Some of the thugs and even police may have been ex-military, but Mikhail had never fought a real Special Forces man. A real American Hero from the movies. Hah. Perhaps if he made this man's death magnificent enough they would make a movie about Mikhail.

The plane climbed steeply into the air, and now the cockpit door slid open. Mikhail cursed in his mind. The door alarm must have been going off. The pilot said something in Spanish. Ten years in Argentina but Mikhail barely spoke the damn language.

Mikhail took a chance and raised his head. There was no sign of the SEAL. The pilot was pulling the emergency exit door closed. He sealed the pressurized door and then stared wide-eyed when he saw Mikhail with a gun.

Mikhail gestured for the pilot to go back to the cockpit. The pilot hurried back to the front, his eyes fixed on the gun. A moment later the cockpit door slammed shut and locked with a loud click.

Mikhail wondered what the pilots would do. The plane kept climbing. Apparently the pilots had not heard the shots through the wind and engine noise earlier. Not surprising.

What was surprising was that the pilot had not noticed the other man slumped in one of the rows of seats. Surely the pilot would have walked past him?

And now Mikhail was certain it was a SEAL. And probably a SEAL sniper. Damyan had been trained as a Russian Special Forces sniper, and he'd told Mikhail about how snipers were trained.

"Most of the job is about keeping still," Damyan had explained once after a long night of ice-cold Russian vodka and hot-blooded Latin women. "So still that your enemy can pass within an inch of your face and not know you are there."

"That is impossible," Mikhail had said from his throat. Damyan could understand Mikhail well enough for them to have simple conversations without the need for the phone-robot.

Damyan had shaken his head and pointed to his eyes. "The secret is to close your eyes. Not just your eyelids but your *eyes*, you understand? Empty your mind and take your attention away from your enemy. All animals have an instinct that tells them they are being watched. You can trick the instinct by this method."

Mikhail hadn't believed Damyan, but now he did. The SEAL must have stayed still as death, closed his eyes, emptied his mind like Damyan said was the trick of the elite snipers.

Too bad you do not have your sniper rifle and scope,

Mikhail thought with a mixture of scorn and relief as he tried to maneuver himself to see if he could find a line of sight between the seats, perhaps reduce the number of seatbacks he would have to shoot through.

But as he stuck his face between the gap in the seats to his front, he suddenly remembered something else Damyan told him about snipers.

How they could approach a target with the stealth of a panther in the night.

Creep like smoke under a door.

Get so close they don't need a scope.

Don't need a rifle.

Don't need more than a nanosecond.

Mikhail's last glimpse of this world was a single green eye staring at him from between the seats of the row in front of him. Below the eye was the black round barrel of a gun. It looked big as a tunnel, it was so close.

Then time slowed down for Mikhail.

The barrel spat yellow flame.

His vision went red.

And faded to the blackness of death.

11

Bruiser watched the familiar pink mist puff into the air as Mikhail's head exploded all over the seat. He'd seen it enough times through his sniper's scope, but it was much more vivid up close. He took no delight in it, but neither did he feel horror or shame. It was his job. His duty. His mission in life. Some men painted pictures. Others designed machines. Bruiser did this. No judgment. No big deal. A man like Mikhail didn't deserve a ceremonious death or a moment of silence.

Bruiser glanced back towards the cockpit. Door still closed. Pilots hadn't heard the shot. It would have sounded like a faint, distant pop behind that thick steel door.

The plane maintained its course. Bruiser clambered out of the row of seats, then stormed down the aisle towards the lavatory.

A sickness flowed through his chest, up his throat, making it hard to breathe. He'd managed to leap onto the plane's wing, but when he looked through the window he didn't see Brenna in the main cabin.

He'd panicked, even though SEALs were trained not to panic. It was a new feeling. Lots of new feelings the past few hours. Right then the primary feeling had been to kill this motherfucker, though.

Do it quick.

Then pray she's still alive.

You'll never forgive yourself if she isn't.

Mikhail was walking towards the back of the plane when Bruiser popped open the above-wing door with his pigsticker. He'd have liked to have used his knife to gut that bastard Mikhail instead of giving him an easy, mostly painless death. But he was frenzied with worry about Brenna.

Was she lying broken and bloody in one of the lavatories? Had he gotten there too late?

There were two lavatories facing each other. He pushed in one door and cursed when he guessed wrong. The other was locked, and he exhaled hard. Locked from the inside was a good thing. He took another breath, raised his right hand, knocked with his knuckles.

No answer. He leaned close, opened his mouth, was about to sound the all-clear.

Then the deadbolt clicked.

The door whipped open.

And something sharp hit Bruiser directly in the face, right above the eye, dead center on that old scar.

"Hey!" he roared, stepping back as he felt warm blood gush down into his eye.

He was blinded for a moment, and felt the weapon come at him again, this time stabbing into the thick muscle of his left pectoral.

It didn't get very far. The muscle was heavy enough

to stop it about a quarter inch deep. Bruiser grabbed her wrist and frowned down at the weapon. It was the center bar of the toilet-paper holder. Brenna had pulled out the spring, straightened the curly wire, then jammed the straightened spring back in and used it to stab him. Not bad.

"It's me," he said as she struggled in his grip, her face peaked with fear, streaked with anger.

Her eyes were wide but out of focus. Bruiser realized there was so much adrenaline and she was so spent, so scared, so wild that she couldn't hear a thing, couldn't process a sentence right now. She was all fight, pure survival instinct right now. She couldn't be reasoned with. Couldn't be calmed down. Couldn't be controlled.

Not until she felt safe.

Safe in a way her frenzied mind and wired body could understand.

And so without another word Bruiser wrapped his big arms around her and pulled her close.

Pulled her so damn hard against his big warm body that she exhaled in a whoosh, letting out all the poison air she'd bottled up for the fight.

She struggled against his chest for a moment, but Bruiser didn't let go, wouldn't let go, damn well *couldn't* let go.

He hugged her as close as he could, as hard as he dared, covering every inch of her scared, shivering body with his protective muscle.

"You're safe, Brenna," he whispered urgently, his face close to her ear, his warm breath curling her open, wild hair. "I promise you, Brenna. You're safe. You're safe with me. You'll always be safe with me."

She tried to pull away again, and Bruiser eased up just enough for her to turn her head up towards him. Her brown eyes were still wide, but there was focus in them now.

Focus, and anger.

"You left me there," she said through gritted teeth. "Left me there with . . . with *him*!"

Fear flamed in her eyes again, and Bruiser took a breath, hating himself for leaving her even though it was the right tactic.

"He's dead," Bruiser said, resisting the urge to explain himself. It was more important that she know Mikhail was dead, his head a pulpy pink mess in row number seven.

She could stay pissed at Bruiser a bit longer. That he could handle.

He couldn't handle seeing the fear in those big brown eyes, though.

He never wanted to see fear in those eyes again.

"Are you sure he's dead?" she whispered. "How can you be sure he's dead?"

Bruiser frowned down at her. He thought back to those moments they'd shared in her cell block. She'd watched him break that warden's neck. She hadn't flinched. Even joked about it. Battlefield humor. This woman was special. She could handle this.

She *wanted* to handle this.

"Come on," he said, turning up the aisle. He stepped in front of her, shielding her with his body, making sure she felt safe.

Brenna's breath caught as Bruiser took a step down

the aisle. She took a hurried step behind him. He waited for her.

Then Bruiser's own breath caught when he felt her press up into his back, her hand urgently reaching for his. The feeling was electric, and Bruiser blinked three times and swallowed twice to get the buzz out of his head.

"You all right?" he said softly, half turning but not daring to look into her eyes.

Not daring to show her his own eyes.

He was afraid of what she'd see in his eyes.

Afraid that she'd see he was defenseless in her presence.

Bruiser swallowed hard. He needed to rein it in. Get himself under control. He was a soldier, a SEAL, an elite warrior. He wasn't a damn teenager on a first date.

She nodded against his broad back. "You keep asking if I'm all right. Can't you tell by now? Isn't my skin flawless? Aren't my eyes clear?"

Bruiser looked over his shoulder, into her eyes now. Her face was still streaked and flushed. The fear was still there, but she was fighting it. That was the definition of courage. To recognize your fear and refuse to be broken by it. This woman had used all her willpower to make that joke.

She was bruised but not even close to being broken.

He felt himself grin. Shit, he felt like that teenager now, didn't he?

She smiled quickly, with trembling lips, then nodded. He nodded back, kept her hand firmly in his big paw, and led her down the aisle. He stopped at row nine, two rows before Mikhail's body. They could see one massive leg stretched stiffly across the aisle.

"It's messy," he warned.

"Good," she said softly, but with unmistakable firmness. "I hope it hurt."

Bruiser sighed. "Sadly no. Less than a second. He probably didn't feel a damn thing before the lights went out."

She dug her cracked nails into his palm. "That's two bad guys you let off pretty easy. For a guy called Bruiser, I gotta say that's less than impressive."

"I'll try to impress you with the next homicidal maniac I kill."

She poked him in the back. It was almost playful. He led her forward. They stopped right by the stiff leg of the maniac formerly known as Mikhail the Tongueless.

"Well," she said after a long pause. "Now he's Mikhail the Headless." She pulled back. "I think I've seen enough. Thank you."

Brenna let go of his hand and Bruiser turned. She looked pale now, the blood rushing out of her head as relief set in. He swooped in and caught her just as she fell. He wasn't going to let her fall. Not now. Not ever.

She hadn't passed out. She was fully conscious, blinking like she couldn't understand why she'd fallen.

"You're completely drained, Brenna," Bruiser said as he carried her to the back of the plane, placed her carefully in the second-to-last row of seats. She felt light like a doll in his arms. He thought he could carry her forever if he had to. Maybe he'd do just that.

"My legs stopped working. No fair," she said with an annoyed frown. She glared at her canvas-covered legs. "I didn't faint. I'm not a fainter." She took a breath, glanced toward the front of the plane, then looked up at Bruiser and shrugged. "Though I did pass out back there in the prison." She crossed her arms under her breasts and pouted up at him. "After you *left* me," she grumped, playfully puffing out her cheeks and rumbling out the air through her lips like a sulky little girl.

Bruiser rubbed the back of his neck, blood rising up his cheeks. "I had to," he said. "I couldn't risk bullets flying all over the place in a closed room. There were guards in the other cell blocks. They were probably all hopped up on amphetamines. AK-47s are wildly inaccurate to begin with, and if—"

"Relax, Soldier," she said with a smile. "Just teasing. It was the right call. We might both be dead if you'd gone full cowboy on those guys." The smile softened, her eyes too. "Though you jumped on a moving plane. That's pretty darned cowboy, I guess. Thank you for doing that."

"Aw shucks, Ma'am," drawled Bruiser, still red in the face but for a different reason now. He grinned and shrugged. It was weird to be thanked, he realized. SEALs did all their work in the shadows, in the darkness, behind the scenes. There were medals and commendations, sure. But it was different to be thanked.

There was a moment of silence as the plane droned on. They looked at each other.

Bruiser rubbed the back of his neck again. Brenna blinked, looked down at her collar, straightened it best she could. It had been hanging low. Bruiser had caught a glimpse of the beginnings of the most incredible cleavage in the history of womankind. He'd quickly looked away.

On any other day, in any other situation, he'd have shamelessly looked. But not when a woman had just been abused and threatened. Not when she was probably still feeling vulnerable. Hell, she was still barefoot. And in some filthy rag of a prison jumpsuit.

"We'll get you some clothes and shoes," he said awkwardly, looking down the aisle, then back up the aisle towards the closed cockpit door.

"How?" she asked.

He looked at her. Thought a minute. Considered calling Benson. Didn't call Benson.

"As of now we're probably on route to South America," he said as his mind snapped into gear and he spun through the scenarios, weighed the options, played out the strategies.

Remembered the mission.

Benson had given him a directive: Make her trust you. Find out why Damyan wants her. Figure out if she's a traitor.

Pretty broad mission. No doubt Benson was holding something back. Common sense dictated that Bruiser call Benson and get clarity, tell him he had Brenna and she was safe.

Shouldn't he just bring her home to the United States? Just kick open the damn cockpit door, tell the bewildered Argentinean stagecoach drivers to set course for Atlanta? Hell, maybe after dropping Brenna off he could make it back to the wedding afterparty at the Axelrod ranch.

But one look at Brenna barefoot and raggedy, bruised

and pale, and something inside him said there was no way he was letting her out of his sight. What would happen if he took a suspected traitor back to the United States? Neither he nor Benson were part of the military or government any longer. She might disappear into the black hole of the counter-terrorism system. A world where being a U.S. citizen didn't mean what the Constitution said it meant. Homeland Security might swoop in and take her away. Put her in a damn interrogation room and sweat her. Hell, maybe they'd ship her to Gitmo with a black hood over her head.

No way.

No damn way he was letting that happen to her again.

She'd just been through hell in a foreign country. He'd just abandoned her and gotten her back. What would happen if he abandoned her again, let her get dragged into another kind of hell? Would he ever get her back?

He wasn't taking the chance.

Not with this mission.

Not with this woman.

Which meant he had to figure this out himself. He already sensed that no way in hell was she a traitor. But Bruiser was logical enough to realize he couldn't know that for sure. She could be playing him. She might see that he was attracted to her. She might use it to her advantage. He was already compromised.

Damn you, Benson, he thought. Maybe you were right. Maybe this shit is out of my skillset.

My mission was to break Brenna, he thought with an inward chuckle.

So why does it feel like I'm the one being broken?

"I could use some breakfast," she said.

Bruiser snapped out of the swirly mess that was his mind. He glanced up the aisle, saw the galley, strode over to it. On the way he twisted Mikhail's leg and jammed it behind the seat. The body would be stiff as a board soon. He was now part of the upholstery.

The galley was small but well-stocked. Bruiser raided the cabinet, hurrying back with his hands full of beef jerky, nuts, and fruit bars. Four bottles of water stuck in his cargo flaps.

When he got back to Brenna he realized he was hungry too. That ribeye steak from the Axelrod Ranch was long gone, burned off to fuel his rescue mission.

He ripped open some fruit bars and packets of nuts for her. She ate like a kid at camp. Bruiser grinned as he chewed through some salt-crusted jerky. It was good beef. Argentina had some good grasslands.

"Wait, we're going to South America?" she said. "Why?"

Bruiser chewed thoughtfully. "Why did Mikhail come for you? What does Damyan Nagarev want with you?" He paused, kept chewing. "Or from you."

Brenna furrowed her brow. "He said something about secret words."

Bruiser raised an eyebrow. "Like a magic spell?"

She smiled, granola-crumbs all over her face. She waved her half-eaten fruit-bar like a wand. "Babayaga," she said, taking a big bite and looking up at him.

Bruiser grunted in surprise. "The witch from the old Russian fairy tales? Haven't heard that word in years."

"Why do you know that word at all?"

Bruiser shrugged. "Russian mother who loved telling stories."

"You're Russian?"

"Half."

"What's the other half?"

"Polish from Chicago. You?"

Brenna finished chewing, took a drink of water. "Mom's a standard American mutt. Dad is Russian. I mean, he *was* Russian, I guess." She went quiet for a moment, stared at the bottle of water, then glanced up at him. "But you already know that, don't you?"

Bruiser took a breath. This was going to be harder than he thought. Benson was right. The easiest part of the mission was when he broke some guy's neck, jumped onto a moving plane, and then won a gunfight against a tongueless monster. Now came the mind games part.

Much more treacherous.

Much more dangerous.

How much should he reveal?

What was his story?

What was *her* story?

"Alexei Yankov," he said finally. "He's dead. You just found out. That's why you were in Russia."

There was a tiny flinch in the little muscle below her left eye. She was thinking too.

Remember that she's smart as hell, Bruiser, he told himself. Princeton grad. Potential traitor.

Yeah, her gratitude was genuine.

The fear was real.

But everything else might be fake.

"Why were *you* in Russia?" she answered after a pause. He noticed that she answered his question with another question.

"Search and Rescue, Ma'am," he said with a half-shrug and a quarter-grin.

"What branch of the military?"

"Who says I'm military?"

"Your walk says so. Your posture says so. Your haircut pretty much shouts it out."

Bruiser frowned and touched his short, thick hair that was buzzed almost to Jarhead level around the sides and back. He glugged down a bottle of water instead of confirming or denying anything.

"OK, so you're ex-Military then," she said triumphantly. "Which means CIA. Or Black Ops."

He chuckled. "Sure. Let's go with that. Doesn't really matter. Now tell me about Alexei. When did you hear from him last?"

"First tell me which branch of the military."

"This isn't a barter system, Brenna."

"Marines?"

Bruiser felt his heat rise. The angry kind of heat. He had wild respect for the Marines, but he was Navy. And he was the best of the Navy. A damn SEAL. She better tread lightly. Don't mess with a Navy man's pride.

"There's stuff going on that you don't understand, Brenna," he said, keeping his voice steady so she wouldn't see she was getting to him. "Just work with me, all right?"

She tapped her lower lip, moved air from one cheek to the other. "Army Ranger?"

Bruiser took a slow breath and let it out through a tight smile. He was going to snap at her but held his cool—on the outside, at least.

She narrowed those intelligent brown eyes at him. Clearly the sugar in the fruit-bars had woken her brain up with a blast of much-needed glucose.

"Well," she said, those eyes darting side to side as she studied his rapidly reddening face. "Maybe Navy SEAL, but I don't think so."

Now Bruiser almost exploded. His right fist clenched. There was a plastic bottle in the fist. It crunched down to the size of a toothpick. Water dripped through his fingers onto the carpeted aisle.

Brenna could barely sustain her smile. "Got'cha," she whispered gleefully. "I knew you were a SEAL the moment I saw you. One of those half-hidden tattoos is Navy, and since you probably didn't sail a battleship up the channel from the Caspian Sea into Ukraine, you gotta be Navy Special Forces. And that's the SEALs. I used to play *Call of Duty* and hang out on the message boards. I know all the branches. And the tattoos. Yup. Knew you were a SEAL all the while."

Bruiser grinned. He dropped the mangled bottle onto the floor and rubbed his eyes. Then he sighed and stretched his arms out wide, turning his neck side to side. It cracked satisfyingly.

"Actually, you didn't. You thought I was Mikhail Gervin when you first saw me," he corrected. "But all right. Fine. OK. I was a SEAL. You got me. Congratulations. Now can we stop playing games?"

"I like this game," said Brenna, her eyes still shining with mischief. But behind those eyes he could see the wheels turning. She was trying to figure things out just like he was.

"Look," he said resting his big elbows on two seatbacks and leaning over her. She was sitting sideways in the row of seats, her back against the window, legs stretched out on the seat. Her bare feet were dangerously close to his crotch, he suddenly realized.

She must have realized it too, because her toes curled and her gaze dropped to the front of his pants. Bruiser immediately felt himself harden. He filled out so damn fast he felt the blood leave his head, making him almost dizzy.

Brenna's breath caught and her eyes widened and she quickly looked away. He saw the color rush to her face, making her round cheeks look like roses in bloom.

Bruiser stood his ground. This was a don't-ask, don't-tell situation. Neither one of them could acknowledge a damn thing. If he turned away or adjusted himself it would be a situation of top-level awkwardness, red-alert tension. It would result in a barrage of embarrassed coughs and serious throat-clearing all around.

Stand your ground, Soldier, he told himself. Hold the line.

Brenna picked up a granola bar and made a production of unwrapping it to defuse the awkwardness. Bruiser gritted his teeth and tried to think about baseball or football or perhaps watching Congress debate a tax bill on C-Span.

Nope. Still hard as the Rock of Gibraltar, big like Mount Rainier.

Maybe if he glanced past Brenna and out the window. He tried.

And it just might have worked if he hadn't glanced *at* Brenna along the way.

His gaze just happened to pass over her chest. She'd had her arms crossed earlier, and the large jumpsuit was pressed tight against her breasts, highlighting their perfect roundness.

Highlighting much more than that.

Highlighting just enough of a little peak to make it clear her nipples were standing straight out like hard, pointy arrowheads.

It was too much for Bruiser. He had to turn away.

Quickly he pulled back, raised his elbows off the seatbacks. He turned so fast his left elbow rammed into the seat-back in front of Brenna. It rocked wildly back and forth.

Bruiser grabbed it to steady it, his face blazing red like Mars at noon. He had to get outta there.

He strode to the galley, yanked open the little fridge, almost tearing it off its hinges. He found a glass bottle of water that was chilled but somehow not frozen. Without thinking, he unscrewed the metal top, raised the bottle to his lips, and drank it down, just pouring it down his damn throat.

It was only when he took a breath and got a strange, pungent aftertaste that he realized it wasn't water.

Breaking Brenna

It was vodka.

Chilled in a glass bottle, Russian style.

He stared at the empty bottle as the alcohol burned down his throat and warmed him from the inside out. Almost immediately he felt the buzz starting to take hold. Bruiser wasn't a big drinker, but he knew what alcohol does to a man.

Makes him walk funny.

Makes him see double.

And oh yeah . . .

Makes him talk his fucking ass off.

Yeah, he knew about alcohol.

And being Russian and Polish, he knew about vodka too.

He knew it was the greatest truth serum known to man.

12

Can I trust this man?

Brenna finished unwrapping the granola bar slowly and carefully. Her peripheral vision was keenly following Bruiser. She didn't know what to make of him. Didn't know what to make of herself around him either. She was smart enough to know that she'd been in a continual state of stress, fear, and shock for a week. Add dehydration, isolation, and starvation to the mix and there is no way in hell you can think clearly.

But can you *feel* clearly, she wondered as she held back a shocked smile at the unspoken moment of supreme awkwardness. She glanced down at her bosom. She'd felt her nipples stand up on their own, get all prickly around the edges, harden like little pebbles.

She looked at her bare toes, curled them again, gasped when she realized she was a little wet between her legs. She looked at the granola bar. It was long and large and made her want to giggle. She pulled the wrapper back over it and stuffed it into the seatback pocket. Then she glanced over at Bruiser again.

Brenna watched him glug down a bottle of water and then make a funny face. He stared at the bottle, then rubbed his eyes and turned his back to her. She sighed and rubbed her own eyes, tried to remember what Mikhail had asked her.

Secret words, he'd said through his phone's robotic voice. Tell me the words. Damyan says you have the words.

What words?

Now Brenna remembered Bruiser saying her father's name. Why did a Navy SEAL sent to rescue her know all of that?

Because he's not a SEAL.

Not any longer, at least, she thought as she studied Bruiser's haircut from behind, took in the sinewy mass of muscle that was his back and shoulders. He's CIA or Black Ops or something like that. He's alone. He's asking me questions. What's going on? What do they think I know? Who do they think I am?

She let her exhausted body relax, let her revitalized brain go over everything she knew.

Then she sat up straight.

Stared at her toes.

Eyes wide open.

A chill of electric realization making her body and head buzz all at once.

Secret words?

Twelve secret words, maybe?

Could it have something to do with that old crypto account?

That *secret* crypto account?

A secret shared only by a father and his daughter?

But that account had been cleaned out a decade ago,

Brenna thought. And surely if her dad had put more money in it before he died he'd have let her know.

Maybe he didn't get a chance.

Maybe the money wasn't for her.

Maybe he was hiding it there.

Now Brenna felt fear creeping up her bare neck. She shivered a little, scrunched her toes up. Even when Alexei was still alive he would come and go like a man of secrets and shadows.

"He's always been like that, Brenna," Nancy had said four years ago when Brenna had brought up the topic again. "He was like that before you were born. He was like that when you were growing up too, remember? He'd show up when he pleased, and when he was gone, he was gone. Do you ever remember getting Christmas cards or long letters or just-checking-in text messages? Did he *ever* do any of that?"

"No," Brenna had said with a sigh.

She'd thought of that solitary postcard that unlocked her college tuition, but she didn't mention it. She'd never told Nancy about the secret cryptocurrency account. She said she got a scholarship and a good part-time job. After all, Alexei had stopped the monthly deposits after sending Brenna that money. Brenna didn't want to drain her mother's life savings. As it was Nancy had quit the DMV before qualifying for her pension.

A shard of guilt stabbed at Brenna as her thoughts drifted back to those days. She knew deep down that she'd hidden Alexei's gift out of a weird distrust for Nancy. She couldn't explain it, couldn't understand it, and couldn't even really admit it to herself. There was nothing about Nancy that justified feeling that way, but Brenna couldn't shake it. Maybe it was that her mom was always around but never really there. In an odd way, both her parents had a very powerful OFF switch, it seemed.

"Why does this damn thing keep turning *off*." came Bruiser's voice through her thoughts.

She looked up, surprised. Was he . . . *slurring*?

She stared as Bruiser emerged from the galley and lurched to his left, slamming against the bulkhead and then flopping down in the front row of seats. He was tapping his phone furiously with fingers that looked big like Polish sausages. He shook the phone like it was a disobedient child, then held it to his ear.

"Benson?" he shouted. "You still there? Damn you, Benson. Next time give me a phone that fucking*works*, will ya? This piece of shit isn't even useful as a weapon. Too small. Too blunt."

Bruiser slid the phone into his left cargo flap and buttoned it somewhat clumsily, like an overgrown child trying to dress himself for the first time. Finally he got the flap closed and grunted. He looked back down the aisle, saw her looking at him, and broke into a huge grin.

"I'm not drunk," he said loudly.

Brenna stared. Then she covered her mouth and snorted out a laugh.

"Ohmygod," she said. "That bottle. Chilled vodka, wasn't it? My dad would always put a bottle of vodka in the freezer when he was in town. They always drink it chilled in Russia."

Bruiser grinned that big-ass grin again. He was clearly a goofy drunk. At least right now he was. He was an angry drunk on that phone call a moment ago.

"Who's Benson?" she asked.

"Darkwater Head of Operations," he said without any filter at all, no hesitation.

"What's Darkwater," she asked, shimmying her butt forward and sticking her bare feet into the aisle.

She sat on the edge of the seat and looked up the aisle towards Bruiser. He was an open book now, she realized with a mixture of guilt and glee. This was like an Ask-Me-Anything on Social Media.

Ah, vodka. The greatest truth serum ever invented.

"Darkwater is . . . a secret," he said, raising his left eyebrow secretively.

"I can keep a secret," she said, curling her toes above the rough carpet. "Tell me."

"No," he said adamantly. He leaned into the aisle from a few rows in front and turned to look at her. One eye was closed like he was seeing double. He pointed a massive forefinger at her. "I'm supposed to find out *your* secrets."

She blinked. Thought a moment. Then she shrugged. "OK. What secrets do you want to know?"

Bruiser heaved himself up from the seat. The plane hit an air pocket and he slammed his palms up against the ceiling to steady himself. He looked massive in the aisle, and Brenna let her gaze drift down his incredibly masculine V shaped frame.

She'd thought he was vaguely handsome even when she believed he was Mikhail the Tongueless, and now that she saw him in full light, that big-ass confident grin on his face, she realized that the handsomeness was more than just vague.

"First question," he said through that wolfish but still-goofy grin. "Do you currently have a boyfriend?"

Brenna felt something in her chest. She realized it was her heart. It was trying to either burst through her ribcage or jump up her throat and escape that way. She swallowed hard and told her heart it wasn't going anywhere.

She cleared her throat, pulled back her horribly stringy, terribly dried out, grossly dirty hair.

"What if I do?" she asked, trying to sound disinterested.

"Well, if you do have a boyfriend," he drawled, taking a step down the aisle, big palms still flat against the ceiling to guide his advance. "Then I would like to have a word with him." He lowered his arms, let them drop to his sides. His fists clenched lazily. His triceps bulged big as footballs. He grinned, cracked his knuckles, shrugged again. "Just a word with the guy. Just me and him, behind the middle-school yard."

Brenna almost choked trying to stifle the giggle. "Aren't you a little big to be beating up middle-schoolers?"

"I'm asking the questions, little lady."

"OK. Next question, then."

Bruiser grunted with satisfaction. "No boyfriend, then. Item One on the list: Check."

Brenna flushed. Looked down at her toes. Up at the overgrown middle-schooler who'd just killed two men to protect her. "What else is on the list?"

He shrugged. Took a step closer. "Nothing."

She laughed. "That's a short list."

Bruiser shrugged again. He was close enough she could smell him. Woodsy with that hint of mesquite, a pungent afterburn of vodka in the air around him.

"Well, maybe there's one more item on my list," he growled.

His shadow loomed over her now. She pulled her toes in and looked up into his eyes. She was wide awake and warm. He was three times her size and drunk off his ass but she felt safe like a bunny in its burrow.

Her body tingled and she took a quick breath, two quick breaths, maybe three. She knew she was filthy and stinking but she felt clean and fresh because of how her body buzzed and her head hummed.

She glanced at his lips and blinked three times. She wondered what she'd do if he came any closer.

If he leaned in, slid his big hand around the back of her neck, pulled her close and brought those lips to hers.

Oh God, what would she do if he . . . if he . . . if he . . .

And then Bruiser was gone.

Gone down the aisle like a bear charging downhill.

All the way downhill to the back of the plane.

Smashing through the lavatory doors.

Dropping down to his knees.

Bowing his head and heaving like a freshman during fraternity rush week.

Paying homage to the porcelain gods.

13

Bruiser splashed water on his face and stared at himself in the tiny airplane mirror. Just one face staring back, which meant he wasn't seeing double.

He pat-dried his forehead and cheekbones and lips with a paper towel that smelled vaguely of lavender. He hated lavender. If he were a bull he'd have spent his prime years destroying fields of lavender.

The thought made him grin. He wasn't so drunk now, but he clearly wasn't all the way sober.

"You all right?" came Brenna's voice from not so far away.

The lavatory door was still open. Bruiser leaned half his body out into the aisle. She was standing three rows away, trying to hold back a smile.

She wasn't making a very good effort. The smile broke through like the sun on a spring morning.

Bruiser grinned back, any hint of embarrassment washed away by her beauty.

"So no boyfriend, right?" he said. He'd meant to either apologize or pretend like that conversation had never happened. Clearly his tongue had other ideas.

She leaned her head back and laughed. Her hair was like straw that had been through a rainstorm and then been dried in a hurricane. She pulled at the clumped strands. Something fell out of the haystack of dark hair.

"Nah," she said with a proud hair-flip that dislodged something else that might have been a fingernail or perhaps a rat-claw. "Been keeping to myself lately. Well, there were a couple of guys interested, but you killed them both."

Bruiser laughed and stepped out into the aisle. Jammed the lavatory door closed. Ran his fingers through his wet hair. The wound from Brenna stabbing him with the toilet paper holder was throbbing afresh. She glanced at it and blinked.

"Sorry for stabbing you in the face," she said.

Bruiser grinned. "In that situation you stab first and ask questions later."

She nodded. Looked down at her toes and then up into his eyes. "We still asking each other questions?"

"You probably already know everything," Bruiser said, shaking his head and rubbing the back of his neck. "What did I say before I got bucked off that horse?"

"Darkwater. Benson. Beating up kids behind the middle school."

Bruiser chuckled. Then his head throbbed and he groaned. "Benson. Shit, I think I called him. Can't remember what he said."

"He probably told you to hand the phone to a grown up," Brenna teased. She turned and looked up the aisle, toward the galley. "How about we get you some real water. Go sit down. I'll bring it to you."

Bruiser was going to protest, but he was momentarily silenced by the sight of her walking away from him. Even that atrociously oversized canvas jumpsuit couldn't hide those womanly curves, that hourglass shape, that large round bottom that made him want to charge like that lavender-hating bull.

He closed his eyes tight and tried to shake the thoughts away. This wasn't the time. It wasn't the place. He shouldn't be staring. Shouldn't be imagining what he was seeing in his mind's eye. She'd just been through hell and she wasn't out of the firepit yet.

Besides, he still didn't know if he was allowed to trust her. He couldn't have told her much, but blurting the name Darkwater and mentioning Benson would raise some flags if she was smart enough. Darkwater sounded like either a private military contractor or a dark ops side project. And mentioning a boss by name instead of rank meant something.

"You aren't in the SEALs anymore, are you?" she asked just as he flopped lengthwise across two seats in row ten. She handed him a plastic bottle of water with the cap already unscrewed for him.

Bruiser sniffed the liquid cautiously before drinking. It was water, and it was much needed. He drained it in two and a half seconds.

"Thanks," he said as she handed him another bottle, also prepped for a quick pour down his gullet. He drank deep and sighed. Tossed the empty bottle over the seat back. "Once a SEAL, always a SEAL," he said stoically.

She rolled her eyes, but he could see she was only pretending to be unimpressed.

"So why am I so important?" she said, sliding those beautiful hips into the seat-row across the aisle. She slid back against the window, placed her feet up on the seat, toes pointing towards him. He could see blisters through the layer of black dirt on her soles. "What did my father do when he was alive? Who was he?"

Bruiser crossed his arms over his chest. He looked at his boots. Then past them into her eyes. "Nobody, according to Benson."

She narrowed her eyes. "You don't think Benson is telling you the truth?"

"Why would you say that?"

"Because of the way you said *According to Benson*."

"Didn't know you were a professional interrogator."

"Don't need to be. You're a terrible liar. You'd make a terrible spy."

"And you'd make a terrible interrogator. Insulting your target isn't gonna loosen his lips."

"In my experience anger works great at making men talk."

"You have a lot of experience with angry men?"

She shrugged. "Some boys get pissed off when a girl proves she's smarter and stronger."

"Boys?"

"If you're going to get all upset because a woman's better than you in every way, then you aren't a man. You're a boy. A child."

Bruiser raised his left eyebrow. "Am I being insulted here?"

She smiled. "You're being interrogated."

Bruiser grinned. "You're good. You haven't told me a damn thing since we got on this plane. Answered every question with a question. Turned every answer into a joke." He relaxed his gaze, set his jaw firm. "If I didn't know better, I'd say you were hiding something."

"Why do you think you know better?"

"You're doing it again." Bruiser glanced at his watch, then at the cockpit door. "Look, we're running out of time. Pretty soon we won't be able to divert this plane to the United States."

She shifted her body and turned to look out her window. It was dark. No stars. No moon. She settled back down. "Because of fuel?"

"Airspace. They've probably filed a flight plan that lets them pass through U.S. airspace en route to South America. But if we pass the southern border and then double-back, it violates the flight plan, violates American airspace." He grinned. "And our fly-boys have itchy trigger fingers."

She smirked. "Whatever. It's not like you hear of the Air National Guard shooting down private planes who've strayed off course. They'll warn the pilots like a million times before sending out a squadron of F-16s. Unless you're flying right into the Pentagon or White House or something. Anyway, can't you just call your boss Benson and call off the dogs?"

Bruiser exhaled. She was right. He'd been bluffing, using the old tactic of setting some sort of deadline. "Lemme guess. You were that super-smart kid who raised her hand to answer every damn question in class. Even the ones where you didn't know the answer. Because you were so confident in your intelligence that you thought you could just wing it."

Brenna narrowed her eyes, studied his face. "Takes one to know one. You were that kid too."

Bruiser frowned. He absolutely was that kid. He also had the longest arms and biggest hands in every class. And the confidence to argue to the death, even if he was plumb wrong.

"Fine," he said with a shrug, making as if he was about to get up. "Next stop Robins Air Force Base in Georgia. Good luck with the *real* professional interrogators."

He took his time getting up off the seat, watching her out the side of his vision. There was a flinch in that tiny muscle beneath her left eye again.

Aha. So she *did* have something to hide.

She held on for a few moments, but Bruiser was willing to carry the bluff all the way through. He didn't particularly want to turn her over to the hard men and even harder women in Homeland Security. But she didn't know that.

At least Bruiser hoped she didn't.

He was two feet away from the cockpit door when she broke.

"Did they tell you about the money?" she said softly, her voice carrying like a melody on the breeze.

He stopped. Turned. Sighed. Shook his head.

Brenna was peeking up over the seatback seven rows down from him. "Well, I *assume* there's money in that old crypto account. There has to be. That's the only reason I'm suddenly in such high demand by big bad men with tattoos and political beefs."

"My politics are pretty simple," Bruiser offered, glancing at his tattooed forearms. "America."

Her eyes shone with something Bruiser couldn't interpret in words but felt in his heart. No way this woman was a traitor. Just no way. Benson was wrong. Kaiser was wrong.

"That *is* pretty simple," she said, blinking and looking away as if she didn't want him to see the light in her eyes.

"What account?" Bruiser said.

She sighed. "I might be wrong about it."

"Can't you check?" Bruiser dug into his cargo flap for his phone. He pulled it out, walked to her row, tossed in onto her lap.

She looked at the phone thoughtfully. Then she shook her head. "If I type in the secret words on that phone, your boss Benson will pick them up. Your phone and messages and all keystrokes are probably being recorded."

"He's not my *boss*," said Bruiser. "Anyway, he can be trusted. He's a good man."

Brenna smiled tightly. "Remember when I said you were a terrible liar?"

Bruiser bristled. "What are you worried about? That someone will steal your money?"

She shook her head. "If that's what everyone is after, then it's the only leverage I have. The only reason I won't be killed—by either side."

"There are things worse than death."

"Is that a threat?"

Bruiser took a breath and let it out hard. "Look, Brenna. I can maybe help you, but you gotta come clean with me, all right?"

"I *am* clean," Brenna snapped, her eyes sharp like darts. "I didn't even *know* about the money. I haven't heard from my dad in a decade. I assumed he was dead. And now he *is* dead. And nobody's told me *anything*, and there's all these people trying to catch me and kill me and do things to get something I don't even know is actually there. And you don't have a team, and you don't have a rank, and you don't trust your boss, and how do I know you aren't another thug after some money I didn't even know I had, and if I give you the secret key to the account maybe I'm no longer useful and I get tossed out like the trash." Her voice trembled, her eyes moistened, but it was all raw anger. She was too wired to be scared. All fire, no fear.

Then she sniffled. Just once. Lips trembling again. Blinking away tears but refusing to cry.

"And I'm filthy," she said. "And I have no shoes. And there's stuff in my hair, like straw and rat poop and bugs. And . . . and . . . there's no one I can trust, Bruiser. I'm alone and filthy and there's no one I can trust."

Tears streamed down her cheeks but she wasn't sobbing, wasn't even really crying. Bruiser had never seen strength like this. He knew it was strength, pure and beautiful.

The tears were involuntary, just the body's reaction to something so deep that was coming out. But her will was stopping her from sobbing, from really crying, from truly breaking.

Bruiser, however, couldn't stay unbroken.

He went to her and reached for her and pulled her up off the seat and took her tight in his arms. She tried to push him away but he just wrapped those arms around her and held her like she was his to protect.

Everything she'd said was logical. She couldn't trust anyone. Hell, if there was big money involved, maybe-*he* couldn't trust anyone either.

But that was a different matter. He'd deal with Benson and Kaiser and the damn spooks later. Right now he needed her to trust him. He wanted her to trust him. It wasn't about the damn mission anymore.

It was about something a hell of a lot simpler.

It was about a man getting a woman to trust him.

And then suddenly everything was simple again for Bruiser. All the complexity of Benson's games and Kaiser's tactics and Damyan's politics dropped away like a useless, heavy coat of armor.

So he dropped the armor. All of it. Stood there defenseless with her. Defenseless but somehow invincible. Shielded only by his need to protect her. A simple, ancient, deadly need. As old as man and woman. As old as the damn universe.

"Everything you said is true except for the last bit," he whispered into her hair. "You're not alone, Brenna. You're never going to be alone again. You're right. You can't trust anyone. But I'm not just anyone, Brenna. I'm yours, you understand? I'm yours and you're mine. It's so damn simple."

She looked up at him from where she'd been burrowing into his chest. Her pretty round face was streaked red. Her brown eyes were shining with tears. She looked at him. Looked down. Looked up at him again.

Bruiser blinked twice. He didn't know why he'd just said that. It had just come out. Maybe he was still a bit drunk. Hell, maybe he was plenty damn drunk. Only a drunk fool says shit that like to a woman he doesn't know, a woman who's in no frame of mind or body to respond to something like that.

And he didn't even mean it anyway.

He couldn't, right? This was the alcohol getting inside his body and Benson getting inside his head and that wedding where Ax and Amy looked so damn happy, so well matched, so perfect for each other that it couldn't have been random chance, had to have been something else, like those crazy coincidences that happen in battle, shit that makes you think about fate, makes you believe in destiny.

"I didn't mean that," he said as she looked at him like she maybe hadn't heard right, hadn't heard at all, oh hell, please let her not have heard him sound like a sentimental romantic idiot.

Her face fell, and immediately Bruiser's heart leaped like the happiest frog in the pond. If she was disappointed that he'd taken it back, then logically it meant she was thrilled that he'd said it.

"Didn't mean what?" she asked, her face small like a

little girl who just opened a Christmas present and found nothing in the box.

"The part where I said I disagree with your last statement." Bruiser sniffed her hair and playfully pushed her away before pulling her back into him. "You were right. You *are* filthy and you most certainly *do* stink. How about I bust open that cockpit door and get those rancheros to land somewhere we can find hot running water and maybe some shampoo?"

She looked up at him, the light flashing back into her eyes, the smile returning to her cracked lips. She nodded against his chest. That feeling was back in his heart. It had never left. It never would leave.

"And some shoes," she whispered up at him. "Some shoes too, please."

14
<u>COSTA RICA</u>
<u>THE NEXT MORNING</u>

"These?" Brenna said hopefully, her eyebrows raised as she examined the red lace-up Converse sneakers in the slanted foot-mirror.

The sales clerk grinned and nodded. He was a pleasant looking Hispanic teenager in a blue floral shirt and a striped necktie that he was using as a belt. Clearly Foot Locker's Costa Rica franchises didn't enforce the company's referee-stripes uniform. Unless this wasn't a real Foot Locker, Brenna thought. The sign had said *Frito Legare*. Didn't that mean Foot Locker in Spanish? Maybe it meant *Frito Lay*.

"Well?" she said, pulling up the legs of the stretch black jeans she'd made Bruiser buy her from the department store while she stayed at the small hotel and showered and bathed and showered again and bathed twice more.

She'd paired the jeans with a black high-necked sleeveless blouse with a dark blue long-sleeved pullover. She'd scoped them all out online and given Bruiser strict sizing instructions.

She'd considered making him pick up a bra and panties, but then decided it might be too embarrassing for both of them. She'd survived a week without underwear. The blouse was thick enough that her nipples wouldn't show obscenely. The pullover was heavy cotton. And black jeans were a strategic choice. No wet spots would show. She could go to church dressed like this.

"Um, hello?" she said for the third time.

Both Brenna and the clerk looked at Bruiser and waited.

He glanced up from his phone, his eyes almost crossed from squinting. "Did you say something?"

Brenna whooshed out a fake exasperated sigh. Shoe shopping with a Navy SEAL named Bruiser. Um, *why* would she think he might be helpful?

"You're useless as a wing-man," she said, eyebrows still raised.

She nodded at the sales guy. His grin was so big and shiny she could see her reflection in his polished white teeth. Then she walked over to Bruiser, feeling awkward when she remembered she had no cash. Or cards. Or a passport. In fact, they were illegals in Costa Rica.

Well, not really. Bruiser had called that guy Benson and had him clear it somehow before diverting the plane to Costa Rica. She figured they'd picked Costa Rica because it was a peaceful democracy on very good terms with the United States. Not so many of those around these days, she'd heard Benson quip on the phone to Bruiser. Benson sounded like a decent guy, she thought. But a decent guy with secrets, Bruiser had told her after he hung up.

"I'll pay you back online when we get to the hotel," Brenna said after Bruiser paid the man with a crisp hundred dollar bill that had been folded about a hundred times. He'd told her that all SEALs carried a few hundreds wrapped tight in waterproof baggies. Sometimes U.S. Dollars loosened more lips than torture, he'd told her.

"Shoes are on me," he said as they walked out the fake Foot Locker and onto the sunbaked sidewalk.

It was just past eleven in the morning local time. They'd landed at midnight, grabbed the pilots, taken a taxi to the closest hotel that had three free rooms, and crashed almost immediately. Brenna didn't have the strength to bathe before the lights went out in her exhausted body and frazzled brain.

The morning after a great night's sleep had felt like a gift from the heavens. And when the hot water of the shower hit her, she felt her life was complete and she could die happy, perfectly satisfied, absolutely content.

Brenna was very content as she felt her squeaky-clean sneakers grip the sidewalk tight. She had strong calves and loved to wear heels with a short dress, but she figured stretch jeans and sneakers were more appropriate for a girl on the run.

Though hopefully she wouldn't have to actually run. She'd been a softball star at Princeton, but it wasn't from chasing down grounders. Being slow in the outfield didn't matter when you could knock them over the fence at bat.

They walked to the corner, where the outdoor cafe where they'd eaten breakfast was filling up with tourists. Mostly Americans, Brenna figured. She scanned the sunburned, sunglassed faces, happy to see people other than Boots and Mikhail.

Then she quickly turned her head away, grabbed Bruiser's hand, and pulled him off the curb to cross the street.

Bruiser was agile for a big man—for any man, really—but he was taken by surprise and stumbled as he was pulled off the curb. His shoulder bumped Brenna, and she lurched sideways into traffic.

Of course, Bruiser had her hand in his, and he yanked her back towards him. Still, the nearest car, a hatchback yellow Honda taxi, slammed on the brakes because running over an American tourist might be bad for business.

The old car's brakes screamed and its tires squealed, and every head in the cafe turned to look.

Which was exactly what Brenna *didn't* want to have happen.

"Brenna? Brenna Yankova?" came the voice as the man stood from the two-person table where he'd been sitting alone, staring intently at his phone, tapping it like he was playing a game. Probably chess. Definitely chess. Trying to figure out how she'd destroyed him with a two-knight offense. "Hey, Brenna! Over here! It's me! Bobby Marshall."

Brenna took a long breath, widened her eyes at Bruiser, then slowly turned and smiled stiffly. She stepped back up on the curb, Bruiser by her side, his arm now firmly around her waist after the not-that-close call with the relieved taxi driver.

"Bobby Marshall . . . from middle school," she said

awkwardly, touching her hair and glancing at Bruiser. She didn't know why she was embarrassed but she was turning red.

Bobby Marshall looked much thinner and much older. She held the forced smile and nodded earnestly, searching for the right words, reaching for a good story, some totally normal reason why she was in Costa Rica with a towering man who looked exactly like what an undercover, black ops assassin should look like.

Bruiser had bought new clothes too, but they were exactly like his old clothes. Black short sleeve T-shirt and black cargo pants.

Ah, you found the ex-military totally-obvious assassin surplus shop, she'd joked.

He'd frowned and looked down at himself like it had never occurred to him. She'd smiled and shaken her head, led him to the cafe in her bare feet. The shoe store hadn't been open yet. Brenna wished she'd found a different shoe store. A different cafe.

"What happened to your face?" said Bobby, his gaze fixing on her cheek, then flicking towards Bruiser, finally back at her. His face paled. His tiny Adam's apple moved as he swallowed.

Shit. Her bruised cheekbone from where Boots hit her.

Bruiser stiffened next to her. She felt like the entire outdoor seating area of the cafe was looking at the two of them now, waiting for her answer. They were all wondering if she was a battered bride or a newlywed on a very rough, raunchy honeymoon.

"Oh, this?" she said, touching her face and just about

stopping herself from saying she walked into a door. That was too cliché, wasn't it? Or wait, maybe it was cliché because it actually happened a lot. To everyone. Just go with it, she thought. "I walked into a—"

But she didn't finish the sentence.

She was jerked away to her left by her arm as something whistled through the air.

Bruiser yanked with such sudden, explosive force that she felt her shoulder pop out and then back in for one sickening moment.

She felt that whistling something whoosh past her in the air as she fell. There was no other sound as Bruiser pulled her down to the sidewalk and covered her with his body.

Then she heard the distant crack of the gunshot. The bullet had gotten there faster than the sound of the shot. Sound travelled so slow.

"Stay down," commanded Bruiser, his mouth close to her ear.

Brenna nodded, the sidewalk rough and hot against her cheek. Her eyes were wide open but she couldn't see straight. The blood pounded in her head like a group of bucket drummers in a subway station. All her senses were heightened but somehow mixed up, chaotic, like she could see sound and hear smell and taste colors. Bruiser smells like a forest, she thought. With lots of wood and brambles and underbrush.

Lots of birds in the forest too, it occurred to her. Making lots of sounds. Gasping. Gaping. Crying. Screaming. What kinds of birds were those?

Finally her eyes stopped doing that blurry thing. Her senses went back to their proper channels. She could see and hear just fine. It wasn't birds, it was people.

They were hiding behind tables, crying, screaming, staring.

Staring at Bobby Marshall lying on the sidewalk, blood pouring out a hole in his right shoulder, eyelids fluttering.

She almost choked. Bruiser's weight come off her.

Then she was being pulled to her feet by his strong arms. Immediately she was dragged into the cafe, Bruiser shielding her all the way, his face completely focused, head turning left and right, scanning every face in the crowd, taking in every entry and exit, every pillar and wall.

"Through the kitchen, out the back," he ordered.

Brenna nodded as Bruiser placed his palm against the small of her back and pushed her along. She cast a hurried glance over her shoulder. Her tummy seized when she saw Bobby Marshall's loafers attached to two twitching feet.

"He was aiming for me," said Bruiser. "Rifle wasn't sighted right. He was using an unfamiliar gun."

Bruiser reached above her head and rammed his first into the swinging kitchen door. He shoved her through as the door swung back like a helicopter blade.

"I'm sorry about your friend. He'll live, though. And I'll get the bastard." Bruiser sounded certain. "First I need to get you safe."

She nodded. Did what he said. Thought about what he'd said to her on the plane.

You're mine, he'd said to her on the plane. She'd kind of heard him, kind of not heard him, couldn't be sure he'd said it, was darn sure he'd said it.

"Tough shot from that angle," Bruiser said as two wide-eyed cooks in white shorts and white shirts and black hairnets and bright turquoise nitrile gloves dived out of the way. "This guy was probably military trained to even try it."

"The bullet got there before the sound," she said as the back door came into sight. It was battered red metal, with silver showing where the paint had chipped. "How did you know?"

Bruiser looped his arm around the front of her waist, swung her around with the grace of a dancer, moved ahead of her in one swift move. He strode to the back door and opened it a crack. There was a green-painted brick wall across the alley. A gunman would have to show himself at the cross street down at the end of the alley to make a shot.

Bruiser glanced at her. She saw an odd hesitation in his green eyes.

"Saw the muzzle flash," he said. "Light travels fastest. Then the bullet gets here. Last thing you hear is the shot."

She nodded. Logical enough. But why had he hesitated before answering? Did he really see the muzzle flash? How do you see a muzzle flash behind you when it's sunnier than hell outside?

Nope. Bruiser hadn't seen shit, she thought.

He'd *felt* it. Felt it in his gut.

A sixth sense that she'd read about once. An interview with an ex-Army General talking about how there were some soldiers who could feel death coming for them, were warned by some unexplainable instinct, something that soldiers were reluctant to talk about because it sounded hokey and superstitious.

"Hope you aren't superstitious," Bruiser said as he pushed open the metal door and beckoned for Brenna to come through. He stayed close when she stepped out into the alley. Kept his body between her and the empty street at the bottom of the alley.

"Why does it matter if I'm superstitious?"

Bruiser spun her around towards the top of the alley, stepping behind her like that impenetrable shield to any possible line of fire. She glanced back at him. He gestured with his head for her to walk towards the dead end.

A dead end leading to a red Spanish-style building with white trimmings around the long windows and arched door.

Above the door was a perfectly positioned white-painted wooden cross.

The doors to the church were wide open to let in the sun and the breeze. The pews were packed, shoulder to shoulder with locals in their best suits and prettiest dresses.

"Because we're about to crash Sunday mass," said Bruiser with a half-grin. "Come on. Run."

Brenna ran in her spanking new red Converse hightops. Her stretch black jeans hugged her bouncing butt very well, made it feel tight and firm even without panties or Spanx.

Her black top didn't do as well on the support front,

though. Her dark blue pullover was tied around her waist, and she didn't have time to maneuver it over her head because Bruiser was behind her and pushing her along as they ran out of the path of danger.

Her boobs almost hit her in the face, but she managed to control the swing well enough that she arrived at the church door with no new facial injuries. She stopped breathless at the threshold, her bosom heaving, the hot sun coaxing out pearls of clean perspiration from her flawless forehead. Her underarms were wet but she smelled of milkthistle soap and green apple shampoo.

Her boobs took their time settling down, though, and many heads turned just in time to take in the sight of a panting curvy woman in a black sleeveless shirt with a bruise below her eye and a towering tattooed beast by her side.

"These seats taken?" Bruiser whispered to a white-haired gentleman who'd hurriedly looked down in guilt and remorse after his wide eyes had settled instinctively on Brenna's chest. He hurriedly crossed himself and nodded as Bruiser sat down hard on the wooden bench and pulled Brenna down by his side.

The entire church was silent. Two elderly women who appeared to be sisters turned in tandem from the row ahead of them. Bruiser grinned wide and looked them directly in the eyes. Brenna smiled as sweetly as she could, hoping she didn't come across as a psycho.

The two sisters frowned at Brenna's bruised face, then glared at Bruiser. He kept grinning, slipped his arm around Brenna's shoulder, then raised his other hand to his lips, thumb sticking up. He leaned his head back and did the universal sign for drinking. Even made a glug-glug sound. A big-ass wink and a sideways glance at Brenna later, the sisters were glaring disapprovingly at her.

Brenna elbowed Bruiser as hard as she could in the side. She wasn't sure if she hit muscle or bone or a concrete wall. It might have been a wall, since Bruiser didn't seem to notice the jab.

"Ow," she grumbled in a pouty whisper. She rubbed her elbow. "You're going to hell for that."

"Nah, I'll just go to the confession booth and get myself off the hook."

"Might as well include the two guys you killed in the past day."

"Those weren't sins."

"Thou shalt not kill, remember?"

Bruiser grunted. "Mom was Russian Orthodox. Dad was Polish Catholic. Apparently I slipped through the cracks."

"Slipped pretty far down," whispered Brenna.

"That's for damn sure."

"Blasphemous!"

"Bless you."

"What?"

"I thought you sneezed," said Bruiser, staring straight ahead like an overgrown choirboy.

Brenna slapped her palm over her mouth, her eyes bugging out as she tried not to burst out laughing. She didn't remember either of her parents taking her to church, but she had no problem with religion.

Then it occurred to her that her parents had never

been married, and she wondered if religion would have a problem with *her*.

"I just realized I'm a bastard child," she whispered to Bruiser as the black-robed priest at the front of the room resumed his sermon in Spanish.

He was tall with a full head of very black hair. He said a few words, then went silent for a moment and two people stepped to the altar before him.

Bruiser shrugged like he was cool with bastards born out of wedlock. He was looking towards the priest and the two people standing with their backs to the congregation.

"And I just realized it isn't Sunday," he said, his eyebrows knitting and then popping up in amusement.

The two people stepped up on a small wooden dais and were clearly visible now. It was a man and a woman. The man was in a shining black suit with a white carnation in the lapel. The woman wore a blindingly white dress that came down past her ankles and was lined with a very tasteful, pretty lace trim.

"So we crashed a wedding," Brenna said when it became clear what was going on.

Suddenly she was very aware of Bruiser's arm around her shoulder. It felt heavy in the wonderful way that a blanket's weight makes you feel secure. She told herself he was just being protective after they'd just been shot at.

Then he looked at her and she stopped telling herself anything. It was hard to think when he was looking at her like that. Hard to even see straight.

Quickly Brenna turned her head and looked down at her hands. They were placed palms-down on her knees.

From the corner of her vision she stole a glance at Bruiser's thick thighs in his new black canvas cargos. His legs were almost touching hers.

Her body was buzzing being so close to him. She'd felt the buzz when he'd held her on the plane. He'd held her twice. She remembered the feeling with a vividness that took her breath away and made her heart thrum like a rabbit on the run.

A quick, furtive glance up at Bruiser again. He'd turned his gaze back to the front, but she sensed that his attention was on her.

Just her.

She knew it.

She felt it.

She loved it.

A warmth rose up her neck. She turned her palms upward, knuckles resting on her knees, fingers slightly curled. Her nails were still cracked and broken but clean and healing.

Beside her she felt Bruiser shift in his seat. It was almost imperceptible but she noticed. Far as she knew, SEALs were trained to keep their bodies absolutely still for hours. A little inner smile of triumph tried to show on her lips. She held it back.

The half-curled fingers on her upturned palm twitched. She felt Bruiser's fingertips on her shoulder move. Tiny moves. Little tells. Miniscule motions that were consuming her attention, like she was hyper-aware of their bodies and their minds, like she was hyper-aware that *he* was hyper-aware.

The priest finished the wedding blessing, made the

sign of the cross, gestured for the breathlessly excited couple to turn their glowing faces to the congregation. Everyone rose, the sound of a hundred people rising reminding Brenna of the tide coming up the beach.

Bruiser took his arm away from her and rose. Brenna rose with him. She let her arms rest by her sides, fingertips curled against her tight black jeans.

Then she gasped and almost swooned when she felt Bruiser's fingertips brush against hers. They brushed past, then came back. Her breath caught and she shot a glance at him. He was looking straight ahead, but his big fingers still teased hers.

Then he took her hand in his fully. Held it with the gentleness of a giant. They stood there hand in hand and watched as the priest presented the newlyweds to the world.

They watched in smiley silence as the couple walked down the aisle, joined together as one. They had no rice to throw. Were people throwing rice? She couldn't tell. She was buzzing too darn hard, smiling too darn wide.

The congregation began to file out behind the couple, family first, friends next, crashers last. The procession went out a side door which opened up into a large stone courtyard protected by a high hedge that was dotted with white-and-yellow blossoms that Brenna couldn't name.

There were long tables set along the far end of the courtyard. Glasses of dark red port and glistening white pinot were being poured while waiters in white shorts and white canvas shoes carried trays of champagne flutes filled with barely a sip each.

"Aw, they must be on a budget," said Brenna when she

saw a woman who perhaps was the bride's mother shake her head at the head caterer to stop him from popping another bottle of bubbly. "Don't take the champagne, Bruiser. Save it for the guests so they can toast."

Bruiser chuckled. "No danger of that. I can still taste the damn vodka in my throat."

He surveyed the crowd in that methodical way that she'd seen outside the cafe. Brenna felt an anxious rush when she realized that she'd almost forgotten about the cafe and the gunshot. She swallowed hard, followed Bruiser's gaze, looked at the people in the crowd.

"Who looks like they don't belong here?" Bruiser said as they watched people mill around and sip champagne delicately and drink wine heartily.

Brenna swept her gaze past the caterers and the servers. Nobody in a mismatched uniform.

Moved on to the crowd, looking for anyone underdressed. She noticed many guests looking at them and whispering. She sighed and raised an eyebrow at Bruiser.

"Us," she said.

He grinned. "Yup. We're sitting ducks here. If a sniper took a shot at us in front of a sidewalk cafe, he's not gonna worry about hitting a damn caterer. Come on. Let's bounce."

"Where?" said Brenna as Bruiser guided her towards the side-door leading back to the church.

"The door we came in from leads back to the alley. I

don't like that. Shooter could have taken up a new position and be waiting for us to come out the door." They stepped into the church. It was empty. Bruiser nodded towards the altar. "There should be a back exit on the other side of the building. Through there, probably."

They hurried down the aisle, their shoes squishing little white flowers that had been tossed at the married couple. They passed the altar, which smelled of frankincense and maybe some palm oil, something sweet and rich like that. Then they circled around the back and stopped.

It was the priest.

He'd taken off his jacket and collar.

Strapped across his white undershirt was a shoulder holster.

It was not empty.

"Que pasa?" said the priest, raising both dark eyebrows and making no move to draw his weapon. He placed his hands on his hips and looked expectantly at them.

Bruiser had stepped in front of Brenna already. She saw his left arm touch his cargo flap. He didn't draw his weapon either. Brenna hoped Bruiser would be the quicker draw if this turned into the Costa Rican version of Dodge City at Dusk.

"I should warn you, Father," said Bruiser with a lop-sided half-grin. "My Espanol is bad enough that you might challenge me to six-guns at dawn."

The priest's dark eyes widened. Then his tanned face

crinkled into a grin. His teeth were very white against his deep brown skin. He kept his hands on his hips, kept the grin on his face.

"I speak English," he said in a thick Latin accent. "What do you want?"

The question was perhaps more direct because of his limited English, but Brenna tensed up nonetheless.

"Safe passage," said Bruiser, gesturing with his head towards a long hallway with a door at the end.

"That is the toilet," said the Priest. "Do you need to pass something there? It is very safe, I assure you."

Brenna bit her lower lip to hold back a giggle. Bruiser laughed openly, a deep rumbling chuckle that make his eyes sparkle like emeralds.

The Priest's face relaxed into a pleasant smile. He turned and gestured with his hand to follow. He led them the other way down the hallway, stopped outside a thick wooden door that was once a slab of a walnut tree's trunk. He noisily unlocked it with a large key of dull gray steel.

"Excuse the mess," he said as he led them through a room that was clearly his private quarters.

It was a large room with a closet on the left and a double-bed on the right. The closet was open. The bed was unmade. There were a pair of women's panties beside the pillow. Purple satin with a dark stain at the crotch. The Priest seemed least concerned about them seeing it. Brenna stifled a smile and glanced at Bruiser.

Bruiser was looking the other way, at the closet. He frowned, then called out to the priest.

"Ah, Policia?" he said.

The Priest stopped, turned, glanced towards his open closet. Brenna followed his gaze and saw two police uniforms on hangers.

"Si," he said, patting his holstered handgun. "Inspector Rodriguez. Come. I show you out to the street." He walked towards another door at the far end of the room, but then stopped and turned. "But let me ask this. You come from where? Americano, yes? But you come from where?"

Bruiser lost the smile and Brenna felt that tension creep up her spine. Great. Just great. They were in a small town and the priest was also the local cop. Did they look suspicious? A big guy who was obviously military, with suspicious bulges in his cargo flaps. A woman with a bruised cheekbone. Crashing a wedding, then trying to leave through the back door. Nope. Not suspicious at all.

Now she wondered whether he knew about the shooting at the cafe. He'd been performing a wedding ceremony, so probably not—unless he was wired for sound and hooked into the police dispatch with some high-tech mini earpieces.

She glanced at his ears. They were quite large and very hairy. No airpods, though.

Then something electronic crackled on his nightstand. A walkie-talkie.

High-octane Spanish blasted out of it. Inspector Rodriguez's expression changed. His dark brown face paled as much as was possible.

Suddenly he reached for his gun, fumbling with the

button on the holster flap. Perhaps he was the quickest draw in Costa Rica, but he would not have made it past sundown in Dodge City.

"Don't," said Bruiser calmly. His weapon was already out. "Please don't, Father. I think Saint Peter will give me a pass for all the others, but this might be pushing it."

15

Brenna pushed the door to the outer rooms shut and locked it from the inside, just like Bruiser had instructed. He still had his gun out, kept it pointed at Rodriguez, right at his chest.

Rodriguez was a well built man, with a broad chest and thick hairy arms. He had a roll of extra weight around his midsection, but was still in decent shape. He was maybe fifty or so. No wedding ring. Those weren't his wife's stained purple panties. Well done, Father Rodriguez.

"Please," Rodriguez said, holding his arms halfway up with palms facing out. He handed his weapon to Bruiser, barrel pointed down.

It was a Beretta 9mm, a very good Italian-made handgun used by the U.S. Army. Rodriguez had kept it clean, which meant he was probably a decent shot. Terrible at the draw, though.

He was nervous. Scared. Almost *too* scared for the situation. What did the guy on the walkie say? It had to be about the gunshot at the cafe. But surely the cops would know by now that the gunman took the shot from far off. No way Bruiser or Brenna could be the shooter. So why was Rodriguez so damn scared?

"What are they saying on the walkie?" Bruiser asked, lowering the gun off to the side but keeping it drawn.

The Spanish chatter was way too rapid for Bruiser to follow. He glanced at the second door, the one that presumably led to the back exit. Surely the cops knew where to find their saintly Inspector. They'd come knocking soon enough. Surprised they weren't already here. The cafe wasn't too far.

"They . . . they found the victims," said Rodriguez, glancing at the gun and swallowing. He looked into Bruiser's eyes, held the gaze for a few seconds, then glanced at Brenna and frowned. "Look, you should surrender to me. They will send someone to find me at the church. It might be a junior policeman. He might do something stupid. Be reasonable. It was bad luck to come this way. God's will. There is nothing to do about it. Turn yourself in. You can call your embassy. They will get you a lawyer. You will get a fair trial. Costa Rica is not some military dictatorship with a monkey court."

"Kangaroo court," Brenna corrected. But she was frowning, her mind probably asking the same question whipping through Bruiser's brain.

"Victims? Plural?" said Bruiser, his instincts already starting to answer the question. "There was only one shot, and I saw the bullet go clean through his shoulder. It hit the sidewalk near the east side of the cafe entrance. Angle says it would have been fired from an elevated position. Couldn't have been us. No way we could have taken the shot and then gotten to the church when we did."

Rodriguez blinked twice, his brows knitting like he

was trying to read if Bruiser was bluffing. Or maybe he was just confused.

"What victims?" Bruiser asked again, dread rising up his spine. He already knew. Damn it. Damn it to hell.

"At the Casa Del Mar Hotel," Rodriguez said, his face darkening. "Two Hispanic men. Tied to the bed posts. Their throats were slashed."

Bruiser took a slow, rumbling breath and let it out. "The pilots," he muttered, pissed at himself. "They killed the pilots."

Brenna stared at Bruiser like she didn't understand. He looked at her and shrugged. "I had to tie them up and gag them. In my defense, I did let them eat and drink and use the little boy's room first. And it was a queen sized bed."

Brenna understood. Her face paled as the seriousness of the situation hit her. Bruiser looked back at Rodriguez.

"Pick up that walkie and tell them you're on your way," he commanded. Then he pointed the gun at Rodriguez's chest again. "Say it slowly so I can understand the Spanish. Two simple sentences. On my way to the hotel. Continue with your work."

Rodriguez nodded, his eyes dark and small, cheeks tight, mouth sullen. He said the words exactly as Bruiser ordered. Sat back down on the wooden chair when Bruiser gestured him over.

Brenna walked up to Bruiser, opposite from his gun hand. Good. She had good battlefield instincts.

"What now?" she whispered.

They both looked at Inspector Rodriguez. He looked

back at them, glanced to his left, at a wooden room-divider that separated the main room into bedroom and what might be a kitchenette and perhaps a sink.

Bruiser frowned, glancing at the unmade bed, those purple panties. The stain at the crotch was dark. Still wet. His jaw tightened. He looked towards the bottom of that wooden room-divider. There was a shadow on the pale wooden floor.

As he watched the shadow, it moved.

"Tell her to come out," said Bruiser softly to Rodriguez.

Rodriguez's face drooped. Now he looked even more scared than when he thought Bruiser was going to blow his head off. He called out in Spanish, his voice resigned, perhaps apologetic.

The shadow moved along under the wooden divider. Then a woman stepped out. She was barefoot, wearing a man's white dress shirt that was buttoned up all the way. The material was thin, and Bruiser could make out the outline of a purple bra. She was tanned but not Hispanic. Her hair was big and blonde and her forehead was very smooth, but she was at least as old as Rodriguez, maybe older.

She also had a very white, very untanned band around her left ring finger. Bruiser glanced at the far side nightstand and saw a gold wedding band sitting next to a platinum ring with a diamond the size of his eyeball. He should have noticed it earlier, but had been distracted by the panties on the bed. He'd glanced at the underwear, then averted his eyes.

Bruiser averted his eyes again, this time for simple decency. The woman's shirt came down almost to her knees, but she clearly didn't have much on underneath.

He looked pointedly at Brenna, who immediately stepped forward, big smile on her face, palms facing out in an open, non-threatening gesture. Yeah. She was good.

"Hi, I'm Brenna," she said earnestly as she stepped forward.

The woman frowned, cocked her head, half-closed one eye.

Her gaze flitted between Brenna and Bruiser.

Suddenly she relaxed, placing a fist on her hip and smiling to show excellent dental work.

"Wait, Brenna? Brenna Yankova? I just heard that name," she said in an American accent that was all Tennessee. Without waiting for a response, she pointed a long painted fingernail at Bruiser. "And you must be Boris Kowalski."

Brenna turned to Bruiser, her eyes wide, mouth agape. Bruiser didn't move, but he felt himself turn crimson. He considered shooting everyone in the room and then himself, just to escape the embarrassment. He decided against it.

Instead he let out a groan, rubbed the back of his head with his gun. Neither he nor Brenna knew this woman.

Which meant there was only one way she could know their names.

"You're the two Americans that John called the Embassy about," she said, breaking into a perfect smile that was somehow both rehearsed and genuine. "He said you guys had your passports stolen or something."

"Or something," Bruiser said with a chuckle. "You work at the American Embassy?"

She glanced at Rodriguez, who looked about as scared as a man of God with a gun could be.

"In a manner of speaking," she said, her tongue snaking out and curling up. It was long enough to touch the tip of her nose. "I'm Patty Duprey. The Consul General's wife."

Rodriguez rubbed his mouth feverishly. Patty turned to him and shrugged. "Oh, they won't tell anyone, Roberto. Look at them. They're clearly not tourists who happened to lose their passports."

Roberto Rodriguez glared at Patty darkly. "Pueden haber asesinado a dos hombres," he muttered.

Patty frowned, touched her delicate chin, looked at Bruiser, then at Brenna. She shook her head. Her big blonde hair shimmied like an overpopulated bird's nest. "Well, I'll concede that Boris is almost certainly in the killing business. But not that kind of killing."

"Bruiser," growled Bruiser.

"What?" said Patty.

"He's sensitive about his real name," whispered Brenna.

"Aren't we all," said Patty. "Right, Roberto?"

"I told you, my name is Robert. I am not some cabana-boy."

"You'd make a terrible cabana-boy. Look at this place. It's a sty."

"You are calling me a pig?" said Rodriguez with a raised eyebrow.

"Well, you *were* grunting awfully loud this morning," Patty teased with that long tongue-curl. Rodriguez flushed dark under his brown skin, but was clearly amused.

Patty tossed her haystack-sized hair back. She smiled sweetly at Brenna. "Let me get some clothes on and I'll take you guys to the Embassy. It's right on the beach."

"They go nowhere but to the Police Station," said Rodriguez.

Patty didn't answer. She strutted over to the bed, snatched up her panties, and scrunched them up tight. Her cheeks reddened. She kept her eyes down and walked quickly behind the wooden divider. Rodriguez's dark eyes followed her all the way.

Bruiser still had his gun out, but kept it down by his side, pointing it at the floorboards. He'd already disarmed Rodriguez, but he was wary that the cop would have a backup weapon stashed somewhere.

Still, the chances of this turning into a firefight were pretty slim with Patty Duprey in the room. Clearly Rodriguez knew he was risking his career, his saintly reputation, perhaps his kneecaps by banging the American Consul General's wife. Putting a bullet in her would pretty much blow the lid off the thing.

Rodriguez sat back down in his straight-backed wooden chair. He leaned back and sighed. They were waiting for Patty to get her panties on. As they waited, the police walkie crackled to life.

Rodriguez listened intently. "It is the Medical Examiner," he said to Bruiser. "May I respond?"

"Let him answer, Bruiser," called Patty from behind the screen. "I'll keep him honest. Mi Espanol muy bien, right, Roberto?"

Rodriguez rolled his eyes, but he was smiling again. He liked her very much, Bruiser could tell. And it didn't appear to be a Catholic Church. Rodriguez probably wasn't breaking any celibacy vows. Bruiser wasn't sure on the adultery part, though. Anyway, that was Saint Peter's problem.

Rodriguez keyed the walkie and rattled off something in Spanish. He waited, cocked his head, listened, and spoke again. Then he put down the walkie and took a long breath.

"He says time of death was no more than forty minutes ago," said Rodriguez stiffly. "Forty minutes ago you both were already in my church, interrupting my wedding ceremony. It could not have been you."

Bruiser glanced towards the wooden divider. Patty walked out in fitted blue jeans, a canary yellow blouse, and a white denim jacket. The jeans and the jacket were speckled with rhinestones. Her hair was stacked up like a beehive.

"He's telling the truth," she said. "That is what the Medical Examiner said. You guys are off the hook."

Bruiser exhaled and nodded. He put his Sig Sauer away, then reached into the other cargo flap and retrieved Rodriguez's Beretta. He wiped off the handle and trigger with the bottom of his T-shirt before placing it on the nightstand for Rodriguez.

Rodriguez grinned and nodded, acknowledging Bruiser's thoroughness. He put the Beretta back in its holster, then stood and walked to the open closet. It took him four seconds to get his Police jacket on over his undershirt. Apparently the black pants worked for both jobs.

"Stay at the American Embassy, please, you two," said Rodriguez.

He buttoned up the smart black-and-gold jacket. His voice took on a tone of authority. Perhaps clothes really did make the man. Bruiser himself liked his uniform because it put him in the mood.

And right now Bruiser's mood was serious as hell. Patty and Roberto were a nice distraction, but there was at least one gunman on the hunt. Clearly someone good with a knife too. He watched as Brenna showed off her new kicks to Patty, then complimented Patty on her rhinestones.

Bruiser walked over to Rodriguez. "You have police databases at the station?"

Rodriguez nodded. "Of course. We are not a desert island."

"And you aren't a cabana-boy," Bruiser said straight-faced.

Rodriguez grinned.

Bruiser lowered his voice. "The gunman was using an unfamiliar weapon."

"How can you tell?"

"Trust me, I can. It means the weapon was either just purchased or it was stolen. Start there."

Rodriguez paused, nodded. "OK."

"It was a hunting rifle."

"How can you tell?"

Bruiser raised an indignant eyebrow. "I know the sound of every military sniper rifle made in the last forty years. This wasn't a sniper rifle. Process of elimination says it was a hunting rifle. And it'll be the same guy who did the murders at the hotel. Probably a local ex-military guy available on short notice as a freelancer. If you can get even a vague description of the guy, that's good enough for me."

Rodriguez frowned. "You have no jurisdiction here."

Bruiser glanced at Patty, then grinned at Rodriguez. "Just call Patty when you have something for me, all right?" he said pointedly.

"You are blackmailing me?"

"Nah. Helping you. No charge. I'll leave the body so you can close the case."

"That is vigilantism."

"You do your job, I'll do mine, OK, Father?"

"Catholic priests are called Father. I am not Catholic."

"So she just calls you Daddy?" Bruiser deadpanned under his breath.

The priest almost spat as he tried to suppress his laughter. Bruiser grinned and thumped him on the back.

"What are you two going on about?" called Patty. She and Brenna were at the outer door, arms locked like they were already friends.

"Original sin," said Bruiser as he strode up to them and walked around them so he could exit first and scope out the street.

He turned the heavy brass key and opened the door a crack. It was almost noon and the heat was like a wall of fire. There were no cops on the street. Between the hotel and the cafe and the shooter's original position, there was probably no manpower to spare.

Bruiser looked through the cracked door and scanned the neighborhood, keeping an eye out for rooftops or terraces or open windows. There was no structure more than two stories high in the street. There were some terraces, but a shooter would have to stand upright and lean over the parapet to get a shot. Bruiser was pretty sure the gunman was holed up for now, probably on the phone with whoever hired him.

Damyan Nagarev.

It had to be.

"How far is the Embassy?"

"Three miles straight east."

"How'd you get here?"

"That," said Patty.

She pointed. Bruiser looked. It was a red Vespa scooter with a side-car. It had local plates.

Bruiser sighed. "Rodriguez must have a car."

Patty shook her head. "Station is a block away. He likes to walk. Hates cars."

"There must be cars at the station."

Patty shook her head again. "They mostly have bikes and scooters. A couple of cars, but they're probably all the way over at the hotel now."

Rodriguez came out and confirmed all of that. He was anxious to get to the station, and so Bruiser told him to go ahead. He could take care of the women.

He thought about calling a cab, then decided against it. The longer they waited, the closer it got to the gunman coming out for another try. Besides, Bruiser was pretty sure he'd been the target. Someone wanted Bruiser out of the way. Someone wanted a clear path to Brenna. And if it was Damyan, he would want her alive.

It had to have been Damyan, Bruiser thought as he

made a decision and hurried the women over to the scooter. Patty immediately swung her right leg around and got in the driver's seat. She turned and smiled at Brenna, patting the fake-leather seat behind her. Bruiser glanced at the sidecar and rubbed his jaw.

He was about to change everything around so he'd be the driver, but decided it was safer this way. If the shooter was around and took a shot, it would be better if Bruiser was separated from Brenna.

"You'll have to drive fast," he warned Patty as he wondered how he was going to cram his big body into a red-painted tincan designed by Italians just to torture men like him.

"I only drive fast," said Patty, starting it up and purring the engine like a raunchy little cat. "Squeeze in quick or you'll be running."

Bruiser sighed and squeezed in. Patty wasn't kidding about driving fast. He had to keep his eyelids down to slits and hang on like it was the magic-saucer ride at Disneyworld. The only good thing was that Patty's hair was so big that the wind pretty much obscured a clear shot at any of them.

It took three minutes and twelve seconds to drive three miles. That made Patty's average speed clock in at 59.74 miles-per-hour by Bruiser's math. It felt like they'd been going a hundred, all downhill into the damn wind. Bruiser was secretly pleased when Patty had to slow down so she wouldn't smash into the U.S. Embassy's gates.

The black metal gates slid open with a mechanical

whir. Two guard-stations on either side were manned by uniformed Department of State Security Officers. They did a double-take when they saw Bruiser grumpily nod at them from his very uncomfortable spot. After they passed, Bruiser glanced in the sideview mirrors and saw the guards grin at each other.

Patty hurtled down the long, tree-lined driveway, screeched around a rotunda-fountain, and stopped outside a white building with columns done in a Spanish style. The Stars-and-Stripes flew high and proud from the red-tiled hacienda-style rooftop. An armed, uniformed guard stood at the top of the stairs, a sidearm in a belt-holster, white gloved and tanned. There was a metal detector and a conveyor belt in front of him.

Bruiser took out his gun and his knife and his phone and Mikhail's phone and his watch and placed them in a green tub and sent them through the x-ray. He stepped through the detector. It went off. He pointed to the steel toes of his military boots. The guard waved him through. He didn't seem concerned about the weapons.

Patty led them through the spacious lobby and across a wood-floored hallway and to the back terrace which was large and open and faced the beach.

The sand was golden like the sun, with heat fumes rising up in the distance. The water was lush blue and frothy. Bruiser almost groaned as he felt that SEAL's need to get to his beloved water, his beloved ocean, feel that saltwater on his skin, taste it on his lips.

"There's bathing gear in the cabana," Patty said, looking at him with a half-smile. "John told me you were a SEAL. And I know how you SEALs get when you see the ocean."

16

"I don't get it," Bruiser said over the sound of the surf. He squinted at her, his face glistening with beads of saltwater. "Do you?"

He was waist deep in the shallows, the waves swirling around him like living things. But the powerful water couldn't budge Bruiser's hard, muscled, heavy body as he lazily walked towards where Brenna reclined on a white-painted wooden beach-chair.

Brenna adjusted her sunglasses and tried to pretend like she wasn't looking at the bumps of ridiculous muscle lining his rock-hard abdomen. His chest was huge, like two slabs of bronzed marble.

The tattoos were perfectly placed, tantalizingly dark. Brenna wanted to get a closer look at them. Maybe trace her fingers along the dark lines. Touch those scars all over his brutally powerful body. Ask him where each came from. Laugh when he said it was classified. Need to know basis. I'll tell ya, then I'll kill ya.

Brenna pressed her thighs together as Bruiser moved up the beach. The waterline was down to his knees now, and his black surf-shorts were plastered against his thighs. His quadriceps were massive, like tree-trunks, straight and thick and pure muscle. The waistband of his shorts was low on his stomach, and Brenna's breath quickened as her gaze followed his deadly V down along those muscle-framed hips that shone in the sun.

She desperately tried to keep her eyes from the center of his trunks, right below the waistband, but it didn't work. She gulped when she saw how big his bulge was, and her toes curled when she felt a tingle beneath the towel she'd laid across her hips.

"Toss me a towel, will ya?" he said as he strode up the beach.

Brenna blinked behind her sunglasses and glanced over at the second beach chair. No towel. Bruiser had been in such a hurry to get to the ocean, he must have forgotten to bring one down to the beach. He'd already been body-surfing the waves when she finally dared to emerge from her cabana.

Brenna was a Jersey girl at heart, and she liked the beach, had enjoyed trips to the Shore all the way through high school and college. She'd never given a damn about showing off her curves, and she was just fine with bikinis.

Today, however. she'd picked out a one-piece suit that was dirt-brown with an ugly pink neon trim all around the edges. She'd put it on and was frowning at the clashing colors when Patty Duprey popped up in the mirror behind her.

"Absolutely not," said Patty firmly. "If I had boobs like that, I'd be on my knees thanking the heavens every Sunday. And I sure as hell wouldn't hide them behind that hideous sack of a suit. It was left behind by the previous tenants. I don't even think it's been washed."

"Ew." Brenna pulled the shoulder straps down and sniffed at them. They smelled clean enough. She looked at Patty, who was in a white bikini and high-heeled sandals. She wasn't skinny, but she was a slight woman with narrow hips and not a lot of curves. She must have been quite athletic when she was younger, Brenna thought, smiling and shaking her head when Patty emerged from the cabana-shelves with a black two-piece that looked much too stringy and way too small.

A round of mild protests and firm arguments later, Brenna was standing in front of that same mirror in the black two-piece. It wasn't as stringy as she'd thought, and it fit quite well. Her large nipples were well hidden by the cups, and the bottoms were full and not thong-y at all. Sure, it would still ride up her big butt at some point, but that couldn't be helped.

Brenna took a breath and nodded. Patty smiled and nodded back, then flashed a wink and walked out of the cabana, heading back towards the main house to get something.

Or so she claimed.

Patty hadn't said anything about Bruiser.

Nothing needed to be said.

"Sorry, what'd you say?" Brenna asked as he stood a few feet in front of her, hands on his glistening hips, grin on his shining face.

"Towel. Need to get this salt off my skin before it dries on there and makes me look like a well-done crab in a bucket."

"Like in Patty's red sidecar?" Brenna teased.

Bruiser raised a grumpy eyebrow. "I'm trying to repress that memory, thank you very much."

"Those guards at the gate will remember it."

"Forget it. I'll get my own towel," Bruiser said, sighing and looking towards the two cabanas in the distance.

Brenna sighed and lifted the towel off her hips and lower belly. Bruiser didn't glance down, but she noticed how his neck tightened and color rushed to his cheeks. She knew he wanted to look. Knowing it made her feel funny under that bikini bottom.

It made her feel nice under that bikini bottom.

Hot, and not from the sun.

Wet, and not from the surf.

She tossed the towel at him and he caught it without turning his head. She sat up and pulled her legs up against her body as Bruiser dried himself off, his muscled arms flexing and relaxing in the most beautiful way. When he was done he hurled the towel back at her. It landed on her face. It was wet and smelled like the ocean.

It smelled like him.

"Gross," she squealed, wrinkling up her nose and placing the towel on the beach chair by her toes. She looked at him. He was grinning like a teenager at the poolside. She grinned back, touched her hair, adjusted her sunglasses.

"You didn't answer my question," he said, still grinning as he turned his body her direction and took a step closer. His trunks were thick material and no longer wet and clingy, but he looked big, bigger than before, big in a way that made her wonder what was going on, what was going down, what he was thinking about . . .

She tried to remember his question but couldn't. He walked around the front of her chair to his chair and leaned forward to pick up his phone. She tried not to stare at his round muscular ass. He picked up the phone and turned it over like he was puzzled. Then she realized it wasn't his phone. It was the other phone. Mikhail's phone. Now she remembered the question.

"No," she said. "I don't get it. If you removed the GPS chip from Mikhail's phone and disconnected the plane's transponder, I don't get how Damyan could have known we were in Costa Rica." She thought a moment. "The pilots would have had to change their flight-plan or something. Maybe they had to communicate with Buenos Aires. Maybe it got back to Damyan that the plane had landed here."

Bruiser reclined down on his chair, dropped the dead phone onto his rock-hard abs, placed his big palms behind his head. "Benson said he'd take care of that. Guess he didn't."

Brenna furrowed her brow. She'd been almost relaxed for a moment back there. Now the anxiety was back. The dread crept up her toes, taking away that wonderful warmth and replacing it with the cold, hard facts:

She still couldn't be sure if she should trust him.

No matter how he looked at her.

No matter how she felt around him.

No matter what her bikini-parts whispered.

No matter what her intuition screamed.

"Damyan could've found out a million other ways," she said, talking her thoughts out loud so she could stop burrowing deeper into the rabbithole of what her body was saying and what his body seemed to be saying too. "Benson knows we're here. And he called Patty Duprey last night. Who told her husband Henry Dupree. Who told one of his aides. Who then called the airport authorities. And then we got to the hotel. And we went to the cafe. And the shoe store. Oh, and before that you went to the department store for my clothes. Thank you for that, by the way."

Bruiser chuckled. "You're welcome." He thought a moment, then turned his head towards her. "Though I gotta ask . . ."

She waited. He didn't finish the sentence.

"What?" she said, her curiosity rising when she saw the mischief in his green eyes.

"Nah, it'll just embarrass you. You've been through a lot. My bad. Forget it."

"I don't get embarrassed easily. Try me."

"Well, maybe it'll embarrass me. Forget I said anything."

"I'd like to see you embarrassed," Brenna said. "Ask me or I'll embarrass you in some other way."

"You're bluffing."

"Then call my bluff."

Bruiser grunted confidently. "Consider it called."

"OK," said Brenna, smiling as she reached down between their chairs to pick up the temporary flip-phone Patty had given her. As she straightened up she thought she saw Bruiser adjust his muscular butt on the chair, turning slightly away from her like he was hiding something. Her face flushed when she glanced down at her cleavage in the bikini top.

She settled back down and flipped open the phone. Pretended to dial Patty's number that was saved in the contacts. "Hey, Patty. Listen, can you pull a clip from the gate's security cameras? From that moment we drove through. All three of us on the scooter. Bruiser in the sidecar. Yes. Just a still-image capture would work great. I'm sure Bruiser's Navy SEAL buddies would *love* to see that. Great. I'll give you my email and you can have the tech guy send it there. Thanks *so* much."

She took her time snapping the flip-phone closed. Then she tossed it onto the sand, and dusted her hands off triumphantly. When she turned her head to Bruiser he was grumping at her.

"All right," he said, sighing and leaning back. "You win."

"So ask me the embarrassing question."

"Well," he said, clearly stalling, clearly weighing the two options and their embarrassment levels. "When I bought your clothes, I noticed a couple of things missing from your list."

Blood rushed to Brenna's cheeks. The underwear. She'd left out the underwear. He'd noticed. He'd been thinking about it. He'd been wondering about it.

"Oh, my God," she giggled, covering her eyes and turning her head to the right, away from him. "I can't believe you noticed. I can't believe you're asking me about it."

"Hey, I said forget it. But you forced my hand. Threatening to humiliate my ass in front of my SEAL brothers means war."

"Well, throwing your wet, stinky towel at my face means war," she shot back, turning her body towards him. She got her foot under the towel on her chair and flipped it across to his chair. "Boris," she whispered wickedly, her eyes dancing.

Bruiser roared and kicked back the towel. It landed on her boobs, wet and cool.

She yelped and hurled it back at his face.

And the game was on.

They furiously sent the poor towel back and forth. Bruiser was laughing, Brenna was screaming. Their arms and feet moved in a frenzy, until suddenly the flailing towel got trapped between the wooden slats of Bruiser's chair.

He leaned forward to pull it free and toss it at her smiling face.

She leaned forward to defend herself from the soggy weapon.

Their heads bumped and they both recoiled, laughing, rubbing their foreheads, smiling giddily, the sun smiling down with them, their bodies shining like the ocean.

Bruiser pulled the towel away from her and tossed it over his shoulder. He leaned forward and took her hands in his, pulled her toward him. He did it firmly but with a gentleness that made it clear he was asking a question, letting her know it was all right for her to back away.

She didn't back away.

She let him pull her across the aisle between their chairs.

She let him bring his salty lips close to hers.
She let him kiss her.
And so he did just that.
He kissed her.
By God, he kissed her.

17

Her lips were sweet like honey, salty like the sea, warm like the sun, cool like the blue depths of the open ocean.

Bruiser could barely see straight as he kissed her deep and long, slow at first, teasing her lips with his tongue before parting them and entering her warm, wet mouth. His hand snaked around the back of her head, up her neck, fingers tightening in her hair. Their knees were touching as they leaned into each other across the beach chairs.

Then he pulled her closer, kissed her harder, felt her thighs against his, her knee pressing into his crotch. He'd been hard since the moment she took that towel off her waist and hips. He'd tried not to stare, didn't want to make her uncomfortable after what she'd been through this week.

But he didn't need to stare to take in the gorgeous expanse of skin smooth like butter, hips wide like a goddess, thighs thick enough for his big hands, that black triangle of a bikini-bottom covering her sex in a way that made him hungry to get his tongue under that lucky strip of spandex, taste the salty sweetness of her sea-bathed slit, inhale the musk of her scent, feel her warmth, her wetness, her wonder.

Bruiser's trunks were peaked higher than the flagpole in the distance, his blood redder than the crimson of the flag, his vision filled with more stars than there were states in the union. He groaned as Brenna's knee touched his hardness, sending his need spiraling to the damn clouds.

He drove his tongue into her mouth, the fingers of his left hand sliding under her bikini-top strap. He pulled her closer by her strap, the cup of her top revealing a sight that could cause a man to launch armies and wage war, inflict destruction and carnage just for the right to claim that prize.

"You are so damn perfect," he whispered hoarsely against her mouth as he looked down at her nipple peeking up at him from behind the cup of her bikini. It was dark and large, round like a saucer, standing out straight and hard like a stone arrowhead. "You taste so sweet. Smell so good."

She shuddered out a breath as Bruiser ran his rough knuckles over her pebbled nipple, pinching it gently between his fingers, then harder, until she arched her neck back and moaned.

Then Bruiser ran his thick tongue down her chin, along her neck, pushing her backwards onto her chair. His mouth closed around her exposed nipple, and he sucked hard, so damn hard she gasped and clawed at his hair.

Now he stood, gently pushed her down on her chair.

She lay back, her right breast hanging out of her bikini top, her creamy skin shining with his saliva, her nipple glistening in the sun. She lay there blinking up at him, her legs moving against the smooth painted wood, her chest heaving as her arousal called to him like a siren.

He stood at the foot of her chair, took in the sunlit sight of a woman who was made for him.

"Damn, Brenna," he said, leaning in and running his hands up her legs from her ankles past her muscular calves around to the outside of her heavenly thighs. She groaned as he moved his hands around to her inner thighs, slowly spreading her as his erection raised its head and fought to burst free of his trunks.

Bruiser tried to remind himself that she'd just been through hell, that they weren't out of the woods yet, that she wasn't safe yet. He glanced over towards the white building in the distance, then out towards the blue horizon over the sea.

There wasn't a soul in sight. No boats on the waves. No planes in the sky. She might not be safe yet, but she was safe now.

And perhaps now would be all they had, Bruiser thought as she arched her neck back and raised her chest just as the back of his hand touched her secret place between those divine thighs.

She was wet like the ocean, and Bruiser's jaw hung open and his eyes glazed over as he ground his knuckles against the front of her soaked bikini bottom. Her wetness was pouring out the sides of the spandex, and his hand was getting sticky with her sweetness.

Her scent came to him thickly as he moved closer, and he inhaled deep and hard, taking in her feminine aroma like an animal in season, a beast in heat.

Slowly he knelt on the sand before her chair, his long body leaning forward, his strong arms pulling her thighs wide apart. He held her like that, reveling in how self-assured she was under the open sky, spreading herself like a butterfly for him.

She looked down past her breasts and into his eyes. Her eyes were glazed and moist, her smile unstable with arousal, quivering with emotion.

"I feel safe with you, Bruiser," she whispered. "I feel protected. I know I shouldn't trust you but I do. I can't help it. Nobody's made me feel like this, Bruiser. This safe. This shielded. Please don't betray that trust, Bruiser. It would break me if you did."

Bruiser looked into her eyes, frowning just a little as Benson's words came floating to him like an annoying voiceover from that mathematical, logical, reasonable part of his mind.

Your judgment might be compromised, Benson had warned.

She might be playing us all, Benson had whispered.

Your job is to break her, Benson had ordered. Not to get broken yourself, Soldier.

Maybe this is beyond your simple seek-and-destroy skillset, SEAL.

Out of your wheelhouse, Navy boy.

Now Bruiser's mind swirled as his cock throbbed. He could smell her in the air, taste her on his lips, feel her on his fingers. He wanted her so damn bad it was scary. Fucking terrifying. So damn terrifying that he suddenly snapped to attention.

Of course he was compromised.

Of course he'd been broken.

Of course he'd walked right into the oldest ambush of all.

The sweetest trap in history.

He looked into her eyes, tried to make sense of the wrenching in his gut, the conflict between his instinct and reason, his body and mind, the mission and the woman. He tried to line them all up, get them to all say the same thing. Bruiser knew his body damn well, understood the intelligence of raw instinct, had trusted his life and the life of his team to it and won every time.

Could this time be different? Could his body be wrong? Could his instincts be failing?

Didn't matter.

Because he wasn't stopping.

"Nobody's made me feel like this either, Brenna," he whispered, stroking her soft inner thighs as she writhed in the sun, her shining body smooth and slick. "I want this damn mission over, Brenna. Get you back to the States, back home."

She nodded, her eyelids fluttering as Bruiser leaned down over her, touched the tip of his tongue to her belly button, dragged it down along her beautifully round belly, started to tease the top of her triangle.

He was in dangerous territory now. This was the domain of the animal, the most dominant need in an alpha beast. To take its mate. To claim and protect.

Maybe she knows that, Bruiser thought.

Maybe she sees that, Bruiser wondered.

Just because she's aroused and wet doesn't mean I'm not being played, Bruiser reasoned.

But his own arousal was like a heat-seeking warhead, controlling his entire body, focusing his mind on the wispy curls of her sex peeking over the top of her bikini. Her scent was invasive, pervasive, warm like the earth, wet like the sand.

He kissed her above her waistband, slowly pulled it down, rolling the stringy straps down her hips with deadly stealth, excruciating focus.

"Going home sounds . . . nice," she muttered as her brown curls bristled in the breeze. "Going home. Safe from tongueless monsters and Russian mobsters."

"I'm not tongueless," he whispered through a wicked grin, his tongue darting out and touching the delicate nub buried in her bush.

She gasped and bucked her hips into his face as he tapped her clit again, her thighs spreading so wide Bruiser could get his entire head down between her legs.

He yearned to drive his tongue deep into her slit, curl it upwards, make her come all over his damn face. But he restrained himself, holding her thighs apart with his hands, then rolling her bikini bottoms all the way off past her ankles.

He leaned back, held the wet cloth to his face, breathed deep and loud as she watched him with a mixture of shyness and fascination.

"You smell damn good," he grinned. "I'm keeping these."

Brenna turned redder than a lobster as Bruiser shoved her soaked black bikini-bottoms into the side-pocket of his surfer-style black trunks. She covered her face and laughed.

"Those aren't mine, you know," she said. "They belong to the United States Government."

"I *am* the United States Government," growled Bruiser against her crotch. He slipped his hands around her thighs and under her ass, digging his fingers into her buttcheeks and squeezing hard. "Tax department. I'll be seizing your assets until further investigation is done into your private affairs, Ma'am."

She giggled, then gasped when Bruiser nuzzled his nose roughly into her private affairs, getting her stickiness all over his face. He was so hard his vision was nothing but a swirling mess, all his senses concentrated on what every man lived his life to claim, to own, to seize forever.

He lapped at her slit, then teased her open with his tongue. She was dripping down his chin, down herself onto the chair, through the gaps in the slats onto the sand.

Bruiser felt Brenna's sweet dark lips open for his tongue, and he entered her quickly and curled his tongue up against the front wall of her vagina. She convulsed and bucked as he pushed deeper, her juices flowing like a waterfall. He was close to losing his mind, about to rip off his trunks, let his beast of a cock do what it was designed to do.

But then something about what he'd said came back to him.

That joke about seizing her assets.

Wasn't there something sketchy in her past when he'd looked? Something about an audit that had been overruled, sealed, dispensed with? Had she cut some deal with the U.S. Government back then? Had Benson been involved? Had he recruited her? She was a Princeton grad. Bilingual. Confident. She fit the profile. Hell, maybe Benson *had* recruited her years ago!

And maybe she'd betrayed Benson.

Maybe she and her Russian father stole American CIA money. Dirty CIA money.

Bruiser knew it was a badly kept secret that the CIA laundered its own money to finance dark operations that were way too sketchy to risk being connected to taxpayer funding. There'd been that big story about how the CIA were running marijuana from Mexico to finance their covert operations against the cocaine cartels of Colombia. They probably had a dozen operations like that to wash dirty money, funnel secret funds.

And the thing about secrets was that they needed to be kept.

Hell, maybe that's why CIA Director Martin Kaiser called Benson, called Darkwater, Bruiser thought. Maybe Brenna and Alexei were the unfinished business, not Damyan Nagarev. Maybe the CIA had assassinated Alexei, only realizing too late that he died with the secret words that unlocked that account, that Brenna was their only chance to recover them.

But why now, after all these years?

Maybe they didn't know Alexei had a daughter? Maybe it was only when she got nabbed in Russia and the name Alexei Yankov showed up that Benson and Kaiser found out? Maybe Alexei was a hacker who could alter records like birth certificates and entry-exit records when he flew into the USA?

Still, even if they just found out, why go through all this? Why not nab her directly and sweat her in some basement in a third-world country?

Maybe they thought Brenna would never break in an interrogation room.

Maybe they thought she'd break out here, in the open, under the sun and the clouds, near the wind and the waves.

Maybe they thought she might break while dodging danger, on the run, protected by a bruising Navy SEAL.

Break without meaning to break.

Break because she trusted him.

Because she loved him.

Which meant the mission was going *exactly* as that wily fox Benson planned.

Now all Bruiser had to do was finish the damn job.

Complete the mission.

Get the information and get the hell out of there.

Bruiser was overwhelmed for a moment, totally messed up by the certainty in his body and the chaos in his mind. He wasn't sure what was up and what was down, who was playing whom. Hell, he wasn't even sure what the damn game was anymore.

But Benson was right about one thing: This wasn't the kind of battlefield he was used to. It wasn't the kind of fight he'd been trained to fight, trained to win, win at all costs, for flag and country.

Then something occurred to him.

What if he didn't want to win this fight?

What if the price was too high?

What if winning meant losing?

What would it do to him—not as a soldier but as a man?

And most importantly, he thought as he looked at her sweet round face, those soft red lips that said she trusted him, that she'd break if he betrayed her now . . . yes, most importantly, what would it do to her?

18

"What are you doing to me?" she moaned as Bruiser's tongue moved inside her and then curled up like a tentacle, tapping a place in her vagina she thought was a myth, a mystery, a darned miracle.

Bolts of ecstasy rocketed through her body as Bruiser's thick tongue invaded her roughly, marching so far into her cunt his nose was buried deep in her bush.

The sun beat down on them from above, the waves roared in the distance like a pride of lions. His big hands firmly gripped her buttocks, and for perhaps the first time ever Brenna felt small and delicate in the clutches of a man.

But more than that, she felt safe under his touch, under his control, under his authority. Bruiser was big as a bulldozer, and she'd felt his astounding strength when he picked her up on the plane. She'd felt like a doll in his arms, a child against his chest when he'd held her close after killing Mikhail.

Even the memory of that monster Mikhail touching her couldn't shake the magic of what was happening right now, Brenna thought. For one darkly private moment she thought that Bruiser was Mikhail between her legs, and she wailed as his thick tongue fucked her deep and rough, exploring her inner walls, claiming her secret cave.

She didn't understand the thought at first, but when Bruiser looked up at her with his clear green eyes she understood. This man had killed Mikhail, shot him in the damn face, destroyed him to save her. It was all intertwined in her memory, and it made her trust him all the more, made her want to give herself to him all the more.

Made her want to love him all the more.

She moaned again as the thoughts swirled through her roiling mind. The feelings came from a place that was distant but deep, like it was ancient and hidden, unacknowledged, uninvestigated, maybe even denied in the modern world.

Was it wrong to want a man who clearly showed he can and will protect you with his strength, defend you with his might, destroy anyone and anything who threatens you, touches you, hurts you?

She'd been taught in school and in college that those feelings came from our evolutionary history, where physical violence was an everyday thing, where having a big beast of a man on your side was the difference between life and death.

But those feelings were to be discarded now, she'd been told.

They were outdated. Morally wrong, even. You have the police and the state and family court and divorce lawyers to protect you now, she'd been told. You don't need no man to protect you.

So grow up. You don't owe this man anything, but maybe you subconsciously feel you do. Well, you're smarter than that. Your brain is in control, not your wet, dripping, oh-so-hot, damn-so-tight needy little pussy. Just because your body is reacting like this doesn't mean it's right.

Doesn't mean it's love.

"What are you doing to me, Bruiser," she groaned again as he pulled his tongue out of that needy little pussy and ran it along her aching, gushing slit in long upward strokes. She stared down at him through her breasts, which were standing up quite well on their own, not flopping down on either side.

The image made her feel very sexy, and the sight of Bruiser's roughly handsome face twisted into a grimace of almost deranged arousal made her even hotter. Clearly the cavewoman in her was very much alive, she thought wickedly as he reached up and pushed the other cup of her bikini off her breast and pinched the hard nipple until she cried out in pleasure.

"Doing my duty, Ma'am," came his muffled voice from down in her muff. She laughed at the joke, but the laughter caught in her throat as the SEAL's tongue breached her border once again.

This time it was too much, and she came with a scream, pulling Bruiser's thick short hair and bucking her hips into his face.

This only drove his tongue deeper into her, and she flailed and thrashed as another orgasm whipped through her like a barrage of Tomahawk Cruise missiles.

Bruiser's hands were back under her tightened ass, and he lifted her off the warm wood and spread her cheeks and ran his fingers along her crack as he tongue-fucked her like the future of the United States depended on it. She felt a monstrous third climax building, and she held on to his hair and lifted her legs and groaned.

Bruiser's touch on her rear crack felt delightfully filthy, and she heard herself moan as the third wicked climax barreled towards her like a freight train going downhill. Then she felt his middle finger stop right on her dark rear hole, tap twice, then carefully enter that forbidden space just as his thick tongue stuck deep inside her cunt and stayed there pressed against her walls.

The feeling of being filled like that, claimed like that, dominated like that was too much, just too damn much. Brenna exploded with a howl, feeling herself squirt all over Bruiser's face as that freight train of an orgasm blasted through the barricades, ripped off the track, launched itself off the damn cliff into freefall.

The climax wrecked her like a battering ram, and Brenna choked on her screams and started coughing and sputtering, laughing and howling, bucking and thrashing.

Bruiser finished her off with a wet kiss between her legs, a hard squeeze for each buttcheek, then clambered onto the beach chair with her and pulled her against his body.

"I can't even understand what just happened," she mumbled, turning to him and burying her face against his neck. "You're filthy," she whispered as he grinned against her hair and reached around to massage her bare bum. He gave her two light smacks, one on each cheek, then nestled four fingers along her rear crack like he damn well owned her. "Ohmygod, you are *so* filthy."

They lay together under the sun, listening to the waves, smelling the sea. Brenna could feel Bruiser hard and thick against her body. He was so long she could feel his shaft all the way along her belly up past her button. The thought hit her that so far he'd only put his tongue and finger inside her.

And both had filled her pretty darned tight.

So what would happen when he . . .

"You all right?" he whispered, kissing her forehead and moving against her. He was hard like stone, thick like a pillar, heavy like a rock.

She reached between their bodies and curled her fingers around his swollen shaft through his trunks. Bruiser groaned under his breath, his green eyes glazing over for a moment. Brenna smiled, her heat rising again when she realized that even though she could palm a volleyball, she couldn't get her fingers all the way around Bruiser's girth. She felt her pussy squeeze out a fresh batch of its sweetness. She wasn't sure if it was excited or alarmed by what was coming its way.

"No," she whispered as she slowly moved her hand up and down. "I am most certainly not all right. I'm wrecked. Ruined. Destroyed. Broken."

Bruiser tried to grin but groaned instead. She moved her hand faster, feeling him thicken under her touch, harden as she handled him.

Soon he was kissing her again. Vicious, savage kisses that made her lips hurt. His hand tightened on her ass, cock throbbed as she jerked him back and forth, delighting in how she was making him feel.

Somewhere in the back of her mind came a whisper that any man with balls gets hard if you jerk him off. It didn't mean a damn thing that his eyes were rolling up in his head and he was kissing her like he was losing control, pawing at her ass like he was moments away from mounting her and filling her, hard and deep, again and again.

The thoughts started messing with her as her arousal started to come back after that backbreaking orgasm. Bruiser was kissing her with savage purpose now, and he rolled her away from him onto her back, descending on her boobs, sucking one then the other, biting her nipples and smacking her boobs with small, quick slaps that made them shiver and shake.

Brenna tried to reach for his cock again, but he slapped her hand away, clambered off the chair, then pulled his trunks down and stepped out of them. His cock sprung out like a booby-trapped log, spraying her with a line of his thick clear pre-cum.

"Oh," said Brenna, blinking as she stared in a mixture of awe and fascination. She didn't have any more words in her Princeton vocabulary. "Oh," she said again like a fool.

Bruiser grinned down at her and stepped to the chair. His cock stood straight out over her body, casting a thick dark shadow across both her breasts. He was monstrously large, a beautiful cock that looked even thicker than it had felt in her hands. He'd been so aroused that his pre-cum had coated his entire shaft, and it shone and glistened like it had been freshly oiled.

Brenna stared agape as a fresh bead of his natural oil oozed from its massive red head, dripping slow and long onto her chest, right between her breasts.

She blinked as he took a step closer. She let her gaze drop to his balls. They were large and heavy, and they looked full in a way that made her pussy tighten again before opening like a mouth between her legs.

"I want you, Brenna," he whispered, reaching down and stroking her cheek with his left hand. His cock bobbed gently up and down, still curved upwards, erect to the extreme.

She nodded up at him, down at him, all around at him. Then she slid up against the slanted seatback of the chair, blinked as she came eye-level with Bruiser's cock.

Slowly he came closer, gripping his shaft and touching his cockhead to her left nipple. She gasped and looked down. Bruiser carefully painted her pert pebbled nipple with his warm pre-cum. Then he slowly straddled her at chest level before doing the same to the other nipple. She gazed down at the long sticky line of his oil connecting both nipples to his cockhead. It looked sublime in the sun. She was wet again between her legs. Ready again between her legs.

Ready again everywhere.

Brenna brought her head forward, glancing up at him and then blinking. She reached out and cupped her hand beneath his mammoth balls. They were warm and heavy and his thick neck tightened and he arched his head back and groaned.

"Oh, Bruiser," she whispered, massaging him, stroking him, her lips parting as he drew close. "Please. I want you too."

She tightened her fist around his cock and he moved up, planted his knees on either side of her breasts, lowered himself as she opened for him.

Bruiser let out a low, guttural groan as he pushed his cock into her mouth. Her lips trembled as she sensed he was restraining himself, barely holding back from driving hard down her throat. His body loomed above her like a wall, the sun casting a monstrous shadow over her as she felt her throat get forced open for him. One hand still cupped his balls, and she felt oddly safe even though he could crush her with his weight, choke her with his size.

She stared to suck him, slow at first, then harder. He moved in her mouth, hunching over and slamming his hands down on the backrest above her head. His fingers slid between the wooden slats, and he started to pump into her mouth.

Brenna's eyes were wide and her throat was open and her lips were stretched to where she could feel them tight in the corners. He was so damn wet her chin was dripping. His aroma was everywhere, inside her and around her, his woodsy scent and the clean ocean salt making her fever rise.

"Hell, Brenna," he groaned through gritted teeth, riding her harder from above. "This is insane. I can't hold on much longer, Brenna."

"Then don't," she gasped, pulling back and taking a heavy, wet breath. His cock throbbed and oozed onto her lips. He was so erect it looked painful. So close it almost made her want to finish him with her mouth, feel him explode down her throat, coat her bare breasts and hard nipples with the death throes of his climax before he collapsed on her.

But there was another part of her that wanted Bruiser deep inside her where it counted, taking her hard between her legs. The need was so strong she was gushing onto the wood and sand like a river in the rain. It was that ancient need bubbling up in her like a brook turning into a geyser.

She didn't question it.

Didn't second guess it.

Didn't fight it.

Bruiser was clearly feeling that need too. He moved down her body with the agility of a tiger, his massive bulk silent and smooth, totally in control, every muscle at his command.

He jammed his elbows down on either side of her head, spreading her thighs with his powerful hips.

His cock was so hard and she was so wet there was no need to guide him.

His cockhead found her opening, split her wide, entered her deep.

"Fuck, you're so warm," he growled as he entered her, opened her, filled her. "So damn tight, Brenna."

She made an odd whining noise, wincing as she felt him spread her labia, push her inner walls out, fill her to a point she knew had never been touched by any man. Her eyes were rolled up so far in her head that everything was colored red. He was impossibly long and insanely thick, and he kept going deeper until finally she felt the heft of his balls slap against her wet underside.

Bruiser stopped, looked down at her, leaned in and kissed her with the awesome gentleness of a king lion. She could barely breathe. It felt like he was so deep inside her that he was filling her throat too.

He kissed her again, running his tongue around the edges of her lips, then sliding it into her warm mouth. She tasted herself on his tongue. Tangy and sweet and a hint of sea salt. Maybe some sand. She let him kiss her again, smiling when he smiled down at her.

"What's that scar from?" she whispered, touching a deep, slashing mark above the red cut she'd given him on the plane.

"It's my good-luck scar," he said, smiling at first and then losing the smile when his gaze rested on her tender but healing cheekbone. "You're gonna have one too, Brenna." His jaw tightened, and she felt his massive quadriceps flex against her inner thighs. "Wish I'd taken my time killing that motherfucker who hurt you."

Bruiser's fists clenched above her head, and although the last thing Brenna wanted to think about was that filthy prison, she couldn't push away the image of Bruiser breaking Boots's filthy neck.

She let it come, watched it in her mind's eye. It was

oddly intoxicating, so much so that it scared her. Her own jaw tightened. Her eyes narrowed as she looked fiercely into Bruiser's green orbs. Her nails were short and cracked, but she felt them digging into Bruiser's back, the sharp edges of the cracks making tiny cuts in his skin, like she was adding her own tattoos to his inkwork. Her pussy clenched around his cock.

"Damn, woman," he growled through a wicked grin. "Something just happened inside you."

She blinked, not sure what to say, not sure what he saw in her.

"It's still happening inside me, best I can tell," she whispered, blinking again.

She moved her hips, tried to pull off the light-hearted joke with a trembling smile. But that dark arousal was surging in her, and for a moment she was scared at where her mind was going.

What kind of a woman takes pleasure in seeing men killed? Was she some sicko who was aroused by blood and death? Or was it just the crushing relief of seeing those men destroyed, broken, defeated.

Defeated by him.

To protect her.

"They hurt you and they deserved to die, Brenna," he whispered, stroking her hair and flexing carefully inside her. "Nothing more. Nothing less. That's not why you're feeling like this. It's because you know I'll protect you. You know I *can* protect you. I *will* protect you. No matter what. No matter who. You're safe with me. Your body knows it. Feels it. Loves it."

He kissed her again with the gentle power of a giant. "This might make the feminists howl and the PC police roar, but there's a deep need for a man to protect his woman, Brenna. And an equally deep need for a woman to feel protected by him. That's why it feels so intense for both of us, Brenna. Violence and sex run on the same engine, use the same energy. Danger and desire too. Same with safety and intimacy. In ancient times, back when it was just a man and his woman against the world, moments of safety were hard to come by." He grinned, moved inside her. "And so our bodies learned to make those moments count."

She giggled, then gasped as she felt herself tighten again, like her pussy was agreeing, like it was saying it might be now or never, that you might never get this chance again, that you were just fighting for your life and you might be fighting for your life again soon.

Sex and violence.

Danger and desire.

Safety and intimacy.

It made so much sense, like a jigsaw falling into place, piece by piece, bit by bit.

Bruiser kissed her once more and then started to move inside her, back and forth as she let herself relax under him, let herself completely trust him, let him completely take her, own her, claim her.

He grunted and started to move faster, driving his powerful hips back and forth with a fever that she could feel rising like the tide. She moaned and dug her nails into his shoulders, felt his rippling back muscles coiling over each other like a pit of vipers. He slammed into her with a ferocious inward stroke, his cockhead dragging against the top wall of her vagina, his hard pubic bone grinding against her stiff, throbbing clit, his balls smacking against her spread-open intersection.

Two seagulls screamed in the distance as Brenna felt the urgency rising, like danger and desire were dancing together again as they fucked under the sun, their glistening bodies wet and shiny like sea creatures on the sand. She was wailing now, her cries rising and falling with each hammering thrust of his need.

Bruiser was grunting deep and hard as he pumped into her, his hands sliding over her hips, fingers digging into her soft sides, holding her tight as he took her again and again, a man on a mission, a beast on the hunt.

He pulled back almost all the way out with each stroke, the bulb of his cockhead teasing her slick entrance for one poignant moment before his powerful buttocks drove his shaft back into her.

She thought he'd been close to coming in her mouth, but now she thought he could go forever. She thought she'd been wrecked when his tongue curled up inside her, but now she understood what it truly meant to be owned from the inside, every damn inch of her secret space invaded and possessed.

Another orgasm moved through her just then, silent like a killer whale taking its victim from below, pulling her down beneath the frothy waves. She screamed like a woman possessed, ripped at the skin on his muscled back, felt his claws almost draw blood along her ass and sides as he pounded her through her climax, pulled her farther beneath the dark waves of ecstasy, took her orgasm to a crescendo that almost broke her into a million pieces.

She was still drowning in that tidal wave of a climax when she felt Bruiser come inside her. One massive thrust and he stiffened like he'd been shot. They both stopped for one eternal moment, like a still-life image of two animals mid-flight or mid-dive or mid-death.

Then Bruiser exploded in her.

A violent, devastating explosion like a dam breaking, releasing jets of pure energy that flooded the land, drowned all the livestock, destroyed all the crops. He roared like an angry tiger as he came, his cock furiously pumping thick warm semen into her. She could feel his heavy balls tighten and release as they pumped their seed so far into her she swore she could taste him in her throat.

Bruiser pulled back and rammed into her again, forcing out another massive load. Her head jerked back and forth like she was convulsing. The climax was unstoppable, hers and his too, and when he finally let out a rumbling, rolling, deeply satisfied breath and collapsed against her panting breasts, she was seeing stars even though it was high noon.

They lay in silence for many long moments. Brenna closed her eyes and felt Bruiser rise and fall as their heavy breathing finally settled. His cock was still inside her, still quite full and heavy, making little jerking movements like it was still coaxing out more of his seed. She ruffled his thick hair, then frowned down at the specks of his blood on her cracked fingernails.

"Lemme know if I'm crushing you," he mumbled from between her boobs.

"Lemme know if I scratched you to death," she replied. "Or gave you rabies from my nails."

"Well," he grunted, raising his head and glancing at her lips. "You *were* frothing at the mouth back there."

"Oh, my *God*," she sputtered, playfully poking her blunt right index finger into his back. "You really are filthy."

"Battlefield humor," he said, smacking her lips and then rolling off her with a sigh. There wasn't enough space for both of them to lay side by side, so she turned on her side, one leg across his naked body. He caressed her thigh and ass, kissed her again, then grinned. "You should hear us when it's just the guys. You'd really understand how close sex and violence really is."

"Who are the guys?" she asked.

Bruiser frowned like he was surprised she didn't already know. She understood why. They felt so close it seemed they should know everything about each other.

Instead they knew almost nothing.

Again that voice of reason, that part of her mind that had been tied up and gagged by the overwhelming force of what just happened, spoke up.

It reminded her that nothing had changed in the outside world. Him fucking her brains out didn't change the facts. She might feel safe and protected, might be all swoony and weak-kneed from the intoxicating mix of danger and desire, but there was more at stake here.

Sex and desire might speak to those ancient instincts, but so did money and power.

Yes, her intuition said Bruiser was a good man, but her intelligence warned her to be careful.

Trust, but verify. That was the logical thing to do, she told herself. Don't just drop all your defenses. For all you know, the only thing keeping you alive are those twelve secret words. Don't give up your insurance policy just because a guy makes you come.

Come hard.

Three times hard.

All over his face like a whore.

All over his cock like a slut.

And then all over again like a woman.

Like a woman in love.

"Love those guys like brothers," he was saying as she watched his eyes shine. "Ax. Cody. Dogg."

She smiled against his neck. "Do all SEALs have names like that?"

"Like what?"

"Like Bruiser. And Dogg."

Bruiser shrugged. "Ax's real name is Jake Axelrod, so that's obvious. I'm Bruiser, and—"

"And that's obvious too," she said, craning her neck and pointedly glancing at the red bruises made by his savage grip on her sides.

He shrugged. Smacked her butt. Didn't apologize. Didn't need to.

She laughed and kissed his neck. They were silent for a while. Then Bruiser exhaled and looked up at the sky, brow furrowed.

"So what happened with the audit?" he asked, blinking and not looking at her.

"Sorry?"

Now he turned his head. "Ten years ago. The IRS audited you. Probably because of that secret crypto account that your dad used to send you a quarter million dollars for college."

Brenna stared, moved a strand of hair from her cheek. "There was no audit. Don't know what you're talking about," she said, her eyes narrowing at the odd question.

Bruiser sighed. "Look, I saw the record. There was an audit. It was resolved or stopped or sealed or something. Can't tell from the record. What happened?"

"I just told you there was no audit, Bruiser."

"What's the big deal? Just tell me. You don't trust me?"

Now Brenna rolled her head away from his chest and glared. "You think I'm lying?"

Bruiser whooshed out a breath. "Never mind," he muttered.

"Oh, my God," she gasped, propping herself up on her elbow even though it hurt on the wood. "You think I'm lying!"

Bruiser let out a rumbling sigh. "I saw the record, Brenna. I don't see what the big deal is. Just fucking tell me, OK? Seriously, if you can't trust me by now, you're in deep trouble, OK? Just trust me."

"OK, that's like the *millionth* time you've asked me to

trust you," she said hotly. "Nobody trustworthy needs to ask even once, let alone a hundred times."

"I thought it was a million times," Bruiser grumbled. He exhaled, then glanced at her, placed his hand on her upper arm, pulled her towards him again. "Anyway, so you didn't get audited. Maybe it was a mistake. After all, it wasn't in the initial file Benson sent me about you."

"They have a file on me?"

"They have files on everyone. Probably get it started on every American when they're in mama's womb. Second trimester. No big deal."

"No big deal? You keep saying that too. Which makes me think it *is* a big deal."

Bruiser looked uncomfortable for a fleeting moment. It was enough to trigger that little voice of reason and caution.

That voice of warning.

Trust but verify.

Or maybe don't trust at all.

"Look," said Bruiser, like he was wrestling with something. She wasn't sure what, but now she knew for damn sure he was holding something back. "Forget I asked. No, I don't think you're lying. I'll check with Benson later. Probably nothing."

"There's clearly something," she said, stiffly lowering her head to his chest again as he pulled her towards him. "You clearly aren't telling me everything."

His chest moved. "Neither are you," he said softly.

Now a chill ripped through her naked body. Suddenly she felt cold in the sun, exposed in the wind. She slowly sat up, took her leg off him, turned to the side. Her bikini bits were nowhere to be seen, but the towel was on the sand. She picked it up, stood, and wrapped it tight around her. It covered her from just above her nipples to just below the edges of her buttcheeks.

"You want those twelve words, don't you?" she said, not sure if she was offended, scared, or just straight up pissed off.

"Lots of people do, Brenna. Bad people. I'm not one of them. You damn well know I'm not."

"Do I? If you were a good man you'd have asked those questions *before* you fucked me, not after."

Bruiser sat up now, his eyebrows arching and then crossing downwards into an angry V. "That's not fair. What just happened was real. As real as anything in my entire damn life, Brenna. Fuck you for saying that."

She stood there barefoot on the hot sand, towel around her boobs and butt. He sat on the edge of the beachchair, his long cock hanging down, balls still full and heavy. There was semen drying all over his shaft. She could feel the same semen slowly dripping out of her, rolling in thick lines down her inner thighs.

But it didn't feel dirty.

It felt right.

Which means you aren't thinking straight, whispered that voice of reason.

Your judgment is compromised.

And if you can't trust yourself right now.

Then you sure as hell can't trust him.

19

Bruiser pulled on his trunks, his back to Brenna. He looked out over the blue sea, narrowed his gaze and then opened it up to take in the broad horizon. As a sniper who sometimes needed to stare through a scope looking for a three-square-inch target for hours, he knew that relaxing your eye muscles also relaxed your entire body.

And he sure as hell needed relaxing right now.

He was pissed at what Brenna had said. Sure, he understood it. Didn't stop him from being pissed off, though. He could usually keep his head cool, but damn, this woman had gotten him turned around.

He turned around, about to say something when a phone rang. It was shrill and annoying. Not his phone.

"Patty, hi," said Brenna, flipping open the phone Patty Duprey had given her.

Bruiser glanced back towards the embassy. No signs of movement. Nobody at the windows. Patty had taken care to give them some privacy. He almost smiled but didn't. Instead he calmed his breathing and listened.

Brenna didn't say much, though. She was listening too. Finally she hung up and looked up at Bruiser, her eyes still sharp.

"That was Patty," she said stiffly.

"I heard," he said gruffly.

"Nobody saw the shooter," she said. "Hotel staff was a dead end too."

Bruiser grunted. He wasn't surprised.

"What about the rifle?" he asked, slowly letting go of his anger as his mind focused back on the mission.

Brenna sighed. "You were right. It was stolen. Early this morning. From the game warden's office at the deer-hunting preserve. Someone broke into the office before dawn."

Bruiser rubbed his chin, picked up his phone, pulled up a map. The deer-hunting preserve was clearly marked. The office was marked too. "Not far from the airport," he muttered. He took a breath and glanced up. "If you just arrived in town and needed a rifle on short notice, where would you go first?"

Brenna looked at him. "Just arrived? You think the shooter flew in? The private terminal where we landed?"

"No. Commercial flight. Shooter could have brought his own weapon if he flew private. This was a last minute thing. Probably couldn't arrange a private flight. Maybe couldn't afford it."

Bruiser looked at his phone again. He tapped a few times and held the phone to his ear, stepping casually away from Brenna, out of earshot.

Benson answered after the first ring. He sounded tense.

"Three commercial flights landed before dawn," Benson said crisply like he'd already gotten there. Patty must have called him first, and Benson must have worked out the rest, just like Bruiser did. "One from Buenos Aires."

He went quiet. Bruiser blinked. Adrenaline ripped up along the muscles lining his spine.

"Do you have access to the airport security cameras?" Bruiser asked quietly. "Do you know for sure?"

"It's him," said Benson softly. "Damyan Nagarev himself. Footage from the customs checkpoint confirms it. Assumed name, fake passport. An identity that wouldn't have showed up on the CIA's radar, which means he just burned a valuable fake name. He can't have many of those."

"Means he's desperate," said Bruiser, strolling farther from Brenna. "Alone. Nobody else he trusts now that Mikhail is rotting in the trash-heap behind the airport."

"It means more than that," said Benson. "It means he's probably broke too. He used up his last favor—or last bundle of cash—to get Mikhail that private flight out to Kiev. So he had to come out of hiding and fly commercial."

Bruiser nodded, stayed quiet. The adrenaline was surging, and he let it flow through his system. He knew what this meant. It meant Damyan Nagarev was up against the ropes, that he was more desperate than even Benson had figured, that whatever was in Brenna's secret vault was worth risking everything for. He was like a wounded animal. A cornered beast.

Which meant Bruiser had the advantage.

"He's alone, without any major firepower," Bruiser said with cool precision. "Had to steal a rifle. A hunting rifle is useless at close range. Too unwieldy. And he won't have a handgun. Not that easy to get one in Costa Rica, and he couldn't have smuggled a weapon with him on a commercial flight." Suddenly Bruiser stopped. "Shit," he said.

"What?"

"Mikhail's Glock," Bruiser muttered. "It's in my hotel room. Stuck it under the mattress along with two extra magazines."

Benson sighed. He was annoyed. "You mean it *was* in your hotel room. Damn. That's going to complicate things."

Bruiser bristled at his mistake. He should have carried both weapons with him. But he was going shoe-shopping. And then to church..

"It's not complicated," he said gruffly. "Now we're evenly matched. I'll take him down, then bring her home."

"You aren't taking anyone down, Soldier," said Benson. He paused. Took a breath. "And you aren't bringing anyone home either. Not yet, at least."

Bruiser blinked. He stared out to sea, then blinked again. His mind spun through everything Benson had said. Then it stopped spinning.

"Wait, you want Damyan *alive*?" he barked. He thought a moment and then groaned. "You cannot be serious, Benson. You still want to recruit him, don't you? You sly mother*fucker*! This whole thing was to get Damyan out of hiding, get him up against the ropes, then . . . then what, flip him like a damn fish on a grill? Dangle the money in front of him and bring him home to the welcoming arms of the CIA, forgive his sins and turn him into an assassin for Kaiser or you? Hell, Brenna was just bait to flush him out, wasn't she? *Wasn't* she, you bastard!"

Benson was quiet. Bruiser could almost hear the man grin. It pissed Bruiser off. He wasn't playing games with Brenna in the line of fire.

"Go to hell, Benson," he said. "I'm putting two bullets in Damyan, one in each eye. Then I'm bringing Brenna home. And you're gonna guarantee that *nobody*—not CIA, not DHS, not some other dark agency—railroads her on some bullshit treason rap. She's innocent, clean, and she's been used and abused. Fuck you, Benson. You make this right, asshole. Promise me, dammit."

"This isn't a negotiation, Soldier," said Benson. "This is a damn order."

"I'm not a soldier anymore," shot Bruiser. "And you sure as hell aren't my commander."

Benson was silent. Bruiser heard him breathe. Wondered if he'd gotten to the wily CIA man. Wondered if he'd won.

He hadn't.

"Then you're free to return home, Bruiser. Or not, of course. You can go anywhere you like, Mister ex-Soldier who doesn't take orders from anyone and can't see the big picture because he's blinded by a warm pussy and a pair of perfect boobs," Benson said smoothly. "Leave Brenna at the Embassy with Patty and Henry Duprey. I'll send someone else to take over for you. Finish the job. Clean up your damn mess."

Bruiser felt the rage rip up his spine. He almost hurled

the phone at a screeching seagull. He thought a moment, then took a breath and smiled tightly.

"Maybe I take Brenna with me," he said coolly. "Maybe we take the money and disappear. Fake our deaths. Fake new lives. Then you get nothing, Benson. Without the lure of the money, Damyan won't be flipped. Yeah, you get nothing, Benson."

Benson chuckled, but Bruiser heard a hint of nervousness in there. "You do that and Director Kaiser will label you *both* traitors and send a wet team after you."

"Bring 'em on," Bruiser growled.

But a moment later he grimaced as the realization hit him cold and clean. He was beaten and he knew it. An American wet team was no damn cake-walk. They'd all be Special Forces or ex-military. And even if he stood a chance against them he'd never strike at one of his own. No way he was going to kill American patriots simply following orders. Maybe Benson was bluffing, but with Brenna involved, he couldn't roll the dice.

Bruiser had to stand down.

Especially since he was bluffing too.

He turned to look at Brenna. She was still in her towel, looking in his direction, her pretty face scrunched up with suspicion.

Would she even go with him if he tried to make good on his threat to Benson?

For a moment Bruiser let his imagination flow free like the waves on the open ocean. He imagined them rich and on the run, hopping from hotel to hotel across South America, Europe, Africa, perhaps the Moon and Mars too. The flight was fanciful but unreal. Bruiser wasn't going to steal, wasn't going to run, wasn't going to hide.

He was going to stand and fight, just like he was trained to do, born to do, sworn to do.

And right now, the opponent was John Benson.

Bruiser believed what Ax had told him about Benson, that the guy was a patriot, a good and righteous man. But a man with secrets, with his own methods, his own way of manipulating the players, his own way of playing the game.

"You just want those twelve words from her, right?" Bruiser said after he'd calmed down and the seagulls had stopped screaming. "She gives up those words, you get the account and what's in it, then Damyan comes to you. End of story. You don't need her once you have the money."

Benson snorted. "You think the United States Government is short on money? It's not that simple. Kaiser and I tried to bribe Damyan, to buy him. He wouldn't take American CIA money then, and he won't take American CIA money now."

"Why?"

"Principles. Some bad guys have them, it appears."

"Just like some good guys don't," Bruiser replied pointedly.

"You questioning my patriotism, Soldier?"

"I'm questioning your methods."

Benson stayed silent.

"So what's so special about this money?" Bruiser finally asked.

"It's his," said Benson plainly.

"Alexei Yankov stole it from Damyan?"

"It appears so."

"But where did the money come from in the first place?"

"It's old UNA funds, recovered from some accounts the Treasury Department missed when they seized everything."

Bruiser frowned. "How much?"

Benson was silent, like he was debating himself. "Current market value is just under nine billion dollars."

Bruiser stared at the seagulls like they were aliens coming in hot. "With a B?"

"Bingo."

"That doesn't add up, Benson. The UNA is small potatoes. Nine billion is . . . hell, with that kind of money Damyan could . . ."

Bruiser didn't even know how to finish the sentence. With nine billion dollars in unblockable, unseizable assets that could be transferred anywhere over the open web, Damyan's limits were set only by his imagination. He could buy a new army. State of the art weapons. He could buy government officials. Military-grade artillery. Guided ground-to-air missiles. Hell, maybe even a nuclear warhead. "Who donated nine billion dollars to Damyan's cause?"

"Nobody," said Benson. "The original amount was less than two hundred thousand dollars all told. Alexei Yankov used the donations to buy cryptocurrency ten years ago. It grew in the account as crypto prices rose."

"And the value skyrocketed to nine billion dollars in ten years?" Bruiser whistled. "I gotta get a new financial advisor."

Benson chuckled. "Alexei Yankov was clearly a good one. Too bad he's dead."

Bruiser took a breath. "Yankov worked for Damyan," he said, not really asking, more like confirming. "Did Damyan know what Yankov was doing?"

"Probably to some degree, at least. But Damyan is old school. Not a luddite, but not particularly tech-savvy."

"So he trusted Alexei Yankov."

"Trusted his skills, at least," said Benson.

"And Yankov betrayed Damyan by stealing?"

"We don't know for sure," Benson said cryptically. "He might have just been stashing the money in that old account. After all, there's no evidence he told Brenna about it. Maybe he was afraid for his life and wanted a bargaining chip. Maybe it was his exit plan. We just don't know. We'll probably never know. Doesn't matter now, anyway."

"It might matter to his daughter," said Bruiser softly. He glanced at Brenna again. She was gone. He looked for footsteps in the sand. Found them. They led back to the cabana where she'd left her clothes.

"That's her problem, not mine. Not yours either, Bruiser. Your mission is damn simple now. And despite you turning into a lovesick puppy, you're close to accomplishing the mission. She likes you. She trusts you. She needs you. So use that, Soldier. Get those twelve words and pass them on to me." He chuckled. "Hell, that'll be a good test, Bruiser. If all that grunting and moaning actually meant something, then she'll spit out those words like pumpkin seeds."

Bruiser held the phone away from his ear, looked at

it. He frowned as he remembered the whole thing with Ax and Amy. Ax had told him about the tech the spooks were using now. Benson could turn on the phone's microphone and camera from a computer anywhere in the world.

"You sick sonofabitch," Bruiser growled.

Benson laughed. "Relax. I have better things to do than watch a SEAL named Bruiser grunt and groan as he takes his mate. I listened just long enough to know that you'd broken down her first line of defense. Good job, Soldier. Now you just need to finish the mission. You're almost there, kid. I think she likes you. Maybe she'll even tell you her secrets if you ask nice. Go down on your knees again. Use that tongue like a deadly weapon."

"I swear, Benson," Bruiser hissed through gritted teeth. "If you get out of this with just a broken nose, consider yourself a lucky man."

"Broken nose I can handle. Finish the damn mission, Soldier."

Bruiser was still breathing hard, but he forced himself to slow it down so Benson wouldn't know that his mind was following Brenna's footsteps back to that cabana. That was real, he wanted to say to Benson. I know it was real, damn it.

Still, Benson's challenge bothered him. Truth is, he wasn't so sure Brenna trusted him enough to give up the one thing she believed was keeping her alive. Yeah, Bruiser was keeping her alive too, but he didn't want to make her have to choose. Not before he had a good grasp on Benson's end game.

So Bruiser pushed deeper into Benson's twisted mind. It was the only way he was going to get Brenna out of this without betraying her, abandoning her, or getting her killed.

"I don't see what good those words will do you, Benson," he said after thinking it through. "So you get into the account and move the money, or offer it to Damyan like a carrot. But that's not gonna work, is it? If you couldn't turn Damyan then, no way you can turn him now. If you believe he won't take CIA money, then you've got nothing on him. If you and Kaiser get the words and get into the account, he'll just disappear again. He'll abandon the money. He has to get the words directly from Brenna, without suspecting CIA involvement. And when he unlocks the account, he's got to see the money in there."

"You're right," said Benson calmly. "He has to get the secret words directly from Brenna. And when he gets into the account, he needs to see all the money in there. Which it will be. We won't move that money. We were never going to move the money. We just want to *watch* the money."

Bruiser blinked, a chill going through him. "But how will that help recruit Damyan? How will it turn him?"

"I never said we're still trying to turn him."

Bruiser thought back. Benson was right. Bruiser had said it, but Benson never confirmed it. Yes, twenty years ago Benson and Kaiser tried to turn him. That wasn't the plan this time.

So what was the plan?

"Follow the money," Bruiser muttered as his mathematical mind put the pieces together. "That's the plan. Follow the damn money. The beauty about cryptocurrency is that it can't be seized, can't be stopped, can't be controlled by any man or nation without the private key. But it can be traced. In fact it can be traced *perfectly*. With dollars you can just convert it into paper money, physical cash. You do that and the trail goes cold. But crypto is pure digital. There's no paper, nothing physical. So you can follow every tiny payment Damyan makes. You can use artificial intelligence and data triangulation to figure out the location of every digital wallet that Damyan sends money to. He'll be like a mole, setting up targets for U.S. covert operations as he buys weapons and bribes corrupt officials and funds genocide or hires hitmen or whatever else. And he won't even know he's a mole. It's like putting a tracker on a guy but without any chance of it getting discovered. There's no login-history or customer support on a crypto account. Damyan would never know the CIA was watching his account, following every payment, slowly building a database of targets all over the world. You take out the targets slow and covertly. And since you have the private key, if Damyan gets too far ahead of you, you can just drain the account and stop him dead. He'll be hung out to dry. Powerless and broke with the click of a button. Then if he's got people doing stuff for him and he can't pay, they'll send their own wet teams after him."

Benson exhaled like he was surprised. Then he chuckled. "Huh. You know, the name Bruiser makes people underestimate you, kid. That's some good big picture thinking. Maybe you can pull this off after all."

Bruiser grunted. "What makes you think I *want* to pull this off?"

"Because you're a patriot. You see how big this can be. You're a soldier, and every soldier is ready to sacrifice for the bigger picture, for something greater than him, greater than us all."

Bruiser tried to roll his eyes but couldn't pull it off. Benson was right. This was big. This was what SEALs were sworn to do, born to do, trained to do.

But it was no longer that simple. He understood the plan, understood its brilliance, understood why it would work beautifully if you looked at the big picture.

But Bruiser didn't want to look at the big picture.

Because the small picture sickened him.

Yeah, Benson was a patriot, maybe even a damn genius.

But he was a cold-hearted machine.

He had to be, to come up with a twisted plan like this.

"Something just occurred to me, Benson," he said, barely holding back his rage. "How were you planning for Damyan to get the secret words from Brenna? You want her to set up a damn play-date for the two of them? A meeting at a cafe? She whispers the words and then walks away? You think he'll *let* her walk away after getting the words?"

"He doesn't need to let her walk away," Benson said coolly. "You do."

"What?"

"Need to me spell it for you?"

"Please do," growled Bruiser. "I wanna hear you say it, Benson. I wanna hear the savage truth straight from your twisted lips, your dark heart, your empty soul."

"Then here it is, Soldier. Get the words out of her. Send them to me. Then walk away. That's all you have to do. Just walk away. Damyan will find her. He'll take her. He'll break her. He'll get the secret words, get his money, and start spending it, just like we want. That's the end-game, Bruiser. That's how it ends for her."

Bruiser stared blankly at the blue horizon, numb inside, sick to his guts. He couldn't speak. Could barely listen.

Benson went on. "It's the only way, Bruiser. The only way Damyan won't suspect it's a set up. A trap. Think about it, Bruiser. Damyan doesn't know who you are. He saw you just once, through a rifle-scope, and you look Russian from that distance. Maybe Ukrainian. At any rate, he won't be certain where you're from. That's good."

Benson paused, took a breath. He sounded excited, maybe even thrilled at how things were working out—for him, at least.

"And stopping in Costa Rica will throw him off the track even more," Benson went on. "Master move, Bruiser."

"It wasn't a *move*, Benson," Bruiser growled, still too numb to think clearly. Instead he just stalled, trying desperately to find another way. A way out. A way for him to do his duty without making a sacrifice he knew he'd never be able to make. "She needed to clean up. There was a dead body to get rid of before it rotted. And I needed some time to think about whether to trust a master-manipulator like you or a woman who'd just spent a week in a prison that was out of some damn horror story. So far it's pretty damn clear, in my opinion." He tried to control his temper, just about managed it. "You're a piece of dried dog-shit, Benson."

"That's a new one," said Benson cheerfully. "Anyway, as I was saying, it was a genius move to stop in Costa Rica. Even if you were just winging it. If you'd taken her to Moscow, Damyan would have suspected you were Russian Intelligence. If you brought her to the States, he'd know you were an American agent. This way he won't be sure who the hell you are. You could be a mercenary, a mafia-thug, a terrorist in your own right."

Bruiser thought about it. He grunted and nodded. Plausible. There were lots of guys who looked ex-military and freelanced for some pretty shady characters. Benson was probably right. Damyan would be wondering who the hell Bruiser was. He'd suspect, but wouldn't be sure. And getting so close to the money might shift the balance, make him take the chance that it wasn't tainted, wasn't a trap. Sometimes when you *need* to believe something, it helps make the thing seem believable.

Bruiser exhaled and spoke. "Yeah, yeah, I get it, Benson. Damyan won't know the CIA has the account number and can track the funds for a while, then drain the account and hang him out to dry. His crypto spending spree will lead us to every terrorist operation and crooked weapons-dealer around the globe. He won't even know he did it."

"Exactly," said Benson. "So get the words and it'll play out perfectly, Soldier. Get the words. Send them to me. Walk away. Mission accomplished."

Bruiser shook his head. "Maybe your mission, but not mine. Look, I'll get the words. Send them to you. But I can't walk away, Benson. Can't do it knowing he'll take her. Torture her. Kill her and dump her in the ocean."

"There's a price to be paid for every mission, Soldier," Benson said. "This mission doesn't succeed if you don't walk away from her, let her get captured. Damyan needs to get the words out of her himself for it to work." He sighed. "Look, kid, I know you two connected. Danger brings that out in people. But you need to look at the big picture, Bruiser. Think about the lives that will be saved if this works. Men, women, children all over the world. Thousands. Maybe millions. You're a mathematician, Bruiser. So do the damn math. One life sacrificed. A million lives saved. Your duty is clear. Just because it's not easy doesn't mean it isn't clear."

"Doesn't feel so clear," Bruiser rumbled, his fingers almost crushing the phone to powder. "There's got to be another way. I'll find another way, Benson."

Benson was silent. Bruiser heard him breathe. It was steady for three breaths, then sped up.

"Well, find it quick then," Benson said finally. "Damyan's probably looking for you right now. If he finds you at the U.S. Embassy, that blows the operation. He'll know you're American. He'll know you're CIA or Special Forces. He'll figure the money's tainted and it's a trap."

"So he'll disappear again," said Bruiser with a cold shrug. "Go underground again. And so what if he does? He'll be powerless. You'll have his money. I killed his only buddy. He's broke and alone. He'll die broke and alone. Not the end of the world."

"Not the end of *my* world, no," said Benson smoothly. "But let me leave you with this thought, Bruiser: Why did Damyan kill those two pilots so viciously? He cut their throats slowly, I was told. All the way to the bone. Why?"

Bruiser shrugged again. Not so coldly this time. Damyan's savage execution of two innocent pilots had reminded Bruiser of why the man was called the Demon. Why he'd been kicked out of Russian Special Forces for being too brutal. The *last* thing Bruiser wanted was a man like that after Brenna.

Right now Damyan needed Brenna alive.

But what would happen if he no longer cared about getting Brenna alive?

What if Damyan discovered the plan was a set up, the money was tainted?

Damyan might disappear, sure.

But would he stay disappeared?

Would a man like that accept defeat quietly?

Or would he let it fester.

Would he think about Mikhail's death at Bruiser's hands. Stew over Brenna's father stealing his money. Fume over almost being tricked by the two of them.

No, Bruiser thought. No way I let Damyan disappear, only to have him pop up years from now, to serve up revenge on a deathly cold platter. There's no retreating from this. There's no running away from my duty.

Even though my duty is in conflict right now.

My duty as a soldier.

And my duty as a man.

"I'll find a way, Benson," he whispered. "I won't fail as a soldier. But I can't fail her as a man. I *won't* fail her as a man."

Without waiting for a response Bruiser hung up. He gazed out over the endless ocean for a long moment. A part of him wanted to swim out to that distant horizon, go as far as his powerful strokes would carry him, let the waves finally take him, relieve him of this conflict that was ripping him apart.

He smiled at that part of him. He knew it well. The secret, dark part of every soldier that wonders about death, perhaps even yearns for it. You don't charge into battle again and again if you haven't made peace with the Grim Reaper, if you can't grin as he stands there in the shadows with his sickle, waiting to take you.

So Bruiser grinned at the Reaper.

Flipped off the hooded being of the underworld.

Told the sucker he'd have to wait.

Then he turned and walked back up the beach.

20

"He's not going to walk away from her," said Martin Kaiser, tapping the ash off a half-smoked Dunhill filter cigarette. "Which doesn't matter, since she's not going to give up those secret words to him in the first place. She's dirty, Benson. Just like her father. Just like all those sons of bitches. Or daughters of bitches. Whatever."

Benson glanced at the glowing red tip of Kaiser's cigarette. They were on the back porch of Kaiser's three-bedroom ranch-style home in Arlington, Virginia. The cream-painted house was nestled on a heavily wooded bluff. They could see the Washington Monument shining in the distance, tall and proud, bright in the afternoon sky. Kaiser had a family, Benson knew. They were not home. Benson knew they hadn't been home for years.

"You're sounding jaded, Martin," said Benson, reaching for a rapidly cooling cup of black coffee. He drained it to the bottom, then looked at the black grounds in the white cup like a fortune teller trying to read the tea leaves. "Where's your sense of wonder? Your belief in humanity? In fate. Destiny." He smiled as Kaiser shifted in his wicker chair and took a long drag. "Where's your belief in love, Martin?" he whispered cruelly, knowing that would put Kaiser over the edge.

It did exactly that. Kaiser flicked the burning butt off the porch. It landed in a patch of dirt that had been a rose garden when Kaiser's wife was still around. He turned and glared at Benson.

"I might be jaded, but maybe you aren't jaded enough, John," he shot back. "Yes, your games sometimes work out. But sometimes they don't. A lot of times they don't."

"If they don't work out, it's only because it wasn't meant to be."

"That's circular logic and you damn well know it." Kaiser shook his head, reached to the table for the open pack of Dunhills. He lit one quickly, dragged deep and blew out the smoke hard. "Anyway, you've got this one wrong. That SEAL is done for. She's played him. She'll stick with him until he kills Damyan. Use him like a shield, a guided missile, a weapon, a damn tool. She'll use him, and then she'll walk away. With the money." He tapped furiously at the cigarette even though it was all cherry and no ash. "It's what women do, John. It's in their DNA. Can't help themselves."

Benson sighed, rubbed his chin. He hadn't shaved this morning. "It's hard being married to the Director of the CIA, Martin. You can't blame Alice for leaving with the kids."

"I wasn't Director when she left."

Benson shrugged. "And maybe you'd never have made it to Director if she'd stayed."

"What do you mean?"

"I mean look at Sally and me. If she hadn't been killed, maybe I'd never have left the CIA, never started Darkwater." Benson took a breath and sighed it out, sliding lower in the large well-worn wicker chair. "Fate isn't always pleasant. Destiny isn't all sunshine and fucking rainbows."

"Oh, please give me a damn break, John."

Benson chuckled darkly. "Look, I know you hate it when I say this, but fate is real, destiny is real, and love is the fundamental energy underlying all of it. There's no way out of it. You might as well accept it, embrace it, use it. That's what I'm doing here, Martin. It's what I've always done."

Kaiser finished his cigarette in silence. Put it out in the ashtray instead of his ex-wife's dead rose garden. Glanced over at Benson and sighed.

"Look, I believe I'm right about her," Kaiser said. "She always knew about the money in the account. She believes Damyan killed her father—which he probably did. That's why she went to Russia. To draw out Damyan. Get revenge for her dad. Then continue her father's work."

"Which was what?" Benson challenged.

Kaiser shrugged. "Don't know. Nobody knows. Doesn't matter. Once Bruiser fails, I'll send in a team to nab her and kill Damyan if he's still alive. Hell, I should give the order right now."

Benson sighed. "Patience, Martin. Wait it out. Just a little bit longer."

Kaiser went silent. He ran his hand through his thinning salt-and-pepper hair and sighed. "No harm in waiting it out now, I guess. I can't send in a team to take Brenna when that Navy SEAL is all protective like a damn caveman. Can't risk getting one of our own killed. So we can wait. Bruiser isn't going to give her up, isn't going to complete the mission if it puts her in danger. Maybe the SEAL kills Damyan. Maybe Damyan kills the SEAL. Yes, I can wait a couple of days before sending in a team to clean up your mess."

Benson nodded. He stood up to go. "Might not be such a mess," he said. "Might work out exactly as planned."

"You got something else up your sleeve you aren't telling me about, Benson?"

Benson shook his head. "It's out of my hands now. You know how I set up these games. Put the players together and let things play out. Well, the players are together now, which means this isn't my mission anymore. It isn't my story. It isn't my fate. If the two of them are meant to be, then destiny will intervene. Give them a shot at their forever."

He strode off around the house towards his dark blue Ford Crown Victoria. Behind him he could hear Kaiser sighing again, probably shaking his head. Benson enjoyed riling up the guy, though sometimes he went a bit overboard with the fate and destiny bullshit.

But at the heart of it he believed his own bullshit. He'd seen his forever in Sally's shining eyes. He'd experienced the magic of that eternal energy that makes the world spin, makes the universe dance, makes a man smile, makes a woman laugh.

Yeah, he'd lost Sally, and he'd never recover from that. Not until he saw her again in whatever came next, when this world used him up and finally broke him.

But losing her was fate.

Her fate.

His fate.

And in a strange way losing Sally had set him free, made him invincible. There was nothing more anyone could do to him. He was alone again, starting a new chapter with Darkwater and these SEALs.

Men who perhaps could dare to see the world the way Benson did.

Men who could keep their eyes on the mission.

Duty on their minds.

But forever in their hearts.

Would Bruiser be one of those men, Benson wondered as he drove down the winding driveway towards the county road.

Would fate intervene for Bruiser and Brenna?

Would the universe give them a chance at forever?

And if it did, would they recognize that chance?

Would they see that fate tests your resolve?

That destiny asks you to risk everything, to prove that you can trust in something bigger than you, stronger than you, smarter than you?

Or would they back away from the challenge.

And let their forever slip away.

21

Brenna slipped the towel off her shoulders and let it fall to the painted wood floor of the little cabana. She glanced towards the open closet area, then frowned when she saw her clothes folded neatly on a white-painted wooden stool. Patty had taken Brenna's clothes back to the house earlier, saying she'd get them washed by one of the housekeeping staff. Apparently that had already happened, because her black top and black jeans and blue pullover were sitting there clean and crisp.

Brenna wondered when the housekeeping person had placed them there. What had they seen? What had they heard? Hopefully what happened at the U.S. Embassy's private beach stayed buried in the sands of secrecy.

Heat rose up her neck as she unfolded her jeans and prepared to step into them. She stopped and sighed. She was still leaking Bruiser's semen down her thighs. She reached for a fresh towel and wiped herself carefully, but she still felt sticky.

Brenna sniffed her underarms and sighed again. Then she glanced towards the back of the cabana. There was a small enclosure near the restroom. A shining metal showerhead with a single knob. It would be cold water, Brenna knew. Good. Maybe it would cool her down—both inside and outside.

The water was cold but not icy. It felt nice. There was a bar of milk-white soap that smelled like a fresh coconut. She finished showering and dried off. Sniffed her pits again. Now she smelled like coconut. Hopefully Bruiser liked coconuts.

"Why do you care what Bruiser likes?" she muttered, her brows crossing as she squeezed into her stretch jeans that appeared to have shrunk in the dryer. She got them up past her ass and over her hips. Thankfully they zipped up and buttoned properly.

She smiled and looked at her ass sideways in the mirror, covering her breasts with her hands like a model. The jeans held her in place better than Spanx, and she felt sexy again, like she had with Bruiser. There was a tingle between her legs, and she pointed at her reflection and glared sternly at herself.

"No," she said. "Absolutely not. Your pussy is a dumb thing that wants what it wants. Your brain knows better. You don't know if you can trust him. You don't know if you can trust your own judgment. So, no. Just no."

She got her black top on and tied her pullover around her waist and looked for her red Converse sneakers. She evened out the laces so they looked like little white bows. Stood and pulled back her wet hair and then shook it out.

There was a stiff-bristled brush on a shelf beneath the mirror. She used it, cleaned a few strands of her hair off it, then put it back on the shelf.

When she turned towards the cabana door, Bruiser was standing there, his back to her, arms on his waist, broad back covering the doorway. He was dressed in his black shirt and matching cargo pants. There was a crisp crease down the middle of the t-shirt. Patty had gotten one of the stealthy housekeeping staff to launder Bruiser's stuff too.

"You look like a freshly minted action figure," Brenna said from behind him.

She'd cooled off, clearly. Maybe it had something to do with the protective way Bruiser stood at the door, his green eyes scanning the horizon for snipers or ships or perhaps seagulls with bombs tied to their beaks.

Bruiser turned, his face red from the sun, his hair glossy from the shower. His expression was serious, bordering on stern. He glanced at her lengthwise, then breadthwise. "And you look like . . ." he started to say. He sniffed the air like a hound. "Is that coconut?"

Brenna nodded. "It was the only soap I could find. You aren't allergic, are you?"

Bruiser took another sniff. Then he took a step closer. "Only one way to find out," he said, finally breaking into a grin as he leaned in to kiss her on the lips.

She turned her head, blushing a little, tingling a lot. His lips grazed her cheek as he missed.

Clearly Bruiser didn't like to miss, because he slid his hand around the back of her head, grasped her wet hair, turned her head and planted his kiss dead center on her nutty lips. It was a wet kiss, full and hard, like he wanted to leave his mark on her.

"I thought we were fighting," she said, trying to sound annoyed.

"I thought I already won."

Brenna neither confirmed nor denied his claim at victory. "Was that Benson on the phone?"

"Were you listening?"

"I tried. But you walked away. I assumed you were discussing where to dump my body after I gave up my secrets."

Bruiser grinned. "I already know where to dump your body," he said wickedly.

Those green eyes darted towards the swell of her boobs in her black top. His hand slid around her lower back, moving confidently down to her ass for a hard, possessive squeeze.

Brenna gasped, going up on her toes, her hips moving towards him like she couldn't help it. She saw the need flash in his eyes, felt her own heat rise. Then abruptly Bruiser took his hand away. He stepped back, but kept his eyes on her.

She curled a strand of hair around her ear, looked up at him. There was something in his eyes besides that flash of mischief, that hint of need, that moment of possessiveness. He was conflicted about something.

About what they'd shared? She didn't know him well enough to read that deep. Couldn't be sure what was behind those sharp green eyes.

"What did Benson say?" she asked, breaking the awkward silence.

She could still feel the pressure where he'd squeezed her

bottom. Her bum tingled. Her head buzzed. She wanted his hand back on her butt. She didn't want all this other drama in her life. She wanted it gone. She wished Damyan wasn't after her. She wished Bruiser didn't have some clearly troubling orders from this guy Benson.

For one wild moment Brenna considered telling him they could go away, disappear somewhere, anywhere. We can take the money and run, Bruiser, she thought of saying. Just you and me, like in a movie or a romance novel. We'll wear disguises, steal motorbikes, ride boxcars across Australia, stow-away on pirate galleons.

The moment didn't last. A hundred objections burst into her mind like fireworks. Her heart sank back to reality.

"What did Benson say?" she asked again.

Bruiser flicked his eyes away from her. "Benson said too much. But somehow still not enough. He's a sly motherfucker. The only reason I'm even listening to his bullshit is because my old SEAL Team Leader Ax swears Benson is the real deal. A trickster and a liar and a manipulative sonofabitch, but somehow still the real deal. So I gotta think it through."

Brenna nodded. Didn't push him. Being close to him made her feel sure about him again, safe with him again. Yeah, maybe she was kidding herself. Maybe she was tricking herself into trusting him because she had no choice. There was no one else. No other option. She needed Bruiser.

She glanced towards the U.S. Embassy in the distance, its white walls shining in the sun, flag flying proudly in the wind.

Um, of course there was another option. The sensible

thing to do would be to hunker down right here. There were armed guards at the Embassy. Patty Duprey was a wild creature but Brenna had immediately liked her and totally trusted her. So why did she feel like there was no option but to stay with Bruiser?

"You should stay here with the Dupreys," Bruiser said just then, like he'd been thinking the same thing.

Except he seemed to have come to the opposite conclusion. She tried not to glare at him as he continued.

"The State Security Officers are well-trained." He paused and thought. "But these guys don't see much combat, don't know what it's like. Most of them have perhaps never even drawn a weapon outside of the range." He took a breath. "But it's still the best option right now, while Damyan's out there. He doesn't know you're here, and let's keep it that way. So you just stay indoors, Brenna. Far away from the windows. No more beach time for now. No strolls around the grounds. Just lay low until I get back."

"You're going after Damyan?"

Bruiser nodded. He beckoned with his head, began walking towards the Embassy. He took it slow. She followed in his bigfoot-sized footsteps. He was still barefoot. She wished she'd carried her shoes in her hands. Her in-soles were grainy and pokey with sand.

"Do you know where he is?" she asked.

"I'll figure it out."

"So you don't know where he is."

"I said I'll figure it out." Bruiser stepped up the pace, like he suddenly wanted to get to the Embassy and lock her in some safe-room and leave her there.

"Is this how a Navy SEAL ghosts a woman?" she

teased, trying to keep it light but letting a bit of an edge into her tone. "Locks her up in a safe-house, puts armed guards at the door, then disappears on some secret, dangerous mission from which he'll never return?"

"I'll be back," he said gruffly.

"What does Benson want you to do?"

He turned his head. Didn't answer. Turned his head away and kept walking towards the Embassy building.

"Damn it, Bruiser," Brenna said, her voice rising. She was hot under the sun and her shoes were unbelievably pokey.

She stopped and went down to her knees and untied her laces. Off came the sneakers. She dumped out the sand, squinting as the sun reflected off the sharp silicon grains.

Then Bruiser's shadow fell over her, giving her relief from the glare. He stood above her like a sentry, his shadow a huge dark V that covered her like a shield.

"He's not going to shoot me if he wants those secret words, right?" said Brenna, tying her shoelaces together so she could sling the sneakers over her shoulder. "You're in more danger than I am, Bruiser. *My* body should be the shield, not yours."

She stood and slung the shoes over her right shoulder. Bruiser smiled, but there was a faraway look in his eyes, still conflicted but with a hint of something else in there.

Something that made her heart sink, made that spiderweb of dread crawl up her back.

"Listen, Brenna," he said, his voice low and calm but with an undercurrent of urgency. "I can't tell you everything that's going on. I wish I could, but . . ."

"But then you'd have to kill me?" she said with a forced smile. "Does the CIA still do that?"

"Nobody's going to kill you," Bruiser said.

Brenna frowned as that sinking feeling came back to her. She could see that something was ripping Bruiser apart from the inside. It was like he was broken inside. Forced to make a choice where he loses either way.

"Tell me," she asked. Her voice trembled. "Please, Bruiser. Let me inside."

He took a breath. Shook his head. "It's not your problem. You're going to be safe, Brenna. I'll kill Damyan and come back for you. You give Benson the secret words. Then we fly home. End of Mission."

She narrowed her gaze at him. Something felt off. "Don't you mean Mission Accomplished? End of Mission sounds like we lost. Like we failed the mission or something."

He smiled. "It's not your problem, Brenna."

"Make it my problem," she said firmly. "Tell me. Please. I know something happened on that call with Benson. I see it in your eyes."

He blinked and looked away. "It's just the sun in my eyes. Come on."

She crossed her arms under her breasts and dug her bare feet into the sand. "Not until you tell me why you look like a soldier who's retreating, surrendering, maybe even disobeying an order. Because of me."

"It's not your damn concern."

"If it's because of me, it *is* my damn concern."

"Let's go inside," said Bruiser. "Damyan could be—"

"You go inside. I'm staying right here."

"Don't be stubborn."

"Don't call me stubborn."

"Then do what I say."

Brenna kept her arms crossed firmly under her breasts. "Why should I do what you say if I can't *trust* what you say? Or don't say, which seems to be the case here."

"You *can* trust me."

"Not if you're hiding something from me."

"This is not a negotiation, Brenna."

"OK. Well, listen. I'm not going inside. I'm not staying here. I'm not telling anyone those secret words. I'm going to find a secure Internet connection, transfer all that crypto out of that wallet, and disappear forever. What are you going to do about it?"

Bruiser crossed his own arms over his own chest. He looked down at her. She didn't budge.

"Nothing," he said. "That's the point. You don't listen to me, I won't be *able* to do anything about it. Benson and Kaiser will send a team after you. Trust me, you do *not* want a team after you."

"Who's Kaiser?"

Bruiser winced. She saw him groan inwardly. Good. He was breaking.

"I guess it's public information anyway," he said. "Martin Kaiser is the CIA Director."

Brenna blinked. "Why . . . why does the Director of the CIA even know who I am?"

"Your father," Bruiser said. He rubbed the back of his neck.

"What about my father?"

Bruiser sighed. "He was probably a terrorist. And a crook."

Brenna stared, gasped in disbelief, then shook her head violently. "No way. He wasn't a great dad and sure as hell wasn't any kind of husband to my mom. But he was better than some. Better than *that*."

"He joined Damyan's Ukrainian Nationalist Army, Brenna. That's classified as a Terror Group by both Russia and the United States."

"I don't care," said Brenna stubbornly, blinking away tears. "He must have had a reason. Maybe he was brainwashed by Damyan. Or blackmailed. Or . . . or maybe he was CIA, working for this guy Kaiser, or Benson." She fought back her tears, tried desperately to come up with a plausible explanation. She didn't care about convincing Bruiser. She just wanted to convince herself. "That's gotta be it, Bruiser. He was CIA or undercover or a double agent or something. Something must have gone wrong and they had him killed. Now Benson and Kaiser want that money. *They're* the crooks, Bruiser."

Brenna looked pleadingly at him. She was starting to believe it herself. It seemed to fit. "He wasn't a bad man," she said. "He told me fairy tales about boys named Ivan and witches named Babayaga."

Bruiser smiled, pity all over his hard face. She hated pity.

"No!" she said when he tried to pull her in for a hug. "Benson and Kaiser are the crooks, Bruiser. It's a cover up. Maybe a money-grab. The CIA's been implicated in that stuff before. They were caught running drugs to make money for covert operations. And . . . and if it's cryptocurrency, then it must be worth a lot now. Crypto has been doubling every year for the last decade. It could be millions. Maybe billions."

Bruiser took a long look at her. He was trying to read her. Trying to study her.

Trying to trust her.

"Nine," he said softly.

"What?"

"Nine billion."

She stared, speechless, almost thoughtless. It was hard to even imagine that kind of money. She blinked and frowned and looked down past her boobs and leaned forward to see her toes. She wiggled them to check if she was still in the real world or if this was a dream. They moved like the little piggies they were.

She looked back up at Bruiser.

He looked back down at her.

Then he started to talk.

Slowly at first, hesitating before each reveal.

Then, when he crossed what must have been the point of no return, he spoke quick and clear, precise with details, colored with insights, laced with a sense of duty that Brenna could almost taste, it was so darned clear.

And now Brenna understood clearly what she'd seen in Bruiser's green eyes.

It was duty.

A conflict between two senses of duty, two moral codes, two sides of the magnificent man standing before her.

It was the duty of a soldier pitted against the duty of a man.

And it was breaking him apart.

"Oh, Bruiser," she whispered as she let it soak in.

All of it. Benson and Kaiser's twisted plan to get the words out of her and then let Damyan take her, break her, toss her away, a casualty of war, collateral damage, a price that had to be paid for the bigger picture.

But although she was sick with anger and burning with indignation, right now it was all small picture for her. The only person in her picture was Bruiser. This hulking hero who was trying to find some way to fulfill his duty as a soldier and as a man.

Her man.

In that moment she understood this wasn't about her father or Damyan.

It wasn't about Benson or Kaiser.

It wasn't even about saving millions of lives.

It was about them.

It was their story.

Their mission.

Their trial.

Their test.

"We'll find a way," she whispered, reaching out and touching her fingertips to his hand, feeling the electricity rip through her body like blue lightning. "I know you won't give me up. I know you won't let me die."

"Damn right I won't," he whispered, his fingers closing around her hand.

"And I won't let you fail," she whispered as their bodies drew close. "I won't let you fail your mission. We'll get those words to Damyan without him suspecting a CIA trap. Directly from me. There's got to be a way."

They stood together as the sun moved behind a cloud. The waves sounded far away. The beach ended less than forty yards up ahead of them. White stone steps led up to the Embassy building on the top of a bluff. Brenna could hear a phone ring somewhere in one of the Embassy offices. She cocked her head and raised a perky eyebrow.

"You still have Mikhail's phone, right?" she said.

Bruiser patted his left cargo flap and nodded. She held out her hand. He frowned, but gave her the phone.

It was large, black, and felt heavier than a cinderblock. She turned it over, saw the marks where Bruiser had pried out the GPS tracker chip on the plane. She turned on the phone and waited for it to start up. She tapped the screen. Everything was in Russian.

Brenna scrolled through the text messages. There weren't many. Either Mikhail wasn't very popular, or he was very organized.

Just three messages from Damyan, acknowledging periodic status updates from Mikhail. There was a message saying Mikhail had been held up outside the gate by the idiot warden. Another message saying he was in through the gates. One last message saying he'd got Brenna on the plane and they were about to take off.

She tapped the header that said DAMYAN in Russian script. It was in all-caps. Mikhail seemed like an all-caps kinda monster. Maybe something to do with having no tongue.

She tapped Damyan's name, then held the phone to her ear.

"What the hell are you—" Bruiser started to say.

She raised her index finger. "Shh. It's ringing."

Brenna turned away from Bruiser, set her jaw, narrowed her eyes, cleared her throat. She needed to get into character. She closed her eyes and pictured herself as a young, curvy Babayaga from a Russian Fairy Tale. Some magic might help, she figured.

After all, she needed to cast a spell on a demon.

The ring-tone suddenly stopped. Brenna glanced at the phone, wondering if it had gotten disconnected.

It had not.

Someone had answered.

Someone was on the line.

"Damyan Nagarev," she said, keeping her tone steady and dead, like it wasn't a question.

There was the sound of breathing on the line. Raspy but measured.

She went on in Russian, cold and monotone, not worrying about the accent but focusing on the words and the message, hoping to hell she could trick a demon with her magic. "I am the daughter of Alexei Yankov. My father is dead, as you must know. But he has left me instructions on how to proceed. I received the instructions by a timed email arranged by my father ten years ago. It arrived just one month ago, bringing me to Moscow, setting this in motion. It is fate. Destiny. Meant to be."

Brenna paused for a breath. There was no reply from Damyan. She tried to anticipate his questions. She needed to pepper the lies with just enough truth to make it palatable. Damyan's desperation would help him believe. She took a breath, and continued.

"The man who killed Mikhail and took me from him spoke Russian, but he may be American, may be Ukrainian. Perhaps he is government. CIA. Russian Intelligence. Maybe some other group. I do not know." She paused, gulped, then continued. "There was a shooting at the cafe. I assume it was you, or ordered by you. You were aiming for the man who killed Mikhail. It missed him, but I escaped in the confusion. I got this phone, this one that he took from Mikhail. It fell from his pocket. I got it and saw your name, knew it was fate for me to find you." She gulped, prayed, inhaled, exhaled. "I'm alone now, but the man is probably looking for me. The faster I can come to you, the better it will be. Tell me where you would like to meet."

She heard Damyan's breath catch. There was enough truth in what she said that her tone must have sounded genuine. She glanced at Bruiser, who was so furious his face was bright red like a beet in the sun.

"My father left me a message," she said again, thinking hard, knowing that was the most implausible part. "It was an automated email triggered by a bot. It is call a death-email. He set up a countdown timer. Set it for ten years. If he was still alive, he would have stopped the timer and the email would not have been sent. He did not stop the timer, so the email was triggered last month."

She paused, listened for his breathing, tried to tell if he was falling for it. She couldn't tell. No choice but to keep going.

"I know about the crypto account. My father used it to send me money for college. If you look at the transactions on the public address for the account, you will see I tell the truth." She swallowed. Her tongue was dry. Head was thundering with blood pounding in her ears. "I have the private key, Damyan. His email said he would never give it to you because the temptation to spend the money would be too great. He wanted the money to grow for a decade. Billions, not millions. That's what's in the account now. You've been watching it, haven't you? Nine billion now. Enough to do . . . big things. Great things. Just like you dreamed of. Just like my . . . my father dreamed of."

She winced, wondering if she was being too vague. But Damyan's breathing quickened for a moment, encouraging her.

"His instructions were to seek you out. He said the money was yours, the vision was yours, and the . . . the glory would be yours." She laughed nervously, then exhaled. "Of course, I had no clue how to find you. I mean, I looked you up, saw who you were, what you'd done." She chuckled. "Couldn't just call up the CIA or NSA and ask for your number, right? So I decided to fly to Moscow, start there. Maybe get to Ukraine. See if I got lucky, stumbled on something." She shrugged, even though Damyan couldn't see her. "Long shot, I know. But sometimes fate works out only if you a chance, gamble on the long shot, right?" She sighed. "Besides, it was my father's dying wish. I had to at least *try*, right? Worst case I figured I'd find my father's anonymous grave and put a headstone on it."

She felt a lump in her throat just then, and choked out a sob that came too quickly to be held back. It was real, no doubt about it. She felt it. She knew Damyan felt it.

Then she glanced at Bruiser and saw that he felt it too.

Felt the hand of fate.

The twist of destiny.

She almost had him. One more hit and Damyan might believe her.

She went back through her memories of Alexei. Back through those exciting times when he'd show up without warning, stay a few days on the green pull-out sofa in the den, fire up his big dark computer screens.

What was on those screens?

Lines of computer code.

Graphs with what looked like stock prices but were probably cryptocurrency charts.

Newsfeed, videos, email, chats.

Nothing special.

Nothing unusual.

Then something popped up in her mind.

Something she'd noticed only once.

The background images on his three big screens.

They'd always been hidden by the dozens of open windows and apps, except one morning when she was maybe five.

She'd walked into the den early, when Alexei was just starting up his computers and screens. She'd seen the background wallpaper. It was colorful, even beautiful. She'd asked what it was. He'd told her it was a flower opening up for the morning rain. She'd closed one eye and looked at it sideways. A flower. Sure. She could see that.

And she saw it again now. She could see those images clearly in her memory.

Beautiful blossoms, rising up like red-and-yellow clouds into a blue sky.

Mushroom shaped blossoms.

Mushroom shaped clouds.

And without stopping to think, Brenna started talking.

"I am ready," she whispered, not what why a sickening thrill raced up her spine. She wasn't sure if it was dread or excitement, but it came through in her voice. "I am ready to prove to you that I am my father's daughter. I am ready to continue his work, the work the two of you talked about so long ago. I am ready, Damyan. Ready for the . . . the mushroom cloud. Yes, the mushroom cloud, remember? Like a . . . a flower opening up."

She stopped and waited, resisted the urge to say another word. She had no idea if the mushroom clouds had any significance, were anything more than a random memory.

She waited. Listened.

It occurred to her that it was too long a shot, too dumb a move, too wild a guess. She winced and held her breath, feeling the embarrassment rise up her cheeks. So lame, she thought.

Then Damyan's breathing stopped.

Just for a moment, but it had definitely stopped.

She tensed up and listened hard. Waited for Damyan to speak, to say something, anything.

Damyan had not said a word yet.

He still didn't say a word.

The breathing was slow and deliberate again.

And suddenly it stopped again.

The line went dead.

Damyan had hung up.

Brenna's heart sank. She felt like an idiot. Blood rushed to her cheeks as she handed the phone back to Bruiser. She shrugged and gave him a little smile.

"Worth a try," she said lamely. "At least now we know what *won't* work."

Bruiser glanced at the phone, then looked into her eyes. "That was reckless. Borderline suicidal. Twisted and insane."

He took a breath like he was relieved.

Truth was, Brenna was kinda relieved too.

Her hands started to shake as the shock of what she'd just tried to do actually sank in.

What the hell was she thinking. How stupid could she get? Who did she think she was? A Superhero in black tights and bitch boots? Whew. Thank God it didn't work.

Bruiser's relief showed in a big grin. Then suddenly his brows knitted in a frown.

He looked at the phone quizzically.

It vibrated in his hand.

Vibrated once more.

Bruiser tapped on the phone, his face paling then hardening. His eyes narrowed and flashed.

"Like I said. That was stupid. Foolish. Twisted. Insane. Reckless. Suicidal." He glanced at the phone again, then handed it to Brenna. "Except it worked."

Brenna's heart almost smashed its way out through her ribcage. She could barely hold the phone, her hand was shaking so much. Finally she focused her eyes on the screen and saw two text messages from Damyan. They were in Russian.

You will send me the twelve words so I can verify they unlock the account.

That will prove you are your father's daughter.

Brenna read the messages again. Then one more time. Her heart thumped harder against the inside of her sternum. She tapped the screen again. Replied to Damyan's message. Thought a moment, then typed another longer message to Damyan. Handed the phone back to Bruiser.

He read her replies and stared, first at the phone, then at her. "Are you crazy? Just give him the damn words, Brenna. That's exactly what we want. It's exactly what Benson wants. This way you don't have to get anywhere near Damyan. It's perfect. Why did you just fuck it up? Why did you insist on meeting? What the hell is wrong with you?"

Brenna shuddered out a breath, sorted out her feelings, cleared her head. Or tried to, at least. "Mushroom clouds, Bruiser."

Bruiser chuckled. "Yeah, I heard that. Where did that come from?"

Brenna blinked. "Doesn't matter. What matters is that he reacted to it."

"Reacted how?"

Brenna shrugged. "Skipped a breath."

"Doesn't make it meaningful. He could've been wondering if you were nuts. After all, there's nothing in

Damyan's profile indicating he ever tried to get a nuclear weapon. He's not that kind of terrorist. The man likes to get his hands bloody. And his idealism leans towards the freedom-fighter end of the psycho-terrorist spectrum. He's not the apocalypse-now kinda madman. He's old-school."

The dreadful feeling snaked up her throat again when Brenna thought back to those wallpaper images. She pushed the sickness back down.

"Look," she said. "Giving him the secret words over the phone is a risk. We don't know how tech-savvy Damyan is, Bruiser. If he understands crypto and digital wallets, he might know how to create a new wallet with a new set of secret words—words that only he knows. So if he gets into my father's account, he might send all the cryptocurrency to his new wallet. He might even be advanced enough to create hidden wallets, write programs to hide the money in hundreds of hidden wallets, make it really difficult for the CIA to follow the payments. He's had ten years to learn, after all. You can learn almost anything on the web now. Maybe I can steer him away from doing that."

Bruiser rubbed the side of his head. "If he sends it to another crypto wallet, this whole operation is a bust. The CIA might still be able track the payments, but they won't be able to drain the accounts and cut Damyan off if things get dicey." He took a breath. "Especially if we're talking mushroom cloud cheeseburgers with extra radiation."

Bruiser tried to smile, but it came out tight and

strained. Brenna knew what he was thinking about. The Soviet Union. The Nuclear Arms Race. The end of the Cold War had left thousands of nuclear warheads in the hands of less-than-trustworthy government officials of the new Russia. The thought was too crazy to take seriously, but only because neither of them had been alive in 1945 to see that it was real as hell not so long ago, could be real as hell again.

Even if it was a tiny risk, the outcome was so vast you couldn't ignore it. Simple math.

Bruiser shook his head. "He's not tech savvy enough. Probably learned over the years, but not that much. I read Damyan's file. He's old school. Was never a spy. His military days were before things got too high tech. He never dealt with anything more complicated than a cell phone. He was pretty clueless about the regular banking systems to begin with—which is why the Russians and Americans seized all the UNA's accounts like taking a chewie from a puppy. I bet Damyan's crypto-knowledge is third-grade level tops."

"Good," said Brenna. "It'll give him more reason to meet. He might need me to show him how it works. Might make him trust me more. Might *force* him to trust me."

Bruiser's forehead crinkled. He shook his head, frowned deeper, then suddenly went wide-eyed. "Oh, shit, you *want* to meet him, don't you? You want to ask him about your father. You want to find out for sure if your father was a true believer in Damyan's violent mission. You want to know if Alexei Yankov, mysterious absentee-father who read Russian fairy tales to his half-American daughter was really a terrorist and a crook, really was capable of joining forces with some madman nicknamed the Demon who wants to burn the world with nuclear hellfire! You want to know what kind of blood runs in your veins, don't you? If you truly *are* your father's daughter."

"I . . . I don't know," Brenna stammered, blinking as Bruiser's words hit home in a way that made her want to curl over and cry.

But Bruiser was right and she knew it.

She did want to know.

She needed to know.

She *had* to know.

They both looked at the phone. It was silent and still. They looked at each other, tension thick in the burning air.

"He'll agree," Brenna said. "I know it. He's alone. He's broke. He doesn't know his way around all this crypto stuff." She blinked desperately, searching for something from the past. "And my father had a way with people, Bruiser. You trusted him, even if you knew he had secrets. You know what I mean? Kinda like what Ax said Benson is like. Secretive. Mysterious. But somehow you felt like trusting him. Something innocent and childlike in him, but also deep, maybe even a bit dark. Hard to explain. He was just . . . authentic. Infectiously authentic. Damyan must have liked my father to give him control of the UNA's finances like that. Which means maybe if Damyan killed him it still hurts in some way. Maybe he even feels guilt. Damyan might want his money, but I don't think he cares about revenge."

Bruiser's gaze narrowed, then relaxed in admiration. He considered her words, then nodded in agreement.

"Damyan was a Special Forces guy," he said softly. "I met some of the Russian Special Forces guys. Deep down we're all the same. We all form strong bonds, learn how to trust our brothers in arms, learn how to trust them with our backs. For all his brutality, maybe Damyan had that going for him. The capacity to form deep bonds, accept that you have to trust a few people in life, trust them completely. Not a lot of people, of course. But you gotta have *someone* you can trust."

Brenna blinked up at him and then nodded. "Damyan had Mikhail. And maybe he also had my father on his side." She paused. "Either way, they're both dead now. Damyan's truly alone now. He must be feeling it. Fear. Loneliness. Isolation. Maybe for the first time in his wretched life."

Bruiser shrugged, then stiffened as the phone vibrated. He looked at the screen and whistled.

"Shit, you got him, Brenna," he said as Damyan's messages started coming through. Bruiser grinned, even though there was worry in the grin, seriousness in the smile. "I guess even a demon feels vulnerable when he's alone. Even a demon wants to believe there's someone on his side."

22

Damyan Nagarev touched the left side of his face, then sat on the tree stump he'd been using as a stool. He'd made his way back to the wilderness preserve, not far from where he'd stolen the rifle. This part of the woods was thick, the trees fighting for territory, their canopies capturing so much of the sunlight that the air looked dark green even in the afternoon.

Damyan stretched out his legs and ran his index finger along the thick scar that ranged from his eyebrow down to the side of his mouth. It had been badly stitched by a mediocre veterinarian who was also a butcher and a barber. The fat-fingered man had practiced all his professions out of the same squalid storefront in the ghettoes of Moscow. Apparently the work blended well. Perhaps a few conflicts of interest, but there were many conflicts in those early days living in the second-floor brothels of those crumbling gray Soviet-era buildings of their ghetto.

Damyan remembered stumbling down the stairs, blinded by his own blood, holding his face together with his eight-year-old hands. The veterinarian had grunted and held out his hand for advance payment. Damyan had spat blood into his open palm.

"My mother will pay you like she always does, you miserly bastard," he'd shouted through his pain.

Of course his mother did not pay in rubles. She paid with her body. Damyan learned early on that a woman's body was valuable, could be used to trade for things. That was one of the reasons he found Mikhail's needs distasteful.

Still, he tolerated Mikhail's perversions. One did not judge a friend, a man who could be trusted, a man who had shown loyalty beyond any doubt.

Yes, it seemed strange to think it now, but Mikhail had been a friend.

A friend who was now dead.

The pilots had told Damyan where to find Mikhail's body. They described the Yankova woman's captor—whoever he was. CIA, Military, Russian, American. One of those or none of those. Either way, he had to believe Yankova. She said things that made Damyan believe. Made him *want* to believe.

Made him want to believe that he had done the right thing all those years ago.

The pilots had begged for their lives, their high-pitched Spanish pleas bypassing Damyan's limited understanding of the language. He cut their throats anyway.

It was not about anger. It was not about revenge. Damyan had long ago defeated the demon of vengeance. He would miss Mikhail, but he would not do something rash in some drive to avenge him. If Mikhail lost a fight, then he deserved to die. That was how it was in battle.

So he killed the pilots with cold calculation, while looking into their eyes. Did it slow and careful, watching the eyes roll up and turn white, then staring at the blood ooze slow at first before exploding when he sliced the artery. He cut all the way to the bone, just like they taught him in Special Forces. Technique was important. Part of it was to make sure your enemy is dead. The other part is to strike terror in the hearts of the ones who were still alive, the ones who found him. War is a game played with both body and mind.

Damyan wondered about the game unfolding with Alexei's daughter. He'd known about her for ten years, ever since Alexei's death. But after paying many agents and investigators to track her down, Damyan had resigned himself to the possibility that Alexei had somehow hacked into computer records and erased all trace of their connection.

Damyan's investigators had not found any marriage records for Alexei. No birth records naming him as a father. They checked Ukraine, Russia, most of the neighboring countries in Eastern Europe for a child born to him.

When nothing turned up, Damyan hired more expensive agents, expanded the search to Western Europe and finally the United States. It was costly to search the United States systems, but it would be worth it to find Alexei's daughter.

She'd been his last desperate hope to get into the publicly-viewable but untouchable crypto account that he watched grow larger and larger. It was like staring at a treasure chest from behind an impenetrable glass wall. Torture in a way that tore at Damyan's insides, especially as his stash of paper dollars dwindled over the years.

But nothing came up in the United States.

Nothing came up anywhere.

Still, Damyan kept the searches going over the years, doing what he needed to pay agents to hack into systems and break through firewalls.

Dead ends.

Month after month.

Year after year.

The untouchable money grew to millions, then billions.

Fate was laughing at Damyan and Mikhail.

Destiny was taunting them.

Then, ten years later, ten days before today, Damyan's agent in Eastern Europe got a hit on Alexei Yankov.

"Russian Secret Police filed a report with Yankov's name in it," the agent told Damyan. "They picked up a woman for questioning in Moscow. American woman who speaks Russian. Her name is Brenna Yankova. She claims to be looking for her father's gravesite. She says her father's name was Alexei Yankov. He is supposedly buried in a government cemetery for unclaimed bodies."

Damyan had scarcely been able to speak. "How did she find out about him?" he asked hoarsely, his mind whipping back ten years, to everything that had happened with Alexei.

It had felt like fate back then.

It felt like fate again.

"She told the Russian Police that she ran her own DNA against some database funded by an offshore non-profit," the agent said haltingly, like he was reading from notes. "Let us see . . . ah, here. A database with DNA of unidentified dead bodies. Human Identification Project. Huh. Who knew of such a thing. Anyway, there was a 50% match with her DNA and DNA taken from an unidentified murder victim in Ukraine. She believes it is her father." He laughed. "Can you believe the Ukrainian police were methodical enough to record a dead no-name's DNA ten years ago?"

Yes, it felt like fate again, Damyan had thought as he listened to the rest of it, formulating a plan that he never thought he'd have the good fortune to make.

And now the plan seemed to be twisting in ways that surprised him. Perhaps there was something about Alexei's proclamations about fate and destiny all those years ago. He'd thought Alexei was a madman—and perhaps he was. But even madmen sometimes speak wisdom in their madness.

Damyan looked at his watch, the shell of that once beautiful Patek-Phillippe. He could not get himself to sell it, instead saving money in other ways. By now he rarely spent money on anything other than food. Mikhail's women had been Damyan's only extravagance. He'd only paid for them because he knew Mikhail would seek to fulfill his need either way. It was better to do it in a controlled manner.

Now his mind turned to the situation. He tried to think with a cold head.

And cold logic told him he could not trust Brenna Yankova. Certainly the man was with her and was a government agent. Alexei Yankov had been dead ten years.

Surely he could not be sending messages from beyond the grave. He had read about such robot-controlled timed emails, though. And if anyone was capable of doing that, it was Alexei Yankov.

Now again doubt clouded his mind. Perhaps Brenna spoke the truth. She was Alexei's daughter, after all. She was also Russian, Damyan reminded himself. So the big man could also be Russian. Perhaps the prison warden leaked that Damyan was interested in a prisoner. Perhaps the man was mafia or freelance, sent to intercept Damyan's prize. It was hard to tell from that one look through his hunting-rifle's scope. It was even harder to tell sitting alone on a tree-stump, out of options, virtually forced to take the chance that she was indeed her father's daughter.

Damyan rubbed his eyes. The eerie green light of sun filtering through dense foliage put him in an odd dreamlike state. There were many inconsistencies that raised doubt in Damyan's mind. Many questions that needed answers before he could be certain about anything.

First, if the man was American CIA, then why not fly straight to America with the woman?

If he was Russian Intelligence, then Moscow was barely two hour's trip from Kiev.

So why stop in Costa Rica? It made no sense. It was a sunny, peaceful democracy. No American military installations. No CIA presence other than perhaps an attaché at the Embassy. The pilots did not know why they had been ordered to land there. They had claimed there was enough fuel, so it was not a refueling stop. Puzzling.

Yes, a puzzle indeed. Could it just be random, Damyan wondered. Misdirection? Deliberately breaking up a pattern to make things seem unpredictable?

Were they hiding? But from whom? Damyan himself? But surely a man who had just defeated Mikhail would not be too afraid of Damyan. Who else might they be hiding from? Who else might they be trying to misdirect?

Perhaps the big man is a rogue agent, Damyan thought as his paranoia ate at him. Perhaps he has been hired by an unknown party who also knows about the money. Others who might have known about Alexei, known he had a daughter.

His thoughts drifted back to Brenna Yankova's voice. Cool and confident, with a subtle intensity. And she was intelligent, just like her father. Damyan had not said a word, yet she had anticipated his questions and answered them, predicted his doubts and addressed them.

She sounded genuine. Authentic.

Perhaps her father Alexei Yankov had been close to her, had talked about colorful mushroom clouds on video screens, dazzled her with stories from when she was a girl with an open heart and a moldable mind.

She had mentioned the mushroom cloud. The flower opening up with colors bold and deadly. That could not just be a coincidence. Too random to be dismissed. Alexei *must* have talked about it.

And if he did talk about it, then perhaps Brenna Yankova tells the truth. Perhaps Alexei's daughter carries on his mission, Damyan thought. Maybe like her father she lives in that world of computer games and robotic trickery, has that same dangerous disconnect from the real world.

After all, she has her father's blood in her.

Perhaps she has her father's demon growing inside her too.

Is that why we are brought together again, he wondered in the misty green glow of the forest canopy.

Fate?

Destiny?

Did I make the wrong choice killing her father?

Is this redemption for me or revenge for her?

Perhaps it is neither. Maybe it is both.

Damyan sighed and touched his scar again, this time running the barrel of Mikhail's Glock handgun along the bump which still showed every amateur stitch from when he was eight. The metal felt cool against his skin.

He tapped the gun lightly against his skull. It made a tinny sound against the titanium plate that covered an old shrapnel wound that had fractured his skull.

"Think with a cold head," he muttered in Russian. "Do not let yourself believe what you *want* to believe. Ask yourself why Brenna Yankova did not come directly to you if she was working with Alexei. Does she suspect I murdered him? Does she *know* I murdered him? Is this revenge? Is she just looking for answers? What is it, Damyan. Think."

Perhaps it is a simpler answer, he decided. She did not know where you were, so she could not come to you directly. That is what she said, and it must be true. After all, Alexei did not have time to voice any suspicions to his daughter before he died. He barely had time to finish his utterance of surprise before Damyan's bullets smashed into him.

The most Brenna would know about Damyan's connection to her father would be if Alexei had told her how excited he was to be working with the great Damyan Nagarev himself.

Of course. That was the answer, Damyan told himself. The simplest answer is usually correct. Do not drive yourself mad. She could not find you, and now she has found you. Fate guided her to you, and now you must follow through.

Besides, what option do you have, old man? You are running low on money, have lost the only man you ever trusted, have been driven insane for ten years watching that money grow beyond your grasp. Think what that money can do for you now. Imagine building an army like you once dreamed.

Nine billion can build an army that can invade Russia if you want, he thought with wild glee, the same kind of boyish delight he'd recognized and liked in Alexei.

Yes, a better army than the group of mercenaries that formed the core of the original UNA, he thought with sad anger. When the UNA's money was seized, all his so-called true believers left for other better-funded causes, and Damyan had to run, taking no one but Mikhail with him. The only true believer Damyan had left. Perhaps the only he had ever had.

For months he and Mikhail hid like dogs, roaming Ukraine's smaller cities, always on the move, always looking for a Russian agent across the street, an American assassin in the shadows. Damyan's reputation was no longer an asset but a liability. The UNA had struck Russian diplomats, had made a mark. They were branded a Terror Organization, which made Damyan Nagarev a terrorist.

So Damyan and Mikhail had to stay anonymous. No money, unable to trade on reputation, they were no more than common street thugs, stealing from drug dealers and pimps, sometimes even the whores that Mikhail could not stop himself from taking in his twisted way.

The downward spiral continued for months, maybe longer, it was hard to say now.

Then Damyan met Alexei Yankov, and everything changed.

Damyan bellowed loudly now, smacking the gun hard against his temple again, banging that titanium plate, sending a sickening shudder through his reconstructed skull. He thought back to his first conversation with the lanky, dark-haired Yankov who reminded him of Rasputin—if Rasputin had been a computer genius.

But not just a computer genius, Damyan thought with a grunt of admiration. A financial mastermind as well. Two hours and twelve vodka-shots into that first meeting, Alexei had used his mobile phone to recover almost three hundred thousand dollars of the UNA's lost funds.

"The U.S. government usually just drains the so-called terrorist accounts it seizes," Alexei had explained in Russian. His accent was distinctly upper class. "It all goes to a slush fund that is held behind the Treasury

Department's Firewall. Very hard to break in without being detected, perhaps tracked. The Treasury Department does not sound as fearsome as the CIA or NSA, but they are more powerful in a silent way. Do not mess with them, is my policy."

He'd rapped his knuckles on the darkwood bar, waited until the heavyset barwoman who smelled like onions refilled their shot glasses from a vodka bottle sitting in a steel tub of half-melted ice mixed with sawdust.

Alexei took his shot, smacked his lips, wiped his beard, and continued, his dark eyes shining like Rasputin whispering secrets to Catherine the Great. "But they missed a few accounts," he whispered excitedly. "Certainly, they froze the funds so no one can withdraw them through the bank. But they did not drain the accounts." He'd tapped his finger to his head. "What they missed, we have recovered." He smiled, wagged his finger. "You kept many accounts at many different banks, Damyan. Diversification. Good strategy."

Damyan had grinned. Perhaps it was the vodka, but he liked this earnest dark-haired man with eyes like Rasputin. He trusted him. Until then Damyan had trusted no one but Mikhail. It made Damyan pay attention. It made him let his guard down. Open up a bit.

"It was not strategy," Damyan said through the grin. "It was because I am disorganized with such things. I did not grow up with phones and computers. I find them tedious." He'd shrugged. "But I learned early in life that you do not trust money to another. Money is like a demon that whispers in your ear, tempts people to betray you. So I handled all of it myself. Not a wise choice, it appears. Now Mikhail and I have to steal just to pay for vodka."

"It is my honor to buy vodka for the great Damyan Nagarev," Alexei had said, summoning the barwoman again. "I heard about you years ago when I was an anarchist graduate student. You had good ideas. Simple, but powerful. I am half-Ukrainian on my mother's side, and because of you I saw the world through Ukrainian eyes. Angry Ukrainian eyes."

Damyan had listened as Alexei Yankov flattered him in his smooth upper-class Russian accent. Flatterers usually disgusted Damyan. They put him on guard, made him feel like he was being set up.

But for some reason Alexei's words felt genuine. They were infused with the awe a boy might have for his father, Damyan imagined. Of course, Damyan was only speculating. His own father was not even a memory in his mother's long list of patrons. And Damyan was not father to any boys himself. None that were still alive, at least.

"Flattery usually gets you killed in my army," Damyan had said with a smile. "My trusted man Mikhail has never bothered to flatter me, yes, old friend?"

They'd both turned to look at Mikhail, who towered above them. The vodka was getting to him too, though not as fast. He was swaying on his feet like an oak tree in a gentle wind. He opened his mouth and wagged his stump of a tongue.

Damyan watched for Alexei's reaction. The typical reaction to Mikhail's mouth was shock or disgust followed by a morbid curiosity. Alexei revealed nothing but his clean white teeth as he laughed. He did not ask about Mikhail's mutilation.

"I saw one of your UNA speeches online," Alexei said. "It struck me to the core. You asked no soldier to bow before you. You said you were a leader not a king, a brother not a father. You said you expect loyalty to the death. But loyalty to the cause, not the man. It was profound. It was real. It brought me here, Damyan. Yes, this is a chance meeting, but I feel like I was brought here, you were brought here. Brought together like fate, like destiny, like it was pre-ordained."

Alexei downed his vodka with a gulp, smacked the thick shot-glass down on the bar, raised a crisp one hundred dollar bill to summon the barwoman.

"You carry American dollars?" Damyan had asked stiffly.

Alexei had shrugged. "It is the only money that does not lose value as it sits in your pocket. All other paper money is good only to clean your arsehole." After paying he'd turned on his stool, leaned close. "Still, U.S. Dollars are far from perfect money. But the beautiful thing is that perfect money has been invented. It is still early, still very technical, very complicated. And that means there is opportunity here." He'd paused, stroked his beard, thought for a long moment. "I have a proposition for you. These three hundred thousand dollars I will recover for you . . . perhaps we consider it a display of my skills. An audition, if you will. A taste of what is possible. For both of us. Yes?"

Alexei went on, his Rasputin-eyes shining as the vodka kept flowing. Damyan had listened. So had Mikhail. Two battle-hardened men from the old world listening to a bright-eyed zealot from a new world they did not quite understand, perhaps did not want to understand.

Before the morning sun came up over the gray buildings Damyan had agreed to Alexei's proposition. Perhaps it was premature, even reckless. But Damyan and Mikhail's old ways appeared to have led to a dead end. What choice did Damyan have but to roll the dice with this strange man who spoke of fate and destiny and electronic money that could not be seized by even the Americans, money beyond the powerful reach of the U.S. Treasury Department who had destroyed the UNA without firing a single bullet.

Over the next month Alexei made good on his promise, showed off his skills. The long-haired hacker moved the three hundred thousand from the frozen accounts, routing them to anonymous wire-services in countries all over the former Soviet Union: Uzbekistan, Kazakhstan, Belarus, and some places even Damyan had not heard of.

When Alexei returned to Kiev a month later, he invited them to the agreed-upon meeting spot, a guest house on the hard side of town. Damyan had recommended it because it was a place where everyone minded their own business. On the neat single bed was a hard-shelled Samsonite suitcase with a combination lock. Alexei turned the tiny dials, popped the top, and stepped back.

Damyan and Mikhail peered into it, their eyes going wide at the sight of stacks of hundred dollar bills, some new, some old, counted out in ten-thousand dollar blocks tied with red elastic bands.

"The places I used charge very high fees for anonymity," Alexei said as Mikhail started to count. "I also deducted my expenses. Travel and lodging. A little food. Plenty of vodka."

Mikhail finished counting and wrote down the number. It was just over one hundred thousand dollars.

Damyan had frowned. "Not to look a gift horse in the mouth, my dear Alexei, but the total you recovered was three hundred thousand. Yes, expenses I can understand, but to spend two hundred thousand dollars on vodka seems excessive, do you not agree?"

Alexei had grinned. "Expenses were nineteen thousand four hundred thirty three dollars and eleven cents. This hundred thousand in cash is for you and Mikhail to go underground, disappear for some time so the trail goes cold for the CIA and Russian Intelligence. They may lose interest. The bounty on your head will eventually slip off the list. People will stop looking. You can live in peace while you prepare for war."

Damyan had seen the fire in Alexei's eyes, felt that inexplicable trust for this man, was infected by his energy. "And you?"

"To go to war, an army needs a war chest," Alexei said simply. "I will build a treasury for your UNA. In a form of money that cannot be seized by the U.S. Treasury and does not need suitcases to transport. Cryptocurrency. I told you about it when we spoke, yes? Magic money that lives only in the computer. Just like everything these days lives behind a computer screen. It is where we will all live in a few decades."

Damyan had blinked, frowning as he tried to make

sense of Alexei's nonsense. He remembered the talk of magic money protected by cryptography and computer programs or something like that. "You will convert the rest of my dollars to this . . . this coded currency?" Damyan asked.

"Cryptocurrency. It is not a conversion but an investment. Seed capital. We will plant the seeds and wait for them to sprout."

"How long will the seeds take to sprout?" Damyan asked after a long pause.

Alexei shrugged. "They are already sprouting. Cryptocurrency grows fast. But mere saplings will do you no good. It is better to wait until they grow into trees. Thick, with deep roots. Many trees. A forest. Endless. Inexhaustible." He'd grinned again. "In two years this money will grow to millions. But in five years it might be billions. In ten years it could be even more!"

Damyan took a slow breath, glanced at his old warhorse Mikhail, then back at Alexei. "Ten years is an eternity. I do not need billions. You can do a lot with just millions," he said. "Buy weapons and supplies for thousands of men."

Alexei snorted. "Thousands of *men*? That is the old way of war. Now with technology even a single well-financed, well-connected man can wage war on nations. Besides, the young men of today have no stomach for marching into war. They rebel on the Internet, fight their battles with memes and tweets. They are inspired by grand imagery and breathtaking violence on the screen. The bigger the better. Drones destroying buses and trains. Missiles raining down on cities. And, of course, the grandest of spectacles: A mushroom cloud, opening like a flower in the rain, streaks of orange, splashes of red, gray-black skies lit up like a painting, poetic imagery that will remind the world that America committed more genocide than everyone else put together, yes?"

Damyan had stared, wondering if Alexei was joking, sincere, or just insane.

Alexei had shaken his head, his long wavy hair shivering like snakes under the yellow light. "Forget that outdated dream of thousands of soldiers with rifles and bayonets, Damyan. Raising an army of men will be a waste. You will simply build another army of mercenaries. The new UNA will be just us, Damyan. With me at the controls we can wage war like it is a game. Which it is, of course. It has always been a game. All boys like to play games, yes? And all men are still boys at heart, are they not?"

Damyan had stared into Alexei's shining eyes, seen the boy in the man, the madness in the mind. He wondered what he was getting into, whether Alexei was playing him like a puppet.

"You can play these games yourself," Damyan challenged calmly, flexing his thigh, dropping his left hand down to his German-made HK 9mm pistol in the cargo flap of his pants. "Why do you even need me? Like you say, Mikhail and I are of the old world. We cannot play these computer games with unmanned drones and computer guided missiles. Mikhail can barely type a coherent text message with his big thumbs. Show him your thumbs, Mikhail."

Mikhail had grinned and held up his hands. Alexei had laughed, but his laughter stuck in his throat when those big hands of the Tongueless One closed around his neck.

Damyan drew his HK pistol but held it down along his thigh. Alexei's eyes went wide, like a kid seeing a real gun for the first time. Damyan was partly amused, partly disgusted.

Alexei was youthful looking, with thick hair and lively eyes. But there were deep lines across his forehead, the beginnings of wrinkles around those sharp dark eyes. He must be in his forties at least, Damyan thought. Perhaps even fifty or older. He was not a man, though. He was a boy, living in his own head, perhaps in the world behind those computer screens.

Yes, Damyan thought as his disgust grew. An overgrown boy. Just like the ones he'd seen in those cafes sitting at long lines of tables, staring at computer screens, pecking at keyboards. Those cafes were all over Eastern Europe now. Full of hunched, skinny men with blotchy skin that had not been exposed to sunlight in years. Staring wild-eyed at screens all day and night. They were boys, not men. Just like Alexei was a boy, not a man.

"Mushroom cloud? Nuclear attack?" Damyan muttered in disbelief. He shook his head. "There is no more cowardly form of war than that. Burning entire cities to dust? Destroying farms and crops and livestock? Ruining generations through radiation that hangs in the air for years, damages the genes? Have you seen the children of Chernobyl? The ruins of Nagasaki and Hiroshima? That is not war." He spat on the floor-tiles, then shook his head again. "Not my sort of war, at least. I go to battle against men, not women and children, not cattle and pigs. I fight soldiers, politicians, whether they be military or mafia, elected or appointed. And if I take an innocent life—and I have taken many—then I do it myself, looking into the eyes of the man I kill."

Damyan shook his head once more, tried to smile, tried to push away the sickness creeping up his spine. He could not understand his revulsion. He had met countless bad men, violent psychopaths, dark-hearted sociopaths, genocidal maniacs. This Alexei was different, though. There was a childish innocence to him, an earnest authenticity. It was what had made Damyan trust the man.

And it was what made Damyan fear the man.

This was a man for whom reality was images on a screen. Colorful explosions. Drones hunting down terrorists and their entire families in Afghanistan. Missiles destroying schools and hospital buildings in Yemen. And ah yes, those beautiful mushroom clouds in slow motion. The most terrible of sights mankind ever conceived. He sees beauty in that? A flower opening up?! Poetry in slow motion?!

What happened to a freedom-fighter actually *fighting* for his freedom? Pushing buttons and watching death on a screen was not fighting. There was no honor in it. Yes, all war was a game. But it was a game that needed to be played in the real world. A warrior needed to feel the warm blood of his enemy. Hear the whip-crack of bullets. Taste the adrenaline. Smell the fear.

Damyan tightened his grip on his HK. He had no illusions about himself. He knew in his dark heart that he had killed many civilians and would do so again. Casualties of war, he'd always told himself.

But it was deeper than that. There was a sickness in Damyan's heart that made him enjoy it. Not like Mikhail, but in Damyan's own way. There was no remorse when he pulled the trigger or broke a man's neck. There was no guilt when he let Mikhail do what he did with the women.

Yes, Damyan did get a thrill that was sickeningly addictive when he smelled warm blood, saw the red juice of life pump out of a man's severed artery or a punctured heart. He welcomed the nickname of Demon, cultivated that reputation out of both practicality and a secret vanity.

No, Damyan was not a good man. He knew it. Accepted it. Loved it. There was a beautiful simplicity to it. Some men were good, others were bad. So easy.

But Alexei was something different. It was the innocence and excitement that confused Damyan. Just like the ambiguous Babayaga witches in those old fairy tales, he truly could not tell if Alexei was a good man or a bad man.

All he knew was that Alexei was a *dangerous* man.

"Answer me, Alexei," Damyan said softly, that gun still by his side. "Why do you need me at all? Why seek me out? Why help me? With your skills you can drain bank accounts and enrich yourself. Do what you do with the cryptographic computer money. Play your video games with drones and robots. Show the world the terrible beauty of your mushroom clouds. What use do you have for a couple of washed up old brutes like us?"

"I told you," said Alexei. "I saw your videos when I was in university. Many years ago, but I remember them vividly. You had thick golden hair back then. It was long like mine is now. Your eyes were very blue. You spoke like a man with a purpose. A vision. A . . . a story."

Damyan frowned, touched his scar, then ran his palm over his close-cropped hair. Was this more flattery? Perhaps. But there again was that spark of excitement in his Rasputin-like eyes. Was this part of Alexei's video game? Was Damyan just a character in this boy-man's made-up world?

Damyan was quiet for a long moment. He glanced at Mikhail, read his old friend's eyes. Then he looked at Alexei and shook his head.

"This is not my vision, Alexei. I am sorry. It is my mistake for not asking enough questions earlier, perhaps not understanding you well enough," Damyan had said quietly. "So here is what we will do: For recovering those lost UNA accounts, you will keep a commission. Let us say twenty percent. What is twenty percent of three hundred thousand?"

Alexei blinked. "Sixty thousand."

Damyan nodded. "And your expenses were twenty thousand?"

Alexei nodded. "Nineteen thousand, four hun—"

Damyan waved him quiet. "So you keep your commission of sixty thousand, plus the expense reimbursement of twenty. Then you return the balance to us. We go our separate ways. That money is plenty of seeds for you to plant in your make-believe garden in the computer screen. I hope they sprout like you say. Then you can play your video games by yourself. Yes?"

Alexei blinked. He glanced at the gun. Looked into Damyan's eyes. Alexei's expression hardened. His dark eyes grew cold. There was a flash of disappointment in there. Maybe a hint of resentment. A boy being rejected by his father.

Damyan brushed it off at first. But then that odd creeping feeling rose up his back again, like disembodied claws climbing up his spine, closing around his throat.

What was that feeling, Damyan wondered. It felt like a mistake, he thought. Like turning Alexei away would be a mistake.

It was almost like Damyan's choice right then would have massive ramifications for the world. What was this damn feeling? Was it the demon in him whispering? Was it an angel in the background fighting for Damyan's forsaken soul?

What had Alexei said about fate? About destiny? About a sense of being drawn to some place, some time, some thing? Was that what Damyan was feeling?

And if so, what should he do about it?

What choice should he make?

"The rest of my money," Damyan said. "Where is it?" He looked towards the open closet for another suitcase, then glanced under the bed. There was nothing anywhere except Alexei's slim black synthetic backpack on a chair by the window.

Alexei grinned. "No more bags of greasy cash handled by a million grubby fingers. The rest of your money is in digital form. Magic money. It is in a crypto wallet. Here. I will show you. Perhaps you will change your mind when you see that even in a month the money has increased in value. The seeds are sprouting. There is still time to change your mind, Damyan. I told you, it is fate that we met, destiny that brought our paths together."

Damyan grunted noncommittally. Alexei hurried over to the desk and flipped open a black laptop computer. A cartoonish picture of a padlock showed up on the screen. Alexei pressed his thumb to a sensor below the keypad. The padlock disappeared and the screen lit up. Alexei's fingers flew over the keyboard. A window with numbers all over the place showed up.

"This long number is the public address for the wallet," Alexei explained. "Crypto wallets are anonymous, but anyone can see the balance just by typing in this public address." Alexei pointed at another number. "This is the balance. Hold on. Let me change the view to show the U.S. Dollar value. There. See?"

Damyan saw, and his eyes went wide at the sight. The money had grown threefold in just one month. It was astounding. Unbelievable. He did some clunky calculations in his mind. His temples throbbed. His heart pumped. His mind felt clear. His head buzzed with the energy of that golden-haired younger man who spoke with vision and purpose, inspired an army only to lose them when he ran out of cash.

Damyan had resented it then, but he understood it now.

He understood immediately that money was power, energy, perhaps even magic. If this magic money grew like Alexei said it would grow, in a year or two the UNA could be financed again, with more men and better supplies than before. Even mercenaries would become true believers with that kind of money, yes?

Yes, he thought. He and Mikhail could hide outside the Ukraine while those magic seeds grew. Just a year or two would do it at this rate. Perhaps they could hide in South America, where money went far and protection was cheap. They could stop living like hunted dogs, regain their strength, their vigor, that old sense of purpose.

That old sense of purpose that was already burning in Damyan like something new.

Something that whispered that Alexei was right about one thing at least:

This was fate.

Destiny.

Meant to be.

It was Alexei's fate that he was led here to Damyan.

To a man known as the Demon.

A man perhaps uniquely qualified to recognize another demon in the making.

A demon who had not yet spread his dark wings.

And never would.

Damyan glanced at the computer screen, at the numerical address of the digital wallet that contained his money. He did not understand all the details, but he could figure them out. He was not a caveman. He knew how to use the Internet. You type questions and receive answers. Find instructions for things such as this. So long as he had that wallet account number, yes?

As Damyan watched the screen, it suddenly went blank. That cartoonish padlock showed up again. Damyan frowned.

"Yes?" said Alexei, pushing down the laptop lid, then turning to Damyan and smiling.

"No," said Damyan softly. "No robots controlled by joysticks from the safety of your computer screen. No mushroom clouds that will destroy millions while you see a flower opening up. One day when I am gone demons like you may roam the earth, but for now you should stay in hell. Mikhail and I will be there eventually. We can meet again in the fiery pit, laugh about fate, drink to destiny. Yes?"

"No!" shouted Alexei, perhaps suddenly seeing Damyan's decision, feeling the fear, tasting the adrenaline. "You idiot, without me you cannot—"

Damyan raised his weapon and fired twice. Both bullets hit Alexei in the chest, sending splinters of bone and shards of flesh all over the room. Alexei's lean body whipped back against the wall. He stood there and blinked, looked down at the holes in his chest, touched the warm blood that his fading heart pumped in spurts.

Then Damyan put a third bullet in his forehead and nodded to Mikhail.

"Knife," said Damyan, kneeling beside Alexei's body.

Mikhail handed him a knife. Damyan extended Alexei's right arm, pressed his palm flat on the tiled floor, and with one clean stroke cut off the thumb at the joint. He briefly remembered that old butcher who cut off all sorts of things in the store below his mother's brothel.

"You know how to use the camera on your phone, yes, Mikhail?" he said, standing and lifting the laptop lid.

The padlock appeared on the screen.

Damyan pressed Alexei's severed thumb to the sensor pad.

Held his breath.

The padlock disappeared.

The screen lit up.

The wallet number was still there.

"Take photos of that number," Damyan ordered. "Check to make sure it can be seen clearly. Send them to my phone. We should both keep copies."

Mikhail held up his phone. Damyan heard the camera sound, a fake shutter clicking. He strode to the bed, closed the suitcase with the cash. It would be more than enough to buy passports, plane tickets to South America. He had heard Argentina was a good place for European fugitives. The Germans had been running there since the 1940s. Many ex-Soviet government people had fled there after Communism fell. Damyan and Mikhail would barely be noticed.

Damyan closed Alexei's laptop, slid it into the backpack, then slung the pack over his broad back. He glanced down at the severed thumb, grunted, and put it into his right cargo flap.

"Take his wallet, keys, phone, anything of value in his pockets," Damyan said to Mikhail. "We can leave him here. No one will check the room until he stinks." He thought a moment. "Cut off the rest of his fingers. Knock out his teeth. Make the face unrecognizable. If we make it hard to identify him, perhaps the police will not bother."

Of course, a body could be identified by DNA tests, Damyan knew, but only if the Ukraine police had Alexei's DNA in the first place. That was unlikely unless he had been arrested for a physical crime, which did not seem to be Alexei's thing. It would also require the Ukraine police to actually give a damn.

Within a week Damyan and Mikhail were settled in Buenos Aires with a suitcase of hundred dollar bills, a laptop computer, and Alexei's thumb which had been smuggled on dry ice and kept in a freezer in the ranch-house they were renting outside the city.

It took another three days before Damyan figured out how to change the padlock-screen to accept his own fingerprint. It felt like a victory, and Damyan had chuckled at how he and Mikhail had struggled with something that had turned out to be quite simple.

But although the old-world brutes stumbled their way down the rabbithole of cryptocurrency admirably, to their dismay they found themselves smack against a dead end, a stone wall, an impenetrable barrier known as C-1559 Cryptography.

And then Damyan was able to finish Alexei's last sentence. A dying declaration that was cut short by reality in the form of two 9mm bullets travelling at the speed of sound.

Without me you cannot move that money, you idiots, Alexei would have said.

The public address lets you look at the money.
But you can't touch it without a private key.
Window shopping only, you fools.

"It appears we need what is called a private key," Damyan had muttered with barely restrained frustration at himself, his own impatience, perhaps arrogance. "It must be on the computer. They say it is represented by twelve English words. It must be somewhere. We will find it sooner or later."

But they found nothing that worked. Not in Alexei's files. Not in his emails. Not in his documents.

They did, however, find something of interest in his image gallery.

A photograph of a younger Alexei, reclining on a black swivel chair, three massive computer screens behind him on a desk, a chubby, healthy baby girl in his arms.

A baby girl with dark eyes that shone with that same energy.

A baby daughter.

Her father's daughter.

23

"What do you know about her father, Benson?"

Bruiser held the phone to his ear as he walked towards the Embassy Gates. He saw the armed sentry who had laughed at the sight of Bruiser overflowing out of a red scooter's side-car. He set his jaw, narrowed his eyes, tried to look as menacing as possible. It wasn't hard. The guard stiffened when he saw Bruiser approaching from across the Embassy lawn.

"Talk fast, Benson," Bruiser said. "I got shit to do here. Brenna's meeting Damyan in thirty minutes. I need to get there before she does, set up for a shot in case things get sketchy."

"Things are already sketchy, Bruiser," said Benson. There were traffic sounds in the background. He was in the city. No idea which city, though.

"Alexei Yankov," said Bruiser impatiently. "His file was so bare-bones that I *know* you're hiding something, Benson. This isn't the damn time to jerk me around with your games."

"Someone's playing games here, but it isn't me," said Benson. "Not this time." He took a breath and went quiet for a bit. The street sounds faded. Benson must have gotten somewhere and parked. "Look, Yankov's file is pretty bare-bones. But not because I'm hiding anything. It's because there's nothing much in there. Born in Moscow to a Russian father and a Ukrainian mother. Upper middle-class but not fabulously wealthy or anything. Brilliant student. Full scholarship to the old Leningrad Institute. No disciplinary problems recorded in school or college. No criminal records. Not even a traffic violation."

"Isn't that *too* clean?" Bruiser said. "He was a hacker, wasn't he?"

"Why do you say that?" Benson asked shiftily.

Bruiser chuckled. "Got'cha. Brenna said he was always hunched over computer monitors." He paused. "Also, there was an IRS audit on Brenna's Treasury Department file that was shut down and sealed. Brenna says she never got notified of any audit. I believe her."

Benson sighed. "We saw that sealed audit too. Looked into it. Kaiser's tech guys say it was clean."

"Definitely clean?"

"Nothing's definite. He says sure, it *could* be a hack, but if so, it was so perfectly done that it was indistinguishable from someone in the Treasury doing it from the inside."

"So if Alexei was a hacker, then he was a great hacker. Is that what you're telling me, Benson?"

Bruiser kept his strides long as he got closer to the nervous sentry. Glanced at the guard's rifle. M-16 standard issue. No scope. Didn't have the range of an M-11 or M-13 sniper rifle, but the M-16 was very accurate from even a few hundred yards. It would have to do. He slowed down a bit to let the sentry stew while he squeezed Benson for more.

"He was killed ten years ago, Bruiser," said Benson. "Hell, the Ukrainian Police report wasn't even digitized. Had to get it translated from a cell-phone picture the Ukrainian PD sent us."

"And?"

"Shot three times. Close range. Two in the chest. One in the head." He paused. "Fingers cut off. Teeth removed. Face slashed beyond recognition. Buried him as a John Doe—or the Russian version of it. Johann Dostoevsky, maybe."

"That's racist, Benson."

"I'll be sure to attend a sensitivity-training class," Benson quipped. He thought a moment. "Had to be Damyan who killed Alexei, don't you think?"

"Yes." He waited a breath.

"Does Brenna know?" Benson asked.

Bruiser stopped a few dozen feet from the sentry. He turned and glanced back to the Embassy. Brenna was on the front steps, arguing with Patty Duprey. He took a breath and exhaled slowly.

"She's smart enough to have guessed it," he said finally. "But she's not going there with revenge on her mind. She just wants to know . . . I guess she wants to know where she came from, what kind of blood runs in her veins."

"Blood isn't destiny," Benson said coolly. "And this isn't a damn soap opera where we all dab our eyes while the heroine faces her demons or whatever."

"What do you care? This works perfectly for you."

"It would if someone actually sends me those twelve words," he said, not as coolly this time. "We cannot let her go to that meeting before getting the words, Bruiser. Once Damyan has her, she's gone. You know it. I know it. She might be under some illusion that she can sit down for a cup of tea with a man called the Demon and ask him to tell her fairy tales about Papa, but that's her problem."

"No, it's my problem." Bruiser huffed out a breath. "There's no way she's going to that damn meeting, Benson. Not without me, at least."

Benson was quiet. "So that's your decision, Soldier? You're going to follow her, take the shot, kill Damyan. Then you bring the heroine home and live happily ever after."

"Something like that. Maybe you get a broken nose somewhere in there, but yeah, that's the general plotline."

Benson sighed loudly. "Well, I guess I can't stop you now." He paused, sighed again. "Your SEAL buddies will be disappointed that you quit on the mission, though. Sad. And this is the first real Darkwater mission. Not an auspicious start. Hell, maybe I should scrap the entire Darkwater thing. Tell Ax to stay on his ranch with Amy, raise cattle and babies, get soft and spoiled, drink beer and talk about the days when the fire still burned. As for Cody and Dogg . . . well, it's over before it even began for them. They won't even get a shot at a Darkwater mission."

Bruiser reddened. "You're bluffing."

"Try me."

"This is blackmail."

"Of course it is. What's your point?"

"I know my brothers better than you do, Benson."

"Of course you do," Benson whispered. "That's why you know I'm right. They'll be crushed that you didn't find a way to finish the mission, do the damn job. Yeah, they'll grin and slap you on the back when you shrug and say you fell in love, that you couldn't sacrifice one person to save thousands, that you said to hell with the big picture, that you decided you're gonna let the forest burn just to save one damn tree."

"I said I'd find a way," Bruiser growled.

"Well, you're running out of time, Soldier." He sighed again. "Look, tell Brenna how Alexei was killed. Tell her about the fingers and teeth. She'll know for sure that Damyan killed her dad."

"She's already guessed that."

"Well, tell her anyway. Maybe it'll scare some sense into her. Then she can send Damyan the twelve words by text. Send me the same text. Then you guys get your happily ever after."

Bruiser glanced towards the Embassy steps in the distance. Brenna appeared to have won the argument with Patty Duprey. The red scooter had been commandeered. Brenna was getting instructions on the controls as a uniformed Embassy guard started to disconnect the sidecar.

"She won't do it," said Bruiser. "She's determined to meet Damyan face to face. She wants to know about her father, Benson. She needs to know what he was. Why he died."

"He was just a smart hacker who got mixed up with

the wrong guys," Benson fumed. "A non-violent criminal who met a violent end." He paused. "Kaiser can put together a fake dossier on her father, if you like. Give Brenna a good story."

Bruiser thought about it. "That won't work," he said. "She'll wonder why the dossier suddenly showed up if you had it all along. As it is she knows you're a damn snake, Benson. It might even make her more curious to find out the truth for herself."

Then something occurred to Bruiser. The fake dossier idea triggered a plan. Not simple. Not without risk. But it might work.

It had to work.

"All right, Benson," he said excitedly, glancing at the sentry's rifle again. "Listen up."

He rattled off the plan. Benson hemmed and hawed, then sighed and agreed.

Within minutes Bruiser had taken the M-16 rifle off the sentry. He still had his Sig Sauer. Two extra magazines for the M-16 from the guard. He counted his bullets. Should be enough, but he grabbed a third magazine from the guard shack. Better to have too many bullets than too few.

After all, there was going to be a fair amount of shooting.

Bruiser just had to make sure nobody got hit.

24

Brenna hit the SEND key on Bruiser's phone. The message shot across cyberspace to John Benson. She handed the phone back to Bruiser and swung her leg over the scooter.

"Twelve words. Count 'em," she said, watching Bruiser check the message she just sent. "Don't you trust me?"

Bruiser looked up and she winked at him. He grinned, but it was forced. She could see he was anxious about this plan, even though he'd come up with the escape plan himself. She was anxious too.

But not about the plan. Nope. She trusted Bruiser with her life. That was the only reason she was able to bring herself to ride a red scooter straight through the gates of hell, right into the lair of the demon she knew must have killed her father.

She was brave, but she wasn't suicidal. Bruiser would protect her. She hadn't been sure exactly *how* at first, but she knew it in her heart. He was a soldier and a man. He would find a way to fulfill both his missions. He would remain true to both his codes. He would not fail his mission.

And he would not fail her.

"Bruiser, listen," she said, glancing at the phone in his hand, then up into his eyes. "If the escape plan doesn't play out the way we hope, then I just want you to know that—"

He shut her up with a kiss. There was an urgency in the kiss, a desperation that she could feel on his rough lips. She sensed how badly he wanted to pull her off that damn scooter, scoop her up in his bearlike arms, hold her close and protect her forever. Then they'd ride off on a rainbow-colored dream-cloud or on a mortar like in a Russian fairy-tale.

But this wasn't a fairy-tale or a dream. It was the real world, and the real world was complex, conflicted, nuanced. Benson was doing what he had to do. Bruiser was doing what he had to do.

And Brenna was doing what she had to do.

Even if she lost everything to do it.

Now the phone buzzed in Bruiser's hand, and Brenna gunned the scooter's throttle and shot off down the Embassy driveway towards the open gates. She glanced in the side-mirrors as she sped through the gates.

Bruiser was staring after her, the phone to his ear.

His face turned red.

His mouth hung open.

Then he started running.

25

"What do you mean she's *gone*?" Kaiser roared into the phone as he kicked an empty swivel chair, sending it spinning across the windowless room at Langley. "Well, go get her back, Soldier. She *lied* to us, Bruiser. She fucking *played* us! She did all of this just to get away from you, to escape with her damn secrets. Hell, did it not occur to you that you should have waited for us to check the words before letting her out the damn gate? You fucked up, Soldier. Now I'm going to mobilize a wet team to take them *both* out before it gets out of hand. Maybe you too if you get in the damn way. Congratulations to both you and Benson. Darkwater, my ass. I should have known better. Benson's lost his damn mind after Sally died. And he's led you down the same path."

It was just Kaiser and Benson and a CIA techie in the room. The techie had confirmed that the twelve words did not in fact unlock jack shit, least of all a crypto digital wallet with nine billion dollars worth of unseizable currency that could be sent anywhere in the world with a click of a computer mouse.

Kaiser hurled the phone at the back wall. The phone

shattered, sending pieces of plastic, glass, and metal all over like shrapnel. The techie appeared unmoved.

Benson stroked his stubble and waited for Kaiser to settle down.

"Martin," he said softly. "Martin, listen to me. Don't send a wet team in just yet. Have some faith in the system."

"What system?" Kaiser growled, walking to the landline phone and dialing. "It's Kaiser," he barked into the phone. "Send me a new secured cell phone. I'm in Room T-196. Yes, now."

"My system," Benson said.

Kaiser looked like he was about to rip the phone off the wall and throw it at Benson. His face turned maroon, then finally paled to a deep red.

"She played him," Kaiser said. "Played *you*. Now she's got the money and is on her way to Damyan."

Benson smiled. "She's on her way to Damyan, I'll give you that. But she isn't playing Bruiser. She isn't playing us." His smile widened. "She's playing the game, Kaiser. The great game. The game we're all playing. Whether we know it or not, like it or not."

"Here we go again," Kaiser muttered. "This is not the time, Benson."

"She trusts him, Kaiser," said Benson. "She trusts him to protect her. That's the only reason she's got the guts to drive a red scooter into a demon's lair. The only reason she's got the courage to face the truth about her father—a truth that she knows in her heart is dark, perhaps terrifying. But she needs to face it, and the only reason she has the strength is because of Bruiser. Her man. She knows he's her man, and she knows he will not fail her. That's why this mission *is* going to succeed. It's because they *are* fated for each other, and they're making choices that prove they trust in their destiny. Choices that are risky, dangerous, even suicidal. But that's what fate watches for, Martin. That's proof that you trust in destiny, are willing to risk it all because you trust in a force that's bigger than you."

Benson stood, his eyes shining gray. "And when you do that, the universe turns in your direction, Martin. Things fall into place. Coincidences that feel like magic. That's the great game, Martin. It's what we all live for. Fight for. Die for. The chance to experience love. The *need* to experience love. That's what all of this comes down to, Martin. This mission. *Every* damn mission."

Benson paused, considered his words, said them anyway. "And so it's always about a man and a woman, Martin. That's the foundational energy of the universe. Sex and violence, protection and destruction, birth and death. It all revolves around that one form of primal energy. Everything starts there and ends there. One man. One woman. That's the only mission. The only story. The only reason anyone does anything worthwhile. The only reason anyone has the guts to risk it all."

"You're insane," Kaiser groaned, rubbing his eyes and cracking his jaw. "I should send that wet team after your ass first."

There was a knock on the door. An aide entered with Kaiser's new phone. He turned it on. Stared at it. Then sighed and tossed it on the table. He sat down hard in a swivel chair, tapped out a Dunhill filter from the pack in his jacket pocket. He lit up, then nodded at Benson.

"All right, I'll wait," he said. "But not forever."

26

It felt like forever, but Bruiser finally saw her on the highway that ran past the airport on the way to the wildlife preserve. A curvy firecracker on a red shooting star.

Her dark hair was open, flying wild like a battleflag in stormwinds. He gunned the engine of the white Jeep Wrangler he'd taken from the Embassy garage. The original plan was for Bruiser to take an alternate route, in the unlikely case Damyan had someone watching the highway for him. But the original plan was gone out the damn window, was speeding down the highway on a red scooter.

"Damn it. Damn it. *Damn* it!" Bruiser shouted, slamming his palms on the leather-wrapped steering wheel. He swerved around a old Chevy pickup driven by two unwashed surfer-dudes smoking a joint. He glared at them as he whizzed past, then overtook a top-heavy truck packed with sad-looking chickens in cages. He glared at the driver of the truck, who didn't look particularly happy himself.

Now Brenna was clearly in his sights, and Bruiser slowed down to stay far enough behind her that he wouldn't be made by anyone watching her. He was burning with embarrassment after talking to Kaiser. The man was right. Bruiser should have known better than to let her go without verifying those secret words were the correct ones. Bruiser had trusted her.

And he'd been played.

Rage surged through his powerful frame. His fists tightened around the steering wheel, almost crushing it to powder. Why had she done that? How could he have been so wrong about her? Had she really been playing them all from the start? Had she been working with her father all these years, picking up where he left off?

"No," he said firmly, taking long, deep breaths to calm down so he could think straight.

No mission with the SEALs had gotten him worked up like this. He was the coolest head in the group. The best sniper. He could stay motionless so long moss could grown on his knuckles. But he was falling apart here. Breaking Brenna had been the mission. So why was Bruiser the one breaking into pieces.

"No," he said again as the structured in-out breaths put his body back in that relaxed state where his mind and muscles got back in synch. "She didn't betray me. Of course she didn't."

He listened to his heart beat.

He thought of what they'd shared.

He thought of what they'd felt.

He thought of what she'd been saying to him when he stopped her with a kiss.

"In case this doesn't work out," she'd said with those

honey-sweet lips, those perfect brown eyes. "I just want you to know that I—"

It wasn't the words, he realized now. It was everything else about that moment. She was saying things with her eyes, her tone, her heart.

Because that first sentence wasn't authentic.

She didn't believe for one damn moment that it wouldn't work out.

She *knew* it was going to work out.

She *knew* Bruiser had her back.

She *knew* Bruiser would figure it out.

Figure out that she hadn't betrayed him.

Which meant she was in more danger than ever.

Because she didn't have the words at all.

Bruiser whipped out his phone and dialed Benson. He answered immediately.

"She doesn't have the secret words at all," Bruiser shouted. "She doesn't know them. She faked us out so I wouldn't stop her from going to meet Damyan. She's determined to find out about her dad, and she trusts me to keep her safe. It's not a double-cross, Benson. It's reckless, dangerous, and it might get her killed for real. But it's not a double-cross. Of course she doesn't remember the words. She's a brilliant woman, but come on, who the hell is gonna remember twelve random words that you saw one time a decade ago?"

Benson was quiet for a bit. "That's not good. If she didn't memorize them, those secret words might be lost forever. We already pulled all her emails from the last ten years and had them scanned. Nothing in Alexei's old emails to her. Kaiser already had Brenna's apartment tossed for old letters, notes, slips of paper hidden in books, you name it. Checked the basement storage locker in the apartment complex. Searched bank records for safety deposit boxes, storage units all over the Tri-State area. Even had a guy break into the family's old house in Jersey, do infra-red and x-ray scans of the walls, search the attics, basements. Nothing. Kaiser's guys know how to do this shit. If those words were written down somewhere, we'd have them."

"Which means she was clean all along," Bruiser growled. "She used the account just once. To pay for college. Then she tossed the words away and never looked at them again. She was just too scared to admit it to me. Too scared of you and Kaiser. Too scared that if we found out the truth, she'd be useless to us. We'd kill Damyan, send her back, maybe hand her over to Homeland Security to be interrogated for treason. Hell, maybe she was even worried that Kaiser would send a wet team to take her out, just to keep things clean."

"Kaiser still might send that team," Benson said quietly. "So you better hope those secret words exist somewhere." He paused as Bruiser's jaw tightened. "And not just because Kaiser's losing patience. Think about it, kid. How patient is Damyan the Demon going to be if Brenna doesn't get him into that account?" Benson chuckled darkly. "If Damyan doesn't get the words out of her, he's going to carve her up until she spills her guts. That's a metaphor. I hope." He chuckled again. "Sorry. Battlefield humor."

Bruiser took a breath. The thought had been foremost on his mind. It chilled him, but he was strangely calm. He knew she was counting on him to find a way. Benson was counting on him to find a way. The damn universe was counting on him to find a way.

A way to have it all.

The mission and the woman.

The glory and the girl.

"In a way, this makes it easier," Bruiser said. "If she doesn't have the words, then nobody can unlock that account. The money will sit there until the world comes to an end. Which means there's no reason to let Damyan live. So to hell with the original plan. I'm not going to risk Brenna getting shot. I'm going to speed up, get there before her, finish this without putting her within a mile of the guy."

"Then you're gonna have some serious explaining to do, Soldier."

"I'm not explaining shit to you."

"Not me. Her."

Bruiser grimaced. He thought of Brenna's reckless determination to meet Damyan face to face. There was something Brenna wasn't telling him. Something she remembered about her father, something that shocked her, saddened her, maybe scared her. She wanted to hear it from the Demon himself. Wanted to look into his eyes when she asked him about her father.

So what would happen when Brenna showed up and found Damyan face down in the mud, those big blue horse-flies already laying their eggs in the bulletholes, Bruiser with a rifle in his arms, a foot on Damyan's head, grinning for the camera like a big-game hunter from the 1920s?

Would she rush into his arms and call him a hero?

Would she sigh and swoon and ask to feel his biceps?

Or would she smack him across the face for making a decision that wasn't his to make.

Say with her eyes that she would never trust him again.

Because trust was the ability to let someone take a risk.

To stand behind them even if it was reckless.

To support them even if it was stupid.

To have their back no matter what.

Bruiser scratched the side of his neck, feeling oddly indecisive. Snipers were never indecisive. They knew the perfect shot only came around once. You might wait hours for that shot, maybe days.

So when it comes, you best be ready to take your shot, Soldier.

Cause that perfect shot only comes around once.

That perfect woman too.

This wasn't about Damyan or Alexei, was it, Bruiser suddenly thought as a chill went through him. It wasn't about Benson and Kaiser, the CIA and the NSA, Russia and Ukraine.

Nah, deep down it wasn't about any of that.

It was about them.

Just them.

A man and a woman.

It was their mission from the start.

Their story till the end.

Now Bruiser could hear Benson almost grinning, like the crafty old wolf was enjoying this.

And why not.

Because it truly *was* a game, wasn't it?

The game of trust.

The game of faith.

The game of man and woman.

The only damn game in town.

Bruiser could see it now. He thought about Ax and Amy, how their choices to trust one another had started this whole thing. Benson's wife Sally being killed. Benson quitting the CIA and starting Darkwater. The former SEAL Team Thirteen going with him to play the game by Benson's rules, the rules of the universe, the rules of man and woman.

And why had the SEALs followed Benson? Left their careers to step into the shadows with a man they barely knew?

Well, they hadn't followed *Benson*. Not really.

They'd followed Jake Axelrod. Ax. Their SEAL Team Leader. A brother to the death.

A brother who'd found his forever in Amy.

Somehow promising the others that they would find their own forevers along this dark, twisted, murky path that Benson was sending them down.

Was that the unconscious reason why Bruiser, Cody, and Dogg had stepped off the ledge, taken the plunge, disappeared into the shadows to play the game by Benson's mysterious rules?

Bruiser thought back to where it had all started for him, at Ax and Amy's wedding that felt like an eternity ago. Benson's questions. Bruiser's answers.

And as he followed Brenna's red dart of a scooter off

the highway towards the dark green borders of the forest, another answer came to Bruiser.

Or rather, a question.

"Hey, Benson," he said, slowing down and pulling off the road while Brenna scooted around a clump of trees. He had the coordinates Damyan had sent to Brenna on Mikhail's phone. He would cut cross-country, do what a sniper does, covering ground on foot, without disturbing a single twig or moving a solitary pebble or squishing a scurrying bug.

"What?" said Benson.

"Her mother," said Bruiser. "What about her mother?"

"Nancy Sullivan. Never been married. She's clean. Unremarkable. Back-office staffer at the DMV in Newark. Quit years ago, before her pension vested. Moved south. Very little contact between the two of them over the years." He grunted. "Kaiser ran her bank accounts. She's living on a small amount of savings that she must have gotten from selling the Jersey house. If she had those secret words, she'd be using that money, I guarantee it."

"Brenna never told her about the account," said Bruiser. "They weren't close. Brenna said Nancy kept to herself, sold the house when Brenna went away to college. She might have the words written down. Maybe in a shoebox of old stuff that Brenna left with her. Did Kaiser send guys to ask her?"

"Kaiser sent a guy into her apartment when she was out shopping," said Benson. "Small place. No storage. No shoeboxes with memories. They were thorough, like Kaiser's guys always are."

"Yeah, but did anyone *ask* her?"

Benson hesitated. "No. Kaiser didn't want to raise any flags in case things went bad and Brenna was killed later. Didn't want to alarm her either. Just the search. No interrogation. We made the call based on her profile. Odds say no way she's got those words memorized. Especially if she didn't even know about the crypto account. She might not even be that computer savvy anyway."

Bruiser shook his head. "Nancy knows her way around computers and tech." He turned off the engine, grabbed the M-16 rifle, slung it over his shoulder, then stepped out onto the tall grass near the forest's edge. "Brenna says Alexei and Nancy met in an online chatroom. Not a dating site, but like a forum. It was for gamers or something. Those elaborate computer games where you collect weaponry and there are backstories and plot twists and ridiculous villains."

Bruiser collected his weaponry, then began to stalk the ridiculous villain who would hopefully give their plot a nice twist with some juicy backstory. He stepped past the line of trees, checked the GPS on his watch, then spoke low into the phone.

"Something doesn't fit," he whispered. "You said Nancy Sullivan worked for the DMV?"

Benson grunted. Bruiser heard him hit some keys on a laptop. "Let's see . . ." he muttered. "Huh."

"What?"

"Shit."

"What is it, Benson? I gotta hang up soon. Within three hundred yards and closing fast. Brenna will be there any minute. I need to be in position."

"Maybe nothing, but I'm checking."

"On what?"

"Employment record for Nancy Sullivan. It's DMV department C-1559."

"So?"

"So C-1559 just so happens to be the Department of Defense code for the cryptography used in . . . wait for it . . . crypto currencies."

Bruiser stopped in his tracks. A bug scurried past his boot. "Coincidence?"

"Probably. But it makes me think of how the CIA would sometimes have a little fun when inventing cover stories for operatives. You know, like giving a black ops agent a job in Department 007 of some innocuous government agency or something cute like that."

Bruiser took a slow breath. "And what innocuous government agency would assign a black ops agent to cryptocurrencies?"

Benson's breath caught. "That would be the U.S. Department of the Treasury," he muttered. "Motherfucker. Those sneaky accountant bastards must have been running Nancy Sullivan. Off the grid. So deep they even kept the CIA out of it. Mother of . . . I gotta call you back, Bruiser. Keep your phone on."

Bruiser nodded. "So Brenna's IRS audit that was sealed so tight it looked like an inside job . . . it actually was an inside job. Mommy taking care of her own," he said casually, smiling as he thought that somehow he understood Brenna a lot better now. She was all secrets and mystery, twists and turns, with more backstory than a soap opera family. Couldn't help it. It was in her blood.

Benson came back on before hanging up. "Kaiser's got a Blackhawk chopper ready to go from Langley. He's already sent a team to pick up Nancy Sullivan and put her on a Marine Nighthawk. We're meeting halfway on a rooftop." He paused. "Eighteen minutes. Then check your phone for twelve words. The mission is still in play, Bruiser. Everything's still in play."

27

"You think you can play with me?" said Damyan Nagarev in Russian.

Brenna stayed where she was in the small clearing surrounded by trees that grew so close together it was like a wall of brown and dark green. She'd parked her red scooter on the path, right next to where Damyan had said would be a fallen tree. She'd found the tree. Now she'd found Damyan.

She stared curiously at the man who'd earned the nickname of the Demon. He was wiry and lean, all muscle and veins, tendons and sinews. His oval, weathered face was scarred from a thousand battles, it seemed. One long scar stretched like a river from above the eyebrow down one eye to the side of his mouth. The eyelid had been cut and not stitched cleanly. It must have happened a long time ago, Brenna thought.

Damyan's once-blonde hair was now almost colorless, close shaved, with a patch on the side of his head where no hair grew. That part of his skull was smooth, like they'd done a skin transplant after surgery. She wondered if he had a metal plate in his skull.

"I have not come all this way to play," she replied in Russian. "This is not a game for me."

Damyan came closer. He wore dark blue cargo pants and a maroon tee shirt. The clothes were well worn but clean. He had a hunting rifle slung across his back. In his right hand was the gun Bruiser had taken from Mikhail and left in the hotel room.

He raised the handgun.

Brenna stiffened. Not because she was afraid Damyan would shoot—surely he wouldn't before getting those twelve words. No, Brenna was nervous that Bruiser might not be able to hold back if he saw Damyan pointing a gun at her. After all, it had been like pulling teeth to get Bruiser to agree to *any* plan that didn't involve putting a bullet in Damyan if he got within ten feet of her.

Still, their escape plan involved Damyan not getting too close. Bruiser and Brenna had agreed that he might search her for weapons or a wire, and it had been a hotly debated issue. Finally they'd compromised: Brenna would leave her pullover with the scooter and approach in her stretch-jeans and tight top. It would be obvious she had nothing beneath her clothes. No wire. No weapons. Oh yeah, and no underwear.

Damyan gestured with his gun for her to turn in place. "Slowly," he said in Russian.

She did a twirl, hands out to her sides. Mikhail's phone was sticking out of her back pocket like a brick. Damyan reached in and slid it out, his fingertips grazing her butt lightly.

Brenna swore she felt Bruiser's finger twitch on the trigger. She hadn't seen or heard him, but she knew he was there. He had to be there. He just *had* to. There was no way she'd even be able to stand up straight right now if she didn't have complete and absolute faith that her man was out there watching over her, would take the shot before Damyan did.

Take the shot and miss.

Miss just right.

"It's too risky," Bruiser had said when they talked about the plan. "The moment he gets the twelve words, you're no longer useful. He might put two bullets in you immediately. He's got to be suspecting a trap anyway. He'll be expecting me to follow you. No way he fell for it when you said you got away from me after the cafe."

"He might suspect it's a lie, but he can't be sure," Brenna had said. "He knows I'm Alexei's daughter. There's a part of him that wants to see me in the flesh."

"Well, there's *all* of me that doesn't want him anywhere *near* your flesh," Bruiser had growled.

They'd argued some more, but finally she broke him. She got him to let her take the risk. She knew it was hard for him. And it felt nice to know.

But what felt even better was that glimmer of admiration in Bruiser's green eyes when he finally nodded and told her to go ahead, that he'd be in the woods watching, finger on the trigger, her life in his hands, their forever on the line.

And it had to be that way. She knew it when she saw

that proud look in the SEAL's eyes. Fate had put them in this position to prove themselves to each other. To test their resolve.

No way was a SEAL's woman going to let her man fail a mission to protect her precious little ass.

So many things came together for her as she finished her twirl and looked into Damyan's eyes again. She was doing this for herself and for Bruiser and for Benson and for the whole darned world. She was doing this for her father too, so perhaps his soul would know she learned the truth about Alexei.

The truth that somehow she already knew.

Yes, she'd felt the truth unfold in her mind like that mushroom cloud opening like a terrible flower. She'd heard the truth in Damyan's breath, the way it caught when she mentioned the mushroom cloud. Then, when he agreed to meet, it was as good as confirming that horrifying truth about the blood that ran in her veins.

"Thank you for killing him," she said suddenly in Russian, the words coming unexpectedly, surprising her, certainly surprising Damyan.

He lowered his weapon, then raised it to tap the side of his head. She heard the thunk of metal on metal, separated only by a thin layer of skin.

"You know?" he asked.

"I do now," she whispered.

Damyan frowned. "You wanted this meeting for revenge?"

Brenna shook her head. She smiled, blinked away a

tear. She hadn't planned any of this, but it felt smooth and natural, liberating and beautiful.

"I do not understand," said Damyan.

"But I understand," she said. "I understand why you killed him, and I'm glad you did."

"You are glad? Why?"

"Because that way I can hold on to the innocent memory of who he was to me," she said. "It doesn't matter what he was *capable* of doing, what he *might* have done, what he *could* have become. It only matters what he actually did. What he actually was." That tear rolled down her cheek like a pudgy bug scurrying downhill. "And what he was to me is a mysterious, exciting figure who showed up now and then, told me fairy tales, and then disappeared again into the shadows." She shrugged. "He wasn't a good father, never gave us any time or attention. But he wasn't the worst father. He did provide for us."

Damyan raised a scarred eyebrow. "He sent you and your mother money?"

Brenna nodded. "Every month from the day I was born. Never missed a month until . . ."

Damyan blinked and looked away. Just for a moment she thought she saw a human in the demon's eyes. The moment passed. Those blue eyes went ice cold again.

"A man's duty is to provide for his family," he said gruffly. "So perhaps Alexei was not just a boy. Perhaps there was some part of a man in him." He shrugged, looked into her eyes, glanced away again. "Perhaps the best part of him found its way to you, eh?"

Brenna stared in shock as the Demon blinked again and looked away for the third time. But not before she saw something in those dead blue eyes again. Something that told her that maybe even a demon isn't completely lost.

"The private keys," Damyan said, flicking his eyes back to her. "They are lost, yes? Alexei never sent you any message. There was no grand plan to continue his mission. That money is locked up behind a glass wall for eternity, yes?"

Brenna took a slow breath. She gazed past Damyan's head towards the thick woods. She didn't respond.

"Who was that man who killed Mikhail?" he asked.

Brenna stiffened. Shook her head. "Told you, I don't know. He spoke Russian like a native."

Damyan grunted, his eyes scanning the treetops like a radar. He looked back at her, narrowed those cold blue slits at her. That moment of mutual vulnerability was gone. That demon was back. The game was afoot.

"I assume he is an American operative," Damyan said casually. "Former Special Forces. They must have picked up my voice on that cell phone call to the prison. Sent a Russian-speaking man to intercept Mikhail—or perhaps just beat him to the punch." He took a long breath, exhaled. "I also assume you are running *with* him, not *from* him. I assumed this would be a trap. Draw me out, then finish me off." He waited, watched her, waited some more. Then he glanced towards the dark woods and shook his head. "But now I am not so sure. If you were followed, I would be dead already." He tapped the gun against his skull again. Broke into a grin. "So if this is indeed a setup and I am still alive, it is only because Benson and Kaiser are involved."

Brenna started, her eyes popping wide, eyelids blinking twice. She couldn't hold a poker face. She just stared and then nodded.

Damyan chuckled. "They tried to recruit me years ago. I told them go to hell. That is where you bastards belong. Yes, I will be going there too, I told them. We can meet and do vodka shots." He laughed. "Drinking hot vodka is real hell for a Russian, yah?"

Brenna kept staring, not sure what to say, what to do, what to think. She looked back at Damyan, watching as he tapped that gun on his metal skull-plate like he was negotiating with the demon inside.

Finally he shrugged his shoulders and sighed. "But I am up against the ropes now. If those twelve words are lost, the money is lost. I have no army. Mikhail is being eaten by rats in the airport dump." He shrugged again, waved his gun casually in her direction. "I could try to hold you hostage, but it would not work. The CIA would shoot both of us and leave us to rot in the woods. So what the hell. What do Benson and Kaiser want me to do? You can hear me, Benson? Where is the microphone? In your ear? Collar?"

Damyan waved his gun again, then suddenly lunged towards her like he wanted to speak into the microphone he assumed was hidden on her.

Brenna heard something in the trees, and she screamed and waved her arms wildly to stop Bruiser.

But she knew Damyan was too close to Bruiser's woman.

No way would Bruiser take the chance.

And she was right.

Bruiser took the shot instead.

28

The shot hit Damyan right in the head.

Or so Bruiser thought.

"Damn," cursed Bruiser, raising the M-16 again and closing one eye to line up the sights for the kill shot.

Damyan was down, but he was still alive. Bruiser was annoyed. He knew his aim was true. He'd sighted the Embassy guard's M-16 and tested it out on the Embassy range out on the far side of the beach. The M-16 was superbly accurate for a general purpose rifle. And Bruiser was superbly accurate for a special-purpose sniper.

Now Bruiser remembered that Damyan had been a sniper too. And just like Bruiser had once flinched out of instinct, Damyan had turned his head just enough that Bruiser's bullet struck a glancing blow on the side of Damyan's close cropped skull. It had made an oddly metallic sound, Bruiser thought. But this was no time for thinking.

"Get out of the damn way!" Bruiser shouted when Brenna put herself in front of the writhing, cursing Damyan. She was waving like a lunatic, screaming something, making wild hand signals that would cause every plane to crash into the control tower if she were on a runway.

Finally Bruiser got the message. He slung the M-16 across his body, swung down from his perch on a thickly concealed branch, and charged towards his woman.

Now stealth was not his primary concern. Dead branches and dried twigs snapped and cracked under his heavy boots. Pebbles and stones flew all over the place like shrapnel. Bugs progressed from scurrying to running for their damn lives.

Within moments Bruiser was on the scene, Sig Sauer drawn, green eyes focused on the demon who dared step within three feet of the protected zone. The blood pounded in his ears as he hurtled past Brenna and landed hard on Damyan, knee in the man's back.

Bruiser pressed the Sig Sauer against Damyan's skull. The man was alive but dazed. He didn't attempt to fight back.

"Bruiser, don't," Brenna shouted breathlessly. "He's surrendered. He says he'll talk to Benson and Kaiser. They tried to recruit him years ago, he says."

"Yeah, but I think it's a bit late for that, buddy," growled Bruiser. He glanced at Damyan's head wound. The bullet hadn't struck directly. It had grazed his skull, ripping off a line of skin. Bruiser did a double-take when he saw the silvery gleam of titanium. Dude was a bionic supervillain. Great.

"Yup, too late. Job offer has expired, dickhead," Bruiser said. "And you are about to expire too."

"Au contraire," came a voice from Bruiser's pocket. He

groaned and took the gun away from Damyan's head. Kept his knee firmly on the Demon's back, though. He'd seen the *Terminator*. Dude with a titanium head is never truly down for the count.

"You gotta stop eavesdropping on private conversations, Benson," he muttered, pulling out his phone, which appeared to have been activated. "Didn't you say this was no longer a recruiting mission?"

"We can be flexible," came Benson's voice. "Can't we, Martin?"

"Sure," came Kaiser's voice from the background. "I'll have my guys beat Damyan with a rubber hose instead of a metal pipe. How's that for flexibility, you piece of terrorist filth?"

"He's just messing with ya, Damyan," Benson said amiably. "The beatings will be mild, I promise. We won't leave any marks. We want you looking sharp for your new job with the CIA." He paused. "Is Brenna OK, Bruiser?"

"I'm fine," Brenna piped in. "Thanks for asking."

"Stop thanking them," Bruiser grumbled. "They used you as bait."

"Can I thank *you*?" she whispered, blinking twice and then looking away.

Bruiser stiffened, trying not to glance at her without that pullover, all sweaty and glistening in a black sleeveless top, stretch jeans over dynamite hips. Eyes front, Soldier.

"Later," he murmured as Damyan groaned and turned to look at them. "Not in front of the Demon."

Brenna giggled. Damyan muttered something in Russian.

"You know that titanium plate in your head wouldn't have stopped a direct hit," Bruiser said in Russian. "You got lucky."

Damyan rolled over, one hand over his bleeding skull. He glanced at Brenna, then looked coolly at Bruiser, and in crisp Russian said:

"So did you."

Bruiser cracked a surprised grin. Damyan chuckled, then groaned again. Something vibrated near his head. It was Mikhail's phone.

Damyan glanced up at Bruiser, who nodded.

Damyan exhaled and reached for the phone. He answered it. Listened with a puzzled frown.

Bruiser glanced at his own phone. He thought he could hear Benson chuckling in the background. Other voices too. A woman's voice faintly came through like she was on another phone line. Then Benson hung up.

Bruiser looked at Damyan. He was holding Mikhail's phone out for Brenna.

"It is for you," Damyan said. "It appears to be your mother."

29
TWO DAYS LATER
CIA HEADQUARTERS
LANGLEY, VIRGINIA

"Bruiser, this is my mother, Nancy Sullivan."

"Pleased to finally meet you, Ms. Sullivan," said Bruiser with a warm smile.

He extended his right arm, palm bigger than a baseball mitt. He was dressed in a dark blue suit, was perfectly shaved, with a clean military haircut. He was freshly showered, and Brenna through he smelled like cedarwood, manliness, and something else that made her blush. He was also grinning like he was auditioning for a role in something big.

Nancy Sullivan smiled wider than Brenna had ever seen before. She shook Bruiser's hand firmly. Nancy had some gray now in her dark red hair, but her light eyes were brighter than Brenna remembered.

She watched Bruiser shake her mother's hand. Then Brenna turned bright red when she remembered where Bruiser's hand had just been not so long ago.

"Sit down, everyone," Benson said from behind the walnut desk. It was Martin Kaiser's spare office in the basement, but Benson appeared quite comfortable in the leather swivel chair.

Brenna sat down in the straight-backed wooden chair with the CIA logo carved into the top of the backrest. She was in a navy blue skirt-suit and black tights. She kept her knees tight together. Nancy Sullivan in a gray pant-suit sat dead center, with Bruiser on the end. It felt strangely formal. Brenna was nervous. She wasn't sure what to expect.

After they'd all been flown back to the States, everyone had been separated. Brenna was put up at an unmarked facility in Virginia with very clean rooms and exquisitely manicured but plain lawns between the dormitory style buildings. She'd been given a thorough medical examination and was pumped with more vitamins and minerals than she knew existed on the periodic chart of elements. She'd been fed until she thought she'd burst. Then she slept for what must have been fourteen hours.

When she woke and showered, she emerged from the bathroom to see two women in black pant-suits standing in her room. They'd asked her detailed questions about everything and everyone. She answered everything honestly and clearly. It felt like a debrief, rather than an interrogation. She was not being railroaded for treason, it turned out.

An hour ago she'd been driven in a shining metallic-gray Crown Vitoria to the CIA Headquarters at Langley. She'd been escorted to the basement, asked to wait in a dimly lit windowless atrium with black walls and a running-water sculpture made of black stone. She'd reached out with her fingers to see if the water was real, but jumped back when she heard footsteps behind her.

"Don't touch a damn thing in this place," came Bruiser's deep voice. "This is worse than the House of Horrors. Everything's alive and watching in here."

Brenna turned and ran to him, not caring that they were dressed in suits and were in the hallowed halls of secrecy and conspiracy. He took her in his arms and lifted her off her high-heeled feet like she was a doll. Before she knew it his lips were against hers, and they were kissing hard, deep, like if these walls couldn't keep a secret, nobody could.

"So damn relieved to see you, Brenna," he growled, kissing her again, hugging her so hard she couldn't breathe. "I would have broken out of my room and hunted you down if Benson hadn't promised me you were OK, that this was protocol, that we all just needed to chill and stay cool while he and Kaiser worked it all out with Homeland Security and the Treasury Department and probably ten other clandestine agencies that nobody knows about and nobody *wants* to know about."

Brenna nodded earnestly, wiping her eyes and holding back a sob. Two days away from Bruiser had felt so weirdly strange, so oddly scary, like she was missing a part of herself. The bond they'd formed through that experience was so deep, so raw, so damn intense that Brenna could feel the crackle of energy in the air when their bodies collided. She was buzzing with his taste in her mouth, tingling with his scent in her nose, desperate for his hands on her body.

Bruiser glanced down at her legs in black tights, dragged his gaze up along the curve of her hips, lingered on the swell of her breasts. When his gaze finally moved up her neck to her face, she saw the need in his eyes.

She saw that he'd been thinking about her every damn second they'd been apart. Dreaming about that stolen moment on the beach in Costa Rica, where they'd made love like it might be the first time and the last time so it damn well better be the best time.

"How much time we got?" Bruiser whispered, cracking a wickedly wolfish smile as he took a step towards her.

"Are you insane?" she gasped when he slid his arm around her waist and pulled her against him so hard she slammed into his hips. She gasped again when she realized he was harder than that stone sculpture oozing its poison water.

"Nobody's gonna know," he growled, sliding his hand down the curve of her lower back, over the rise of her rump, down to the base of her ass.

He palmed her ass and squeezed hard. She felt wetness in her panties, already seeping through her tights. Her butt was tingling, her pussy tightening.

"Um, *everyone's* gonna know. This is CIA headquarters," she said, putting her hands against his chest to push him away.

Instead her arousal pulled her closer when she felt his massive pectorals tighten under her tender touch. She remembered how Bruiser's chest had looked like slabs of bronze marble when he stood above her in the sun, his cock coating her nipples, anointing her with his oil.

"There are probably cameras everywhere in this place," she whispered, trying to squirm away, not trying very hard.

"Hell, no. This is the most private place on earth," Bruiser said. "You think these double-dealing, backstabbing, two-timing spooks want all their secrets caught on camera? No chance in hell. Come on. You're wasting time arguing. Besides, we're American taxpayers, Brenna. We have a right to use this place. It's in the Constitution."

"Um, I'm pretty sure *that's* not in the Constitution," she gasped as Bruiser's hand slipped under her skirt from behind and somehow clawed its way down the back of her tights, down her panties, until the SEAL's palm was resting squarely on her bare bottom.

"Damn, that's a wicked stealth move," she whispered as his fingers teased her rear crack wide and thrummed against her tight pucker like it was totally the thing to do in the dark basement of CIA headquarters.

"Snipers are trained to get into tight situations," Bruiser growled against her ear. He licked her neck as he squeezed her ass, then hiked her skirt all the way over her big round butt and got both hands down her panties. "In and out before anyone even knows they were there. No trace of penetration. No sign of exit."

"Yeah, well, I think some signs are showing," she said, reaching down and placing her palm against his bulge. She almost moaned in delight as he went stiff all the way, thickening against her palm until he was the size of a pillar.

Bruiser took her lips inside his mouth and bit like an

animal seeking blood. She couldn't hold back her moan as he ravished her face like a hungry bear, but the sound was drowned out because they were against the cold black stone of the fountainhead spewing dark water.

The yellow overhead lights cast strange shadows that seemed to move as Bruiser pulled her tights down to her ankles, rolled her panties down past her knees, then turned her to face the blackstone wall surrounding the sculptured fountain. She was wet down her thighs, panting as she heard Bruiser unzip behind her. She felt him press his cockhead against her ass, push down on her lower back with his palm.

Then he took his hand away, and just as she was wondering what he was doing, it came back quickly against her bare ass, Bruiser's baseball-mitt sized palm smacking her twice on each buttcheek, the slaps stinging in the most beautiful way.

"Ohmygod," she gasped, her face red and peaked. "Did you just *spank* me at CIA headquarters?"

"Discipline is important in the Navy, Ma'am," said Bruiser, his voice wicked with mischief, his tone heavy with his need. She could already smell his pre-cum that must be coating his beautiful cockhead, oozing down his glistening shaft.

"Well, I'm not in the Navy," she said, an open-mouthed smile emerging as she felt her ass quiver in the most delightful way. "And neither are you, by the way."

"My mistake, Ma'am," he whispered coolly though his breath was hot against her neck.

He reached around her chest and kneaded her breasts

beneath her suit jacket. Then he slid those big palms down her front, between her legs, rubbing her wet pussy rough and dirty, making her sick with need, wet with urgency, like she needed to be fucked now. "I guess I'll be going now, Ma'am," he whispered as he petted her bush until her soft curls were matted with her thick juice.

"Don't you dare leave before the mission is complete, Soldier," she groaned in delight as Bruiser's thumb pressed down on her clit, sending ecstasy ripping through her curves. "Do your duty, Soldier. You need to do your damn duty."

"Yes, Ma'am," Bruiser murmured. "Would you like it Navy SEAL style or Army Ranger style?"

She giggled. Then she gasped when Bruiser's massive cock pressed up against her butt. "Um, what's the difference?"

"SEALs do it deep. Rangers do it dirty."

Brenna almost choked with a mixture of arousal, shock, and laughter. "Navy, I think. Let's go with Navy for now."

Bruiser rumbled out a laugh, bit her ear from behind, reached beneath her, and guided his cock to her slit from below. "Good choice, Ma'am."

She sighed out a groan as Bruiser entered her like a torpedo launching into the deep blue sea. He felt thicker than she remembered, and she was tighter than she imagined possible.

Bruiser pushed himself deep into her, the last few inches ramming into her with a quick upwards pump of his deadly hips.

He slid his fingers into her hair from behind, held her firmly against the black stone ledge, then started to pump urgently into her. Each stroke was quiet but powerful, his hips driving her ass up as he pounded into her.

The fountain gurgled and growled as they panted and groaned. The sound of dark water trickling onto cold stone muted the hungry slapping of skin against skin, the stealthy slither of well-lubricated entry and exit, the urgent progress towards the mission, deep and hard, in and out, back and forth, always and forever.

Bruiser came with a silent explosion that rocked Brenna's body and wrecked her mind. She hunched over the ledge, almost choking on her scream as her own orgasm came riding in like the dark horses of the apocalypse. She felt the rush of warm wetness inside her cunt, then along her thighs. She knew she was coming all over him even as he came inside her.

They rocked back and forth like a multi-legged beast in the dark depths of the CIA basement, finishing against the black stone, gurgling and gasping like that fountain that had been patiently watching. Slowly she felt him recede inside her, then pull out. She turned and he kissed her hard on the lips.

A kiss of possession.

A kiss of commitment.

"You're mine, Brenna," he said to her, his green eyes shining with sincerity. "I knew it the first day we met. I'll know it till the last day I'm alive. You're my damn woman, Brenna. You were the mission. And from now on, you're *always* going to be the mission." He paused, took a breath, exhaled hard. "Two days without you made me even more certain this is real, Brenna. Listen, once we're done with this meeting, done with whatever loose ends Benson wants tied up, we're going to seal this up tight. Seal *us* up tight. I want to make sure you're mine forever, you got that?"

She looked at him, not sure what he was asking, but totally sure that her answer was yes, whatever the damn question.

She nodded, unable to speak though the lump in her throat. He grinned, kissed her again. She smiled, blushed, looked down at the two of them. Her tights and panties were around her ankles. His pants too, cock hanging out, dripping onto the stone tiles paid for with taxpayer dollars.

"We should . . . um . . ." she stuttered, blinking as she felt the sticky wetness against her soft inner thighs.

"Yeah. Benson. Meeting. Right," he grumbled. He kissed her again, rubbed her ass lovingly, then reached into his jacket pocket.

He pulled out a black silk handkerchief, went down on his knees and wiped her thighs dry. Then he leaned in and kissed her pussy gently, taking a deep breath that made her shiver. Finally he rose, pulled his pants back up, zipped up, cleaned up.

And six minutes later, while Brenna could still feel the Navy SEAL's semen warm inside her, they were in Benson's office, and Bruiser was shaking hands with her mother.

30

"So you didn't know your mother used to work undercover for the Treasury Department," Bruiser said, glancing at Brenna past Nancy Sullivan. "But you guessed she had the twelve words that unlocked the private key. When did you guess?"

Brenna shrugged. "When you told me about the IRS audit that I never knew about. I figured someone had to have got into the Treasury Department system and nixed the audit, sealed the record. I thought it might have been my father at first. But the Treasury Department is by far the most protected firewall in the world. After all, that's ground zero for the U.S. Dollar, the most powerful weapon of both peace and war. No way even the best hacker in the world is getting into the nerve center of the world economy." She shrugged again, glanced at her mother, flashed a quick smile. "So I thought that maybe . . . just *maybe* it was Mom."

Benson smiled. "And you were betting Bruiser and I would get to the same conclusion. Which we did."

"Not soon enough," said Bruiser. "But it worked out."

Nancy smiled. She had sharper features than Brenna,

a longer, more angular face. But her eyes had the same mix of hard intelligence and soft understanding. Nancy's eyes were a bit sadder, Bruiser thought. Keeping secrets for so long does that to a person, he guessed.

Benson, the master of secrets, looked at Nancy and nodded. "Kaiser got it cleared with the Treasury Department, Nancy," he said. "You can talk freely about what you did for them back then. All the way back then."

Nancy's lined face paled. She blinked and touched the neat bun at the back of her dark red hair. She glanced at Brenna, then back at Benson, her jaw tight, eyes darting left to right.

"I . . . I don't know if I can," she said, shooting another look at Brenna, then glancing away. "How can I tell her what I did?"

"Because you did it for the right reasons," said Benson. "You did it because you were a patriot. Just like everyone in this room, in this building. You followed orders, made difficult decisions, and paid the price alone. In silence. Building a wall between you and your daughter. A wall within yourself." Benson took a breath. "I know what that's like, Nancy. Everyone who works in the shadows knows that's the price we pay."

Brenna frowned. She turned her chair slightly towards her mom. "What's he talking about, mom? What did you do? Nailed someone for tax fraud? Mom? Why are you looking so sad? So worried? It can't be *that*bad. It's not like you killed anyone, did you?"

Nancy's thin red lips trembled. She blinked twice, then a third time. Finally she turned towards her daughter, pulled her chair close, took Brenna's hands in hers.

She looked into Brenna's eyes. Then she started to speak.

"Alexei and I didn't just happen to meet in that gamer chatroom," Nancy said, her voice hesitant at first. "I was in there looking for him. Well, not him specifically. Someone like him. Someone who fit the profile."

"What profile?" Brenna asked.

Bruiser stiffened in his seat, his instincts telling him this wasn't going anywhere good. Treasury Agents didn't sound as bad-ass as CIA Operatives, but they could spin up some serious sketchy when it got down to it.

"Hacker. Gamer. Anarchist." Nancy sighed, touched her bun again, shook her head. "Someone who could be steered, guided, directed."

Brenna blinked, her eyes flashing. "Wait, what?"

Nancy's face was almost drained of blood. But she kept going like the words she'd held inside so long were being let out and they weren't going to stop.

"Back then the Treasury Department was worried about this new thing called cryptocurrency. They feared it might threaten the U.S. Dollar, make America lose some of the power we get from having the world's strongest currency." She shrugged. "So they came up with a plan. They cultivated a few agents like me, trained us in cryptography and how these currencies worked, then unleashed us on the wild open web to find a patsy."

"A . . . a patsy? You mean to set someone up?" Brenna asked, her jaw tightening.

Nancy nodded. "The idea was to find someone who

fit the profile, guide them towards a mental place where they do something with cryptocurrency. Something big enough, bad enough, grand enough that it makes the news."

"Oh, my God," Brenna shouted. "And then they'd say, Oh, look at what bad people do with cryptocurrency! It's the tool of the devil! The instrument of the terrorist! Was that it? The Treasury Department wanted to protect the Dollar by winning the battle in the court of public opinion instead of the currency markets or economy?"

Nancy took a breath, looked down at her hands, nodded. "At the time it made sense. We were all on board. Sure, the methods didn't sit well with us. But we understood that some men and women who work in the shadows have to use methods that . . . that . . ."

"That belong in the shadows," said Benson. He was looking intently at Nancy. Bruiser could see the wheels turning in Benson's crafty, shadowy brain. "Go on, Nancy. You're doing fine. Nobody's going to judge you. Not in this room." He paused, surveyed all three seated before him. "Not in this team. Not in this family. We all trust each other, know each other's hearts. Go on, Nancy. Let it out."

Brenna frowned at Benson, her face streaked with emotion. She looked at Bruiser, and he nodded warmly back at her, then looked at Nancy and smiled.

"No judgment from me, Ma'am," he said firmly. "I've been in the shadows. Darker than most." He shot a pointed glance at Brenna, then back at Mom. "Your daughter has too. She's not going to break. She's not going to bawl. She's got the best of you in her. The best of her father too, I bet."

A sob burst out of Nancy, but she caught herself before another got through. She dabbed her mouth with a white silk square and nodded. Then she forced a smile and continued.

"Alexei and I chatted for weeks online. He fit the profile, and how. There was a streak in him. Dark. Dangerous. But untapped. Not yet fully alive. So we kept chatting, I kept pushing, doing what my handler said would get him closer to our goal." She paused, cleared her throat. "Things started to get personal. My handler said to keep going. We sent pictures to each other. Alexei asked to meet. I was scared, but I agreed." She took a breath, sighed it out. "I was young then, barely out of college, doing something big and important for my country. I was *so* nervous, Brenna. And Alexei was so cool and confident. So much boyish energy even though he was older than me. That long dark hair, those eyes like Rasputin's might have been." She smiled, shrugged, looked away dreamily. "We met at a bar near the old part of Moscow. We drank vodka. We talked half the night. We danced the other half of the night. Then he took me home." Nancy's eyes misted over. She looked at Brenna, a faraway smile that was somehow intimate and loving came to her lips. "And we made you. We made you together, Brenna. One night. A magical night. The best night of my life, because it created you."

Brenna's shoulders shuddered. She was trying not to bawl. She leaned into her mother and hugged her tight. Bruiser looked away, gave them their privacy. When he looked back, the color had returned to Nancy's face. She was smiling like the sun.

"I flew back to Washington the next day," Nancy said. "Told my handler I couldn't do it. Not with Alexei, at least. My handler was pissed. Gave me a huge guilt trip on how much they'd invested in me. I didn't budge. They took over my chatroom account, probably had someone else pretend to be me. They warned me never to contact Alexei. Warned me that everything was classified, that it was my patriotic duty to stay silent."

"So you never contacted him after leaving Moscow?" Brenna asked.

Nancy shook her head. "Never heard from him until the week after you were born. That's when the first deposit came through into my bank account. It was a wire transfer from Moscow International Bank. I was petrified that the Treasury Department would find out."

"Why didn't they?" said Bruiser.

"Fate," said Nancy. "Just before Brenna was born, there was a major criminal ring busted on the dark web where they were all using cryptocurrency for stuff like human trafficking and hiring hitmen and crazy shit like that. So the Treasury Department got the bad press they wanted for crypto without having to run agents like me who could potentially get blown and cause a huge faceplant. So they shut down the operation, reassigned that handler, pretty much forgot about me."

"What about later? The IRS never tagged you for those wires from Moscow?" Benson asked, one eyebrow raised, a half-smile on his lips.

Nancy shook her head. "Alexei always stayed below

the reportable threshold, so my local bank wasn't obligated to report to the IRS or the anti money-laundering group." Then she winked at Benson. "Also, I still worked for the Treasury back then. Still had access to all their systems. Still knew how to get in and out without leaving a trace."

Benson grinned, leaned back in his chair, rubbed his chin. Bruiser knew he had something cooking. Did Darkwater need someone like Nancy on its shadowy payroll? Bruiser thought it best to leave that to Benson. It was above his paygrade.

"So you intercepted Brenna's IRS audit when Alexei sent her the college money and she converted it to U.S. dollars from the crypto account," said Benson. "Then you quit the Treasury. Sold the house. Moved to Florida. Why?"

Nancy shrugged. "When I saw that Alexei had sent Brenna almost a quarter million in crypto, I got scared. I wasn't sure where his mind was at, what else he had going on. I mean, I knew Alexei wasn't on a CIA watchlist or anything. He'd been visiting every couple of years to see Brenna."

"And to see you, Mom," said Brenna. "But you'd always leave the house when he was around. Never eat with us. Never hang out with us."

Nancy almost broke. "I know, honey. I . . . I felt like such a fraud, you know? And I couldn't tell anyone. Not him. Not you. I just . . ."

"It's all right, Mom," Brenna said, forcing a brave smile. "You're telling me now. Go on. What else?"

"Well, nothing else, really. After seeing the IRS audit stuff, I traced your account back to the crypto wallet. Then I looked through your mail, knowing Alexei would have sent you the twelve-word private key on old-fashioned paper, not on email that could be hacked. I memorized the private key words, just because I'm a numbers person and I thought it might be useful someday. Then I destroyed the paper."

Brenna took a breath and exhaled hard. "So *that's* why I never found that letter when I looked for it a few years ago. I thought I lost it when we moved out of the house." She bit her lip, cocked her head. "Why'd you destroy the key?"

Nancy's eyes narrowed. "I was worried your father was progressing. Reaching his . . . potential, I guess. I didn't want him to involve you. Maybe I was scared you might *want* to get involved. Either way, I didn't want you connected to him—especially not to his crypto accounts. That stuff is anonymous, but you can still trace locations of digital wallets using transaction triangulation and artificial intelligence algorithms."

Benson leaned forward abruptly, his palms hitting the walnut desk with a thump. "Speaking of nerdy stuff like transaction triangulation and artificial intelligence, how are things progressing with Operation Demon Stalker?"

Bruiser and Brenna both stared at Benson. He was looking at Nancy Sullivan. She straightened the collar of her gray jacket. Touched her bun again. Cleared her throat. It appeared that family time was over. It was all business now.

Darkwater business.

"Kaiser's letting Darkwater handle the tracking part of Damyan's operation," Benson said. He nodded in Nancy's direction. "And Nancy's running the systems that track the crypto he's going to be spending on various weaponry that's never gonna quite get sold because Kaiser's men will be there to intercept the delivery boys, put black hoods over their screaming heads, and transport them to places where even the goats have more civil liberties than assholes who wish harm against the United States and its friends."

Bruiser cocked a brow. "Operation Demon Stalker? Pretty subtle, Benson. Not grandstanding at all. Man, you gotta hire someone else to name our operations going forward. Coz you suck at it."

"Says the man named Bruiser," Benson grumbled. "Or should I say, Bor—"

Bruiser's head almost exploded as he roared out a protest that was closer to bear language than Russian or English. He lunged at Benson, swiping at the wily bastard with his big right paw. Benson pushed his swivel chair away from the desk with surprising strength, rolling out of reach of the swinging SEAL.

Laughter echoed off the dark wood-paneled walls of the windowless CIA room. Bruiser and Benson sparred playfully as Nancy clapped and Brenna tried not to get an elbow in the face. The shenanigans continued until the desk phone rang like the end of school recess.

"What?" said Benson, listening and then wincing. "Shit. I was going to cancel that." He sighed. "All right. Thanks. Yeah, I'll handle it, I guess."

Bruiser straightened his suit jacket. He was warm under there, but still cooler than when he and Brenna had turned up the heat in the fountain-room. He stole a glance at his woman. She was in her straight-backed chair, knees tight together. Her skirt hugged the curves of her hips and thighs in a way that made him sick with need. He felt himself hardening, expanding, rising.

Quickly he glanced at the wall and tried to think of something besides Brenna's boobs in his mouth. He wished he'd taken her top off earlier. Pinched those sweet pink nipples until they were dark red and hard.

Shit, he was hard as a pipe now. He crossed one leg over the other knee in an attempt to hide his rising flagpole. Not in front of her mother, he ordered himself. Stand your mast down, Navy man.

"What was that?" asked Nancy. Bruiser froze, then exhaled when he saw she was talking to Benson. Asking about that phone call. Maybe it was about Operation Demon Stalker.

Being reminded of the ridiculous codename made Bruiser momentarily forget about Nancy's daughter's breasts. He glanced at Benson.

"That was . . ." Benson started to say. He stopped, shook his head, smiled, then leaned back in his chair. He looked at Brenna, then at Bruiser. "Actually, why don't you take this one. Tell her about your brilliant escape plan, you guys. You laughed at me for coming up with Operation Demon Stalker, right? Well, let's have a good laugh at Operation Fake Her Death and Hope Damyan Is Stupid Enough to Believe It."

"Fake whose death?" said Nancy.

Brenna rubbed the back of her neck. She looked at Bruiser, who reddened and shifted in his uncomfortably tight tailored pants.

"Doesn't matter now," Bruiser said gruffly. "We didn't need to use that plan."

"Thank your lucky stars for that," said Benson. He chuckled. "You're a good sniper, Bruiser. But you're trained to make hits, not misses. And not just misses, but misses that look like hits." He laughed again, turned to Brenna. "And it's not easy to just play dead, you know."

"It wouldn't have been for long," Bruiser said hotly. He turned to Nancy and explained. "The plan was for Brenna to give Damyan the words at the meeting, then make sure she stepped a few feet away from him. I'd put down a line of bullets between them, send Damyan diving for cover. Brenna would scream as if she were hit, go down hard, lay still long enough while I hammer the ground with more bullets, driving Damyan into the woods. I figured once he already had the words, he'd keep running."

Nancy looked a bit cross at him. Benson was grinning like he was loving it. Bruiser kept his composure.

"It would have worked on our end, I'm sure of it," Bruiser said. "No, Damyan wouldn't have been certain Brenna was hit, couldn't be sure Brenna was dead. But once you did your bit, Benson, he'd believe Brenna was dead."

"Um, why did my daughter need to be dead once Damyan had the codes?" Nancy demanded.

Now it was Bruiser's turn to grin. "Ask the puppet master. John? You care to explain?"

Benson lost the grin, ran his hand through his silver hair. "Kaiser and I believed Damyan would abandon the money if he thought the CIA also had the private key. He'd figure the money was tainted, that there was some kind of trap. The idea was that he gets the private keys directly from Brenna, then . . . um . . . well . . . then he . . . you know . . ."

"Then he kills my daughter to make sure you and Kaiser can't get the codes from her," said Nancy, raising two well-plucked, highly indignant eyebrows. "Did I seriously just agree to work for you?"

"Brenna was never in danger," Bruiser said. Logically he knew he was lying, but it felt like the truth. "If that bastard raised his weapon or came within a foot of her, I'd have emptied the entire M-16 magazine into his bionic brain."

"And you'd have failed the mission," said Nancy, her eyes shining. "For her."

Bruiser shook his head firmly. "Failed Benson's mission. Failed Darkwater's mission. But not my mission." He glanced past Nancy to Brenna, then focused on his soon-to-be mother in law. "Your daughter is my mission, Nancy. She was always the mission, will always be the mission from now on. I promise you that." He took a breath, gazed past Nancy into Brenna's shining brown eyes. "And I promise you that too, Brenna. You're the mission now. Always and forever."

Nancy blinked away a tear. Brenna didn't bother to blink away hers. From his peripheral vision Bruiser thought he saw Benson glance away to hide something that might be construed as emotion.

"Well, before this gets out of hand and we all start hugging each other on camera," Benson said, standing and holding his arms out like a minister blessing the bride and groom. "You two should know that I came through with my end of the plan."

Bruiser frowned. Then he chuckled. "Operation Fake-Her-Death?"

Benson nodded. "Forgot to pull the plug on what I'd set in motion. Patty Duprey got a fake police report filed in Costa Rica. And Kaiser's guy just put a dramatic news story in the Newark Daily about a local girl killed during a hunting accident in Costa Rica."

"Um, so now what?" said Brenna.

Benson shrugged. "Well, it's not worth the trouble to undo all that. Better to just wait for a few weeks. It'll get lost in the newsfeed churn. Then you can return to the land of the living. Nobody will notice."

"Nobody will notice? Well, that's a little insulting," grumbled Brenna.

"Don't take it too personally," Benson said. He slid open a desk drawer, pulled out a brown manila envelope, tossed it on the table. "Here. We even got you a fake identity. And since you're dead, you can't go back to your apartment until you come back to life, so there's a hotel suite booked in your new name. Honeymoon suite, by the way."

Brenna blinked, flushing with excitement. She tore open the envelope like a kid on Christmas morning. Then her eyes went wide and she glared at Benson.

"Babayaga Kowalski?" she said. "Are you serious? And *where* did you get that photograph?"

"DMV, honey," said Nancy. "Remember, I used to work there. Kind of."

Bruiser frowned, rubbed his jaw, narrowed his eyes at Benson. "Kowalski is *my* last name," he said.

"Yes, obviously. I did say honeymoon suite, didn't I?" said Benson. "There are two sets of IDs in that envelope. One of them is yours."

Bruiser snatched the envelope from Brenna and pulled out the second set of credentials.

"Boris Kowalski," he said, reading the name off the plastic cards. "Very creative."

"Thank you," said Benson even though it wasn't a damn compliment. "Enjoy your honeymoon, Mr. and Mrs. Kowalski." He glanced at Nancy, gestured with his head. "You have a wedding gift for the newlyweds?"

Nancy nodded. She reached into her jacket pocket, pulled out a folded piece of white cardstock paper, handed it to Brenna.

Brenna unfolded it, raised her eyebrows, then showed it to Bruiser.

Twelve secret words.

"Is this what I think it is?" said Brenna.

Nancy nodded. "A new crypto account. We moved some of that money. Damyan isn't going to spend nine billion before he gets caught by some terrorist who figures out he's working for the CIA." She shrugged. "Besides, it wouldn't be nine billion if not for your father. So enjoy your fake death and fake honeymoon, you two. Try not to kill anyone, OK?"

Bruiser took Brenna's hand in his. He glanced at his fake ID with his real name. Raised an eyebrow at Benson.

"It's gonna be real hard not to kill anyone before I leave this damn room, Benson." He glanced at his fake wife, looked down at her curvy body, winked at her Rasputin-like eyes. "Shall we, Mrs. Babayaga Kowalski?"

Everyone laughed except Brenna. She turned to pull away from him but he held on tight. He led her to the door, opened it wide, but stopped her from stepping past the threshold.

"What?" she said, puzzled.

Bruiser didn't reply.

Instead he swept her up into his big arms.

Lifted his curvy Russian wife clean off the floor.

Then he carried her across the threshold.

Out of the old world and into the new world.

Out of the past and into the future.

Their future.

Their always.

Their forever.

∞

EPILOGUE
THREE MONTHS LATER
HINDU KUSH MOUNTAINS
AFGHANISTAN

"Hey, Ax?"

"Bruiser."

"You nervous?"

"Hell, yeah, man," said Ax. "Aren't you?"

Bruiser gulped, nodded, then crawled back down from the gravelly rise from where he'd been scoping out the target. They were still a hundred yards out of range. A group of armed Taliban were crossing the ravine in front of them, and although Ax, Cody, and Dogg would have loved to join Bruiser in raining hellfire down on the bastards from above, that wasn't the mission. Not this time. The Army Rangers who were still running unofficial operations in the Hindu Kush could handle that.

"Fuck yeah, I'm nervous," said Bruiser. "Scared out of my damn mind, Ax. And we only just found out that Brenna's pregnant. You and Amy have known for months now, right?"

Ax checked his weapon, looked up, nodded. "Doesn't get any less terrifying, though. Gotta make sure Amy's eating right, sleeping right, no stress, that kinda stuff."

"And then there's the birth," said Bruiser. "The trainers at BUD/S didn't prepare us for this level of stress, man. So glad this mission came up. It's so relaxing out here in the freezing, windswept mountains with nothing but enemy combatants crawling the hillsides."

Cody and Dogg came crawling down the rise from opposite directions.

"Just the usual," said Cody. "Goat herders with no goats but a shitload of AK-47s and RPGs."

"The goats took off when they smelled you coming, Cody," Dogg said.

Cody chuckled. "Yeah, well, they'll come bounding back when they hear you bleating after I stick my bayonet up your ass."

"You mean your toothpick, don't you?" Dogg whispered.

"What happens in the Hindu Kush, stays in the Hindu Kush," Cody deadpanned.

Cody and Dogg snickered like schoolboys, then glanced at Bruiser and Ax.

"What's with you two?" said Dogg. "You guys look scared shitless."

"Since when do a couple dozen Taliban with rocket-launchers scare you two?" scoffed Cody.

Bruiser sighed. "You wouldn't understand, man."

Ax nodded. "They'll find out sooner or later."

Dogg and Cody shrugged at each other. Bruiser raised his finger to his lips. He crawled up the rise, looked through the scope of his M-13 Sniper rifle. The group of Taliban had crossed and were headed east into the sun.

Bruiser called for the team to follow. It took them about twenty minutes to cover the hundred yards of hard mountainous territory. When they got to the small rocky plateau past the ravine, Bruiser could hear the screams coming from outside the village.

"Looks like we're at the end of the line with Damyan," Benson had told him the previous day. Bruiser and the rest of the team were at a Darkwater meeting at the Axelrod Ranch in Georgia. "Operation Demon Stalker has concluded. The Demon will be doing no more stalking for us."

The guys had nodded. They were all aware that Damyan Nagarev had been reviving old contacts all over the world with his newfound billions. Tracking Damyan's payments from the crypto account meant that Damyan didn't have to risk wearing wires or tracking devices on his body.

Nancy and Benson had a pretty efficient process: Damyan would cut a deal with a crooked military supplier or a bent politician for serious weaponry. He'd pay half up front, the other half upon delivery.

Except there would be no delivery, of course.

Kaiser's operatives would track the initial payment, then swoop in on the crooked sellers before they ever made the shipment. The CIA black ops folks worked silent and clean, and Damyan hadn't been made yet.

Of course, Benson and Kaiser knew it was only a matter of time before Damyan got made.

And Damyan probably knew it too.

Or if he didn't, he sure as hell knew it now.

"Damyan cut a deal with a splinter group that supposedly had stolen a bunch of U.S. military equipment we abandoned in Afghanistan. Wanted to sell it," Benson had said. "Deal went wrong. They got Damyan before Kaiser's operatives were able to get the guys. Kaiser pulled out his guys, called off the strike, cut Damyan loose. End of the line."

Bruiser had shrugged. Both he and Brenna knew this would happen eventually. Even three months was pretty good to keep a sting operation like that going.

"So Damyan's dead," he said. "I'll let Brenna know. She's not going to celebrate a man's death, but it'll bring some closure. Guy did put three bullets in her father, after all."

"Sure. I understand. You should tell her," Benson had said casually. Then he'd shrugged. "I mean, technically he's not dead yet, but he will be in a couple of days."

"What do you mean? He's been captured? He's being interrogated? By whom?"

Benson swiped at the air. "Doesn't really matter. Nancy moved the remaining money out of that crypto account. It's part of the Darkwater treasury now. And Damyan's not going to talk anyway. The splinter group isn't interested in the inner workings of the CIA. They were just a Taliban village who wanted to sell some stolen U.S. equipment. Last thing Kaiser's guys saw before leaving were the tribesmen cutting out Damyan's tongue, feeding it to the goats."

Bruiser had stiffened. So had the rest of the team.

They were all aware of what happened in those mountains. The Taliban and other Afghani tribes had fought the Russians for years before the Americans ever arrived. The tribesmen learned back then that scaring your enemy was a very effective tactic. They'd perfected brutal methods of inflicting horrible pain while keeping a man alive for days, screaming for hours, begging for death. They would often wrap a victim's head in cloth so he couldn't knock himself out by banging his skull on the flat rock where he was tied down.

Bruiser had taken a long, slow breath as he thought about it. Outside the Axelrod Ranch house the cattle were lowing, the horses whinnying. It was a beautiful day in Georgia, warm and sunny, green grass and blue sky. The Hindu Kush mountains would be dry and cold, barely enough scrub-grass for a skinny goat to survive. No sane man would ask to go out there.

"Let me go out there," Bruiser had said to Benson. "I'll go alone. Brenna will understand."

"You're not going alone anywhere," said Ax coolly to Bruiser.

"Who's going where?" said Cody. "I wanna come too."

"Count me in, motherfuckers," growled Dogg.

"Nobody's going *anywhere*," barked Benson. "I'm not risking the entire Team Darkwater on some rescue mission for Damyan Nagarev. He's helped put down some bad guys, but he's a long way from redeeming himself. That's gonna be between him and Satan in the fiery underworld. Fuck him. There's no rescue mission, and that's final."

Bruiser stood, shook his head. "Not a rescue mission, Benson." He took a breath, gazed at his team, nodded at them. "A mercy mission."

And now Bruiser lined up his shot. He acquired the target in the scope of his M-13. Stroked the trigger. Waited for the wind to die.

Through the clean glass scope he could see Damyan Nagarev tied on his back on the flat rock that was streaked with blood both old and new. He was shirtless. His mouth was crusted with blackened blood. There were no tribesmen around. They'd cut him open without damaging his organs or cutting any major blood vessels. He could last for days like that. Nobody deserved to die this way.

Not even a demon.

And so Bruiser took aim, patient as a tree, waiting for the perfect shot.

The wind died just then, and in that moment Damyan Nagarev raised his head.

His eyes were unfocused, almost blind with blood and pain.

Then for one poignant moment the pain left Damyan's face.

It was the sniper's instinct that knows when a fellow sniper has you in his sights.

And as Bruiser squeezed the trigger, took the shot, his mercy and his woman's mercy flying to Damyan with that bullet, he saw the Demon's broken lips move, saw the forsaken but forgiven man mouth a single word in Russian:

"Thank you," said the Demon.

"You're welcome," said Bruiser.

Then he nodded at his team, his brothers, his fellow SEALs, his family. They nodded back. Nobody grieved, but nobody celebrated either. It was just something that had to be done.

And there was a whole lot more to be done, they all knew as they hiked back to the pickup site, the mood lightening again as they remembered they were men on missions, two with women at home, the other two being watched by the mischievous eyes of fate, the devious gaze of destiny.

Because fate was coming for them too.

Destiny riding hard on their heels.

Riding in fast.

Riding in hot.

Riding in soon.

Hooyah.

∞

FROM THE AUTHOR

I hope you enjoyed that one!
Because there's so much more coming.

Navy SEAL Cody's story is next in CAPTURING CATE, the next full-length standalone romantic thriller in this wild, action-packed series! Get it now!

And do consider joining my private list at
ANNABELLEWINTERS.COM/JOIN
to get five never-been-published forbidden epilogues from my SHEIKHS series.

Love,
Anna.
mail@annabellewinters.com

∞

Printed in Great Britain
by Amazon